FORTUNES OF WAR

FORTUNES OF WAR

Stephen Coonts

ORION

689616

The right of Stephen Coonts to be identified as the author
of this work has been asserted by him in accordance with
the Copyright, Designs and Patents Act 1988.

First published in Great Britain in 1998 by
Orion
An imprint of Orion Books Ltd
Orion House, 5 Upper St Martin's Lane, London WC2H 9EA

A CIP catalogue record for this book is available
from the British Library.

ISBN 0 75282 168 7

Printed in Great Britain by
Clays Ltd, St Ives plc

To Deborah

ACKNOWLEDGMENTS

The author solicited technical advice from experts for various portions of this book. For their kindness, the author wishes to thank publicly Ray A. Crockett, Charles G. Wilson, and Captain Sam Sayers, USN Ret. A special tip of the flight helmet goes to Colonel Bob Price, USMC Ret., and his colleagues, the test pilots at Lockheed-Martin, who watched the author fly the F-22 cockpit concept demonstrator and didn't laugh.

CHAPTER ONE

● THE TWO TELEPHONE company vans moved along the traffic-choked boulevard beside the Imperial Palace at a snail's pace, precisely the speed at which everyone drove. Traffic in Tokyo this June morning was heavy, as usual. Reeking exhaust fumes rose from the packed roadways into the warm, hazy air in shimmering waves.

In the lead van, the driver kept his eyes strictly on the traffic. The driver was in his mid-twenties, and he looked extraordinarily fit in his telephone company one-piece jumper. He wore a blue company billed cap over short, carefully groomed hair. Concentrating fiercely on the traffic around him, he drove with both hands on the steering wheel.

The passenger in the lead van was a few years older than the driver. He, too, wore a one-piece blue jumper and billed cap, both of which sported the company logo. This man examined with sharp, intelligent eyes the stone wall that surrounded the palace grounds.

Between the fifteen-foot wall and the boulevard was a centuries-old moat that still contained water. Atop the wall was a green tangle of trees and shrubs, seemingly impenetrable. There were actually two moats, an outer moat and an inner one, but here and there they had been permanently bridged. In many places, they had just been filled in. Here in the heart of Tokyo, the remaining hundred-foot-wide expanses of water populated with ducks and lined with people were stunning, inviting, an inducement to contemplation.

The passenger of the lead van paid little attention to the open water or the crowds. He was interested in police cars and palace security vehicles, and he mentioned every one he saw to the driver. Occasionally, he checked his watch.

When the two vans had completely circled the royal compound, the man in the cargo area of the lead van spoke a few words into a hand-held radio, listened carefully to the reply, then nodded at the man in the passenger seat, who was looking at him. That man patted the driver on the arm twice.

In a few seconds, the vans turned into a service entrance. The inner moat had been filled in here, and the vehicles went through a narrow gate in the wall to a courtyard. A uniformed security officer in a glassed-in guardhouse watched the vehicles park. There were two armed officers by the gate and two by the door of the building. All four of them watched the passenger get out of the lead vehicle and walk over to the guardhouse.

The security officer's little window was already open, apparently for ventilation.

The passenger gave a polite bow, just a head bob. "We are the telephone repairmen. They told us to come this morning."

"Identity cards, please."

The passenger passed them over.

"Yes. I have you on the list." The officer gave the cards back.

"Where should we park?"

"Near the door." He gestured vaguely. "There should be no conflicts. How long will your repairs take?"

"I don't know. We will have to inspect the failure, ensure we have the proper equipment to repair it."

"You must be out of the palace by four o'clock."

"And if we cannot fix it by then?"

"You will have to call the Imperial Household Agency, describe the problem, and make an appointment to return."

"I understand. First, we must diagnose the problem. We have some test equipment to take inside."

The security officer nodded and gestured to the two armed policemen standing near the door.

It took a bit to get the vans parked and unloaded. One of the security officers went over and spoke for a moment to the man in the guardhouse while the telephone men checked their equipment. The four men each hoisted a share. One of the security officers held the door open for them, and another followed them inside.

"I will show you where the problem is," he told the four, then took the lead. "The agency has a telephone technician on the staff. If you wish, I will have him summoned and he can tell you what he learned when he examined the system."

"We may have to do that," the man who had been the passenger in the lead van said. "We will look first."

They went up a staircase to the second floor and down a long corridor. They were inside an equipment room when the garroting wire went over the guard's head, startling him. The wire bit deeply into his neck before he could make a sound. He was struggling against the wire when one of the men, now in front of him, seized his head and twisted it so violently that his neck snapped.

The repairmen took the guard's weight as he went limp. They placed the body in a corner of the room, out of sight of anyone who might come to the door, open it, and look in. The murder had taken no more than sixty seconds.

The men picked up their equipment. Outside in the hallway, the passenger from the van ensured the door was completely shut and latched.

Their rubber-soled shoes made no noise as the four men walked the marble corridors deeper and deeper into the huge palace.

The bubbling, laughing children circled about the empress with carefree abandon. They giggled deliciously as they danced around her arm in arm on the manicured green lawn, among the shrubs and flowers growing riot in lush beds, under a bright sun shining down from a gentle blue sky, while temple bells chimed in the distance. Stately, measured, the bells proclaimed the beauty of an ordered universe.

Emperor Naruhito was probably the only person to pay any attention to the chiming temple bells, which he thought the perfect musical accompaniment to the informal lawn ceremony in front of him. The children's bright, traditional dress contrasted sharply with the deep green grass and captured the eye as they circled around the empress, who was wearing a silk ivory-colored kimono trimmed with exquisite organdy. The other adults were removed a pace or two, ceding center stage to the empress and the happy children. The photographers shooting the scene stationed themselves ever so slightly out of the way. They were dressed in nondescript clothing, rarely moved, and, in the finest tradition of their profession, managed to fade into the scene almost like shadows.

The natural world certainly had an innocent charm that human affairs lacked, the emperor mused bitterly. For weeks now he had been brooding upon the current political situation. The new prime minister, Atsuko Abe, seemed bent on forcing the nation onto a new course, a course that Emperor Naruhito regarded with a growing sense of horror.

The Japanese political situation had been drifting to the right for years, the emperor thought as he watched the empress and the children.

He reviewed the sequence yet again, trying to make sense of an avalanche of events that seemed beyond human control.

Each government since the great bank collapse had lasted a short while, then was swept from office and replaced by one even more reactionary. As the emperor saw it, the problem was that politicians were not willing to tell the Japanese people the truth. Their island nation was small, overpopulated, and lacked natural resources. The prosperity of the post–World War II era was built on turning imported raw materials into manufactured products and selling them to the American market at prices American manufacturers could not compete with. Japan's price advantage rested on low labor costs, which eventually disappeared. Sky-high real estate and hyperinflated stock values fell sickeningly as Japan's economic edge evaporated. The government propped up the overextended banking system for a while, but finally it collapsed, nearly bankrupting the government. Then tensions in the Mideast rose to the flash point and the Arabs cut off the sale of oil to force the developed world to pressure Israel.

The oil was flowing once again, but the damage was done. Japan found it could not afford Mideast oil at any price. The yen was essentially worthless, the banking system in ruins, huge industrial enterprises couldn't pay their bills, and disillusioned workers had been laid off in droves.

Maybe the Japanese were doomed. The emperor had moments when cold anxieties seized his heart, and he had one such now.

Perhaps they were all doomed. To be led into the outer darkness by a poisonous ultranationalist like Atsuko Abe, a demagogue preaching against the evils of foreign values and foreign institutions while extolling the virtues of the ancient Japanese nation—was this the Japanese destiny? Was this what the nation had come to?

Ah . . . Japan, ancient yet young, fertile yet pure and unspoiled, home for the select of mankind, the Japanese.

If that Japan had ever existed, it was long gone, yet today Abe waved the racial memory like a flag before a dispirited, once-proud people betrayed by everything they trusted. Betrayed, Abe claimed, by Western democracy. Betrayed by bureaucrats. Betrayed by captains of industry . . . betrayed by capitalism, an import from a foreign culture. . . .

Japan, Abe thundered, had been betrayed by a people who refused to hold its values dear, the Japanese. *They* were guilty. And they would have to pay the price.

All of this was political rhetoric. It inflamed half-wits and foreigners and gave newspapers much to editorialize about, but it was only hot air, spewed by Abe and his friends to distance themselves from other, more traditional politicians, and to win votes, which it did. Only when he was firmly ensconced in the prime minister's office, with the reins of power in his hands, did Atsuko Abe began to discuss his true agenda with his closest allies.

Friends of the emperor whispered to him of Abe's ambitions, because they were deeply troubled. Abe's proclamations, they said, were more than rhetoric. He fully intended to make Japan a world power, to do "whatever was required."

Naruhito, always conscious of the fact that the post–World War II constitution limited the throne to strictly ceremonial duties, held his tongue. Still, the burden of history weighed oppressively upon him.

A personal letter from the president of the United States shattered Naruhito's private impasse. "I am deeply concerned," the President said, "that the Japanese government is considering a military solution to aggravating regional and economic problems, a solution that will rupture the peace of the region and may well trigger worldwide conflagration. Such a calamity would have enormous, tragic implications for every human on this planet. As heads of state, we owe our countrymen and our fellow citizens of the planet our best efforts to ensure such an event never occurs."

There was more. Naruhito read the letter with a sense of foreboding. The president of the United States knew more about the political situation in Japan than he, the emperor, did. Obviously, the president got better information.

Near the end of the letter, the president said, "We believe the Abe administration plans an invasion of Siberia to secure a permanent, stable oil supply. The recent appeals of the indigenous Siberian people for Japanese aid in their revolt against the Russians are a mere pretext orchestrated by the Abe government. I fear such an invasion might trigger a world war, the like of which this planet has never seen. A third world war, one more horrible than any conflict yet waged by man, may bring civilization to a tragic end, throwing the world into a new dark age, one from which our species may never recover."

Here, in writing, were the words that expressed the horror the emperor felt as he observed the domestic political situation. Even though he lacked the specific information that the president of the United States had, Naruhito also felt that he was watching the world he knew slide slowly and inexorably toward a horrible doom.

"I am writing you personally," the president concluded, "to ask for your help. We owe it to mankind to preserve the rule of law for future generations. Our worldwide civilization is not perfect; it is a work in progress, made better by every person who obeys the laws and works for his daily bread, thereby contributing to the common good. Civilization is the human heritage, the birthright of all who will come after us."

Naruhito asked the prime minister to call.

Although the emperor had met Atsuko Abe on several occasions since he had become prime minister, he had never before had the opportunity to speak privately with him. Always, there were aides around, functionaries, security people. This time, it was just the two of them, in the emperor's private study.

After the polite preliminaries, the emperor mentioned the letter and gave Abe a copy to read.

Atsuko Abe was unsure how to proceed or just what to say. A private audience with the emperor was an extraordinary honor, one that left him somewhat at a loss for words. Yet this letter . . . He knew the Americans had spies—spies and political enemies were everywhere.

"Your Highness, we are at a critical juncture in our nation's history," Atsuko Abe said, feeling his way. "The disruption of our oil supply was the final straw. It wrecked the economy. Japan is in ruins; millions are out of work. We must repair the damage and ensure it never happens again."

"Is it true?" the emperor asked, waving the letter. "Is your government planning an invasion of Siberia?"

"Your Excellency, we have received a humanitarian appeal from the native Siberian people, who are seeking to throw off the Russian yoke. Surely you have been briefed on this development. The justice of their situation is undeniable. Their appeal is quite compelling."

"You are evasive, sir. Now is the time for speaking the blunt truth, not polite evasion."

Abe was astounded. Never had he seen the emperor like this, nor imagined he could be like this.

"The time has come for Japan to assume its rightful place in the world," the prime minister said.

"Which is?"

"A superpower," Abe said confidently. He stared boldly at the emperor, who averted his eyes from the challenge on Abe's face.

Then, ashamed, he forced himself to look the prime minister in the eye. "Is it true?" the emperor asked obstinately. "Does Japan plan to invade Siberia?"

"Our hour has come," Abe replied firmly. "We are a small island nation, placed by the gods beside a growing Chinese giant. We *must* have oil."

"But you have signed an agreement with the Russians! They will sell us oil."

"That, Your Excellency, is precisely the problem. As long as we are buying Russian oil, we are at their mercy. *Japan must have its own resources.*"

The son of an industrialist, Atsuko Abe had spent the first two decades of his adult life in the Japanese Self-Defense Force, the military. Although he was selected for flag rank, he left at an early age and obtained a post in the defense ministry. There Abe made friends with politicians across the spectrum, rose in influence, won promotion after promotion. Finally, he left the bureaucracy and ran for a seat in the Diet, which he won handily. He had been there for almost ten years, surfing the political riptides that surged through the capital.

He was ready now, at sixty-two years of age. *This* was his moment.

The emperor refused to look away. "*Our* hour? How dare you? This nation has never been in a shadow. Our way of life is honorable; we have kept faith with our ancestors. Our nation has made mistakes in the past, for which our people have paid dearly, but our honor is un-stained. We need no hour of conquest, no triumph of violence, no blood on our hands."

"You are born to your position," Abe said bitterly. "What do you know of struggle, of triumph?"

The emperor fought to maintain his composure. "Russia has nuclear weapons, which the Russians might use to defend themselves. Have you the right to risk the very life of this nation?"

"We are in a grave crisis, Your Excellency."

"Don't patronize me, Prime Minister."

Abe bowed. When he straightened, he said, "Forgive me, Excellency. The fact you do not know is that Japan also is a nuclear power. I am convinced that Russia will not risk nuclear war to retain a wasteland that has never earned her a single yen of profit."

The emperor sat stunned. "Japan has nuclear weapons?" he whis-pered.

"Yes."

"How? How were these weapons developed and manufactured?"

"With the greatest secrecy. Obviously." The manufacture of these weapons was Abe's greatest triumph, a program reluctantly agreed to by politicians watching their world collapse, then accomplished under a security blanket worthy of Joseph Stalin.

"The government did this without the consent of the Diet? Without the knowledge and consent of the Japanese people? In violation of the constitution and the laws?"

Abe merely bowed his head.

"What if you are wrong about Russia?" the emperor demanded. "Answer me that. What if Russia retaliates with nuclear weapons?"

"The risk is as great for Russia as it is for Japan, and Russia has less at stake."

"They may not see the equation as you do, Prime Minister."

Abe said nothing.

The emperor was too astonished to go further. The man is mad, he thought. The prime minister has gone completely mad.

After a bit, the emperor recovered his voice sufficiently to ask, "What do you suggest I tell the president of the United States in answer to his letter?"

Abe made an irritated gesture. "Ignore it. No answer is necessary, Your Excellency. The president does not know his place."

Naruhito shook his head ponderously from side to side. "My grandfather, Hirohito, received a letter from President Roosevelt on the eve of World War Two, pleading for peace. Hirohito did not answer that letter. He refused to intervene with the government. All my life, I have wondered how history might have been different had my grandfather spoken up for what he believed."

"Emperor Hirohito believed that the government was acting in the nation's best interests."

"Perhaps he did. I am not convinced that your government is now."

Abe shook himself. He had come too far, endured too much. He faced the emperor like a sumo wrestler. "The government must speak for you, and the nation, which are the same. *That* is the law."

"Do not speak to me of law. Not after what you have told me."

Abe pounded his chest. "You reign, I *rule*. That is the Japanese way."

Abe took several deep breaths to compose himself. "If you will give me a copy of the letter, I will have the foreign minister prepare a reply."

The emperor didn't seem to hear. He continued, thinking aloud: "In this era of nuclear, biological, and chemical weapons, war is obsolete.

It is no longer a viable political option. The nation that plunges head-long into war in the twenty-first century will, I fear, merely be com-mitting national suicide. *Death,* sir, is most definitely not Japan's destiny. Death is final and eternal, whether it comes slowly, from natural causes, or swiftly, in a spectacular blaze of glory. *Life,* sir, must be our business. *Life* is our concern."

Before Abe could think of a polite reply, the emperor added softly, "You carry a very heavy burden, Prime Minister. You carry the hopes and dreams of every Japanese alive today and those of our honored ancestors. You literally carry Japan upon your back."

"Your Excellency, I am aware of my responsibilities," Atsuko Abe retorted, as politely as he could. He struggled to keep a grip on his temper. "Keenly aware," he added through clenched teeth.

"In your public speeches that I have read, sir, you speak as if Japan's destiny were as obvious as the rising sun on a clear morning," Emperor Naruhito said without rancor. "I suggest you consult the representatives of the people in the Diet before you make any major commitments."

He could think of nothing else to say to this fool facing him. . . .

"Follow the law," the emperor added. That was always excellent advice, but . . .

"The Japanese are a great people," the emperor told the prime min-ister, to fill the silence. "If you keep faith with them, they will have faith in you."

Abe forced his head down in a gesture of respect. The skin on his head was tan, the hair cropped short.

Naruhito could stand no more of this scoundrel. He rose stiffly, bowed, and walked from the room.

That had been two days ago.

Naruhito had forsaken his ceremonial, almost-mystical position as head of state to speak the truth as he believed it, for the good of the nation. He had never done that before, but Abe . . . advocating the un-thinkable . . . telling the emperor to his face what his duty was—never in his life had Naruhito been so insulted. The memory of Abe's words still burned deeply.

He had written a letter to the president of the United States, written it by hand because he did not wish to trust a secretary.

The truth was bitter: He could not affect events.

The children were singing now, led by Naruhito's wife, Masako. A flush of warmth went through the emperor as he regarded her, his dearly beloved wife, his empress, singing softly, leading the children.

Truly, he loved life. Loved his wife, his people, his nation ... *this* Japanese nation. His life, the nation's life, they were all bound up together, one and inseparable. A profound sense of loss swept over him. Time *is* running out. . . .

Captain Shunko Kato stood concealed by a curtain at a second-floor window in the Imperial Palace, watching the ceremony on the lawn below. Behind him stood the other three erstwhile telephone repairmen, *his* men, standing motionless, seemingly at perfect ease. They weren't, Kato knew. He could feel the tension, tight as a violin string. Military discipline held them motionless, silent, each man in communion only with his thoughts.

The sunlight coming through the window made a lopsided rectangle on the floor. Kato looked at the sunlit floor, the great frame that held the window, the hedge, the lawn, the people, the bold, brazen sky above. . . .

He was seeing all this for the last time. Ah, but to dwell on his personal fate was unworthy. Kato brushed the thought away and concentrated on the figures before him on the lawn.

There was the emperor, shorter than the average Japanese male at five feet four, erect, carrying a tummy. Surrounding the group were security officers in civilian clothes—most of these men had their backs to the ceremony.

Kato retreated a few inches. He ensured he was concealed by the shadow of the drape, hidden from the observation of anyone on the lawn who might look at this window. Satisfied, he scanned the security guards quickly, taking in their state of alertness at a glance; then he turned his attention back to the royal party.

The emperor stood slightly in front of a group of officials, watching the empress and the children, seemingly caught up in the simple ritual. No doubt he was. He certainly had nothing else to worry about. The emperor, Kato was sure, was quite oblivious to the desperation that had ravaged so many lives since the bank collapse. How could it be otherwise? The emperor certainly didn't move in ordinary circles.

Yet the man must read newspapers, occasionally watch television. How could he miss the corruption of the politicians, the bribes, the influence peddling, the stench of scandal after scandal? Could he not see the misery of the common people, always loyal, always betrayed?

He never spoke out against corruption, avarice, greed. Never. And never condemning, he silently approved.

Kato felt his chest swelling with indignation. Oh, that they called such a man "Son of Heaven!" An extraordinary obscenity.

The empress was saying good-bye to the children. The ceremony was ending.

Kato turned, surveyed his men. Still wearing the blue jumpers and caps of the telephone company, they were as fit as professional athletes, lean, with ropy muscles and easy, fluid movements. Kato had trained them, hardened them, made them soldiers in the Bushido tradition. In truth, he was proud of them, and now that pride showed on his face. The men looked back at him with faces that were also unable to conceal their emotion.

"For Japan," he said softly, just loudly enough for them to hear.

"For Japan." Their lips moved soundlessly, for he had told them to make no sound. Still, the reply echoed in Kato's ears.

"Banzai," he mouthed.

"Banzai!" The silent reply lashed his soul.

The security guards escorted the emperor and empress toward the door of the Imperial Palace. One of them held it open for the emperor, who always preceded his wife by two paces. The security men did not enter the hallway; they remained outside. The entire palace was inside a security zone.

Inside the building, away from other eyes, the emperor paused to let Masako reach his side. She flashed him a grin, a very un-Japanese gesture, but then she had spent years in the United States attending college before their marriage. He dearly enjoyed seeing her grin, and he smiled his pleasure.

She took his arm and leaned forward, so that her lips brushed his cheek. His smile broadened.

Arm in arm, they walked down the hall to the end, then turned right.

Four men stood silently, waiting. They blocked the hallway.

The emperor stopped.

One of the men moved noiselessly to position himself behind the royal couple, but the others did not give way. Nor, the emperor noted with surprise, did they bow. Not even the tiniest bob.

Naruhito looked from face to face. Not one of the men broke eye contact.

"Yes?" he said finally.

"Your wife may leave, Your Excellency," said one of the men. His voice was strong, even, yet not loud.

"Who are you?" asked the emperor.

"I am Captain Shunko Kato of the Japanese Self-Defense Force." Kato bowed deeply from the waist, but none of the other men moved a muscle. "These enlisted men are under my command."

"By whose authority are you here?"

"By our own."

Naruhito felt his wife's hand tighten on his arm. He looked again from face to face, waiting for them to look away as a gesture of respect. None of them did.

"Why are you here?" the emperor asked finally. He realized that time was on his side, not theirs, and he wished to draw this out as long as possible.

Kato seemed to read his thoughts. "We are here for Japan," Kato said crisply, then added, "The empress must leave now."

Naruhito could read the inevitable in their faces. Although the thought did not occur to Captain Kato, Naruhito had as much courage as any man there. He turned toward the empress.

"You must go, dear wife."

She stared into his face, panic-stricken. Both her hands clutched his arm in a fierce grip.

He leaned toward her and whispered, "We have no choice. Go, and know I love you."

She tore her eyes from him and swept them around the group, looking directly into the eyes of each man. Three of them averted their gaze.

Then she turned and walked back toward the lawn.

From a decorative table nearby, Kato took a samurai sword, which the emperor had not previously noticed. With one swift motion, the officer withdrew the blade from the sheath.

"For Japan," he said, grasping the handle with both hands.

The sword was very old, the emperor noticed. Hundreds of years old. His heart was audibly pounding in his ears. He looked again at each face. They were fanatics.

Resigned, Emperor Naruhito sank to his knees. He would not let them see him afraid. Thank heavens his hands were not trembling. He closed his eyes and cleared his thoughts. Enough of these zealots. He thought of his wife and his son and daughter.

The last thing he heard was the slick whisper of the blade whirring through the air.

Masako walked slowly toward the door where just seconds ago she and her husband had entered the palace. Every step was torture, agony....

The men were assassins.

Masako, in her horror, had sensed it the moment she saw them. They had no respect; their faces registered extraordinary tension—not like loyal subjects meeting their emperor and his wife, but like assassins.

She knew her nation's history, of course, knew how assassins had plagued rulers and politicians in times of turmoil, how they always murdered *for Japan*—as if their passionate patriotism could excuse the blood, could excuse slashing the life from men who had little or no control over the events that fired the murderers—then atoned for their crimes in orgies of ritual suicide.

The bloody melodrama was terrible theater, yet most Japanese loved it, reveled in it, were inspired by it. Ancient racial memories were renewed with flowing fresh red blood. New sacrifices propitiated savage urges ... and mesmerized the audience.

Patriotic murder was sadistic, Masako thought, an obscene perversion that surfaced when the world pressed relentlessly in upon the Japanese, as it had in the 1930s, as it had in December 1941, as it apparently was ...

Now?

She could scarcely place one foot in front of another.

Oh, Naruhito, beloved husband, that we should have to face this ... and I should not be at your side....

She turned and hurried back toward her husband. Toward the evil that awaited them both.

She ran, the length of her stride constrained by her skirt.

Just before she reached the corner, she heard the singing of the sword and then the sickening *thunk* as it bit into flesh.

She turned the corner in time to see her husband's head rolling along the floor and his upright torso toppling forward.

She saw no more. Despite her pain—or perhaps because of it—she passed out, collapsed in a heap.

———

Shunko Kato did not look again at the emperor's corpse. There was little time, and staring at the body of a man who had failed Japan would be wasting it.

He arranged a letter on the table where the sword had rested. The letter was written in blood, the blood of each man there, and they had all signed it.

For Japan.

Kato knelt and drew his knife. He looked at his chief NCO, who was standing beside him, his pistol in his hand. "Banzai," he said.

"Banzai."

Kato stabbed the knife to the hilt in his own stomach.

The sergeant raised his pistol and shot Kato in the back of the head. Blood and brains flew from the captain's head. The sound of the shot made a stupendous thunderclap in the hallway. In the silence that followed, he could hear the tinny sound of the spent cartridge skittering across the floor.

Air escaping from the captain's body made an audible sound, but the sergeant was paying no attention.

He looked at his comrades. They, too, had their pistols out.

Brave men, doing what had to be done.

The sergeant took a deep breath, then raised the barrel of his pistol to his own head. The others did the same. The sergeant inadvertently squeezed his eyes shut just before he pulled the trigger.

CHAPTER TWO

● "CAPTAIN KATO AND his men were all dead when the security men got there," Takeo Yahiro told the prime minister, Atsuko Abe. "Apparently they committed suicide after they beheaded the emperor. The empress was the only person alive—she was passed out on the floor."

Abe's astonishment showed on his face. "The emperor was beheaded in the presence of his wife?"

"It would seem so, sir. She was lying on the floor in a faint when the security officers came upon the scene."

Abe shook his head, trying to make the nightmare easier to endure. To assassinate a powerful official for political reasons was certainly not unheard of in Japan, but to do so in the presence of his wife . . . the *empress*? He had never heard of such a thing.

What would the public think?

"Captain Kato left a letter under the sword scabbard, sir, a letter written in blood. It gave the reasons for his actions."

The prime minister was still fixated upon the presence of the empress at the murder scene. With his eyes closed, he asked, "Did the assassins touch the empress?"

"I do not know, sir. Perhaps the doctors—"

"Has the press gotten this detail?"

Takeo Yahiro spoke softly, yet with assurance. "No, sir. I took the liberty of refusing to allow any press release until senior officials were notified."

Abe breathed deeply through his nose, considering, before he finally opened his eyes. He nodded almost imperceptibly, a mere fraction of an inch.

"Very well, Yahiro. Inflaming the public will not accomplish anything. A tragedy, a horrible tragedy . . ."

"There was a letter, sir. The assassins were disciples of Mishima."

"Ahh . . ." said the prime minister, then fell silent, thinking.

Yukio Mishima had been an ultranationalist, a zealot. Unfortunately he had also been a writer, a novelist, one with a flaming passion for the brutal, bloody gesture. Thirty-eight years ago he and four followers stormed into Japan's military headquarters in downtown Tokyo, barricaded themselves in the office of the commanding general, and called for the military to take over the nation. That didn't happen, of course, but Mishima was not to be denied. He removed his tunic and plunged a sword into his belly; then one of his disciples lopped off his head before killing himself, as well. The whole thing was neatly and tidily done in the grand samurai tradition. Mishima seared a bold political statement into the national conscience in a way impossible to ignore. And, incidentally, there was no one left alive for the authorities to punish—except for a few people on a minor trespass charge.

In the years since Mishima had become a cult figure. His ultranationalistic, militarist message was winning new converts every day, people who were finally coming to understand that they had an absolute duty to fulfill the nation's destiny, to uphold its honor.

"Public dissemination of the fact that the empress was a witness to her husband's assassination would accomplish nothing," Abe said.

"The empress may mention it, sir."

"She never speaks to the press without clearing her remarks with the Imperial Household Agency. She has suffered a terrible shock. When she recovers, she will understand that to speak of her presence at the murder scene would not be in the national interest."

"Yes, sir. I will call the agency immediately."

The prime minister merely nodded—Yahiro was quite reliable—then moved on.

"Prince Hirohito must be placed on the throne. In a matter of hours. Ensure that the ancient ceremony is scrupulously observed—the nation's honor demands it. He must receive the imperial and state seals and the replicas of the Amaterasu treasures." The actual treasures—a mirror, a sword, and a crescent-shaped jewel—could be traced back to the Shinto sun goddess, Amaterasu, from whom the imperial family was descended, so they were too precious to be removed from their vault.

"Arrange it, please, Yahiro."

"Yes, Prime Minister. By all means."

"The senior ministers will all attend. The empress may attend if the doctors think she is strong enough."

The prime minister was almost overcome by the historic overtones of the moment and was briefly unable to speak. *The emperor was dead.* A new emperor was waiting to be enthroned.

He shook his head, trying to clear his thoughts. So much to be done . . .

"Clear my calendar and send for a speechwriter," the prime minister told the aide. "And the protocol officer. We must declare a period of national mourning, notify the foreign embassies—all of that—then set up a state funeral. Heads of government from all over the world will undoubtedly attend, so there is much planning to do."

"Yes, sir."

"Ensure that a copy of Captain Kato's letter is given to the press. The public is entitled to know the reason for this great calamity."

"Yes, sir."

"We are on the cusp of history, Yahiro. We must strive to measure up to the vastness of our responsibilities. Future generations will judge us critically."

Yahiro pondered that remark as he went out of the office, but only for a few seconds. He was a busy man.

Prime Minister Abe waited until the door closed on Yahiro; then he opened the door to the conference room that adjoined his office and went in. Two men in uniform were sitting at the large table. Small teacups sat on the table before them.

One of the men was chief of the Japanese Self-Defense Force. The other was his deputy.

The two soldiers looked expectantly at Abe's face.

"It is done."

The soldiers straightened in their chairs, looked at one another.

"His wife was with him. . . . She saw it."

"A bad omen," one said. Careful planning, dedicated men, and then this horrible slipup.

"We'll try to keep the public from learning that fact," Abe said. He made a gesture of irritation. "We must move on. There is much to be done."

The generals got to their feet, then bowed. "For Japan," the chief of staff said softly.

When Masako awoke, she was in her bed in the royal residence, a Western-style home on the grounds of the Imperial Palace. A physician and nurse were in attendance. The nurse was taking her pulse; the doctor was writing something.

She closed her eyes. The scene came back so vividly she opened them again, focused on the ceiling.

The nurse whispered to the doctor; the doctor came to check her head. He pressed on her forehead, which was sore. Apparently, she had hit it when she had fallen.

"Please leave me alone," she asked.

It took a while, with much bowing by the nurse, but eventually the professionals left the room and closed the door behind them.

Masako kept her eyes open. She was afraid of what she might see if she closed them.

They killed him.

She wondered if she was going to cry.

When it became apparent that she was not, she sat up in bed, examined her sore head in a mirror. Yes, she had fallen on her forehead, which sported a vicious bruise. She fingered the place, felt the pain as she pressed, savored it.

They killed him! A shy, gentle man, a figurehead with no power. Murdered. For reasons that would be specious, ridiculous. For reasons that would interest only an insane fanatic, *they killed him.*

She felt empty, as if all life had been taken from her. She was only an unfeeling shell, a mere observer of this horrible tragedy that this woman named Masako was living through.

She sat upon the bed, unwilling to move. Scenes of her life with Naruhito flashed through her mind, raced along, but finally they were gone and the tree outside had thrown the room in shadow, and she was merely alone, in an empty room, with her husband dead.

In Washington, D.C., the president of the United States was getting ready for bed. He was going to bed alone, as usual, because his wife was at a soiree somewhere in Georgetown, playing the First Lady role to the hilt. The president was chewing two antiacid tablets when he picked up the ringing telephone and mumbled, "Uumpf."

"Mr. President, the emperor of Japan was assassinated in the Imperial Palace about two hours ago. The report is that he was beheaded." The voice was that of Jack Innes, national security adviser. He would have been called about this matter by the duty officers in the White House situation room.

"Who did it?"

"Apparently a junior officer in the military and three enlisted men. They got into the palace by posing as telephone repairmen. Lopped off the emperor's head with a four-hundred-year-old samurai sword. Then they committed suicide."

"All of them?"

"All four. The officer stabbed himself in the gut; then someone shot him in the head. The three enlisted apparently shot themselves."

"Jesus!"

"Yes, sir."

"Right-wing group?"

"Apparently they were followers of some right-wing cult, Mishima something. They left a letter written in blood, full of bullshit about Japan's destiny and national glory."

"Have we received any answer from the emperor to my letter?" the president asked.

"Not to my knowledge, sir. I'll check with the Tokyo embassy and the State Department."

"Do we even know if he received it?"

"It was delivered to the Japanese government by our ambassador. That is all we know for certain."

"We are fast running out of options."

"We should know more in the morning, Mr. President."

"When you know more, wake me up."

"Yes, sir."

President David Herbert Hood cradled the instrument and lay down on his bed. He was very tired. It seemed that he was always in that condition these days.

So Naruhito was dead. Murdered.

And the letter had accomplished nothing.

The president, Jack Innes, and the secretary of state had sweated for three days over the wording in that letter. After careful consideration, they had decided not to mention the fact that the United States had a secret military protocol with Russia promising military aid if Russia's borders were ever violated. The protocol was three years old, negotiated and signed as an inducement to Russia's fledgling democratic government to speed up the pace of nuclear disarmament. Even he, David Herbert Hood, had personally told the Russian president that the secret protocol was a solemn promise: "Russian territory is as sacred as the boundaries of the United States."

Well, a promise is a promise, but whether the promise would be honored was a different matter entirely.

The president got out of bed and went to the window. He stood there looking at the lights of Washington. After a bit, he sank into a chair and rubbed his head. He had spent the last twenty years in politics and he had seen his share of unexpected disasters. Most of the time, he had learned, the best thing to do was nothing at all.

Yes, nothing was usually best. The Japanese had another crisis on their hands, and the Japanese were going to have to solve it.

He should get some sleep.

The news from the far side of the Pacific had been getting steadily worse for years. Democracy in Russia had been a mixed blessing. Freed at last from Communist tyranny and mismanagement, the Russians soon found they lacked the ability to create a stable government. Corruption and bribery were endemic everywhere, in every occupation and walk of life. A dying man couldn't see a doctor without bribing the receptionist. Apparently, the only people doing well in the post-Communist era were the criminals. Ethnic minorities all over Russia had seized this moment to demand self-government, their own enclaves. If the Russian government didn't get a grip soon, a new dictator was inevitable.

In the United States, the public didn't want to hear bad news from overseas. The recent crisis in the Mideast had doubled the price of oil, here and around the world, a harbinger of shortages to come. Still, America had oil, so it didn't suffer as badly as Japan did. And the oil was flowing again. All in all, life in America was very, very good. And David Herbert Hood had the extreme good fortune to be riding the crest of the wave, presiding at the world's greatest party. His popularity was at a historic high; the nation was prosperous and at peace. . . . He would go into the history books with a smile on his face, children would read his biography in grade school for the next century, at least, and . . . Japan was about to invade Siberia.

The president stared gloomily at the lights out there in the night. He had this feeling that, for some reason just beyond the edge of the light, mankind had been enjoying a rare interlude of prosperity and peace. They certainly hadn't earned it.

The emperor . . . murdered. My God! The man was the benign symbol of all that was best in the Japanese culture. And they cut off his head!

———

Captain Jiro Kimura sat on the small balcony of his flat, staring between apartment and office buildings at Mount Fuji and drinking a beer. Although he was looking at Fuji, in his mind's eye he saw Pikes Peak, stark, craggy, looming high into the blue Colorado sky. "The Peak of Pike," his fellow cadets had called it, back when they were students at the U.S. Air Force Academy.

It was in his second or third year that three of his friends convinced themselves, and him, that they should run up the mountain. And back down. They tried it the second weekend in September, a Pikes Peak marathon, thirteen miles up and thirteen down.

Jiro Kimura smiled at the memory. What studs they had been back then, whippet-lean, tough as sole leather, ready to conquer the world! They actually made it to the top of the mountain and back down. Still, the last few miles going up, the pace was not what anyone would call a run. Not above twelve thousand feet!

Although that weekend had been almost twelve years ago, Jiro could recall the faces of those boys as if it were yesterday. He could see Frank Truax's shy, toothy grin; Joe Layfield's freckles and jug ears; Ben Franklin Garcia's white teeth flashing in his handsome brown face.

Garcia had died six years ago in an F-16 crash, somewhere in Nevada. They said his engine flamed out and, rather than ejecting, he tried to stretch a glide. That sure sounded like Ben Garcia, "the pride of Pecos, Texas," as they called him back then. He had been tough and smart, with something to prove, something Jiro Kimura could never quite put a finger on. Well, Ben was gone now, gone to wherever it is God sends those driven men when they finally fall to earth.

Truax was somewhere in the states flying C-141s, and Layfield was getting a master's degree in finance.

And Jiro Kimura was flying Japan's top-secret fighter plane, the new Zero.

His wife, Shizuko, came out onto the balcony with another beer. "Colonel Cassidy will be here soon," she said, a gentle reminder that he might wish to dress in something besides a T-shirt and shorts.

Jiro smiled his thanks.

Bob Cassidy. He had been a major back then, a young fighter pilot at the Academy for a tour. He had been commander of Jiro's cadet squadron. He took a liking to the Japanese youngster, who had nowhere to go for weekends or holidays, so he took him home.

Cassidy was married then, to Sweet Sabrina, as he always called her.

Never just Sabrina, always with the adjective before her name, and always with a smile. Sweet Sabrina ... with the long brown hair and a ready smile ...

She and the boy died in a car wreck two years after Jiro graduated. Cassidy never remarried.

He should have married again, Jiro Kimura told himself, and he involuntarily glanced through the open door at Shizuko, busy within.

Perhaps Cassidy had never found another woman who measured up to Sweet Sabrina. Perhaps ...

Ah, if only he could go back. If only he could go back and relive those days, go back to the patio in Cassidy's yard with Truax and Garcia and Layfield, with Sweet Sabrina serving cold beer to boys not yet twenty-one while Bob Cassidy pretended not to notice, someone tuning the radio to the station called "The Peak" because it played all the top hits.

Just one day ... that wouldn't be asking too much. A hot day, in the high eighties or low nineties, so the sweat on your skin would evaporate as fast as it appeared, a hot, high, dry day, with that Colorado sun warming your face and a faint scent of juniper in the air and the shady side of Pikes Peak purple in the afternoon.

Jiro missed those days.

He missed those people. Or most of them, anyway. He certainly didn't miss Major Tarleton, the physics professor, whose two uncles had died in the western Pacific, "fighting the Japs." That was the way he'd phrased it, wasn't it, while staring at Jiro as if he had personally ordered the attack on Pearl Harbor? There had been others, too, officers and enlisted, who went out of their way to let him know they didn't appreciate the fact that a Japanese soldier was training at the U.S. Air Force Academy.

Tarleton had been more than prejudiced—he had tried to ruin Jiro's academic career, gave him a failing grade for quiz after quiz, even though every answer was correct. Afraid, alone, Jiro endured in silence. Then Tarleton accused him of cheating on an exam. An ice-cold Bob Cassidy called the young cadet into his office, grilled him until he had it all.

The following Monday morning, Tarleton was gone, and Jiro heard no more about the alleged honor code violation.

Cassidy was like that. He would risk everything to save one scared kid.

Jiro Kimura took another drag at the beer and stared with unseeing eyes at the snowcapped cone of Fuji.

Maybe what he missed was America.

He wiped the tears from his eyes.

They had never asked who his father was, what he did, how much money he had. Not once. They took him for who he was, what he was. And they made him one of them.

Cassidy was a colonel now, the Air Force liaison officer at the U.S. embassy in Tokyo. He was still trim, still grinned, although maybe not as readily as he used to when Sweet Sabrina was alive.

He worked too hard now. Jiro was sure of that. Good colonels work a lot more than captains, and Cassidy was a good one. In fact, he was one of the best.

Back then some of the guys had called him "Hopalong" behind his back. Or "Butch." They had to explain the references to Jiro. He never did understand exactly how nicknames were derived or bestowed, although he did acquire the American taste for them. Still, for him, Cassidy was always Cassidy.

Or Bob. How American! "Use my first name. That shows that you like me."

Jiro was in the bedroom changing clothes when he heard the knock on the door and the sounds of Shizuko greeting Cassidy.

"Oh, Colonel, so good to see you." Shizuko's English was not so good, but Cassidy had never had too much trouble understanding it.

"Have you heard the news? About the emperor?" Cassidy's voice was hard, very concerned.

"What news?" He could hear the worry in Shizuko's voice.

"He was assassinated. They just announced it."

Shizuko said something that Jiro didn't hear, then several seconds later he heard the sound of the television announcer.

He quickly finished dressing and hurried into the living room. It was a small room, about a third the size of the one Cassidy used to have in Colorado Springs. Jiro shook his head, annoyed that that irrelevant thought should distract him at a time like this.

He said hello to Cassidy, who gave a tiny bow while remaining intent on the television.

"Sit, Colonel. Bob. Please."

Cassidy knew some Japanese, apparently enough to follow the television announcer without too much difficulty.

Shizuko hid her face in her hands.

"Perhaps this isn't a good evening . . ." Cassidy began, but Jiro waved him into silence.

They sat on the mats in front of the television as the last of the afternoon light faded from the sky. It was completely dark when Jiro turned off the set and Shizuko went into the small Pullman-style kitchen to make dinner.

Cassidy was about six feet tall, a wiry man with a runner's build. Tonight he wore civilian clothes, dark slacks and a beige short-sleeve shirt. He had blue eyes, thinning sandy-colored hair, and a couple of chipped teeth, which had been that way for years. A cheap watch on his left wrist was his only jewelry.

"Beer?"

"Sure."

"Good to see you, Bob." Kimura spoke like an American, Cassidy thought, with fluent, unaccented English.

"When I heard the news on the radio, I almost turned around and went home," Cassidy told his host. "Thought you and Shizuko might want some privacy. But I figured that these get-together times are so hard to arrange that . . ."

"Yeah. I needed to talk to you. This assassination is not good." Jiro Kimura thought for several seconds, then shook his head. "Not good. Japan is on a strange, dangerous road."

Cassidy looked around the apartment, accepted the offered beer. Kimura turned on a radio, played with the dial until he got music, then resumed his seat just across from his guest.

"They are preparing to move the planes to forward bases," Jiro said. "We are packing everything, crating all the support gear, all the special tools, spare engines, parts, tires, everything."

"You mean bases outside of Japan?"

"Yes."

Robert Cassidy sat in silence, digesting Kimura's comment. Finally, he sipped his beer, then waited expectantly for his host to decide what else he wanted to say. For some reason, at that moment he recalled Jiro as he had first known him, a lost, miserable doolie at the U.S. Air Force Academy. A more forlorn kid, Cassidy had never met.

Of course, the Japanese had sent their very best to the United States as an exchange student. Jiro finished second in his class, with a 3.98 grade point average—in aeronautical engineering. The first person in the class was a black girl from Georgia with a 180 IQ. After graduation, she didn't spend a day in uniform; she went on to get a Ph.D. in physics on the Air Force's dime. The last Cassidy heard, she was doing fusion research at the Lawrence Livermore Laboratory.

Jiro became a first-rate fighter pilot—for Japan. Now he was flying an airplane that had been developed in the utmost secrecy. Until Kimura mentioned the new Zero to him six months ago, Cassidy had not known of the plane. Judging by the startled reaction his report caused in Washington when he sent it in, no one there knew about it, either. Since then he had received a blizzard of requests from Washington for further information on the new plane, and he had had just two further conversations with Jiro.

The first occurred when he invited the Kimuras to dinner in Tokyo. Jiro didn't mention his job during the course of the evening. Cassidy couldn't bring himself to ask a question.

It was obvious that Jiro had wrestled with his conscience long and hard before he violated the Japanese security regs the first time.

Cassidy decided that the next move was up to Jiro. If he wanted to tell the U.S. government Japanese secrets, Cassidy would convey the information. But he would not ask.

Last month he and Jiro had attended a baseball game together. In the isolation of a nearly empty upper deck of the stadium, Jiro discussed in general terms the dimensions of the Japanese military buildup that had been under way for at least five years. Some of that information Cassidy knew from other sources; some was new. He merely listened, asked questions only to clarify, then wrote a detailed report that evening when he got home. That afternoon Jiro had been short on specifics.

Whatever internal battle Jiro was fighting then was apparently over now. Tonight he met Cassidy's gaze. "The new Zero is the most advanced fighter on earth. Very maneuverable, stealthy, good range, speed, easy to fly. Very sophisticated radar and computer, GPS"—this was the global positioning system—"all the goodies. And it has Athena."

"I don't know what that is," Cassidy said.

"Athena is, or was, the American project code name for some very advanced stealth technology, an active ECM protection system. Somehow Japan acquired the technology, which had almost died in the United States due to a lack of development funds."

Cassidy nodded. American spending on research and development of military technology had slowed to a trickle since the end of the Cold War.

Jiro continued. "Athena arrived here just when the government was looking to spend serious money on developing a military tech edge.

They latched onto Athena and made it the centerpiece of the new Zero."

"Explain to me how it works."

When Jiro didn't immediately reply, Cassidy added, "You know you don't have to tell me anything, Jiro. I didn't ask you for anything."

"I know! I want to tell you, Bob." Jiro Kimura searched for words. He stood and went out on the balcony. Cassidy followed.

"I was born in this country. I live here. But America is also my home. Do you understand?"

"I think so."

"I have two homes, two peoples. I will tell you what I can, and you must pass it on in great secrecy. If the Japanese find out I have even spoken of these matters, I will be in serious trouble."

"Up to your ass in it, kiddo. I understand."

"The world is too small for loyalties based on race. Or nationality."

"That is sort of an advanced idea, but I'll grant you—"

"Just don't think less of me because I need to tell you these things. I don't ever want to fight against Americans."

He was facing Cassidy now, looking straight into his eyes. "Do you see how it is, Bob?"

"Yeah, kid. I see."

Jiro rested his forearms on the balcony railing and looked between the high-rises at the white ghost of Fuji, just visible against the late-evening sky. "Athena is active ECM." ECM meant electronic counter-measures. "It detects enemy radar transmissions, then radiates on the same frequency from antennas all over the plane to cancel out the incoming transmissions. Uses a small super-cooled computer."

"Uh-huh."

Jiro Kimura could see from the look on Cassidy's face that he had no appreciation of the advantage that Athena conferred on the plane it protected. "What Athena does, Bob, is make the Zero invisible to ra-dar."

Cassidy's eyebrows went up.

"Low-observable—stealth—technology began when designers tried to minimize the radar return by altering the shape of the craft. Then designers used radar-absorbent materials to the maximum extent prac-ticable. Athena is stealth technology a generation beyond shapes and materials, which, as you know, limit the performance and capabilities of a stealth aircraft.

"The Zero is a conventional aircraft made of composites—a damn big engine, gas tanks stuck everywhere, vectored thrust, boundary layer control on a fixed wing, really extraordinary performance. It's got all the electronic goodies to help its pilot find the enemy and kill him. Athena hides it."

"Sounds like a hell of a plane."

"It is that, Bob, one hell of a fighter plane. It can do simply unbelievable things in the air, and the brass wants us to use it as a straight and level interceptor. Find the enemy, launch missiles, fly home to an instrument approach. Sounds like something a bunch of brass-hatted desk pilots thought up from the safety of a corner office, huh?"

"Well, if you have enough missiles..."

"There are never enough."

"How many Zeros are there?"

"About a hundred. The number is classified and no one mentions it. I have been trying to count nosewheels, so to speak."

After a bit, the American colonel asked, "So where is the Japanese government planning on using these things?"

"Russia, I think. But no one had confirmed that."

"When?"

"Soon. Very soon."

"Abe is very nationalistic, advocates a larger role for the military in Japanese life. What do the folks in uniform think of all this?"

"Most of them like Abe, like what he is saying. The officers seem to be with him almost to a man." Jiro paused to gather his thoughts. "The Japanese have much more respect for authority than Americans. They like being part of a large, organized society. It fits them somehow. The American concept of individual freedom..." He shook his head negatively and shrugged.

"What about the Mishima disciples?" These ultra-right-wing nationalists were back in the news again, claiming converts in the military and civil service.

"Mishima was a fanatic zealot, a fossil, a relic of a bygone age. Everybody knows that. But he preached a return to the noble-warrior concept, the samurai spirit, and that still fascinates a lot of Japanese."

Bob Cassidy rubbed his face hard, then said, "I guess I have trouble taking Mishima, Abe, this samurai warrior shit—I have trouble taking any of that seriously. All that testosterone ranting and posturing... man, that crap went out everywhere else when gunpowder came in.

There is no such thing as a noble death in the nuclear age. The very term is an oxymoron. Didn't Hiroshima and Nagasaki teach the Japanese that?"

A grimace crossed Jiro's face. "Bob, you're talking to the converted," he said. "My morals were corrupted in Colorado Springs years ago. I'm just trying to explain."

"The only noble death is from old age," Cassidy continued, "but you gotta get there to get it, amigo. That's getting harder and harder to do these days."

Shizuko came out of the kitchen carrying a large dish.

"Thanks, Jiro."

"I wish Shizuko and I were back in Colorado Springs, Bob, sitting on your patio with Sweet Sabrina."

"We can't ever go back," Cassidy told him. "When the song is over, it's over. I know. I wanted to go back so badly, I almost died."

In the middle of dinner, Jiro said, "The United States is going to have to take a stand, Bob. Atsuko Abe and his friends are crazy, but I don't think they are crazy enough to strap on the United States."

"I hope to God you're right."

Shizuko acted as if she didn't understand the English words.

"What if *you* aren't?" Cassidy asked in a small voice.

Jiro pretended he hadn't heard.

Bob Cassidy's thoughts went to Sweet Sabrina. It was good, he thought, to be with someone who remembered her fondly.

The U.S. ambassador to Japan was Stanley P. Hanratty, who owned a string of automobile dealerships around Cleveland and Akron. He was balding, overweight, and smart. His middle initial stood for Philip, a name he hated, yet he thought his name looked too informal without a middle name or initial or something, so he used the *P.*

Stanley P. had spent twenty-seven years of his life getting to Japan. He started out selling used cars, mortgaged his house and soul to acquire a used-car sales lot, and then a second, and a third, finally a new car dealership, then another and another and another.

He was arranging the financing on the second dealership when he made his first big political contribution. Occasionally men from humble backgrounds have large ambitions, and Hanratty did: he wanted someday to be an ambassador to a big country.

For years, he listened to windy speeches, shook hands, wrote checks, and watched the political hopefuls come and go. By the time he had eight dealerships, he was giving to political parties in a six-figure way. Finally, he was rewarded with an ambassadorship.

Stanley P. had never forgotten the conversation when one of the members of the new president's transition team called him about the position.

"The president-elect would like to send your name to the Senate. Mr. Hanratty, he wants you *on his team.*"

"Guinea-Bis what? How did you say that?"

"Bissau. It's in Africa, I think."

"North or south of the equator?"

"Well, sir, I don't know. I seem to recall that it's on the west side of the continent, but don't hold me to that."

Through the years, Stanley P. had invested a lot of money in his quest, so he didn't hesitate. With feeling, he said, "You tell the president-elect that I'm honored he thought of me. I'll be delighted to serve his administration anywhere he wants."

After he hung up the telephone, he looked the place up in an atlas. U.S. ambassador to Guinea-Bissau!

In Guinea-Bissau, Hanratty did more than luxuriate in the ambassador's quarters of the embassy, which in truth were not all that luxurious; he studiously applied himself to learning the business of diplomacy. He attacked the State Department's paper-flow charts and the ins and outs of Bissauan politics with the same common sense, drive, and determination that he used to sell cars. He made shrewd evaluations of local politicians and wrote clear, concise, accurate reports. He didn't once blame conditions in Guinea-Bissau on United States foreign policy, an attitude that State Department professionals found both unusual and refreshing. He also proved to have an extraordinary quality that endeared him to policy makers in Washington: if given instructions, he followed them to the letter.

After he correctly predicted that a military coup would occur in Guinea-Bissau if a certain person won an election, Hanratty was named ambassador to a nation in the Middle East endangered by fundamentalist Islamic zealots. He performed superbly there, too, so when the U.S. ambassador to Japan dropped dead of a heart attack, the secretary of state was relieved that he could send Stanley P. Hanratty to the American embassy in Tokyo.

Hanratty had been in Tokyo for thirteen months when the emperor was assassinated. During his habitual sixteen-hour workdays, he had become expert in the myriad aspects of U.S.-Japanese relations and made many friends in key places. This evening, just hours after the emperor's murder, with the world still in shock, he was sitting in his office with the television on, putting the finishing touches on a private letter to the secretary of state, when he heard the knocking on the door.

"Come in," he called loudly, because the doors were thick and heavy.

"Mr. Ambassador, I wonder if I might have a few moments of your time?"

"Colonel Cassidy, please come in."

Stanley P. liked the Air Force attaché, who occasionally dropped by to inform him firsthand of developments in the Japanese military that he would eventually read about weeks later in secret CIA summaries. The senior CIA officer, on the other hand, never told him anything. It was almost as if that gentleman thought the ambassador couldn't be trusted with sensitive information, which frosted Stanley P. a little.

"It's been a long day, Colonel. How about a drink?"

"Thank you, sir. I'll have whatever you're having."

Stanley P. removed a bottle of bourbon and two glasses from his lower desk drawer. He poured a shot in each glass and passed one to Cassidy.

"I've been speculating, Colonel. Speculating with no information. Speculate with me a little."

Cassidy sipped the whiskey.

"Do you think it's possible that a faction, shall we say, in the Japanese government might have had a hand in the emperor's assassination?"

"I had dinner this evening with an officer in the Japanese Self-Defense Force, the air arm, and he said the officers are with Abe almost to a man. They think he's going to save the nation."

"The killers were soldiers, I believe."

"That's what the government is telling the press. I suppose some high official might have enlisted some zealots to undertake a suicide mission. There is historical precedence, as I recall."

"There is precedent by the page," the ambassador admitted. He concentrated on savoring the golden liquid.

"The assassination is going down pretty hard with the guy on the street," the colonel said. "I rode the train back to Tokyo. The people in the subways and trains seem pretty upset."

"Murder is a filthy business," the ambassador muttered.

"This officer I had dinner with tonight . . . he told me some things that he shouldn't have. Perhaps the news of the assassination made him feel that . . . Oh, I don't know!"

Cassidy brushed the thought away, unwilling to try to analyze his friend or make polite excuses for him. Jiro did what Jiro felt he had to do. "The Japanese have developed, manufactured, and put in service about one hundred new, highly capable fighter planes." The colonel weighed his words. "They are more capable than anything in our inventory, according to my source."

"How good is your source?"

"Beyond reproach. One hundred percent credible."

The ambassador poured himself another drink, offered more to the colonel, who refused. Cassidy could see his and the ambassador's reflections in the window glass. Beyond the reflections were the lights of Tokyo.

"The thing my source confided in me that I believe you should know, sir, is this: His squadron is packing for deployment in the near future."

"Deployment where?"

"Russia, he thought."

"The appeal for Japanese help by the native minorities—there was a television broadcast about them last night. According to the government, they are the racial cousins of the Japanese." The ambassador channel-surfed with his television remote. He had picked up more than a smattering of the language. ·

"Perhaps they will just move your source's squadron to another base here in Japan," Stanley P. suggested to Cassidy.

"That is possible, sir. My source didn't think so, though. He thinks the squadron is going a lot farther than that."

CHAPTER THREE

● WHEN MASATAKA OKADA returned to his office after lunch everyone in the department was watching television—a day after Emperor Naruhito's assassination, the television types were still microanalyzing the implications. Okada's office was fairly large by Japanese standards, about ten feet by ten feet, but all the walls above waist level were glass. Apparently the architect believed that the best way to keep spies in line was to let them watch one another.

Okada had spent the morning decoding the message from an agent with the code name of Ten, or Ju in Japanese. Alas, it was forbidden to input messages this highly classified into the computer, so the work had to be done by hand.

He had completed the decoding, a tedious task, then did the translation and typed the result before lunch. Now he removed the file from his personal safe and read the translation again.

The message was important, no question.

Very important. In fact, Masataka Okada suspected that the future of both Japan and Russia hinged on the contents of this two-page message from Agent Ju. Of course, Okada had no idea who Ju actually was, but he obviously had access to the very top leadership in the Russian army. He also had access to the contents of the safes of the top leadership, because some of this information could have come only from official documents.

Boiled down, the message was that the last of the guidance systems had been removed from the Russians' submarine-based ballistic missiles. The Russians had finished removing the guidance systems from their land-based ICBMs last year; their tactical nuclear warheads had been removed from service and destroyed five years ago.

Russia was no longer a nuclear power.

Okada knew that the United States had secretly insisted upon nuclear disarmament as the price of the massive foreign aid needed by the current, elected regime to solidify its hold on power. That fact came from intercepted American diplomatic traffic. The United States hadn't even briefed its allies.

Well, the secret had certainly been well kept, even in Russia. Not a whisper of this earth-shattering development had appeared anywhere in the public press in Russia or Western Europe: Okada would have seen it mentioned in the agency's press summaries if it had been. Part of the reason was that only the top echelon of military commanders in Russia knew that *all* the guidance systems had been removed in a series of maintenance programs nominally designed to test and return to service every system in the inventory.

Disarmament was such a political hot potato that the Russian government had kept it a secret from its own people.

By some tangled loop of Kremlin logic, this course of action made perfect sense. As long as no one outside the upper echelons of government knew that the nuclear weapons delivery systems were no longer operational, no one lost face, and no one lost votes. The domestic political crises never materialized. And as long as no one outside Russia knew, the missiles continued to deter potential aggressors, just as they always had. Deterrence *was* the function of ICBMs, wasn't it?

Now the Japanese knew. And the Russian government didn't know they knew.

That is, the Japanese would know as soon as Masataka Okada signed the routing slip and sent the message to his superior officer, the head of Asian intelligence for the Japanese Intelligence Agency.

From Okada's boss, the news would go to the head of the agency, who would take it to the prime minister, Atsuko Abe.

What Atsuko Abe would make of this choice tidbit was a matter to speculate darkly about. Masataka Okada did just that now as he chewed on a fingernail. Abe's national-destiny speeches leapt to mind, as did the secret military buildup that had been going on in Japan for the last five years. And now there was the assassin's letter, written in blood, which had been leaked to the newspapers by someone in the prosecutor's office investigating the assassination. The letter demanded that the military take over the government and lead Japan to glory. Okada's friends and acquaintances—indeed, the whole nation—could talk of little else. Amazingly, the ritual suicides of the emperor's killers had given the ultranationalistic, militaristic views of the Mishima sect a mainstream legitimacy that they had never before enjoyed.

Watching this orgy of twisted patriotism gave Okada chills.

What would be the consequences to Japan if military force was used against Russia?

Okada well knew that there would be consequences, mostly unpredictable and, he feared, mostly negative. He certainly didn't share Abe's faith in Japan's destiny.

Okada's father's first wife died at Hiroshima under the mushroom cloud. He was a son of the second wife, who had been severely burned at Hiroshima but had survived. As a boy, he had examined his mother's scars as she bathed. When he was ten she died of leukemia—another victim of the bomb. Forty years had passed since then, but he could still close his eyes and see how the flesh on her back had been burned, literally cooked, by the thermal pulse of the explosion.

He fumbled for his cigarettes, lit one, and tried to forget his mother's back as he inhaled deeply, savoring the smoke.

What if . . .

What if this message merely reported that some of the guidance systems had been removed?

Masataka Okada scrutinized the message carefully. Well, it would be easy enough to write another translation. If he deleted this third sentence, changed this phrase, added a sentence or two at the bottom, he could make it appear that the Russians were still years away from complete disarmament.

His superiors would catch him eventually.

Or would they?

It wasn't like the head of the agency was going to Moscow any time soon for a personal chat with Agent Ju.

The other people in the office were still intently watching the television set.

I must be going mad. Crazy. The pressure is getting to me. The first rule, the very first rule, is never, ever put anything in writing that creates the least suspicion. Leave no tracks.

But what I'm contemplating is not espionage; it's sabotage.

He intertwined his fingers and twisted until the pain brought tears to his eyes.

At some point, a man must make a stand.

This is insane! You are merely buying time.

Okada scrolled a sheet of paper into his typewriter, glanced yet again at the backs of his colleagues, and began to type.

You are buying time at the cost of your own life, fool. No one will care. Not a single, solitary soul will care one iota.

After two lines, he stopped and stared at the words he had written. This wouldn't work.

Ju was certain to send follow-up reports; indeed, he might have already sent other reports on this subject. It was probable that he had. Both previous and future reports might be given to another cryptographer to decode. It was just a stroke of good fortune that Okada had been handed this particular message.

He took the sheet of paper from the typewriter and inserted another.

The best way to discount the message wasn't to change the facts related, but to change the way they were related. Okada knew his boss, Toshihiko Ayukawa. The man had an uncanny ability to separate gold from dross. Intelligence agencies inevitably gathered huge amounts of dross: idle rumors, wild speculations, inaccurate gossip, outright lies, and, worst of all, disinformation passed as truth.

Through the years, Okada had become a connoisseur of intelligence reports. As he had first typed it, Agent Ju's report seemed to be pure gold—it contained eloquent facts, lots of them, crammed into as few words as possible, yet the source for each fact was carefully related. What if the style was changed, not too much, but just enough?

It would be dicey—the message would have to appear to someone who knew Ju's style to be indubitably his, yet the tone had to be wrong—not clearly wrong, just subtly wrong, enough to create a shadow of doubt about the truth of the facts related in the mind of a knowledgeable reader. The tone would be the lie.

God knows, Toshihiko Ayukawa was a knowledgeable reader!

Okada lit another cigarette. He flexed his fingers.

His colleagues were still glued to the television in the common area.

He took a last drag, put the cigarette in an ashtray to smolder, and began to type quickly.

The thought shot through his head that Ayukawa might ask another cryptographer to decode the original of this message again.

True, he might, if he thought Okada had done a sloppy job.

And if he did that, Okada would be in more trouble than he could handle.

He would just have to rely on his reputation, that's all. He was the best. The boss damn well knew it.

Oh well, every man's fate was in the hands of the gods. They would write a man's life as they chose.

His fingers flew over the keyboard.

When he finished the message, he read it over carefully. He had it the way he wanted it.

He put the fake message into the official envelope and signed the routing slip in the box provided for the cryptographer.

The people outside were still watching television, milling around, talking. No one seemed to be looking his way.

Okada held the copy of the real message under his desk and folded it carefully. He then slipped the small square of paper into a sock.

He took the envelope in his hand, weighing it one last time. When he walked out of this office with this envelope in his hand, he was irrevocably committed.

He swayed slightly as the enormity of what he had done pressed down upon him. He had to struggle to draw a breath.

Ayukawa knew Ju's work. This fake message might stand out like a police emergency light on a dark night.

If so, Masataka Okada was doomed.

His eye fell upon the old photo of his family that stood on the back of his desk. It was perched precariously there, almost ready to fall on the floor, shoved out of the way when he made room for the usual books and files and reports that seemed to grow like mushrooms on his desk. That picture must be at least ten years old. His daughter was grown now, with a baby of her own. His son was in graduate school.

What would they look like with their skin black and smoking and hanging in putrid ribbons from their backs? From their faces?

Masataka Okada took a firm grip on the envelope and walked out of his office.

At six that evening, Okada's superior officer, Toshihiko Ayukawa, got around to opening the classified security envelope containing the decoded message from Agent Ju. He'd had a feeling when this message first came in that it might be very important, but he had spent the afternoon in meetings and was just now getting to the red-hot matters awaiting his attention in his office. It was a wonder his desk hadn't melted, with a belligerent China, civil unrest in Siberia, and riots in the streets of Hong Kong. Yet the assassination of the emperor and the coming state funeral took precedence over everything.

"No," he had told the agency director, "we have no indication whatever that any Asian power had anything to do with the emperor's murder."

As Ayukawa read the message, he frowned. It sounded like Ju, cited the proper codes, yet... He read it through again slowly, his mind racing.

He looked at the envelope for the signature of the cryptographer. Okada.

Then he called his confidential assistant, Sushi Maezumi. He held up the envelope where Sushi could see it.

"Why did you give this to Okada?"

The assistant looked at the signature, then his face fell. "I apologize, sir. I forgot."

"I had another copy of this message for decoding." Ayukawa consulted his ledger. He believed in keeping his operation strictly compartmentalized. It was unfortunate that the aide had to know that he occasionally handed out duplicates of the messages to be decoded and translated, but unless he had the time to do everything himself—and he didn't—he had to delegate. The use of duplicates allowed him to check on the competency of his staff. And their loyalty. And if the message was important, he would have two versions to compare, for they were never exactly the same.

"Number three four oh nine," Ayukawa said. "Where is it?"

"Here, sir." Sushi removed the envelope from the bottom of the pile.

Ayukawa ripped it open and scanned the message. He didn't even bother to compare this with Okada's short story.

"You disobeyed my order. I told you not to give any sensitive item to Okada without my express approval."

"I forgot, sir."

The avoidance of direct confrontation was one of the pillars on which Japanese society rested. Ayukawa had little use for that social more. "That's no excuse," he said bluntly to his aide, who blanched. "My instructions must be obeyed to the letter. *Always.* I am the officer responsible, not you. And you know that we have a mole in this agency. ... But enough—we'll discuss it later. Go see if Okada is still in the building. Now, quickly."

Speechless after this verbal hiding, Sushi Maezumi shot from the office as if he had been scalded.

In the Shinjuku district neon lights tinted the skins of visitors red, green, blue, orange, and yellow, all in succession, as they moved from one garishly lit storefront to the next. Beyond the light was the night, but here there was life. Here there was sex.

This was Tokyo's French Quarter, only more so, a concentration of adult bookstores, peep shows, porno palaces, and nightclubs, with here and there a whorehouse for the terminally conventional. The whorehouses ranged from bordellos specializing in cheap quickies to geisha houses where the evening's entertainment might cost thousands of dollars.

The crowds were an inherent part of the district's attraction. A visitor could blend into the mass of humanity and become an anonymous voyeur, savoring sexual pleasures denied by social convention, which is the very essence of pornography.

Masataka Okada moved easily through the swarms of people. He enjoyed the sexual tension, a release from the extraordinary, heart-attack stress he had experienced that day, as he did every day. The flashing lights and weird colors, highlighted on the men's white shirts, seemed to draw him and everyone else into the fantasy world of pleasure.

Okada bought two square cakes of fried shark meat from a sidewalk vendor. The heat of the evening and closeness of the crowd made the smell of the cooking fat and fish particularly pungent.

He walked on, adrift in this sea of people. The lights and heat and smells engulfed him.

Somewhere on this planet there might be an occupation more stressful than that of a spy, but it would be difficult to imagine what it would be. A spy played a deadly game, was always onstage, spent every waking moment waiting for the ax to fall. In the beginning it had been easier for Masataka Okada, but now, as the full implications of his choices became increasingly clear, just getting through each day became more and more difficult. Every gesture, every word, every unspoken nuance had to be examined for a sinister meaning. Any slip would be fatal, so every choice came laden with stress.

The truth of the matter was that Masataka Okada was burning out. He was nearing the end of his string.

As he strolled and watched the crowd this evening, his thoughts turned to World War II. Every Japanese had to come to grips with World War II in some personal way. Every living person had lost family members in that holocaust—grandfathers, fathers, brothers, uncles, cousins, mothers, aunts, grandmothers—all gone, like smoke, as if they had never been. Yet they *had* been; they *had* lived, and they had been cut down.

About 2.1 million Japanese had perished in that war, over 6 million Chinese and, however the apologists dressed it up, the fact remained that the war in the Pacific had begun with Japan's full-scale assault on China in 1937. Once blood had been drawn, Japan's doom became inevitable: the rape of Nanking, Pearl Harbor, the Bataan death march, the firebombing of Japanese cities, Okinawa, the obliteration of Hiroshima and Nagasaki—it was a litany of human suffering as horrific as any event the species had yet endured.

Okada had long ago made up his mind who was responsible for that suicidal course of events: Japan's government, and its people, for governments do not act in a vacuum. When you thought about it dispassionately, you had to question the sanity of the persons responsible. A crowded island nation about the size of California willingly had sought total war with the most powerful nation on earth, one with twice its population and *ten* times its industrial capacity.

And so, in a tragedy written in blood, an entire generation of young men had been sacrificed on the altar of war; the treasure of the nation—accumulated through the centuries—had been squandered, every family ripped asunder, the homeland devastated, laid waste.

All that was history, the dead past. As long ago and far away as the Mejii restoration, as the first shogun . . . and yet it wasn't. The war had scarred them all.

An hour's strolling back and forth through the neighborhood brought Okada to a small peep parlor. With a long last look in a window at the reflections of the people behind him, he paid his admission and went inside.

The foyer was dimly lit. Sound came from hidden speakers: Japanese music, adenoidal wailing above a twanging string instrument—just noise.

From the foyer, one entered a long hallway, each side of which was lined with doors. Small red bulbs in the ceiling illuminated the very air, which was almost an impenetrable solid: swirling cigarette smoke, the smell of perspiration, and something sickeningly sweet—semen.

The walls seemed to close in; it was almost impossible to breathe.

An attendant was in the hall, a small man in a white shirt with no collar. His teeth were so misshapen that his lips were twisted into a permanent sneer. A smoldering cigarette hung from one corner of his

mouth. He looked at Okada with dead eyes and lifted his fingers, signaling numbers.

Thirty-two.

Okada looked for that number on a door. It was beyond the attendant.

He turned sideways in the narrow hallway to get by the attendant.
As he did so, the man behind him opened a door. For a few seconds,
Okada and the attendant were isolated in a tiny space in the hallway,
isolated from all other human eyes.

In that brief moment, Okada pressed the message into the attendant's hand.

He found booth 32, opened the door, and entered.

There were ten of them waiting for him to come home, but Masataka Okada didn't know that. They were arranged in two circles, the
first of which covered the possible approach routes to the apartment
building, and the second of which covered the entrances. Two men
were in the apartment with his wife, waiting.

The man in the subway station saw him first, waited until he was
out of sight, then reported the contact on his handheld radio.

Okada was nervous, wary. The sensations of Shinjuku had been
wasted upon him tonight. He hadn't been able to get the message from
Ju off his mind, couldn't stop thinking about the murder of the emperor, couldn't stop thinking about his mother's scarred back. Despite
being keyed up and alert, he didn't see the man in the subway.

A block later, he did spot the man watching the side entrance to
the building where he lived. This man was in a parked car, and he
made the mistake of looking around. When he saw Okada, he looked
away, but too late.

Masataka Okada kept walking toward the entrance as his mind
raced.

They had come. Finally. They were here for him!

His wife . . . she was upstairs. Fortunately, she knew absolutely nothing about his spying, not even that he did it. So there was nothing she
could tell them.

It shouldn't have to end like this. Really, it shouldn't.

He had done his best. He didn't want future generations of Japanese
to go through what his parents had endured, and he had had the courage to act on his convictions. Now it was time to pay the piper.

Well, the Americans had the message from Ju, as well as all the others, all the copies of documents that he had made and passed on detailing the secret arms contracts and the buildup of the military that had been going on for the last seven years. They knew, and Abe didn't know they knew.

Abe would find out, if these men managed to arrest him. They would get the truth from him one way or the other. Okada had no illusions on that score. They would use any means necessary to make him talk; there was just too much at stake.

The dark doorway of the building loomed in front of him.

If he walked through that door, they had him. Some of them might be inside just now, waiting to grab him, throw him to the floor, and slap handcuffs on him.

Even if they let him go up to the apartment, they would come for him there. They would never let him leave the building.

These thoughts zipped through his head in the time it took for him to take just one step toward the doorway.

He would not go in.

He turned right, down the sidewalk, and began to walk briskly.

Glancing back over his shoulder, he saw the man in the car looking his way and holding a radio mike in front of his mouth.

Even though he knew he shouldn't, Masataka Okada began to run.

He had had a good life, and he didn't want to give it up. Those fools who killed the emperor, committing hara-kari, voluntarily ended the only existence they would ever have. Ah, was life so worthless that a man should throw it away, as if it didn't matter?

He darted into the street and managed to avoid an oncoming bus. He made it to the sidewalk on the other side and swerved into an alley. Down the alley a ways was a brick wall, which Okada climbed over with much huffing and puffing, severely skinning his ankle.

He found himself inside a cemetery. The headstones and little temples looked weird in the reflected half-light of the city, sinister. *This* was Japan's future—he saw it in a horrible revelation: a nation of tombstones and funeral temples, ashes in urns, a nation of the dead.

Sobbing, Okada threaded his way through all this masonry and crawled across the wall on the other side. His ankle hurt like fire, but the collapse of his world and his vision of the future hurt worse.

His wife . . . what would she think? Oh, how he had abandoned her, poor, loyal woman.

He was now in another alley, this one lined with little wooden houses, relics of old Japan. He thought about stealing a bicycle but couldn't bring himself to do it.

At the end of the alley was a street. Although he was severely winded already, he managed to work himself into a trot. As he rounded the corner, he met a man running the other way. Fortune favored Okada—he reacted first and got his hands up, bowling the other man over as he went by.

He didn't look back, just ran. Alas, his gait was a hell-bent stagger, his lungs tearing at him as he gasped futilely, unable to get enough oxygen.

Ahead was a subway station. If he could catch a train, he could get off anywhere, could lose himself in Tokyo, perhaps even make his way to the American embassy.

Those Americans, they said that someday this might happen. He had refused to believe, even when he knew they spoke the truth.

He was close to passing out from the exertion, almost unable to think. He smoked several packs of cigarettes a day, had done so for years, and he never exercised.

Okada could hear footsteps pounding the pavement behind him.

There—the stairs into the subway! He ran down them, grabbed the turnstile, and leapt over.

More stairs. He took them two at a time.

He could hear the running feet behind him, closer and closer, but he used the last of his energy, forcing himself to run even though he could scarcely breathe and was having difficulty seeing. Spots swam before his eyes.

A train was coming.

If they catch me ...

The train was still moving at a pretty good clip when Masataka Okada did a swan dive off the platform, right in front of it.

CHAPTER FOUR

● HE COULD SEE it above him, at least two miles up, a flashing silver shape in the vast, deep blue. Jiro Kimura used the handhold on the canopy bow to hold himself upright against the G forces. He grunted, kept his muscles tense so that he would not pass out, fought to keep his eyes on that flashing silver plane so far above.

If he lost sight of that plane, it might take several seconds to reacquire it, seconds he could ill afford to lose. The other pilot was undoubtedly looking down at him, watching him twist and turn, waiting for an opening when he could come swooping down with his gun blazing—like an angel of doom. Or the bloody Red Baron. To kill.

Jiro Kimura knew all of that because he knew the other pilot. His name was Sasai. He was just twenty-four, rarely smiled, and never made the same mistake twice. This was only Sasai's third one-on-one flight, but he was learning quickly.

Just now, Kimura wanted to make Sasai think that he had an opening when he really didn't.

Kimura rocked his wings violently from side to side, first one way and then the other. He was also feeding in forward stick, unloading the plane and accelerating, but Sasai couldn't see that from two miles above. All he could see were the wings rocking, as if Kimura had momentarily lost sight and was futilely trying to find his opponent.

Sasai turned to arc in behind Kimura and put his nose down, committing himself.

Kimura waited for several seconds, maybe four, then lit the afterburner and pulled his nose up. The G felt good, solid, as the horizon fell away. Jiro Kimura loved to fly, and this morning he acknowledged that fact to himself, again, for the thousandth time. To fly a state-of-the-art fighter plane in an endless blue sky, to have someone to yank and bank with and try to outwit, then to go home and think about how it had been while planning to do it again tomorrow—what had life to offer that could possibly be sweeter?

When he was vertical, Kimura spun around his longitudinal axis until his wings were perpendicular to Sasai's flight path; then he pulled his nose over to lead Sasai, who was now frantically trying to evade the trap. Because he was slower, Kimura could turn more quickly than the descending plane, could bring his gun to bear first.

Jiro Kimura pulled the trigger on the stick.

"You're dead, Sasai," Kimura said on the radio, trying to keep the satisfaction out of his voice. "Let's break it off and go home."

Sasai rendezvoused on Kimura, who consulted his GPS display, then set a course for base. They were over the Sea of Japan above a broken layer of low clouds. Kimura checked his fuel, verified his course on the wet compass, then stretched. The silver airplanes, the sun high in the blue vault overhead, the sea below, the clouds and distant haze—if heaven was like this, he was ready.

If Shizuko could go, too, of course.

He felt guilty that he was contemplating paradise without Shizuko. Then he felt silly that he was even thinking these thoughts.

Well, maybe it wasn't silly. Real combat seemed to be coming, almost like a terrible storm just over the horizon that no one wanted to acknowledge. We make plans, for next week, next month, next year, while refusing to acknowledge that our safe, secure little world is about to disintegrate.

Jiro looked across the invisible river of air flowing between the planes and saw Sasai in his cockpit. He was looking Jiro's way. They stared at each other's helmeted figures for a moment; then Jiro looked away.

Kimura was the senior officer, and leader, of his flight. Then came Ota, Miura, and Sasai. They would fly together as a unit whenever possible.

Alas, Sasai was green, inexperienced. He knew how to use the new Zero fighter as an interceptor, utilizing the radar, GPS, computer, and all the rest of it, but he didn't know how to dogfight, to fight another aircraft when it was out of the interception parameters.

Neither Ota nor Miura was particularly skilled at the craft, either. The colonels and generals insisted that Zero pilots be well trained in the use of the state-of-the art weapons system, that they know it cold and practice constantly, so all their training had been in using the aircraft's system to acquire the target, then fire missiles when the target came within range.

"What will you do," Kimura asked the three pilots on his team, "if the enemy attacks you as you are taking off?"

His junior wingmen looked slightly stunned, as if the possibility had never occurred to them. Their superior officers, none of whom were combat veterans, reasoned that the plane's electronic suite was the heart of the weapons system, the technological edge that made the new Zero the best fighter on earth: the airframe, engine, and wings existed merely to take the system to a point in space where it could be employed against the enemy. The never-voiced assumption almost seemed to be that the enemy would fly along straight and level while the Japanese pilots locked them up with radar, stepped the computer into attack, and watched the missiles ripple off the racks and streak away for the kill.

The senior officer in the air arm had been quoted as saying, "Dog-fighting is obsolete. We have put a gun in the Zero for strafing, not shooting at other airplanes." Indeed, the heads-up display—HUD—did not feature a lead-computing gunsight.

Jiro Kimura didn't think air-to-air combat would be quite that easy. Whenever they were not running practice intercepts, he had been dog-fighting with his flight members. They didn't get to do this often; still, they were learning quickly—even Sasai.

They should be able to handle the Russians.

Ah yes, the Russians. This morning at the weekly intelligence briefing, the wing commander had given them the word: Siberia, two weeks from now. "Study the Russian air force and be ready to destroy it."

"Two weeks?" someone had murmured, incredulous.

"No questions. This information is highly classified. The day is almost upon us and we must be ready."

Jiro raised his helmet visor and used the back of his glove to swab the perspiration from his eyes. After checking the cockpit altitude, he removed his oxygen mask and used the glove to wipe his face dry.

He snapped the mask back into place and lowered his visor.

"It will be a quick war," Ota had predicted. "In two days they will have nothing left to fly. The MiGs, even the Sukhoi-27s, will go down like ducks."

Jiro Kimura said nothing. There was nothing to say. Whatever was going to happen would happen. Words would not change it.

Still, after he had suited up in his flight gear, before he and Sasai went out on the mat to preflight their planes, he had called Bob Cassidy at the American embassy in Tokyo. Just a short chat, an invitation to dinner three weeks from now, and a comment about an alumni letter Jiro had received from the Air Force Academy in Colorado Springs.

He dismissed Russia and Cassidy from his mind so he could concentrate on the task at hand. The clouds ahead over Honshu looked solid, so he and Sasai were going to have to make an instrument approach. Jiro signaled his wingman to make a radio frequency change to air traffic control; then he called the controller.

Three men were waiting for Bob Cassidy when he came out of the back entrance to the embassy. At least he thought there were three— he arrived at that number several minutes later—but there might have been more.

As he walked along the sidewalk, they followed him, keeping well back—one behind, one on the other side of the street, and one in a car creeping along a block behind. The guy in the car was the one he wasn't sure of for several minutes.

This was a first. Cassidy had never before been openly followed.

He wondered about the timing. Why now?

The one behind him on his side of the street was about medium height for a Japanese, wearing glasses and some sort of sport coat. His stride proclaimed his fitness.

The one across the street was balding and short. He wore slacks and a dark pullover shirt. Cassidy couldn't see the driver of the car.

If there were three men he knew about, how many were there that he didn't?

Undecided as to how he should handle this, he walked the route he always took toward his apartment. When he'd reported to the embassy fifteen months ago, he'd had the choice of sharing an apartment inside the embassy compound or finding his own apartment "on the economy." He chose the latter. Without children in school or a wife who wanted to socialize with other Americans, it was an easy choice.

These men had been waiting for him. They must know where he lived, the route he usually took to get there. They must have followed him in the past and he just hadn't paid attention.

Well, maybe his conversation with Jiro had made him apprehensive, so that was why he was looking now. Actually, he admitted to himself, he felt guilty. Jiro shouldn't have talked out of school.

Oh, he was glad he had, but still . . . Cassidy felt guilty.

A block from home, just before turning a corner, he paused to look at the reflection in a slab of marble siding on a store. The balding man was visible, and, just turning the far corner, the car.

Bob Cassidy went into his apartment building. He collected his mail at the lobby mailbox, then rode the elevator to his floor and unlocked the door to his apartment. He didn't turn on the light.

He sat in the evening twilight, looking out the window, trying to decide what to do.

They must be monitoring the telephones at the base, or at the embassy.

Jiro was the only member of the Japanese military who had ever told Cassidy anything classified. Oh, as air attaché, he routinely talked to Japanese military men, many of whom were personal friends. A dozen of his contacts even held flag rank. The things these soldiers told him were certainly not secrets. He collected common, everyday "this is how we do it" stuff, the filler that military attachés all over the world gather and send home for their own militaries to analyze. Finding out the things that the Japanese didn't want the Americans to know was the job of another agency, the CIA.

So did the tail mean the Japanese knew that Jiro had talked?

One of Cassidy's fears was that his report of the conversation with Jiro had been compromised—that is, passed right back to the Japanese. Alas, the United States had suffered through too many spy scandals in the last twenty years. Bitter, disappointed men seemed all too willing to sell out their colleagues and their country for money. God knows, the Japanese certainly had enough money.

He would have to report being tailed to the embassy security officer; perhaps he should do that now, and ask him if anyone else had reported being followed. He picked up the telephone and held it in his hand, but he didn't dial. This phone was probably tapped, too. If he called embassy security and reported the tail, it would look like he had something to hide.

He went to the window and stood looking at the Tokyo skyline, or what little he could see of it from a fifth-floor window. He checked his watch. Two hours.

He was supposed to meet Jiro in two hours. Jiro had mentioned Colorado Springs when he called earlier that day. Two days ago, when Cassidy had dinner at the Kimuras', he and Jiro had agreed that the mention of that city would be the code for a meet at a site they agreed upon then.

The code had been Jiro's idea. Cassidy had a bad taste in his mouth about the whole thing. Neither one of them was a trained spy; they were in over their heads. They were going to compromise themselves.

Even if they didn't, Cassidy had this feeling deep down that this episode was going to cost him a close friend.

He turned his mind back to the problem at hand.

Jiro had called, and a plainclothes tailing team had been waiting when he left the embassy compound.

Perhaps they were monitoring all the calls from Kimura's base and had intercepted this one, then decided to check to see if Kimura was meeting people he had no good reason to meet.

Or maybe they were onto Kimura.

Maybe they knew he had spilled some secrets to the Americans. Maybe they were trying to rope in Kimura's U.S. contact.

Maybe, maybe, maybe...

Cassidy changed into civilian clothes while he mulled the problem over, then went into the kitchen and got a beer from the refrigerator.

Hanging on the wall was a photo of himself at the controls of an F-16. The plane was high, over thirty thousand feet, brilliantly lit by the sun, against a sky so blue it was almost black. Cassidy stood sipping beer as he looked at the photo. What he saw in his mind's eye was not the F-16, but the new Zero.

He had actually seen it. Last week. From a hill near the Japanese air base at Niigata. He had hiked up carrying a video camera in a hard case on a strap over his shoulder. He had videotaped the new fighters taking off and landing. Although the base was six miles away, on the climb-out and approach they came within a half mile of where he was standing.

He had also gotten some still pictures with a 35-mm camera from just under the glide path. He had driven into a noise-saturated neighborhood beside the base and snapped the photos from the driver's seat of his car as the planes went overhead.

The CIA had sent him a gadget to play with as the new Zero flew over, a device that resembled a portable cassette player and could pass for one on casual examination. It did, however, have a three-foot-long antenna that he had to dangle out the window.

Cassidy did all this high-tech spying in plain sight. Only one person had paid any attention to him, a youngster on a tricycle, who sat on the sidewalk four feet away and watched him fiddle with the cassette player and antenna as the jets flew over.

He remembered the sense of relief that came over him when he was finished. He had started the car and slipped it into gear while he took one last careful look around to see if anyone was watching.

It was amazing, when you stopped to think about it. The Japanese designed, manufactured, and tested the ultimate fighter plane, one invisible to radar, put it into squadron service, and the United States knew nothing about it—didn't even know it existed, until one of the pilots sought out the U.S. air attaché at the American embassy and told him.

Perhaps, Cassidy thought as he looked out the window to see if the tails were still waiting, the Japanese are too far from war. As it has for Americans, war for them has become an abstraction, an event of the historical past that students read about in school—dates, treaties, forgotten battles with strange names. War is no longer the experience of a whole people, the defining event of an entire generation. Today the only people with combat experience are a few professional soldiers, like Cassidy.

As a young man, he had flown in the Gulf War—he even shot down a MiG—and he dropped some bombs in Bosnia. His recollections of those days seemed like something remembered from an old B movie, bits and pieces of a past that was fragmentary, fading, irrelevant.

Today war is sold as a video game, Cassidy decided. Shoot at the bad guys and they fall down. If the score is too low, put in another coin and play the game again. You can't get hurt. You can't get . . . *dead*! All you can lose are a few coins.

Cassidy had to make a decision.

Kimura had called, had wanted to see him. The tails were out there. If he didn't go to the meet, Kimura was safe, for the time being anyway, and he would not learn what Kimura wanted the American government to know. On the other hand, if he went, he might be followed, despite his best efforts, and Kimura might wind up in prison, or worse. Hell, Cassidy might wind up in prison, which would really be a unique capstone for his Air Force career.

Jiro seemed to have a lot of faith in the U.S. government, Cassidy mused. Cassidy had long ago lost his. Still, Jiro had to do what he thought right. Indeed, he had an obligation to do so. That *is* what they teach at the Air Force Academy, isn't it?

He finished the beer, tossed the empty can into the trash. He belched.

Okay, Jiro. Ready or not, here I come.

Bob Cassidy was standing near the large incense burner at the Asakusa Temple when he saw Jiro Kimura buy a bundle of incense sticks.

He lit them at one of the two nearby braziers, then tossed them into the large burner. Cassidy went over and the two stood in the crowd, waving the holy smoke over their hair and face.

"I was followed," Cassidy said in a low voice, "but I think I lost them."

"Me, too. I've been riding the subways for an hour. Sorry I'm late."

"They've tapped the phones at the embassy or your base."

"Probably both places," Jiro said under his breath. "They are very efficient." He led the way to the water fountain, where he helped himself to a dipper, filled it with water, and sipped it.

"God only knows what you'll catch drinking out of that. You'll probably shit for a week. Your damn teeth are gonna fall out."

"Uh-huh." Jiro handed the dipper to the person behind him, then moved on. Few Japanese spoke English, so Cassidy's remarks didn't disturb anyone.

Jiro went into the Buddhist temple and tossed some coins into the offertory. He moved forward to the rail and prayed while Cassidy hung back.

At the door, he moved over beside Cassidy.

"It's Siberia. Our wing commander told us this morning in a secret intel briefing. In two weeks, he said."

"He has a timetable?"

"Yes. We were told to be ready to tackle the Russian air force and destroy it."

"Did he say why you are going?"

"Just what I've told you. Cryptic as hell, isn't it?"

Cassidy walked with Kimura out of the temple. They stood for a moment on the steps watching the people around the incense burner.

"Happy, aren't they?" Cassidy said.

Kimura didn't answer. He went back into the temple, to the fortune drawers on the right side of the altar.

"I may not see you before you go," said Cassidy, who had followed Jiro back into the temple.

"You won't. Ten to one, when we go in tomorrow, they'll close the base, lock us up. It's a miracle they didn't think of that today."

"Maybe they wanted to see who you would talk to."

"Maybe," Jiro muttered. He put a hundred-yen coin in the offering slot and picked up a large aluminum tube. He shook it, then turned it upside down and examined the opening. The head of a stick was just visible there. He pulled it out. "Seventy-six," he said, and put the stick back into the tube.

"I'm trying to tell you, amigo. They may already have burned you."

"I wish to Christ we were back in the Springs."

The sudden shift of subject threw Bob Cassidy. "Those were good times," he said, because he could think of nothing else to say.

"With Sweet Sabrina," Jiro said. He opened drawer number seventy-six and took out a sheet of paper. He closed the drawer, moved a couple of steps back, then glanced at the paper.

"Yeah," Cassidy said. He had a lump in his throat.

Jiro didn't seem to notice. He folded up the paper and put it in his pocket. "We'll meet again someday. In this life or the next."

" 'This life or the next,' " Cassidy echoed. The words gave him goose bumps—the cadets at the Academy used to say that to one another on graduation day.

He pointed toward Jiro's pocket, the paper from the drawer. "Was your fortune good?"

"No."

Cassidy snorted. "That stuff is crap."

"Yeah."

"A racket for the monks, to get money from suckers."

"I gotta go, Bob."

"Hey, man."

"*Vaya con Dios.*"

"You, too."

Jiro Kimura turned and walked out of the temple. He kept going without looking back.

Bob Cassidy felt helpless. He was losing Jiro, too. Sabrina, little Robbie, now Jiro . . .

"This life or the next, Jiro." A tear trickled down his cheek. He wiped it away angrily. He was losing everything.

The next morning Jiro went straight to the office of his commanding officer and knocked. When he was admitted, he told the colonel that he had been followed the previous night.

"I have no idea who that man was, sir, but I wish to make a report so that the incident may be investigated. I have never before been fol-lowed—that I know about anyway."

The colonel was surprised. He apparently had not been told that Kimura was a suspicious character, Jiro concluded, or else he should be on the stage professionally. It was with a sense of relief that Jiro described the man in the train station.

"Perhaps this man wasn't really following you, Captain. Perhaps you are too suspicious."

"Sir, that is possible. But I wish you would report the incident so that the proper authorities may investigate. In light of what the wing commander said yesterday . . ."

"Yes. Indeed. I will make a report, Captain Kimura. This incident should be investigated. Japan is filled with foreigners who cannot be trusted."

On that illogical note, Jiro was dismissed.

And he was right about the base closure. Just before noon, the colonel called an officers' meeting and made the announcement that all officers and enlisted were confined to the base until further notice.

CHAPTER FIVE

● THE FIRST PERSON in Russia to learn that Japan planned to invade Siberia was Janos Ilin, who heard the news an hour after the American national security adviser, Jack Innes, told the Russian ambassador to the United States.

Ilin got the news from a FIS officer in the Russian embassy in Washington. The FIS officer had much less bureaucracy to work through, so his news arrived in Moscow first.

Ilin was at his desk in the Foreign Intelligence Service—which had replaced the old KGB—building in Dzerzhinsky Square. He read the translation of the encrypted message completely and carefully, laid it on his desk, cleaned his glasses, lit an American cigarette, then read it again.

Janos Ilin was not a Communist. He wasn't anything. He was old enough and wise enough to know that the reason Russia was a sewer was because Russians lived there. In his fifty-five years on earth he had come to believe that in their heart of hearts, most Russians were selfish, lazy peasants who hated anyone with a ruble more than they had.

From Ilin's office window, looking above the tops of the buildings across the square, he could see the onion spires of the Kremlin.

These were the days of Kalugin, who now ruled the tattered remnants of the czars' empire. In truth, the empire that the Communists had inherited and held with grim determination for seventy-five years was now irretrievably gone; only Russia and Siberia remained. Still, Russia and Siberia were huge beyond imagination. In towns and villages and isolated cottages out in the vastness of the steppe, the long grass prairies, and the boreal and subarctic forests, Kalugin was just a name, a photo or flickering image on the television. Life went on pretty much as it had since the death of Stalin, when the secret police stopped dragging people away. The winters were still long and fierce, work hard, food scarce, vodka too plentiful.

Kalugin fought his way to the top, promising to restore Russia's glory and build an economic system that worked. His plan was to legitimize the vast criminal enterprises that were actually feeding, clothing, and housing a significant percentage of the population, and making the people who ran them rich beyond the dreams of avarice.

Kalugin was one of those rich ones. He could orate long and loudly on the glory of Mother Russia, and he had never paid a ruble in taxes. Now he was in the Kremlin, surrounded by men just like him.

Janos Ilin took a deep breath and sighed. War again. Against Mother Russia.

Now we find out what Kalugin is made of, he thought.

He finished his cigarette before he went to see the minister.

Washington, D.C., was overcast and dreary in the rain. The soldier at the wheel of the government sedan had little to say, which was just as well because Bob Cassidy was whacked from jet lag. He felt as if he hadn't slept in a week. His eyes burned, his skin itched, and he was desperate for a long, hot shower and a bed. Alas, it was six in the evening here and his orders were to proceed directly to the Pentagon. The driver had been waiting for him when he got off the plane at Dulles Airport.

He rode along for a while watching traffic, then leaned back in the seat and closed his eyes. He hadn't slept a wink on the all-night flight from Tokyo to Seattle, nor on the cross-continent flight to Dulles. He hated airliners, hated the claustrophobia brought on by being shoe-horned into too small a seat. But that was past. He felt himself relaxing as he enjoyed the motion of the car, the rhythm of the wipers.

"We're here, Colonel. Sir! We're here."

Cassidy levered himself erect and looked around. The soldier was parked outside the main entrance, and he was offering Cassidy a security badge. "You need to show this to the security guard inside, sir."

"You'll wait for me?"

"Yes, sir. I have your luggage. I'll wait right here."

Cassidy took the security badge and climbed from the car. He paused to straighten his tie—he was wearing a civilian suit—then marched for the main entrance. The rain was still falling, a medium drizzle.

Inside, one of the security guards led him along endless gray corridors, up stairs, along more corridors. He was completely disoriented within two minutes. Once, through an open door, he saw a window that appeared to be on an outside wall, but he wasn't sure.

Finally, he arrived at a decorated corridor, one with blue paint and original artwork on the walls, carpet on the floor.

The security guard led him into a reception area, introduced him to a Marine Corps lieutenant colonel, who asked him to take a seat for a minute. The marine disappeared into an office. In minutes, he was back. "It will be just a few minutes before the chairman can see you, Colonel. Could I offer you a soft drink or a cup of coffee?"

"Coffee would be perfect. Black, thank you."

The headline in the newspaper on the table screamed at him: SE-CRET MILITARY PROTOCOL WITH RUSSIA REVEALED. Under the head-line, smaller type said, "President committed U.S. to defense of Russia. Key congressional leaders approved secret pact."

Tired as he was, Cassidy picked up the paper and read the story. When the marine returned with a paper cup full of steaming black fluid, Cassidy sipped gratefully as he finished the story. The marine waited patiently.

"Do you have a room where I could wash my face and brush this suit?"

"The general will see you in just a few minutes, sir. Believe me, you don't have to put on the dog for him. He knows you just got off the plane."

They made small talk for several minutes; then the telephone buzzed. Thirty seconds later, Cassidy was shaking hands with the chair-man of the Joint Chiefs, General Stanford Tuck.

The marine aide left the room and pulled the door closed behind him.

They sat in leather chairs facing each other, on the same side of the large desk. "I'm sorry for the short notice, Colonel. Things are hap-pening quickly, which is par for the course around here. I don't know just what they told you at the embassy in Tokyo, so let me summarize. It appears that Japan will invade Siberia in the very near future."

Cassidy just nodded. Apparently the bigwigs believed Jiro's tale.

Tuck continued: "We project that Japan's new Zero fighter will destroy Russia's air force within a week, if the Russians are willing to keep sending their planes up to get shot down. Due to the dearth of decent roads in Siberia and the vast distances involved, both sides are going to have to rely on air transport for all their food, fuel, and ammo. Baldly, the side with air superiority will win."

Tuck's gray eyes held Cassidy transfixed.

"It is doubtful if the United States will take sides in this regional conflict," the general continued.

"I saw the story on the military protocol in the paper."

Tuck gestured at the heavens. "We are toying with the idea of loaning Russia a dozen of our best fighters to take on the Zeros. That's where you come in."

"What kind of airplanes, sir?"

"F-22 Raptors."

"These will be American airplanes?"

"No. We are going to sell or trade them to the Russians. These will be Russian airplanes, and the Russians will hire qualified American civilians to fly them. They just don't know it yet."

"When will they know it?"

"We'll bring this subject up after the shooting starts. You understand?"

Cassidy shook his head. "No, sir. I don't pretend to understand any of it."

"A refreshing attitude. I'm not sure I understand much of it, either. Still, if we decide to go through with this proposal, your job, Colonel, would be to command the Russian F-22 squadron."

Cassidy just stared. This trip to Washington had occurred on two hours' notice. No reason given, just a summons to be on the afternoon plane. He had speculated all the way across the Pacific, which was one reason he hadn't had any sleep. He had concluded that the folks in the Pentagon wanted to ensure they had everything he knew about the new Japanese Zero fighter. He certainly hadn't suspected this.

It occurred to him to ask, "Why me, sir?"

Stanford Tuck thought that a logical question. He said, "You know as much about Asia as any senior flight officer, and you are F-22–qualified, so we won't have to waste weeks teaching you how to fly the darn thing. Amazingly enough, when we put our criteria into the idiot box, your name was at the head of the very short list that popped out."

"I don't know what to say, sir."

"Don't say anything. That's normally best." The general smiled.

"I'll have to think about it, sir. This is right out of the blue. I'm not sure I could do the job."

Cassidy looked tired, the general thought.

"As you might suspect, there are political complications," the general continued, "so there are some serious wrinkles. The political types think we are skirting dangerously close to the abyss if we have a serving U.S. officer in combat against a friendly power, so you'll have to retire from the Air Force."

"Well, I—"

"Another is that the Air Force chief of staff doesn't want any of his active duty F-22 pilots resigning to accept commissions in the Russian air force. I think he's afraid of starting a precedent."

The general's eyes solidified, like water freezing. "He didn't want to lose you, either, but he didn't have a choice. Still, the politicians don't want to ruffle the chief of staff's feathers—they're going to get quite enough flak over this as it is—so you'll have to get your recruits from Raptor-qualified folks who just got off active duty or retired. There aren't many retirees, but there are one or two you can talk to. We'll give you a list."

Cassidy had recovered his composure and got the wheels going again. "Most of those people will have plans, sir. They're not just leaving active duty—they're going *to* something. They won't be interested in going to Siberia."

"Your job is to recruit the people you need, out of uniform or in." Tuck leaned forward and his voice hardened. "You let me know who you want, and I'll see that he or she is an available civilian pretty damn quick."

"If I say yes, when would I start, General?"

"The politicians haven't committed to this adventure yet. They're considering it. I won't go along until more details are ironed out."

"We'll need qualified maintenance people, intel, weather."

Tuck nodded. "My aide, Colonel Eatherly, will go over the nuts and bolts with you. Fixing problems is what he does best. He can smooth the road, help straighten it out."

"Maybe you should give him this job, sir," Bob Cassidy said, and tried to grin. "I've never even been to Russia."

Tuck got to his feet. "Go get some sleep, Colonel. Come see me in the morning, let me know what you think then. As I said, your name came up. The folks around here tell me you are F-22–qualified, you got us most of the info on the Zero, and you understand the Japanese as well as anyone in uniform. The U.S. ambassador to Japan highly recommends you, as do two of your old fighter bosses I've talked to. They tell me you can pull this off if anyone can. It's your decision."

"I'll have to think about it, sir."

As Stanford Tuck shook the colonel's hand, he said, "You're a professional fighter pilot, Cassidy; this will probably be all the war you'll ever get."

The general looked Cassidy right in the eye. "It's going to be a genuine sausage machine. A lot of people are going to die. The process

10

will be damned unpleasant and ugly as hell. The elected leaders of your country refuse to declare war. Do you want to risk your life for Russia, for the Russians? Sleep on it. See me tomorrow."

"Yes, sir."

"Everything we have discussed is top secret, Colonel. *Everything.*"

Out in the reception area, one of the enlisted people volunteered to lead Bob Cassidy toward the main entrance and the waiting car.

Combat. People dying.

Lord have mercy.

Kalugin looked like a wolf, an old gray wolf of the taiga from a Russian folk story. He had small black eyes and a fierce, hungry look that hid whatever thoughts were passing behind the features of his face.

Aleksandr Ivanovich Kalugin was a shrewd, calculating paranoid without morals, ethics, or scruples of any kind, a gangster willing to do whatever it took to enrich himself. He had no loyalty to anyone except himself. He was a perfect political animal, ready to strike any pose and make any promise that he thought his listeners wanted to hear.

Like politicians in Western democracies, he paid "experts" to tell him what it was "the people" wanted. He was willing, of course, to try to deliver on his promises, if the cost was low and the prospect of personal profit high. The man was a case study for those fools who believed that a politician's character didn't matter as long as he was on their side. The truth was that Kalugin had no side but his own: he was as ready to devour his supporters as he was his enemies.

Today he fixed that wolfish stare on the minister of foreign affairs, Danilov, as the minister expounded on the conversation in the White House between the American national security adviser and the Russian ambassador to the United States.

A vein in Kalugin's forehead throbbed visibly. Finally, he muttered, through clenched teeth, "The damned Americans are lying."

"Mr. President—"

"They are lying, you doddering fool! They have lied to us ten thousand times and they are lying again. The Japanese are not stupid enough to get trapped in Siberia this winter. That icebox is the most inhospitable hell on this planet in winter, which is what, three, maybe three and a half months away? By October the temperatures will be below freezing and dropping like a stone. Only Russians would be crazy enough to endure that bleak, frozen outhouse that God never visits. The damned Americans are lying. Again!"

"I think that—"

"Get the Japanese ambassador into your office and ask him to his face. Ask him if his country plans to invade Russia. Ask him!"

Kalugin pointed toward the door. Danilov went.

What if the Japanese did invade? The event would ignite a wildfire of patriotism. Business as usual would come to a rapid halt.

Kalugin began to mull the possibilities. It seemed to him that if the Japanese invaded Siberia, an extraordinary window of political opportunity would open for a man fast enough and bold enough to seize the moment. If a man played his cards right . . .

Inadvertantly, Kalugin's eyes went to Stalin's portrait, which he kept on the wall even though the dictator was out of fashion in most quarters these days. For a moment, Kalugin fancied that he could see a gleam in the eye of the old assassin.

Bob Cassidy got a room in a hotel in Crystal City, one of those modern buildings with glass walls. By some quirk, his room had a good view of downtown Washington even though the desk clerk assured him he was only being charged the military rate.

He couldn't really get to sleep. The room wasn't dark: light from the city leaked in around the curtains. He dozed at times, and dreamed of being aloft in a cockpit. He was in and out of clouds, the missile warning flashing and sounding in his ears, telling him of invisible missiles racing toward him at twice the speed of sound. He was trying desperately to escape, but he couldn't. The missiles were streaking in. . . .

He awoke each time sweating profusely, his mouth dry, his skin itching.

Finally, he fixed himself a drink from the wet bar and drank it quickly. The alcohol didn't help.

He pulled the drapes back and sat looking at the lights. He could just see the capitol dome and the Washington Monument.

A war was coming and all these people were oblivious. Even if they knew, they wouldn't care—as long as the bombs didn't fall here.

General Tuck would want to know his decision in a few hours.

Maybe he should ask about after the war. If he survived, could he get back into the Air Force?

Would he want back in?

F-22s versus Zeros. Jiro Kimura was flying a Zero.

My God, he might end up shooting at Jiro.

He finally dozed off in the chair. The flying dream didn't return. In the new dream, he was young again, just a boy in Kansas, watching clouds adrift on a summer wind in an infinite blue sky.

He awoke for good at 3:00 A.M. It was hopeless. There was no more sleep in him. He took a shower and put on a uniform.

Could the F-22 survive against the Zero? The Raptor was very stealthy, but with Athena, the Zero was invisible, or so Jiro said. How do you fight a supersonic enemy that you cannot locate on radar?

"Taking a squadron of F-22s to Siberia will be a challenge, General," Bob Cassidy told Stanford Tuck the next morning. The general was sitting behind his desk in his shirtsleeves, drinking coffee. His jacket hung on a hook near the door.

"Logistics will make or break the operation," Cassidy continued. He sketched out the problems he saw with basing, logistics, early warning, and keeping his people healthy and flying. "Even the food will have to come from the States."

"Siberia," the general muttered, just to hear the sound of the word.

"The logistics problem would be easier if we were taking a squadron to Antarctica."

The general punched a button on the telephone. In seconds, a door opened and the general's aide appeared.

"This is Colonel Eatherly. I want you to go over everything you've talked about in greater detail with him. He'll take notes and brief me on what he thinks. The president wants to make a powerful political statement against armed aggression. He doesn't want to embroil the United States in World War Three. Yet if we commit a dozen planes to combat in Russia, they must have at least a fighting chance of accomplishing their mission. If the Japanese sweep them from the sky— for whatever reason—we will be worse off than if we did nothing. Offering hors d'oeuvres to a hungry lion is bad policy."

Tuck loosened his tie and rolled up his sleeves.

Bob Cassidy took a deep breath. He appreciated the stakes involved, but he knew what trained pilots could do with the F-22.

"Subject to the qualifiers we discussed, sir, I think a Raptor squadron could go toe-to-toe with the new Zero. With the right pilots, we can give them a hell of a fight."

"A dozen planes is all we can give you," Stanford Tuck said, "so you are going to be outnumbered by a bunch." He laid both hands flat on his desk.

"You may as well hear all of it," the general said. "We cannot give you the new, long-range missiles. The politicians refused. You can take AMRAAMs and Sidewinders, but nothing that has technology we don't want the Japanese or Russians to see." AMRAAM stood for advanced medium-range anti-aircraft missile; it was also known as the AIM-120C.

"Sky Eye?"

"No. The thinking is that if foreign powers learn how good Sky Eye is, they will target our satellites in any future conflict."

"Our satellites are already targets."

"Low-priority targets."

"But—"

Tuck raised a hand. "I'm not here to argue. I didn't make that decision. We have to live with it."

"Why the hell buy it if we can't use it?" Cassidy asked with some irritation.

"This country's future isn't on the come line just now," Tuck said with his eyes half-closed. He seemed to be trying to measure Cassidy. "You and I are on the same side."

"I'm sorry, sir. I didn't mean—"

"Go talk to Eatherly."

As Eatherly led Cassidy from the room, he stuck out his hand. "My friends call me John. Did you get along okay with the old man?"

"I think so."

In his office, Eatherly pulled a chair around for Cassidy and got out a legal pad.

"Does the general really think an F-22 squadron in Siberia has a chance?"

Eatherly looked surprised. "What are you saying?"

Cassidy frowned. "Or does he want me to give him reasons to say no?"

"I believe he was hoping you could show him how this proposal could be made to work," Eatherly replied thoughtfully. "If you think it can."

Cassidy rubbed his face hard. "I—"

"*You* are going to be leading this parade, Colonel. The tender, quivering ass on the plate this time is yours."

Bob Cassidy sat lost in thought for a long moment. Then he said, "My source in Japan says the Zeros are invisible to radar. He says the Japanese acquired—stole—an American project called Athena."

Eatherly nodded. "There was a black American project with that name. I checked when I saw your report on the Zero. The American project died years ago."

"How did it work?"

"It was active ECM. When the signal from an enemy radar was detected, the raw data was put through a superconductive computer, which then used other antennas buried in the aircraft's skin to emit an out-of-sync wave that effectively canceled the enemy radar signal."

"But what about scatter effect? Radar A transmits a signal, but B receives it?"

"The computer knows the scatter characteristics of the airplane it is protecting, so it emits the proper amount of energy in all directions. That was the heart of it."

"Why didn't we develop it?"

Eatherly shrugged. "Ran out of money."

"Terrific."

"The F-22 is very stealthy," Eatherly mused. "With your radar off, you might escape detection until you are into visual range."

"It isn't that stealthy," Bob Cassidy replied. "And the human eyeball isn't that good. What we're going to need is Sky Eye. The satellites are going to have to find these guys and tell us where they are."

"I'll talk to the National Security people."

"And we're going to need something to protect our bases. We won't have the planes to stay airborne around the clock. We need an equalizer."

"Sentinel," John said, and wrote the word on his legal pad.

"Explain."

"Sentinel is an automated weapon—highly classified, of course. You deliver it to a site, turn it on, and leave it. When it detects electromagnetic energy on a preset frequency, it launches a small, solid-fuel, antiradiation missile that seeks out the emitter. The missiles have some memory capability, so they can track targets that cease emissions—the capability of these new computer chips is really amazing. Anyway, as I recall, Sentinel has a magazine capacity of forty-eight missiles. The missiles have a range of about sixteen miles."

"Electrical power will be a big problem in Siberia."

"Sentinel has rechargable solar cells. All you have to do is reload the magazine occasionally."

"So Zero pilots are going to be down to their Mark I, Mod Zero eyeballs."

"Sentinel will definitely encourage them to leave their radars turned off."

"Nasty." Cassidy grinned.

"Doesn't the F-22 have the new camouflage skin that changes colors based on the background?" Eatherly asked after they discussed logistics for several minutes.

"The newest ones do," Cassidy told him. "Active skin camouflage, or smart skin. The skin has to be installed on the assembly line."

"How good is it?"

"It really works. Against any kind of neutral background, such as clouds or ocean or haze, the plane is extremely difficult to locate visually when it's more than a couple hundred yards away. Some people can pick it up with their peripheral vision, sometimes. Occasionally you see movement out of the corner of your eye, you know it's there, and yet when you look directly at it, you can't pick it up. It's scary."

Eatherly made a note. "Talk to me about maintenance. How many people, how many spares?"

After a morning of this, John Eatherly and Cassidy went back into the chairman's office for lunch. As they ate bean soup and corn bread, Eatherly briefed the general. He ran through proposed solutions to every major problem: personnel, logistics, maintenance, weapons and fuel supply, early warning.

"So what is your recommendation?" the general asked Cassidy when Eatherly was finished.

"Isn't there any way to prevent this war from happening, sir?" Cassidy was staring into the bean soup. He had no appetite.

"The politicos say no." Stanford Tuck shrugged. "War happens because a whole society screws itself up to it—it isn't just the fault of the politicians at the top. That society will quit only when the vast majority believes their cause is hopeless."

"So the F-22 outfit is supposed to help convince them. Show them the error of their ways."

"I want you to nibble at 'em, worry 'em, shoot down a Zero occasionally, target their air transports, convince the Japanese that they've bitten off more than they can chew."

"Sir, the Japanese have active ECM that makes their plane invisible. Athena. They will blow us from the sky unless we use the satellites to find the Zeros and point them out to us."

"The White House says no."

"I am not taking Americans to Russia to be slaughtered. Without Sky Eye, there is no way. I want no part of it."

Stanford Tuck helped himself to another spoonful of soup, then put the spoon down beside the bowl. "You've been in the military for twenty-some years, Cassidy. There's not much I could tell you about this business that you don't already know. I will try to get authorization to use the satellites."

"I'll be lucky to bring half of them home."

"I'll do the best I can. That's all I can promise."

"Those who do come home—can we get back into the Armed Forces?"

"I'll get a letter to that effect from the president. I'm sure he'll sign it."

"Good."

Then Tuck added softly, "Is there anything else you want to tell me, Colonel?"

"I know one of the Zero pilots pretty well, General."

Stanford Tuck glanced at Eatherly, then cleared his throat. "After spending a year in Japan, I'd be surprised if you didn't know several," he said. "I hate to press you like this, but time is running out. Can you do this job?"

"I can do it, General. My comment about the Zero pilot is personal. The job you are offering is professional, in the best interests of the United States. I know the difference. I just pray to God my friend lives through all this."

"I understand." Tuck's head moved a tenth of an inch. It was a tiny bow, Cassidy noted, startled.

"Colonel Eatherly will help you get the ball rolling," the general said. "Let's see what we can make happen."

"Yes, sir," Cassidy managed to say as Stanford Tuck stuck out his hand to shake.

Tuck held his hand firmly and looked him in the eye. "Check six, Colonel. And remember what the Good Book says: When you're in the valley, fear no evil."

CHAPTER SIX

● THE FIRST PEOPLE in Siberia to discover something amiss were the radar operators at the Vladivostok airport, a facility the military shared with the occasional civil transports that had flown the length of Siberia or over the Pole. There weren't many of those anymore. Fuel was expensive, money to maintain aircraft in short supply, and the navigation aids in the middle of the continent were not regularly maintained. Anything or anyone that really had to get to Vladivostok came by rail or sea. Still, the radars that searched the oceans to the east and south were in working order and operators were on duty, even at two o'clock in the morning, near the end of another short summer night.

In Russia change occurred because the government agency responsible ceased paying the bills and, to survive, the people who had lived on that trickle of money wandered on to something else. Money to make the radars work still dribbled in occasionally from Moscow. The task of safeguarding Mother Russia was too sacred for any politician to touch.

The only operator actually watching the screens was also perusing a card game that the other members of the watch section were playing. Occasionally, he remembered to glance at the screens. It was on one of these periscope sweeps that he saw the blip, to the south. Three minutes later, when the blip was still there, and closer, he called the supervisor to look. The supervisor put down his cards reluctantly.

There were no aircraft scheduled to arrive from that direction—there were no aircraft at all scheduled to arrive in Vladivostok until the next afternoon—and repeated queries on the radio went unanswered. As the blip got closer, it separated into many smaller blips, apparently a flight of aircraft.

The radar supervisor called the air defense watch officer on the other side of the base and reported the inbound flight, which would penetrate Russian airspace in about twelve minutes if it maintained the same course and speed.

Two Sukhoi Su-27 fighters were in the usual alert status, which meant each was fully fueled and armed with four AA-10 Alamo missiles and a belt of shells for its 30-mm cannon. The ground crews were asleep in a nearby hut. The pilots, wearing flight suits, were playing chess in another nearby shack. Usually at this time of night, the alert pilots would be asleep, but these two had attended a wedding dinner earlier in the evening and weren't sleepy.

When the duty officer telephoned, ordering a scramble, they dropped everything and ran for their planes as they shouted to awaken the ground crews. One of the pilots opened the door to the ground crew's shack and turned on the light.

At the aircraft, the pilots donned their flight gear as the ground crewmen came stumbling across the mat.

The Sukhois rolled onto the runway eight minutes later, lit their afterburners, and accelerated. The mighty roar washed over the sleepy base like thunder.

After a modest run, the wheels lifted from the concrete and the pilots sucked up gear and flaps. With the afterburners still engaged, the two fighters moved closer together. The pilots then pulled into a steep climb and punched up through the overcast as the leader checked in with the ground control intercept (GCI) controller, who was the same man who had seen the incoming blips, for what was originally one blip had now separated into five, sometimes six, individual targets. The supervisor and most of the watch section were now gathered behind him, watching the scope over his shoulder.

The blips were doing about 250 knots. Probably turboprop aircraft. But whose? Why were so many aircraft coming from the southeast? Why hadn't Moscow transmitted a copy of their flight plans?

The tops of the lower layer of stratus clouds were at fifteen thousand feet tonight. Another cloud layer far above blocked out most of the glow of the high-latitude sky. As they climbed above the lower layer of stratus clouds, the Sukhoi pilots eased their throttles back out of burner and spread out into a loose combat formation. They then killed their wingtip lights, so only the dim formation lights on the sides of the planes enlivened the darkness.

When the fighters were level at twenty thousand feet, the GCI controller turned them to a course to intercept the large formation heading toward Vladivostok.

The leader's attention was inside his cockpit. Although the Su-27 had a HUD, the pilot wasn't using it. Even if he had been, he would probably have died anyway.

He concentrated on flying his aircraft on instruments, and on adjusting the gain and brightness of his radar screen. The task took several seconds. As he examined the scope, he glanced at his electronic countermeasures panel, which was silent. Yes, the switches were on.

A shout on the radio. He automatically raised his gaze, scanned outside.

At eleven o'clock, slightly high, a bright light . . . brilliant!

Missile!

The thought registered on his brain and automatically he slammed the stick sideways to roll left, away from his wingman, and pulled.

The responsive fighter flicked over obediently into 220 degrees of bank. The missile arrived a second and a half after the pilot first spotted the exhaust plume: The fighter's nose had come down no more than ten degrees.

The missile missed the Sukhoi by about six inches. The proximity fuse detonated the warhead immediately under the cockpit area. The shrapnel punched hundreds of holes in the belly of the plane. In less than a second, fuel from punctured fuel lines sprayed into the engine compartment, starting a fire. A half second later, the aircraft exploded, killing the pilot instantly.

The wingman had instinctively rolled right—away from his leader—when he spotted the inbound missile. He also shouted into his radio mike, which was contained within his oxygen mask. It was this warning that the leader heard.

The wingman only rolled about seventy degrees, however, so he could keep the oncoming missile in sight. Still he laid on six G's. He saw the missile streak in out of the corner of his eye and saw the flash as it detonated under the leader's plane.

The flash temporarily blinded him.

Blinking mightily, he slammed the stick back left and pulled while he looked to see if his leader had successfully avoided the missile. He keyed his radio mike, opened his mouth to call.

The wingman never saw the second missile, which impacted his plane in the area of the left wing root and detonated. The explosion severed the wing spar, so the wing collapsed. The hot metal of the warhead ignited fuel spewing under pressure from the ruptured wing tank. Then all the fuel still in the wing exploded. The sequence was over in a few thousandths of a second. The pilot died without even knowing there had been a second missile.

The blossoming fireballs from the two Sukhois were visible for twenty miles in this dark universe.

The pilots of the four Japanese Zeros—White Flight—cruising at max conserve took their thumbs off the fire buttons on their sticks, where they had been hovering in case further missiles were necessary. The leader had been the only plane to fire.

Now White Leader began a gentle left turn to carry the flight back in the direction of Vladivostok. He hoped to orbit in this area to the east of the city in a racetrack pattern, ready to shoot down any other aircraft coming out of Vlad or the bases on Sakhalin Island to harass Japanese aircraft delivering paratroops.

Flying as number three, Jiro Kimura checked the location of the other aircraft in the formation on his computer presentation. The planes used pencil-thin laser beams to keep track of one another. No external lights were illuminated; consequently, the airplanes were invisible in the darkness.

Confident that all four planes were where they were supposed to be, Jiro's thoughts moved on. He banked to keep the leader in position.

Why did he not feel elated? The first two victories of the war had just been won. The Athena devices on the Zeros made them invisible to Russian radar, so the GCI controllers had no clue whatsoever that the Zeros were even airborne. They had launched the Sukhois to investigate the incoming transports. The Sukhoi pilots had been ambushed without warning . . . without mercy, without a chance in hell. They were executed.

That was the truth of it.

Jiro felt no pity or remorse, only a tiredness, a lethargy, and a sense of profound sadness.

Flash, flash, two explosions seventeen miles away in the night sky . . . and two men were dead. Presumably. Jiro thought the odds of surviving explosions like that must be very slim.

Bang, bang.

Just like that—two men dead.

That was the way he would die, too. The revelation came to him now in his cockpit as he sat there tired, hungry, thirsty, and very much alone. He would die in this cockpit someday just as those two Russians had, without warning, without luck, without a moment to reflect, without an opportunity to make his peace with the universe.

And he had chosen this destiny! Just last evening, his commanding officer had sent for him, showed him a message from the Japanese Intelligence Agency demanding a loyalty investigation. "You telephoned an American Air Force officer?"

"I attended the American Air Force Academy, sir, as you are aware. I know many Americans. I have kept up my contacts with several of them through the years."

"Of course," his CO said. "These bureaucratic spy fools have not looked at your record. But you see how it is, Kimura. You see how easy it is to compromise yourself. Be more careful in the future." With that admonition, the CO tossed the message in a pile of paperwork that a clerk was placing in boxes for storage.

"I called this American to—"

His commanding officer didn't want to hear it. He cut him off. "Kimura, we are going to have a war. You and I will both be in combat within twenty-four hours. I have better things to do just now than write letters to bureaucrats. An investigation, they want. If we are both alive a month from now, I shall write them a letter saying that you are a loyal soldier of Japan. If you are dead, I shall tell them how gloriously you died. Like cherry blossoms falling—isn't that the way the old poems go? If I am dead . . ."

The CO had shooed him out.

Now the Russian GCI controller came on the air, calling to his dead pilots. He didn't know they were dead, of course, but they had disappeared from his radar scope, so he was calling, albeit futilely.

Jiro could not understand the words, but he could hear the concern and frustration in the controller's voice.

Jiro kept a wary eye on his electronic warfare (EW) warning indications—they were comfortably silent—monitored the tactical display, and concentrated on staying in proper position in his formation as the controller called and called to men who would never answer.

The ten aircraft approaching Vladivostok were C-130 Hercules, J-models, the most advanced version of the late-twentieth-century military transportation workhorse. Each aircraft was crammed with troops.

The first flight of four aircraft began descending seventy miles from the city. They dropped into a trail formation by alternately dropping gear and flaps. The pilot of the lead plane delayed his dirty-up the longest—he dropped his gear just as he intercepted the instrument landing system (ILS) glide path. He couldn't yet see the runway since the visibility was only three or four miles in this gentle rain.

The ILS was working fine, which was amazing considering how little money the Russians had devoted to their airways system over the last few years. Even if the ILS had been disabled, he would have flown exactly the same approach using the GPS equipment and computers in his cockpit. Still, the flight leader was delighted the ILS was operating. Had it been off, he would have had to worry about how much warning the Russians had had and whether or not the runway was blocked. Since the ILS was functioning, he felt confident the runway would be clear. Just to be on the safe side, however, he compared the ILS indications he was receiving with the computer presentation derived from GPS and the onboard inertial. All the instruments agreed.

The copilot chortled merrily, as did the leader of the paratroops, who stood behind the pilot looking over his shoulder.

The second flight of four C-130s kept their speed up as they dropped toward the city. Level at three thousand feet, in the overcast, the crews opened the rear cargo doors. The paratroopers lined up and connected their static lines.

The planes continued descending toward the city in trail, three miles apart, the paratroopers waiting. Many of the soldiers stood with eyes closed, lips moving as they prayed to their gods and their ancestors. A night parachute jump was hazardous enough, but the Russians had antiaircraft missile batteries and artillery spotted around the city; if they opened fire the C-130s were going to fall like ruptured ducks. And the city was on a peninsula, with water on three sides. Paratroopers hated water. When the chart was unveiled, revealing the location, several gasps were heard as the men saw all that water.

The guns and missile batteries remained silent. The Hercs swept in at 200 knots, slowing to 150 as they dropped lower and lower toward city lights glowing in the cloudy, rainy darkness.

Two of the planes dropped their paratroopers over the old closed Vlad airport, which was being rebuilt.

The other two planes dropped their men north of the wharves along Golden Horn Bay. The first planeload of these troops landed mainly on the streets and small grassy areas, but a gust of wind seemed to catch the last several dozen men of the second stick. The men hanging in their parachutes drifted toward the black water of the bay lying immediately to their right.

Silently, without a cry or shout, the soldiers dropped into the oily waters of the bay and went under. Each man was wearing almost a hundred pounds of gear and weapons, so they had no chance. They were the first Japanese to die invading Siberia.

In the airport tower, the supervisor was unable to establish communications with the approaching aircraft. He spoke into the microphone only in Russian. Trying to communicate with the incoming planes in English, the universal language of international aviation, never once occurred to him.

The thought did occur to him, however, that he had better personally notify the military of the presence of the unknown planes.

He dialed the telephone number of the commanding officer of the army unit that provided airport security. Since it was the middle of the night there was no one in the office to answer the telephone. The army ran a strictly business-hours operation. Consequently, the four ZPU-23 antiaircraft artillery units parked around the airport perimeter that could have shot the incoming Japanese C-130s to bits with just a few bursts of aimed fire were never manned. This was, perhaps, just as well, because near each gun was a Japanese commando in civilian clothes, armed with a sniper rifle equipped with a starlight scope.

The tower supervisor also turned off the airport lights—the runway, taxiway, and approach lights. Vlad airport instantly took on the appearance of the black water that bordered it on three sides.

The lead C-130 broke out of the overcast a mile and a half out on the ILS glide slope. As a precaution, the aircraft was displaying no exterior lights. The pilot looked in vain for the approach and runway lights, then correctly assumed that they had been turned off. He spoke this conclusion aloud to the battalion commander standing behind his seat. The words were just out of his mouth when the ILS needles locked up and the off flag appeared on the face of the instrument. The tower supervisor had ordered the instrument landing system turned off, too.

The copilot was now flying the plane. The ILS failure bothered him not at all. He continued to follow GPS lineup and descent commands on the heads-up display.

At a hundred feet above the runway, the pilot saw lights reflecting off the wet concrete and called it. The copilot saw it, too. The pilot had his hand on the switch to turn on the landing lights, but he decided not to take the risk. There was just enough glare from the city reflecting off the clouds for the copilot to flare the Herc and set it on runway centerline. The pilot pulled the props into reverse thrust and, when the plane had slowed, turned off on the first available taxiway.

The battalion commander slapped the pilot on the shoulder, then turned and went aft to where his men were waiting.

Six minutes after the first Herc was on the ground at Vlad airport, Japanese troops were in the airport control tower and Japanese controllers were running the radar and talking to inbound traffic.

The transition occurred with only the most minor of glitches: The tower guard, a young Russian policeman armed only with a pistol, pulled it from its holster as six soldiers in strange uniforms trotted out of the darkness toward him with their assault rifles at high port. The gesture was futile. No one had told the policeman anything; he had not the least glimmer of an idea that Siberia—the airport—was being invaded. Still, his nervous reaction was, perhaps, understandable.

A pistol was a pistol, so the corporal trotting up with his squad shot the policeman with a burst of three rounds. The soldiers, all wearing body armor, jerked open the door of the building and went thundering through.

The policeman's body lay where it had fallen for the rest of the night. A passing Japanese officer finally noticed the pistol—a seventy-year-old Webley relic from the heady days of World War II Lend-Lease. He picked it up and stuck it in his belt. No one touched the body.

The paratroopers landing at the former closed airport assembled and counted heads. Several of the men had landed in construction ditches and one had fractured a leg by striking a bulldozer that had apparently been employed tearing up concrete. Surpisingly, the Russians were ripping up the crumbling old runways and putting in new. They were also in the process of installing sewers, water, and power lines.

Miraculously, all the paratroopers had somehow missed a construction crane towering a hundred feet in the air. Landing in a major construction site complicated the paratroopers' arrival somewhat, but so far, no one had paid them the least attention.

In accordance with the invasion plan, a company of soldiers assigned to guard the perimeter moved to the fences and took up their positions. The remainder of the soldiers laid out flares and tiny radio transmitters to outline a landing zone in the event the airport runway lights failed for any reason. Some of the larger pieces of construction equipment, including the construction crane, were marked with red warning lights. Then the men waited for the additional paratroopers scheduled to arrive. Within fifteen minutes, more soldiers floated from the misty clouds on white parachutes as the hum of turboprop engines echoed from the surrounding buildings and hills.

When the second wave of troops was on the ground and out of the way, containers carrying machine guns, ammo, and communications gear began to drop from the clouds. The Japanese were dropping most of the men first, then the containers of supplies, just to be on the safe side. Still, they had hoped for only light opposition. So far, there had been none.

Occasionally, a container would drift too far west and fall into Amur Bay amid the fishing and industrial boats moored there, but not too many drifted that far, so no one paid much attention. People were visible on the boats, watching the military operation. No one made any attempt to interfere or even get closer to kibitz better.

Meanwhile, in the heart of the old city of Vladivostok, four unarmed Japanese commandos in civilian clothes watched as a small coaster eased through the gentle swells of the black water inside the Golden Horn, moving toward the public pier. There were no policemen or Russian soldiers anywhere about, the commandos had made sure of that. For the past two days, they had had this area under surveillance. During the hours when they weren't on watch, they played the role of Japanese businessmen at a local hotel and ran up prodigious bills—which they had no intention of paying—for food, vodka, and women.

Two of the commandos walked out to the bollards and caught lines thrown from the coaster's deck. Soon she was against the pier, with two gangways over. Troops in combat dress trotted ashore. They kept right on going across the pier and sidewalk and parking area, stopping at the first major street and forming a perimeter guard.

When the coaster's contingent of fifty men was ashore, the lines were taken in and it backed out into the strait. Another coaster eased out of the darkness up to the pier.

The next day, several major cargo ships would appear in the roadstead, ships carrying tanks, artillery, and all the other supplies and equipment necessary to keep a division fighting for weeks.

Across the bay at the Churkin wharves, a similar scene was being played out. Two of the Japanese cargo ships could get in against this wharf, but the cargo cranes were broken. The Russians had been unloading cargo by hand. The following day, these soldiers would have to have the military situation in Vladivostok well enough in hand that a portable crane could be off-loaded and erected.

The soldiers certainly had encountered no opposition thus far. That would soon change. Telephones were ringing all over Russia; the news from the airport was being discussed in Moscow. Locally, the authorities were hearing of the paratroops' arrival.

At the ferry slip on the west side of the bay, the captain of *Ivan Turgenev,* a ferry loading passengers for Russian Island, across the strait from Vladivostok, saw strange troops in battle dress on the Churkin wharves and called his dispatcher on the radio. The dispatcher was incredulous.

With the diesel engine of his ferry still idling, the captain went ashore. The boozy barflies waiting to be taken home after an evening on the town paid no attention. Some of them were already vomiting over the railing.

At a public telephone in the little terminal, the ferry captain asked the operator for police headquarters. The officer on duty there did believe the captain's story, got the facts as quickly as possible, and even thanked him for calling.

After he hung up, the captain stood watching the troops for a moment from a window in the terminal; then he heard another ferry tooting. *Ivan Turgenev* was late on her departure. He ran back to the boat and headed for the bridge. Invasion or no, the ferries had to keep running.

A half hour after the destruction of the two Su-27s from the Vladivostok airport, the combat air patrol of Zeros known as White Flight was nearing the end of its on-station time. A new flight of four—Yellow Flight—scheduled to enter the area in five minutes was at least fifteen minutes behind schedule. White Leader had listened a few minutes ago to Yellow Leader talking to the tanker on Station Alpha, two hundred miles southeast. Yellow Leader was in a foul mood—the tanker was having equipment problems—but verbal rockets over the radio seemed to have little effect. So that flight was late, and it was not escorting the transports carrying more troops and supplies to Vlad.

There, on the very edge of his tactical screen, something coming west from Sakhalin Island. . . . White Leader adjusted the scale of the screen.

Four planes, still climbing. His computer identified them as MiG-29s. Definitely hostile.

He decided to continue to orbit, to let the MiGs come to him. If he flew toward them, he was leaving the back door open for planes coming south from Khabarovsk in the Amur valley.

"White Three, you will fire two missiles at the easternmost targets, upon my command." This transmission went out over the encrypted radio circuit.

"Roger, White Leader." That was Jiro Kimura, White Three.

Max range for the missiles under the Zeros' wings was sixty nautical miles. White Leader decided to shoot at fifty, in case one of the missiles had less than a full load of fuel. He studied the tactical display as he orbited.

The MiGs were high, over thirty thousand feet, up where airliners cruise. Airliners . . . Where were the transports? They should be just offshore . . . coming north from Hokkaido. Shouldn't they?

White Leader checked the watch on his wrist. He adjusted his tactical screen, pushed buttons. The transports should be identified on this presentation, if they were on time.

Nothing. Drat!

"White Three, White Lead. Do you have any friendly transports on your tac screen?" This transmission was encoded in a discrete, impossible-to-intercept beam of laser light that was aimed only at the other planes in the formation.

"Affirmative. They are—"

Even as Jiro spoke, the MiGs changed course, ninety degrees to their left. Southwest. And the transports appeared on White Leader's tac screen, the very edge of it. The MiGs were on course to intercept.

"White Three, watch the back door. White Two, come with me." White Leader stroked his afterburners.

The Zeros had been cruising at a very economical .8 Mach. Now the fuel flow increased dramatically, as did the airspeed. The two Zeros slid through the sonic barrier with nary a buffet. Mach 1.2 . . . 1.6 . . . Mach 2 . . . 2.3 . . . 2.4. The airspeed stabilized at Mach 2.5.

Below, people asleep in coastal villages and towns awoke to twin thunderclaps, so close together that some people heard only one loud sonic boom. The booms reached the ground miles behind the speeding Zeros, streaking to intercept the MiGs before they got within range of the transports.

Above the clouds, the brilliant glow of the white-hot flames from twin afterburners shot across the sky like missiles. As the planes got away from the land, the stratus clouds thinned to wisps. Here and there, the sky was clear.

The intense heat signature of the two planes appeared as targets on several infrared scanners on coastal antiaircraft missile batteries, batteries recently alerted by telephone calls from frantic men in distant headquarters. One of the missile crews got an IR target lockup and tried to confirm via telephone that the target they were seeing was hostile. While this conversation was taking place, the targets passed out of range and lockup was lost.

The second crew was less professional. The danger of firing a surface-to-air missile at Russian fighters did not occur to them until later. When they got an IR lockup, they pushed the fire button.

Their SAM-3 missile leapt from its launcher as a sheet of dazzling flame poured from the solid fuel rocket motor. The missile accelerated away into the darkness, chasing that hot target.

Unfortunately, the battery crew had committed their missile to a futile stern chase. The missile exhausted its fuel before it closed half the distance to those fleeing Mach 2.5 targets. When the engine fell silent and the missile nosed over, a self-destruction circuit sensed the absence of acceleration and exploded the missile harmlessly.

White Leader got a glimpse of the explosion in his rearview mirror, but he was extremely busy and didn't give it any thought until later, much later, during mission debrief.

He was closing on the MiG-29s at almost a right angle, actually eighty-eight degrees. This would be a full deflection missile shot at nearly maximum range, the worst kind: the missile might not be able to make the corner. Should he wait and turn in behind before shooting? That would increase the chances that a missile would track, but it would let the MiGs get closer to the transports. The MiGs were at seventy-five miles now, closing at a sixty-degree stern angle.

There were two flights of MiGs, two to a flight, and the flights were about three miles apart.

For a second, White Leader wondered if the MiGs knew he was

there, knew they, too, were being hunted. He shook the thought off. No time for that now.

Sixty-miles range. He fired one missile, then made a short left turn. This would let the MiGs extend out, put him astern. He still had a ton of closure—they could be doing no more than Mach 1.5. He would get astern and shoot again.

"White Two, shoot on my command."

"Roger."

Now, a sixty-degree angle of bank turn to the right. Yes. He was only forty-five degrees off, still closing.

The first missile must have missed, because the MiGs were turning hard, hard right, into the direction that the missile had come from.

"Out of burner, now."

White Lead and his wingman came off the juice. They slowed as they turned to place the turning MiGs at their twelve o'clock.

Very nice. Range forty miles. Well within the missiles' performance envelope. White Leader triggered his last missile at the leading MiG, the one farthest to his right.

"I've shot at the leader, Two. Blaze away at the rest of them."

Two said nothing. He answered with missiles. One after the other, two seconds apart, three missiles came off his rails.

Seconds ticked by. The Russian second-element wingman, Tail-end Charlie, lost sight of his lead during all the maneuvering and turned hard left, back toward the transports. He picked the nearest and locked him up with his radar. Just then, White Leader's missile impacted the lead MiG-29 in front of the tail and detonated. The tail was severed from the aircraft, which entered an uncontrollable tumble. The pilot tried to eject, but the tumbling was so violent that he passed out before he could do so. Within seconds, the plane broke up.

From the corner of his eye, Tail-end Charlie saw the fiery streak of the first missile coming in and the flash as it impacted, and he correctly guessed what it was. He had his firing solution on one of the Japanese transports at max range, seventy miles, so he pushed the fire button on his stick and held it down.

The firing circuit had a one-second delay built in before it ignited the missile's rocket engine, a delay designed to prevent inadvertent missile launching. This second was the longest of the young pilot's life. As he waited, he saw in the canopy rail mirror the flash as a Japanese missile exploded just above the cockpit of his element leader. This was the first missile fired by White Two.

Now Charlie's long-range Alamo missile came off the rail and seared the darkness with its cone of white fire.

Instinctively, the MiG pilot rolled upside down and pulled the nose ninety degrees down, straight down, toward the black ocean below.

The second missile from White Two arrived right on time, fatally impacting the other surviving MiG.

The missile aimed at Tail-end Charlie nosed over to track him and increased its speed. Charlie lit his burners, accelerated toward the waiting ocean.

The missile nosed down farther, gravity making it go even faster . . . and it overshot. It exploded harmlessly when its internal computer concluded it had missed.

At the flash of the explosion, Charlie began to pull. He was passing twenty thousand feet, eighty degrees nose-down at Mach 1.6. He came out of burner, pulled until he thought the wings would come off, then pulled some more. The nose was coming up, but not fast enough.

He fought to stay conscious.

Pull, pull, pull, scream into the mask, pull to stay alive.

Nine thousand . . . seven . . . nose thirty degrees down . . .

Nose twenty degrees down . . . ten degrees, passing three thousand feet . . .

At one thousand feet, only three hundred meters above the sea, Tail-end Charlie bottomed out. He was below Mach 1 at this point, but he was alive.

As the nose came above the horizon and he relaxed the G, the Russian pilot glanced at the radar scope on the panel before him. Nothing. It was blank. He laid into a turn in the direction from which the missiles had come. The enemy had to be up there, if only he could point his plane in the proper direction. Unlike the Zero, the MiG-29 lacked computers and passive sensors; the pilot had only radar to enable him to see his enemy.

A streak of fire in the sky caught his eye—another missile!

He was low and slow, trapped against the sea. He did the only thing he could—pulled the nose of the MiG straight up and lit the afterburner.

The missile went through the left wing, snapping it cleanly in two.

With his plane rolling out of control, the pilot of Tail-end Charlie ejected.

His parachute opened normally and he rode it down into the black ocean.

After floating in his life jacket for two hours, he died of hypothermia and exhaustion. During that time his only consolation was the fact that he had fired a missile at a transport before the unseen enemy got him. He never knew that his missile failed to guide.

White Three—Jiro Kimura—watched the spots of flame that were the afterburner exhausts of White One and Two accelerate away into the darkness. They receded more slowly than missile engines, but they did resemble missiles, or wandering stars, points of light growing smaller and smaller as the night swallowed them.

Jiro glanced at his wingman, then turned back toward Vladivostok. He kept his turn shallow, less than a ten-degree angle of bank, so he would not present the belly of the plane to an enemy radar to use as a reflecting surface.

He watched the tactical situation develop on his multifunction tac display. He saw the transports, saw the MiGs go for them, and saw White One and Two dash to cut them off. The missiles that were fired were not displayed, but the disappearance of the MiGs from the screen one by one spoke volumes.

We are winning.

That thought has sustained fighting men for thousands of years. It helped Jiro now, gave him a sense of confidence that no amount of exhortation could.

He was eying his fuel gauges nervously and toying with the idea of breaking radio silence when the tactical display presented a target coming down from the northeast, from the direction of Khabarovsk. A Sukhoi. Now two.

Where is Yellow Flight?

Jiro leveled his wings heading toward Vlad. The Sukhois were about a mile apart, heading southwest. If everyone maintained heading, the Sukhois would pass White Three and Four several miles to the left.

"Three, this is Four. My gadget has overheated. I'm turning it off."

This unexpected transmission on the plane-to-plane digital laser system shook Jiro. He had just been basking in the glow of Athena's technical excellence, and now his wingman's unit had failed.

It was high time to be out of here. Where is Yellow Flight?

Without Athena to cancel incoming waves of electromagnetic energy from enemy radar, Four was now plainly visible on the screen of every Russian radar looking. Apparently, several of them were looking with interest. Jiro's electronic countermeasures panel lit up—someone was tracking them in high PRF, the firing mode of an antiaircraft missile radar. Actually they were tracking the wingman, but Jiro was close enough to the targeted aircraft to receive the indications on his equipment.

"Break away, Four. RTB." This meant return to base. "I'll be right along."

"My fuel is bingo," Four said, trying to cushion the embarrassment of his Athena failure.

Jiro's fuel was also getting desperate. But if he didn't cover Four's withdrawal, Four was in for a very bad time.

"RTB," Jiro repeated. "Now!"

The other Zero turned away hard. Jiro watched the tactical display and ensured the wingman steadied up as he headed toward Hokkaido.

The Sukhois from Vlad turned fifteen degrees to the left and launched a missile. Two.

Four was too far away for the discrete laser com. Jiro keyed the radio, which was scrambled, of course. Still, he was radiating. "Two missiles in the air, White Four. Sixty-three miles behind you." Four should have the missiles on his tactical display, if he had the proper display punched in. Jiro was taking no chances.

The Sukhois were too far away for Jiro to shoot. The Russian missiles had more range than the Japanese.

Perhaps the Sukhois could be diverted with another target. Jiro turned off his Athena device.

The visibility was too poor to see the Russian missiles' exhaust. They were out there, though, thundering along at almost Mach 4, covering two miles every three seconds. The missiles had been fired at nearly maximum range, so White Four was trying to outrun them. He was accelerating too, dumping fuel into his exhaust in exchange for speed. That was not a wise maneuver for a man without fuel to spare, but he was trapped between the devil and the deep blue sea.

Four was accelerating through Mach 2.

Well, he was safe. The missiles would never catch him in a stern chase before they exhausted their fuel.

"Three, this is Four. I'm changing freqs, calling for a tanker. I need fuel to get home."

"Roger."

Jiro devoted his attention to the Sukhois, which had turned in his direction. He checked his fuel gauges. He didn't have any to spare on speed dashes, either.

Missile launch. One . . . two from the Sukhois.

Where in hell is Yellow Flight?

"Yellow Leader, White Three. State your position and expected time to arrive on station, please."

Jiro and the Sukhois were closing head-on at a combined speed of Mach 2.5. The missiles were coming at Mach 4. Closure speed with the missiles, 1.2 miles per second.

He was going to be in range for his missiles in five seconds. They were armed and ready to fire. He had only to punch the fire button on the stick.

Four . . . three . . . two . . . one . . . the in-range symbol appeared on the scope.

If he waited for a few seconds, he would have a better chance of scoring hits. But the fuel . . .

Jiro pressed the fire button and held it. One potato . . . and a missile left in a gout of flame. He released the button, waited for the ready symbol on the HUD, then fired again.

With his left hand, he reached for the Athena switch. He turned it from the standby to the on position. The yellow light stayed illuminated.

Damnation!

He cycled the switch to off, then back to standby. Now to the on position. There was a ten-second warm-up delay built into the circuitry, so that many seconds had to pass before the gear began to radiate, canceling incoming radar waves.

Meanwhile, he dumped the nose and turned hard to the southeast. Nose well down, gravity helping him accelerate.

The incoming missile warning was flashing, showing twenty-one seconds to impact.

He was tempted to engage the afterburners; he eyed the fuel gauge again. No, he didn't have enough. If he did the burner trick, he might end up trying to swim to Japan.

Going down hard. He pushed the stick forward another smidgen, steepening his dive.

Fifteen seconds to impact. He looked outside, tried to see the oncoming missiles.

There!

And he went into the top of the stratus cloud deck.

That was stupid. If he had kept the missiles in sight, he would have had a better chance to outmaneuver them, if Athena refused to work.

Stupid. A stupid mistake.

You are fast running out of options, Jiro, options to save your silly butt.

At twelve seconds to impact, the green light appeared on the Athena panel.

The missiles were still coming. He watched them close on the tactical display. Were they tracking him?

One way to find out. He slapped the stick sideways and turned hard into the missiles. Six G's. Inadvertently, a groan escaped him.

The missiles didn't follow. They passed harmlessly behind and to his left.

Jiro got his nose up, started climbing, and lowered a wing to turn back to the southeast. He needed to get up to at least forty thousand feet for the trip to the tanker at Station Alpha.

He was climbing when he saw his missiles and the Sukhois merge on his tactical display. Target merger, and the Sukhois were gone.

He lived; the Russians died.

Just like that.

Jiro wiped the sweat from his eyes.

CHAPTER SEVEN

● THE SOVIET NAVY was always something of a floating oxymoron, the seagoing service of the world's largest land power. It never received the prestige, money, or priority accorded to the Soviet army. The navy's hour of glory came after the 1962 Cuban missile crisis, when capable blue-water combatants were built in sufficient numbers to form a credible threat to the U.S. Navy and America's global interests. These sleek, heavily armed gray ships sailed the seven seas in packs, proudly waved the red flag, and never fired a shot.

When the bankrupt Soviet Union imploded in 1991, the surviving republics divided up the navy's ships. Russia received the majority, a dubious honor, for she lacked the money to sail or repair them. There wasn't even money to pay the sailors or buy them food. Some of the ships were sold to Third World nations for badly needed foreign exchange, but most were left to rust at their piers.

About half of the Russian far eastern fleet was tied to piers at the three naval bases near Vladivostok when squadrons of four destroyers each steamed into the harbor of each base.

The Japanese navy opened fire from less than a mile away with 127-mm 54-caliber deck guns. Not a single Russian ship fired back.

Most of the Russian ships had no crews, and even the ones that did have sailors aboard were in no condition to get under way, much less fight. At the two bases east of Vlad, all the ships were cold iron, without steam up. In Vlad, only two ships were receiving electrical power from the shore. These were tied to the westernmost pier in Golden Horn Bay. The rest looked, by day anyway, like exactly what they were, rust buckets abandoned to their fate.

It wasn't as if the nation or the navy didn't care about these ships, which had been purchased at an enormous cost, but they could never reach a decision about what to do with them. Every choice had enormous emotional and political implications. So they did nothing. Most of these vessels were now so far gone that they would be useful only if salvaged for scrap.

The Japanese ships steamed slowly in trail, one behind the other, acquired their targets as if this were an exercise, and banged away mercilessly. The explosive shells shredded the upper decks of the Russian ships and punched holes in unarmored hulls. Here and there minor fires broke out, but the ships contained no fuel, no explosive fluids, nothing that would readily burn. All those materials had been stripped off the ships years ago by naval yard workers and sold on the black market.

The two ships that had power and lights received special attention from the Japanese destroyers. Ironically, neither was a combatant. One was a fifty-year-old icebreaker, the other a large oceangoing tug. Both sank at their piers under the Japanese hammering.

Finally, after thirty minutes of shelling, the Japanese were satisfied. Still in trail, keeping to the channel, the four destroyers of each squadron turned smartly and steamed for the entrance of the bay.

The naval base five hundred miles northeast, at Gavan, received a similar treatment, quick, surgical, and vicious. Alas, this base was almost a mirror image of the bases at Vladivostok, a place to moor abandoned ships, but here and there were a few active units, ships that had received some modicum of attention through the years and still had a crew.

One of those craft was a low-freeboard monitor used by the border guard to patrol the Amur River when it was free of ice. The crew, directed by a very junior officer who had the night watch, managed to get one of the vessel's two 115-mm antitank guns unlimbered and loaded.

Their first shot missed, but the second punched a nice hole through the hull of a Japanese destroyer, starting a hot fire.

The Japanese turned the fire of their flotilla upon this one gunboat. The gunners in the armored turret of the 115-mm gun got off two more rounds, both of which missed, before Japanese shells severed all electrical power to the turret.

Later, as the destroyers steamed away, on their way to shell Aleksandrovsk on Sakhalin Island, then Nikolayevsk, at the mouth of the Amur River, the flag officer in charge of the flotilla pondered about that gun crew. Against overwhelming odds, they had fought back bravely. Conquering the Russians, he mused, might not be as easy as wardroom gossip predicted.

Captain Second Rank Pavel Saratov was the skipper of *Admiral Kol-chak,* a Russian diesel/electric attack submarine cruising between the southernmost of the Kuril Islands and the Japanese island of Hokkaido. Normally, in accordance with navy doctrine, Saratov would be well out of sight of land while he ran on the surface charging his batteries, but to irritate the Japanese Moscow had ordered him to cruise for the last three days back and forth just outside the Japanese twelve-mile limit, often near the Japanese port of Nemuro.

The boat left its base at Petropavlosk, on the eastern coast of the Kamchatka Peninsula, two weeks ago. Her first task had been to deliver two navy divers to a shipwreck blocking the channel into Okhotsk, a tiny port on the northern shore of the Sea of Okhotsk that had given the sea its name. Normally, maritime demolition jobs were assigned to the Border Security Forces, but for reasons known only to a bureaucrat buried in Moscow the navy got this one. Saratov couldn't find the wreck. He went ashore and was told by the port manager that the wreck he sought had blocked the channel for ten years, until last winter, when the badly rusted superstructure was destroyed by pack ice, which closed the port annually from December through May. There was nothing left to demolish.

An hour before dawn this rainy, misty morning, Saratov was on the bridge of his boat, the cockpit on top of the sail, or conning tower, pondering his fate. He had once commanded an *Alfa*-class nuclear-powered attack submarine, but the nuke boats were all laid up several years ago when Russia agreed to disable their reactors in return for foreign bank credits. Saratov had not complained—the reactors were sloppily built, old, and dangerous. They had never been properly maintained. Actually, he had been relieved that his days of absorbing unknown quantities of leaking radiation were over.

Many of his fellow submarine officers left the navy then, but Saratov had decided to stay. The entire nation was in economic meltdown; he had no civilian skills or job prospects. He opted to use his seniority to get command of a diesel-powered sub, one that could actually get under way. Not that there was much money for diesel fuel. Twice he had traded torpedo fuel for food and diesel fuel so he could take his boat to sea.

Four and a half years later, here he was, off the coast of Japan, still in command, still eating occasionally. His crew consisted of twenty officers and twenty-five warrants, or *michmen*. Only five of the crew were common enlisted. The Soviet navy's enlisted men had all been draftees, few of whom had the skills or desire to stay past the end of their required service. Those few willing to stay for a career had been promoted to *michmen*. After the collapse of communism the new Russian navy was forced to use the same system since there was no money to attract volunteers. The officers and *michmen* on board, and the five volunteer recruits, were 25 percent of the survivors of the Soviet far eastern submarine fleet. Three other conventional diesel/electric subs were similarly manned—just four boats in all.

It was enough to make a grown man cry.

Admiral Kolchak was a good old boat. She had once been known as *Vladimirskiy Komsomolets,* commemorating a municipal organization of Communist youth, but after the collapse of communism she was renamed—for an anti-Communist hero. She had her problems, of course, but they were repairable problems that came with age and use, not design defects. The crew always managed to get her back to the surface, where her diesel engines could usually be coaxed into life. And none of the sailors had come down with radiation sickness. Two years ago the Libyans almost bought her, then elected to take a boat from the Black Sea fleet instead. That had been a close call.

The communications officer interrupted Saratov's reverie with a radio dispatch from Moscow. It was highly classified and marked with the highest urgency classification, so it had been decoded immediately and brought to him.

He read the paper by the light of the red flashlight he carried. A Japanese attack on Vladivostok?

He went below and read the message again under the good light in the control room.

The message directed him to take his boat to Vladivostok and attack any Japanese ships he encountered. First priority, according to the message, were warships; second, troop transports. Presumably, the troops would be on deck waving Rising Sun flags, which would be visible in the periscope, so he wouldn't waste a torpedo on a ship laden with bags of cement or rubber monster toys.

The navigator was at his station in the control room. Saratov handed the message to him to read as he examined the chart on the navigator's table. The navigator started whispering excitedly with the officer of the deck.

Saratov was measuring distances when he heard the *michman* of the watch say in a normal tone of voice, "P-3 radar signals." This would be the fourth P-3 flyover in the last three days.

"Where?" Saratov asked sharply.

"Bearing one one five, estimated range fifteen."

"Dive, dive, dive! Emergency dive!" Pavel Saratov shouted, and personally pushed the dive alarm.

The P-3 Orion was a large four-engine turboprop airplane with a crew of twelve. Made by Lockheed for the U.S. Navy and periodically updated as electronic technology evolved, P-3s were military versions of the old Electra airframe. They were a much bigger success as antisubmarine patrol planes than they ever were as airliners. The Japanese Self-Defense Force had operated them for decades.

The crew of the P-3 that found *Admiral Kolchak* knew that the submarine had been operating on the surface near the port of Nemuro. Tonight they had been overflying radar contacts and positively identifying them with their 100-million-candlepower searchlight.

Then one of the contacts ahead began to fade.

The radar operator sang out enthusiastically, "Sinker, sinker, sinker. Thirteen miles, bearing three five zero relative."

"Estimated course and speed?" That was the TACCO, the tactical coordinator, exasperated that the radar operator had to be asked.

"About zero nine zero magnetic, speed six knots. He's definitely a submarine, going down, down, down."

The operator was brimming with excitement. *This* was war. After all those years of training, this was the real thing. Ahead was a Russian submarine, diving for the thermal layer; the crew of this airplane, which most certainly included the radar operator, was going to destroy it.

The TACCO, Koki Hirota, was working hard. The submarine had undoubtedly detected the P-3's radar, then dived for safety. Hokkaido was eight miles south; the sub had been cruising eastward on the surface. Once submerged, the submarine would probably turn to complicate the tactical problem. Which direction was it likely that the skipper would pick? Certainly not south, or a course that would take him back into the restricted waters of the strait. But then again . . .

No, no, no. No shortcuts tonight. Let's do it by the book, get this submarine. We'll start a general search, pull the net tighter and tighter, then kill him with a Mk-46 homing torpedo.

The pilot, Masataka Yonai, had finished restarting the number one and four engines. He had been cruising on just two engines as they conducted a general search. With all engines running, he put the plane into a gentle descent. He leveled at two hundred feet above the water and engaged the autopilot. Doctrine called for night searches to be carried out at five hundred feet, day searches at two hundred, but the magnetic anomaly detector, or MAD gear, was slightly more sensitive at the lower altitude. Yonai had his share of the samurai spirit: he wanted this submarine, so the book be damned—he would fly at two hundred feet.

Tension was high in the aircraft as the crew laid a general search pattern of sonobuoys. Some were set to listen above the thermal layer, which should be about 350 feet deep here, and others were set to listen below. It would take several minutes for the deep listeners to get their microphones down.

The northernmost shallow sonobuoy picked up faint screw noises. "Contact, contact," the operator sang out. Koki Hirota flipped switches so he, too, could listen. He concentrated very hard. Yes, he could just hear it: a sub.

Thank heavens this is a Russian boat, Koki Hirota thought. If it had been an American submarine—the quietest kind—one plane would have a poor chance of pinning it. In his ten years in patrol planes, Hirota had only found one American boat, and that time, he freely admitted, he had been very lucky. Russian or not, if this skipper down under us is any good, we'll need luck to get him, too.

Hirota ordered a four-thousand-yard barrier pattern to the north of the northernmost sonobuoy.

Yonai complied immediately. He had complete confidence in Hirota, whom he believed to be the best TACCO alive. Yonai now had the airplane thundering along at two hundred knots indicated airspeed, two hundred feet above the water.

He and his copilot concentrated fiercely on the flight instruments. There was no margin for error, not at two hundred feet. The P-3 was a big plane; they were flying it right against the surface of the sea.

The sonobuoys went out of the bay with split-second precision. Hirota selected the ones he wanted from among the sixty-four buoys in the bay and the order in which he wanted them dropped; then the computer spit them out. Forty of the buoys were the cheap LOFAR, or low-frequency, buoys. Eighteen were DIFAR, or directional, buoys used in tight search patterns. And six were the new doppler-ranging buoys that had been developed in secret by Japanese industry. Should the crew need them, more buoys were stowed in the plane and could be dropped manually by the ordnance technician.

The crew had good tools, which they knew how to use. They spent their professional lives practicing.

A murmur went through the plane each time a sonobuoy was dropped. The tension on a contact always racheted to violin-string tautness, which was why most of these men did this for a living. Hunting submarines was the ultimate team sport.

With the string down, the operators pressed their headphones against their ears and listened intently for the slightest stirring in the ocean below, the tiniest hint of screws pushing a man-made leviathan.

"I have it," shrieked the number-one sensor operator. "Third and fourth buoys. He's still above the layer."

Koki Hirota flipped switches and listened intently. He closed his eyes, concentrating with all the power of his being.

The TACCO got just the subtlest of hints, the most exquisite nuance amid the cacophony of the noisy ocean. There was the noise of sea life, rhythmic surf sounds from Hokkaido, and the hum of at least ten ships. Amid all that noise, the submarine was there, definitely there. The sound seemed to be part screw noise, part deck-plate gurgle, maybe a hint of a loose bearing.

The submarine was fading now, perhaps slipping down below the thermal layer, trying to hide.

Hirota switched to the deeper buoys.

Yes, he was quite audible on this buoy.

Hirota checked another. Louder still. Hirota's fingers danced on the computer keys in front of him, and a blip appeared amid the search pattern on the screen.

The submarine skipper was turning, coming back to an easterly heading. Still, he was moving very slowly to minimize his noise signature, maybe three knots. Four at the most.

Should he drop a two-thousand-yard pattern, or a thousand-yard one? Hirota had only a limited number of sonobuoys, so he couldn't afford to dither.

He was chewing a fingernail on his left hand as he flipped back and forth between the channels, listening alternately on different buoys. He checked the computer, which agreed with his assessment. There was the track, turning back to the east.

They had caught this Ivan in shallow water, and he was trying for deeper.

The TACCO lined the pilot up for another buoy run—keyed the computer for a tight string, a thousand yards between buoys, a bit north of east. He elected to put a DIFAR at each end of the string and a doppler buoy in the middle.

He wanted to wait, to drop the string after the sub steadied out on a new heading, but that was not going to be possible since the sub was fading from buoys already in the water.

Hirota thought the sub skipper's most probable new course would be about 090. The shortest route to deep water was in this direction. Still, Hirota was merely making an educated guess. Or perhaps he sensed the Russian captain's thoughts.

Masataka Yonai turned the P-3 using the autopilot heading selector. Level on the new heading, he corrected his altitude—the autopilot had lost twenty feet in the turn—and reengaged the thing. When he was a new aircraft commander he had insisted on flying all these patterns manually; and he had stopped that nonsense only after Hirota convinced him the autopilot could do the job better than any human could.

"Be alert, men. We are tightening the net," Yonai said over the intercom.

The tension was palpable.

Out went the sonobuoys, like the ticking of a clock.

The last two buoys in the string were still in the airplane when the operator screamed over the intercom, "I've got him."

Hirota checked. Yes. The computer was plotting. . . . There! Heading 085, speed four knots.

"Yonai, do a slow two-hundred-seventy-degree turn to the left and roll out heading zero eight five degrees for a MAD run. I will direct your turn. We will fly right up his wake."

Yonai twisted the autopilot heading selector as the flight engineer nudged the throttles forward a smidgen. The extra power would help hold airspeed in the turn. The airplane's altitude was down to 150 feet above the sea. Yonai disconnected the autopilot, concentrated fiercely on the instruments as he coaxed the airplane back to two hundred feet, still in the turn. When the plane rolled level out of the turn, he reengaged the autopilot.

Every man in the plane was concentrating intently on the displays before him. The men listening to the sonobuoys could hear the screws, urgent, insistent.

"He's turning again. We will have to drop a short pattern. Come right ninety degrees and stand by for another heading."

Hirota stared at the computer display. He was trying to read the mind of the Russian submarine commander.

"He is turning back north," Hirota declared. "He knows we're onto him. He may climb back above the layer. Let's put this pattern a thousand yards apart. New heading three six zero, pilot; then I'll call a right turn."

Silence on the intercom. Everyone was concentrating on doing his job to perfection. Yet even as the new sonobuoy pattern went into the water, the computer lost the track of the submarine. The sub was there, and then it wasn't.

Hirota listened intently on each channel, as did his enlisted specialists. Nothing. The sea was as quiet as the grave.

He must have stopped his engines, Hirota decided, or be moving very slowly, just maintaining steerage.

"He's probably very deep by now," someone offered.

Hirota triggered an active ping by one of his middle sonobouys in the new pattern, then waited for the others to pick up the echo.

Even before he heard the echo, he heard the thrashing of the submarine's screws. It was a thunder, quite loud.

"He's going to full power," the number one sensor operator said. "And I think he's going deeper."

Yes. Full power. In just a few minutes, the sub would be doing in excess of twenty knots. Maybe twenty-five. If that was a nuclear boat, the speed might be as high as forty-five knots. Hirota's one American sub two years ago had disappeared over the horizon at fifty-two knots.

The computer began a plot.

"I have him," Hirota told the others, his voice tight with excitement. "We will do a MAD run. Yonai, come right to zero four five."

Yonai laid the plane into a forty-degree banking turn. Hirota could feel the increased g.

We are going to nail this sub!

"On around to zero nine zero degrees ... steady ... steady ... We are closing, coming up his wake."

The damned submarine was still accelerating, making over twenty knots now.

"MAD, MAD, MAD!" shouted the radar operator, who also ran the MAD gear. The needle pegged as the plane flew over the magnetic field of the submarine.

A short, fervent cheer on the ICS. These were disciplined men, but this was a life-or-death game. Yonai positively encouraged enthusiasm in his crew; in the past he had canned people who didn't demonstrate fighting spirit.

Now Yonai laid the big P-3 into another forty-degree-bank right turn. He needed to turn for 270 degrees and come across the submarine again from the beam. If the MAD operator sang out and the TACCO gave his okay, Yonai would drop a Mk-46 homing torpedo.

The torpedo would go out of the bomb bay. When it hit the water, it would turn right and begin a passive sonar search for its target, which, if the P-3 crew had done its work properly, should be within five hundred yards. Once the torpedo detected the sub, the torpedo's seeker would switch to active pinging and home on the submarine. In American movies, submarines outturned and outran torpedoes, but Yonai knew that was pure fiction: the pinging of a Mk-46 torpedo zeroing in was the last thing the submarine crew would ever hear.

Masataka Yonai had the plane over hard, turning tightly. "Open bomb-bay doors," he ordered.

"They will not open," the copilot reported.

Yonai looked at the indicator.

Still closed. Damnation!

"Check the circuit breaker. Quick."

This was intended for the flight engineer, because the armament panel circuit breakers were aft of him, beside his right elbow.

The autopilot, which had lost altitude in the turns earlier in the search, was doing it again. Just now the plane was passing a hundred feet above the water, descending gently, but no one noticed.

"Sir, the circuit breakers are all in." All the flight engineer had to do to establish this was run his hand over the panel and ensure none was sticking out.

"Well, cycle it." Yonai wanted the engineer to pull the bomb-bay breaker out, then push it in again.

"I can't find it," the engineer confessed, his voice frantic.

Matasaka Yonai was beside himself. They were almost to weapons release, and then this! "You idiot! It's on the armament panel."

The copilot turned around, pointed the beam of a flashlight at the panel. "Right there," he said. "It's right there."

Yonai felt the plane slew as the right wingtip kissed the crest of a wave. He slammed down the autopilot disconnect button and twisted the yoke to the left as he pulled it toward him.

Too late! The right wing buried itself in the next swell.

The drag of the wingtip through the water yawed the nose right, hard, toward the sea. That dug the wingtip deeper into the water. The plane cartwheeled.

The uncontrollable yaw threw the ball in the turn-and-bank indicator as far left as it would go. Yonai felt the yaw and instinctively mashed in full left rudder as his eyes shot to the turn-and-bank indicator. It was the last thing he would ever do.

The cockpit struck the water first. All three of the cockpit crewmen died instantly.

The men in back were flung forward, then crushed as equipment and seats broke free and smashed forward. Then the left wing hit the sea and the fuselage of the airplane came apart.

The splash was stupendous, and almost a minute passed before the roiling waters became calm.

The remains of the P-3 and the men who flew it began the long descent to the seafloor.

In the control room of *Admiral Kolchak*, Captain Pavel Saratov heard the splash. He was wearing headphones so that he could also listen to the sonar as the sonarman called out bearings to sonobuoy splashes. The navigator was plotting the bearings based on range estimates supplied by the captain. Saratov decided where to take his boat based on the picture developing on the chart before him. The chart was crude, the method long abandoned in better-equipped navies, but this was all Saratov had.

The huge splash surprised him, baffled him. It was far too large to be a sonobuoy or torpedo. He closed his eyes and listened intently as rivulets of perspiration coursed down his face and dripped off his chin.

The sonarman spoke first. "The engine noise is gone."

He was correct. The background vibration from the four aircraft propellers was no longer audible.

Saratov could hear something grinding. Perhaps the fuselage being crushed?

Could it be? No engine noise, a gigantic splash? Were they miraculously delivered?

Pavel Saratov opened his eyes. Every eye in the control room was on him.

"He crashed," the captain said.

His listeners couldn't take it in.

"He crashed," Saratov repeated. "He hit the water."

Cheers. Screams. They laughed so hard that tears ran down their cheeks.

Ah, life was sweet.

Jack Innes stood in the doorway of the Oval Office and watched President Hood finish with a group of Eagle Scouts. The photographers snapped away; the president shook hands, smiled, pretended he didn't see Innes. One of his skills was the ability to concentrate totally on the people in front of him, make them feel that during their moment they were his sole concern.

The aide ushered the Scouts and their leader from the office right on the tick of the clock. They had had their five minutes.

As the president seated himself behind his desk, Innes said, "Japanese forces are invading Siberia. They began around midnight there, which is about an hour ago. The news just came in."

"I wondered how long Abe would wait."

"The Russians arrested the leader of the Siberian independence movement eighteen hours ago. Abe went on television at midnight. The native people of Siberia have suffered enough from Russian oppression, he said. The Japanese, their blood brothers, are taking up the standard of their kinsmen."

Innes continued, telling Hood everything he knew. The president swiveled his chair, looked out the window while he listened. He swiveled back around, glanced at his schedule. When Innes finished, he asked a few questions.

"Okay," Hood said. "You know the drill. Get the National Security Council over here, the majority and minority leaders of both houses, all the usual suspects. We'll see what the consensus is."

"Yes, sir."

"They'll dither and wring their hands and advise doing nothing."

"Surely they'll condemn Japanese aggression?"

"Words. Just words. You watch. They won't want to actually *do* anything."

"You are going to try to make them take action, aren't you?"

"Sooner or later, Jack, we are going to have to screw up the courage to start doing the right thing."

"The difficulty is knowing what the right thing is."

"No, sir. It is not. Overeducated quacks and New Age gurus can never see the right thing, but to people with a modicum of common sense the right thing is usually obvious. What everyone wants to avoid is the *cost* of doing the right thing. Take Bosnia, for example, in the early nineties: the Serbs began murdering Muslims, committing genocide, killing every person who might exert an erg of leadership in the new Serbian utopia. They wanted to make the Muslims a slave people. This was a conscious choice, a policy choice of the Serb leadership *because they thought they could get away with it.* For three years, they did. For three years the American leaders wrung their hands, dithered, refused to use force against the Serbs. Genocide! Mass murder! Adolf Hitler's final solution one more time. We condoned it by refusing to lead the effort to stop it, by refusing to pay the price."

"Bosnia might become another Vietnam, the liberals said."

Hood took a deep breath, sighed deeply. "When you refuse to lift a hand to stop evil, you become a part of it. That's as true today as it was two thousand years ago. You watch, Jack. Tonight these people will argue about the dangers—the cost—of standing up to Japan. They will argue that Russia is a corrupt, misruled den of thieves with no one to blame but themselves for the fix they are in. The newspapers lately have been full of it. They will argue that we can't afford to get involved in someone else's fight. They will argue that this mess isn't our problem, that the United States is not the world's policeman. They will refuse to confront evil. Just watch."

"People don't believe in evil anymore," Innes reflected. "It's obsolete."

"Oh no," the president said with conviction. "Evil is alive and well in our time. The problem is that too many people have made their peace with it."

The first real resistance to the Japanese occupation of Vladivostok came from squad- and platoon-sized groups of young troops led by junior officers. Without orders or coordination, they blocked streets and started shooting. These pockets of resistance were easily surrounded and wiped out. Still, Japanese troops attempting to link up and form a front across the peninsula were delayed. They called for tanks and armored cars to help mop up points of resistance. All of this cost time.

Two hours after dawn, several thousand Russian infantry were actively engaged. The belch of machine guns and the pop of grenades was widespread in the northern parts of the city. Smoke from burning buildings and cars wafted over the city and the bay.

There was no resistance on Russian Island and in the area of the city around Golden Horn Bay because there were no Russian troops there. The police, outnumbered and grossly outgunned, surrendered without a shot. The unarmed civilian population had no choice; they merely watched and tried to stay out of the way.

By 7:00 A.M., a squadron of Zero fighters was on the ground at Vladivostok airport, being refueled and rearmed with missiles and ammunition helicoptered in from a supply ship anchored a half mile out. A dozen helicopter gunships came ashore from another ship, and soon they were attacking Russian positions in the northern areas of the city.

Rain continued to mist down.

The sky was a clean, washed-out blue, with patches of long, thin, streaky clouds down below. On the horizon, the distant Rocky Mountains were blue and purple.

Against this background, Bob Cassidy was looking hard for airplanes. There were two smart-skinned F-22s out there, he knew, and they were joining on him. The damn things are like chameleons, he told himself, marveling that he couldn't see planes less than a mile away.

"Two, do you see me?"

"Got you, Hoppy Leader. I'm at your three o'clock, level. I'm heading three zero five degrees."

"Lead's three one zero degrees, looking."

He was looking in vain. The sky appeared empty.

"Three's at your nine o'clock, Hoppy. Level, joining heading three one five."

Cassidy glanced left, caught something out of the corner of his eye. When he tried to focus on it, it wasn't there. He glanced at his tactical display in the center of his instrument panel. Yep, a wingman on each side, closing the distance, joining up.

He saw the man up-sun at about three hundred yards. He first appeared as a dark place in the sky, then gradually took the shape of an aircraft. He didn't see the down-sun man until he was about two hundred yards away. He was there, then he wasn't, and then he was, almost shimmering.

"This chameleon gear is flat terrific," he told his wingmen over the scrambled radio channel.

The three fighters entered the break at Nellis Air Force Base in Las Vegas, Nevada, and landed in order, one, two, three. The chameleon gear was off, of course.

They taxied to the ramp and shut down.

The hot, dry summer wind was like a caress on Cassidy's damp head when he removed his helmet. He waited until the ground crew got the ladder in place, then unstrapped and climbed slowly down.

He took a deep breath, removed his flight glove from his right hand. With his bare skin, he touched the skin of the airplane. It felt cool, smooth, hard.

An officer in blues came walking over. He saluted. "Colonel, we had a call for you from Washington, a Colonel Eatherly. Japan has attacked Vladivostok. They want you back in Washington immediately. They are sending a plane to pick you up. And he wants you to call as soon as possible."

"Thanks."

So it was really true. The shooting has started.

Bob Cassidy walked slowly around the F-22, inspecting it with unseeing eyes while he thought of the Japanese officers he knew and the Americans in Japan. He found himself standing in front of the wing root, staring at the little door that hid the mouth of the 20-mm Gatling gun.

He turned and walked quickly toward the maintenance shops. They would have a telephone he could use.

The late-evening meeting at the White House went about as the president expected. The evening had been long, filled with depressing news. The Japanese were overrunning the Russian Far East.

National Security Council staffers used maps and computer presentations to brief the group. When they finished, the mood was gloomy.

The consensus of the group was voiced by the Speaker of the House: "America must stay neutral: this is not our fight. We must do what we can as a neutral to stop the bloodshed."

The president didn't say anything. Jack Innes argued the president's position in an impassioned plea.

"This *is* our fight. Every American will be affected by today's events.

Every American has a stake in world peace. Every minute we delay merely increases the cost of the final reckoning. This is our moment. We must seize the initiative now, while we are able."

Alas, his audience refused to listen.

On the way out of the meeting, the Senate leadership paused for a quiet conversation with the president.

"Mr. President, we hear that you are putting very severe pressure on the United Nations to censure Japan, to pass some binding security resolutions."

"We are talking with other nations at the UN, certainly," the president said suavely.

The Senate majority leader spoke carefully. "In my opinion, sir, it would be a major foreign policy mistake to maneuver the UN into the position of advocating the use of armed forces against Japan. My sense of the mood of the Senate is that my colleagues will not support such a policy. You might find yourself dangling from a very thin limb, sir, with no visible means of support. That would be embarrassing, to say the least."

"Most embarrassing," the president agreed. There was no smile on his face when he said it.

CHAPTER EIGHT

● "ANY GAS, JACK?"

Bob Cassidy had driven from Washington, D.C. He poured himself a cup of coffee and was standing at the cash register in a gas station/convenience store on the outskirts of Baltimore. He could hear the distinctive sounds of a ballpark announcer coming from a radio, apparently one behind the counter.

"Are you Aaron Hudek?"

The man behind the counter looked him over before he nodded affirmatively. The announcer at the ballpark was getting excited. Hudek reached down and turned up the volume slightly. A home run.

Hudek was in his late twenties. His jeans were faded and his blue service shirt had a patch over the breast pocket that bore the name Bud. He was about six feet tall, maybe 180 pounds, with a well-developed upper body. An old blue Air Force belt held up his jeans.

"Your mom said you were working here."

"Why don't you pay your bill and let the man behind you pay his?"

"Pump three, and coffee." Cassidy forked over money. "My name's Cassidy. I need to talk to you."

"What about?"

"A job."

"I got one." Hudek looked at the man behind Cassidy, who held up a quart of oil.

After Hudek pounded the register keys and finished counting the change, Cassidy added, "It's a flying job."

Hudek's eyes flicked over Cassidy again. "I get off in about ten minutes, when the girl working the next shift comes in. We can talk then."

"Okay."

It was closer to twenty minutes, but a tree beside the pavement threw some shade on a concrete bench. Cassidy was there when Hudek came walking over. He didn't sit.

"How'd you get my name?"

"From the Air Force files."

"So you're government?"

"Colonel Bob Cassidy, at least for a few more days."

"What's the job?" Hudek asked matter-of-factly. He showed no interest in sitting. He didn't seem nervous or in a hurry. He just stood with his arms crossed, looking at Cassidy.

"Have you heard that Japan invaded Siberia?"

"It's been on the radio for a couple days."

"I'm looking for people with F-22 experience." Cassidy went on explaining while he watched Hudek's expression. He might as well have been talking in Hindi for all the impression he made. Hudek's expression didn't change an iota. Looking at him you would find it hard to believe he was an honors graduate in electrical engineering from MIT. One of the "10 percenters," as Cassidy called them. The military flight programs had been so competitive the last twenty years, a person had to be in the top 10 percent of his class at every stage of his life— high school, college, and flight training—if he expected to fly the hot jets. Hudek was brilliant, a superb student, athletic, in perfect health, and he could fly the planes. Yet somewhere, somehow, it had all gone wrong for him.

When Cassidy stopped speaking, Hudek turned his head, checking the vehicles going into and out of the service area, then turned back. "Russia, huh?"

"Yeah."

"Well, it's amazing."

"What is?"

"That you're here. Didn't you read my last evaluation? My last skipper thought I was a stupid son of a bitch, and he said so in just about those words."

"I read it. I don't give a damn about paperwork or saluting or parking-lot etiquette."

"You *did* read it."

"I need fighter pilots."

"Well, I really ain't interested. All that is behind me now. I haven't flown in three months. Don't miss it. Don't miss the pissy little Caesars in their cute blue uniforms, either."

"This isn't the peacetime Air Force. This is war, the real thing. I guarantee you, there will be no strutting martinets, no shoe polish, no bullshit."

"I've heard that song before," Hudek said with a sneer. "Now I'm supposed to raise my right hand, then sign on the dotted line. What if you just happen to be wrong? What if your little operation is more of the same fucked-up fire drill I just got out of? Then I'm already in and it's my tough luck, huh?"

"I'll be right there with you. If I'm wrong, we'll still be in it together."

"You're going to be there?" Hudek was incredulous.

"Yep. Are you?"

Hudek put his hands in his pockets and flexed his shoulders. "Don't believe so," he drawled finally. "Even if it's what you say, I've got some other things going. I've done the military thing and it's time to move on, go on down the road. There's this girl. . . . She sorta likes me, wants me to settle down, have a kid. Got a deposit down on a little tract house going up in a subdivision near here. Ain't much, but it'll be all mine."

"Uh-huh."

"I'm tired of dicking with paper-pushers, tired of always doing what some fathead who happens to be senior to me thinks we oughta do . . . tired of trying to *look good*!"

Cassidy got up and dusted his trousers. Then he passed Hudek his card, on which he had written the telephone number of his hotel in Crystal City. "Call me. Let me know what you decide."

"I'm doing that very thing right this minute, Colonel. I'm letting you know. I have definitely decided. Absolutely decided. I don't want to go to a fucking Siberian icebox."

"Call me."

"I am *not* going to call you. Listen! *I don't want to go.* I don't even like their food!"

"Tonight. Late. I have another guy to call on. Maybe you know him—Lee Foy?"

"Damnation, can't you hear me? Ain't my mouth working right? I ain't calling you tonight or any other time. I'm telling you right here and now—*I'm not going to Russia.* I don't do Third World shitholes. And I never heard of Foy."

"He said he knows you. Said he met you a couple years back during the F-22 op eval. Said you were a real good stick but you had a shitty personality. Said you'd give me a ration of crap."

"Oh! Foy Sauce, the California Chink. Yeah, I know that lying little slant-eyed bastard. Is he going?"

"Maybe."

"Jesus, taking Foy Sauce—you clowns must be scraping the bottom of the barrel. They're going to shoot all you people down. You'll all be dead in a week."

"Call me tonight."

"Where is Foy these days, anyway?"

Cassidy didn't reply. He unlocked his car and got behind the wheel.

Hudek stood watching Cassidy as he piloted the rental car slowly toward the street. He was still standing there when Cassidy went through the light at the corner and glanced back, just before he turned left.

Lee Foy was living in McLean, Virginia. He was an up-and-coming real estate agent. "I'm making a ton of money," he told Cassidy. "I don't speak a solitary word of Chinese, but the company assigns me to every Hong Kong businessman or Chinese official coming to the Washington-Baltimore area. I always make the sale. Being a hyphenated American has its advantages. I'm getting rich."

"I've always wondered what a number two in a Stanford graduating class did with his life."

Lee Foy beamed. "Couldn't happen to a nicer guy, believe me."

"Number one in your flight school class, number two in your class at test pilot school. That right?"

"All that is behind me. I'm making serious money now."

"Uh-huh. Well, I talked to Hudek. You were right about him. He's a jerk of the first water."

"Good stick, though. Funny thing, but I never met a saint flying a fighter plane."

"So, are you going to give up all this good living and easy money and come fly for the Russians?"

"Hell no. I told you that yesterday."

"That was your wallet talking. The shooting has started. Now I appeal to your patriotism, your manhood, your sense of duty."

"My wallet covers all those things. I'm making good money and I like it a lot."

"It'll still be here when you get back."

"When I get back, some other Charlie Chan will be sopping up the gravy, Colonel. The world doesn't stand still for anyone. And we both know that my chances of coming back aren't red-hot."

"The chances aren't bad, or I wouldn't be going."

"Don't shit me, Colonel. If you make it, you'll come back a brigadier.

General Cassidy. You'll retire on a general's pension. You'll spend the rest of your days lying around some 0-club sucking suds, fat and sassy, schmoozing about the good ol' days with old farts in yellow golf slacks and knit shirts decorated with ponies and alligators while you wait for the next retirement check to show up in the mail. Me, if I live through this little adventure, I'll come back a year or two older and a whole lot poorer, with a bout or two of dysentery and a couple cases of clap on my medical record. I'll have to rent apartments to crack addicts to make a buck. Thanks, but no thanks. I'll stay right here in the good ol' US of A and keep the good times rolling."

"How did you ever become a fighter pilot, Foy, a cynical, money-grubbing bastard like you? You're a damned civilian."

"I could make that plane dance, Cassidy. Ask Hudek. But that wasn't a living. Selling real estate to the 'Ah so' crowd is a living. Making the sale is my thing." He pointed downward. "See these shoes? Damn things are alligator. Cost five hundred bucks a pair on sale for thirty percent off."

"What's your point?"

"I'm tired of being poor, man. My wall is covered with diplomas I can't spend. I've seen the money and I want some."

"The Russian government will pay five thousand for every Japanese plane you bag."

"Five thousand what? Bongo bucks? Yuan, yen, pesos, rubles? Man, that stuff is toilet paper."

"U.S. dollars."

"That'll be easy to earn. I'll go up every morning and knock down two bad guys before breakfast. Seriously, Colonel, I make that much selling a condo and I don't have to risk anything to get it. I don't have to bleed, either."

"Hudek told me not to take you to Siberia. Said you'd be dead in a week. He called you Foy Sauce. Said you can't fly for shit."

"Fuck Fur Ball. And tell him I said so." Hudek's nickname was fighter pilot jargon for a dogfight, so named because a computer presentation of two or more three-dimensional flight paths resembled something from a cat's tummy.

Cassidy shrugged.

"Hudek and I weren't butt-hole buddies, but he knew damn well I could fly that plane."

Cassidy fingered his card. He had written the telephone numbers on it in ink.

"You look at my evals, Colonel. My skippers knew what I could do."

Cassidy tucked his card in Foy's shirt pocket and turned away.

"You see Fur Ball again," Foy called, "you tell him I'll kick his ass on the ground or in the sky. His choice."

Cassidy rented a car at the airport in Cheyenne and drove. He went through two thunderstorms and passed close to another. By the time he reached Thermopolis he estimated that he had seen four hundred antelope.

He got directions at the biggest filling station in town. "Which way to Cottonwood Creek?"

The house was at the end of a half mile of dirt road. It had a roof, four walls, and all the windows had glass, but it didn't look like it would be very comfy during a Wyoming winter, when the cold reached twenty below and the snow blew in horizontal sheets. The thought of a Wyoming winter reminded Cassidy of Siberian winters, and he shivered.

A man in bib overhauls came out of the dilapidated little barn next to the house.

"You Paul Scheer?"

"Yeah."

"Bob Cassidy."

Scheer came strolling over. "Somebody called from Washington, said you were coming, but I told them you were wasting your time. Did they give you that message?"

"I got it."

"Well, it's your time. I got a couple beers in the fridge."

"Okay."

There was a redbone hound on the porch. Only his tail moved, a couple of thumps, then it lay still. "He came with the ranch," Scheer said, nodding at the dog. Cassidy lowered himself into one of the two porch chairs while Scheer went inside for the beer.

The wind was blowing about ten or twelve knots from the northwest, a mere zephyr. The brush and grass near the house were low, sort of hunkered down, not like the flowers and lush bushes in Japan and Washington, where the winters were milder and the summers twice as long. Cassidy took a deep breath—he could smell the land.

When he and Scheer were drinking beer from cans, Cassidy asked, "How much ranch you got here?"

"About thirty thousand acres. Fifty-five hundred acres are deeded; the rest is a BLM grazing lease."

"How many cows?"

"Three hundred and thirty cow-calf units."

"Sounds military as hell."

"Doesn't it?"

"As I understand it, Paul, you left the Air Force in 1995 after ten years of active duty, worked for Lockheed-Martin as a test pilot in the F-22 program until last year, then quit and moved to this ranch out here in the middle of Wyoming."

"That's accurate."

"If you don't mind my asking, what's a place like this worth?"

Scheer grinned, displaying perfect teeth. The thought crossed Cassidy's mind that some women would consider Scheer handsome.

"What it's worth and what I paid for it are two completely different things. I paid two million. Now, your next question is, 'Where did ol' Scheer get two million dollars.' The answer is, 'Out of my four oh one (k) plan.' I'm single, live modestly, don't have any expensive vices. The stock market has been doing fine the last fifteen years, and I have, too. Saw an ad for this ranch one day, got to thinking about it. You know, as I was looking at that ad, it came to me that the time had come. The time had come to cash out and do something stupid. Haven't regretted it one minute since."

"Have you heard about Siberia?"

"You mean lately? Don't get the paper here and I don't own a TV."

"Japan invaded Siberia."

Scheer took a long pull on his beer and crushed the can. "It's a crazy world," he said finally.

"Yeah. I'm recruiting fighter pilots. We're giving an F-22 squadron to the Russians, and they are hiring qualified pilots. You were highly recommended."

"By whom?"

"The head test pilot at Lockheed-Martin."

Scheer shrugged. "I miss the flying. The F-22 is a great machine, really great. But..." Scheer took a deep breath and sighed. "This is where I'm going to spend the rest of my life."

Cassidy looked at his watch. "I got a few hours. How about a tour."

"Okay. Let's take the Jeep."

The road was a washed-out rut with huge mud holes that almost swallowed the Jeep. "Got to do something about the road," Scheer muttered.

"What was last winter like?"

"Cold and long."

Cassidy asked questions to keep him talking, about raising cattle, the weather, the range. Finally, he asked, "Do you really think this is the place for you?"

Scheer took his time before he replied. "I'm only the third white man to own this land. Last owner was from Florida, a real estate broker whose wife divorced him after the kids were grown and out of college. He lasted four years. He bought the place from the original homesteader, who was nearly ninety when he sold. He's in a nursing home in Cheyenne now."

Scheer pointed to some of his cattle, then indicated his boundaries with a pointed finger or a nodded head. After a bit, he remarked, "Hard to believe, isn't it, that the original white settler is still alive? The country is young."

Finally Scheer brought the Jeep to a stop on a low ridge. He pointed through the windshield. "See that low peak? Way out there? My line cabin is just under that peak. It's twenty-five miles from the house to that line cabin."

"This ranch isn't *that* big!"

"But it is. Most of it lies along this creek, and up there is the head of it. The ranch is the watered grazing land. Everything else belongs to the government. Pretty, isn't it?"

"You could come back to this, after the war."

"Let's not kid ourselves, Mr. Cassidy. A lot of the guys you recruit are going to get killed."

Cassidy didn't say anything.

"I'm going to do my living and dying right here, waking up every morning to this."

"Why don't you level with me?" Cassidy asked. "You didn't have a wife of twenty years divorce you. You didn't get fired from your job; you aren't hiding from the law. You aren't a hermit, an alcoholic, or a dope addict. Why are you rusticating out here in cow-patty heaven, smack in the middle of goddamn nowhere?"

Scheer looked at Cassidy. He turned off the engine and climbed out.

"You're the first one who asked," he said. "Oh, they asked, but not like that."

Cassidy got out, too, and stretched.

"I'm HIV-positive," Scheer said. "Anally injected death serum. Had it for years. Lived longer than I thought I would."

"So?"

"It's a death sentence."

"Man, life is a death sentence."

"We all go sooner or later. I'm one of the sooners."

"Your 'the time has come' speech—that's for the local yokels, right?"

"You're a real smoothy, aren't you, Cassidy?"

"Come to Russia with me. It'll be a hell of a fight. You live through that, you can come back here to wait for the Grim Reaper, watch the cows chew their cuds, listen to the wind, think the big thoughts when the temp drops to twenty below."

"You're a colonel, right?"

"Right."

"I didn't get AIDS by licking toilet seats, Colonel."

"Did you get in any trouble in the Air Force? Or at Lockheed?"

"No."

"You must have kept your love life and your professional life separate. Keep doing that."

"So you'd take me to Russia?"

"Of course."

"You're the first blue suiter I ever told about my sexual orientation."

"I wouldn't tell any more of 'em, if I were you."

"But you still want me?"

"You're healthy, right?"

"No symptoms."

"I don't think we'll do physicals. My branch of the Russian air force won't be very picky. We'll need to fit you for a full-body G suit if they don't still have the one you wore at Lockheed. We will do all the shots. Don't want anyone getting diphtheria or cholera or some other weird disease."

"I already got my disease."

"Take me back to my car."

They got into the Jeep and Scheer started up.

"Here's a card with my telephone number. You know the airplane inside out, and you can teach it. I need you, Scheer, or I wouldn't have made this trip. Think it over and call me."

They rode the rest of the way back in silence. Scheer didn't drive any faster than he had coming out, but he didn't bother to slow for the mud holes and fords. Cassidy hung on with both hands.

When they pulled into the yard by the house, Scheer killed the engine and said, "I'll come. Take me a few days or so to find someone to keep an eye on the cattle while I'm gone."

"Okay."

"Lockheed oughta still have my G suit. My weight hasn't changed, so it should still fit."

"I'll call them."

"I'm assuming that you'll keep this conversation to yourself," Paul Scheer said.

"I'm making a similar assumption about you," Cassidy replied, and stuck out his hand to shake.

"What's the Russian air force pay, anyway?"

"I don't know exactly. Washington is still working out the details."

"I hope the money covers the cost of hiring a hand to look after this place."

"Well, it will if you get a Zero or two. Probably pay a bonus for every one you knock down."

"Whose idea was that?"

"Not mine, rest assured. Some Russian experts in the State Department suggested a bonus for every confirmed victory. They say that will impress the Russians with our seriousness."

"Seriousness."

"Seriousness is very big in Russia. They didn't just adopt capitalism, they swallowed it."

Bob Cassidy got into the rental car, headed for the hard road. A mule deer leapt from the brush onto the road in front of him. He checked that his seat belt was fastened.

Cassidy waited in the break area outside the building. The sun felt hot on his arms and face; the breeze coming in off the Pacific felt soothing. He leaned his head back against the wall and closed his eyes. If only he could forget the problems for a little while and just relax, enjoy the heat and the breeze.

"Are you Colonel Cassidy?"

He started to stand, but she motioned for him to stay seated.

The woman before him was of medium height, with short brown hair that framed her face. She cocked her head as she looked at him, and her eyebrows arched slightly.

The thought occurred to him that she was lovely, in a way.

"You're Daphne Elitch?"

"Please! Dixie. Even my mother calls me Dixie."

"Have a seat, Dixie. Pleased to meet you."

"So what brings you to Orange County, Colonel?"

"Recruiting." Cassidy launched into his spiel.

Dixie Elitch listened politely, saying nothing. The breeze played with her hair. Cassidy watched her eyes, which were dark brown and restless. They scanned the other students in the break area, the sky, the grass, and the colonel. Those intelligent eyes didn't stop moving.

Dixie had been a middle-distance runner at the Air Force Academy and had almost made the U.S. Olympic team. She got her degree in astronautical engineering, number two in the class, and turned down an assignment to Cal Tech, where she would have gotten her doctorate. She went to flight school instead, finished first in her class, got F-22s— even though the program was closed at the time—because the commanding general called the chief of staff.

When Cassidy finished, she didn't say anything. After a bit, Cassidy asked if she had questions.

"No. I'm just trying to visualize how it will be. The F-22 is a good plane, but obtaining spare parts, weapons, and fuel will be a horrific nightmare. Everything will be a problem—intel, early warning, basing, everything. What will you do for hard stands? If the enemy catches you on the ground, they'll wipe you out unless the planes are in revetments."

"We're working on that."

Dixie examined his face with those restless eyes. "You aren't going to discuss it because you don't know the answer, I haven't signed on, or you don't want me to bother my pretty little head with men's problems? Which is it?"

"I don't know the answers."

"You're leading with your chin. What is it you want me to volunteer for?"

"I want you to fly with us."

"You can't even assure me you're going to fly."

"I'll solve the problems or live with them, as they arise. That's all I can do."

"I'm out of the 'yessir' crap now," she said. "I've got two more weeks of class; then I'm going to be a stockbroker."

"I see."

"Cold-call people, explain why they should let me show them the best investments."

"Uh-huh."

"How they can get rich in the stock market."

"Sounds exciting."

"Why they should pay commissions to my company."

"Uh-huh."

"Even though I have no money myself and couldn't take my own advice, even if I were foolish enough to want to." She laughed, a pleasant, full-throated woman's laugh.

Bob Cassidy felt warm all over. He bit his lip. He wasn't supposed to feel like *that*. This is a professional relationship, he told himself stiffly, and looked away from Dixie Elitch.

"The market is in freefall this afternoon. The Dow industrial average is down to eighteen thousand five hundred, off eighteen percent from its high last week."

"Sounds like a hell of a time to start selling stocks."

"Oh, the market will come back. Sooner or later. It always does."

"So you're not worried?"

"Colonel, we've just been presented with one of the greatest buying opportunities of our age, courtesy of the Japanese government. They will make a lot of people very rich. I hope to be one of them."

"I see."

Dixie shivered. "I'll be glued to a chair in this suburban utopia, wearing my little designer telephone headset, sweet-talking Orange County plutocrats into buying nursing home stock. Meanwhile, you and your friends will be shooting down those poor innocent Japanese boys in their shiny new airplanes, blowing them out of the sky."

"Something like that," Cassidy allowed. He passed her a card with his telephone numbers.

Dixie pressed on the sides of her head. "Why did I ever think I could do this? I couldn't sell cold beer to a man on his way to hell. I should have my head examined at the funny farm." She rubbed her face, then glanced at her watch.

"Win the war for us, Colonel. Speaking for myself, I will enjoy the money."

She stood and held out her hand to shake.

"We could use you in one of those cockpits," Cassidy said.

"I have committments here."

"You're not a stockbroker. You're a fighter pilot."

"Used to be," Dixie Elitch acknowledged, then joined the other students returning to the classroom.

"Siberia!" Clay Lacy pronounced the word as if it were a benediction. He took a deep breath and said it again.

Bob Cassidy couldn't suppress a smile.

They were sitting in the student union at Cal Tech, where Lacy was working on a masters in electrical engineering. With his military haircut, trim physique, and neat, clean clothing, he looked out of place among the longhaired, sloppily dressed techno-nerds, or so Cassidy thought. But to each his own. Isn't that the mantra of our time?

"Russia."

"I suppose you've been reading the news, watching the mess on TV?" Cassidy said conversationally. CNN was devoting half of each day to the invasion and half to the falling stock market, which was down to 17,800 now. Just now scenes from Vladivostok were showing on the television at the other end of the room, although the commentary was inaudible. There, a map, showing the Japanese thrusts. Two students were watching. The rest were eating, reading textbooks, holding hands, talking to one another. One was playing a portable video game.

"Oh, a little," Clay Lacy replied, glancing at the television. "But I'm so busy. If the world were coming to an end, I wouldn't have time to do more than glance at the headlines."

"This story is not quite that important," Cassidy acknowledged. "Still, we could use you in Russia. You could go back to school when it's over, maybe in a year or so. Do some flying, pocket some change, help out Uncle Sam."

"It didn't look like we were ever going to have a war," Clay Lacy explained. "At least during my career. That's why I got out. That 'Peace is our profession' BS is a real crock."

Cassidy finished his coffee.

"You aren't CIA, by chance?" Lacy asked.

"Just plain old U.S. Air Force."

"You wouldn't say if you were CIA, would you? You'd say you were in the Air Force."

"You'll have to trust me, Lacy."

"No offense, sir."

"Ask me no secrets and I'll tell you no lies."

Cassidy's mood was growing more foul by the second. Lacy was a flake. Perhaps he would be better off without him.

After a bit Lacy said, "The F-22 is one hell of an airplane," almost talking to himself.

"So is the new Zero, they tell me," Cassidy muttered.

"If a man missed this fight, he might regret it all his life."

"I doubt that," Cassidy snapped. Jiro Kimura flashed into his mind. He bit his lip.

"All his life, he might wonder," Lacy insisted.

"It won't be easy," Bob Cassidy remarked, more than a little unhappy with the way this conversation was going.

Lacy looked intense. Too intense. Now Cassidy was almost certain the man was a nut.

"Flying was almost a religion with me," Lacy said after a moment. "With me and my friends. We all thought that way. Didn't think I would ever leave it, but ..." He shrugged. "That's the way things go. I got tired of the peacetime routine. Got tired of the annual budget slashing in Congress. Tired of the eternal cutbacks and resizing and reductions in force. It's a conspiracy, slashing the defense budget so far that America can't defend itself. It's a conspiracy by foreigners, to throw open our borders. They've always been against everything American."

Cassidy said nothing.

Lacy went on, "Of course, I've never been in combat. Can't honestly say how I'll handle it, because I don't know. I *think* everything will be fine. I won't pee my pants. I won't forget to retract the gear or arm the gun. I will manage to do what they trained me to do."

"Hmm," Cassidy said.

"I always thought I could kill someone if I really had to. If there were no choice. Then I could do what I had to do. But to go to Siberia to strap on a plane to fight Japanese pilots ... well, the whole thing is slightly unreal. Sitting here, I can feel the doubt. It's tangible. I don't know if I could kill anyone, Colonel."

"Well, if you have tangible doubts, Clay, you—"

"I think I could, you understand, but I don't know for a fact."

"Uh-huh."

"No one could know, until it happened to them."

"Not everyone is cut out for—"

Lacy mused, "Maybe that's why I'm here, instead of still in uniform." He frowned.

Now he looked at Cassidy with a start, as if suddenly realizing he was talking to a colonel. "I probably shouldn't be saying these things," he added hastily.

"It's a complicated world we—"

"I'll think about it, sir. Let you know. Do you have a telephone number?"

Cassidy thought for several seconds before he gave the man a card. "Don't do anything rash," he told Lacy.

"At night, I miss the flying the worst. I can close my eyes and feel myself blasting through space."

"Think about it carefully."

"Maybe I—"

"Kill or be killed. The Japs are pretty damn good, Lacy. The Zero drivers will punch the missiles off the rails and they'll be coming hard. If you don't handle it right you're gonna be toast. Even if you handle it right, you may get zapped."

"I—"

"You tell me you want to go, Lacy, you better be sure. I don't want your blood on my hands. I'm toting enough of a load through life as it is."

"I'll think it over and call you, sir," Clay Lacy promised.

When Lacy had gone to class, Cassidy put a check mark beside his name on the list. Okay, he's a nutcase, but if he can fly the plane and pull the trigger, he'll do.

CHAPTER NINE

● "SVECHIN HAS BEEN into the torpedo juice again."

"Anybody else?"

"Three or four of them have been sipping it, Captain. They do it because Svechin eggs them on."

Pavel Saratov eyed the chief of the boat, a senior warrant, or *starshi michman,* who averted his gaze.

"They haven't been paid in five months, sir."

"I know that."

"They ask why we are here."

"There is a war. We defend Mother Russia."

"Ha! There is no money. There is no food. There is no clothing. The electricity is off half the time. There is no medicine, no vodka, no tobacco. The politicians are all thieves, children are sick, people are dying from pollution, industrial poisoning."

Saratov rubbed his face, then his head.

The chief continued: "We don't have a country. That is what the men say. We left our families to starve in the dark and sailed away to drown at sea. If the Japanese want Siberia, let them have it. We might be better off under the Japanese. I hear they eat regularly."

"The men say that?"

"Yes, Captain."

"What is your opinion?"

"That is what the men say."

"And you? Answer me."

The chief's Adam's apple bobbed up and down. "The men think we are doomed. That we have no chance. The P-3s will find us again. We should surrender while we are still alive."

"And you?"

"I am a loyal Russian, Captain."

Saratov said nothing.

"We might sail to Hawaii," the chief offered tentatively. After a moment of silence, he added, "Or the Aleutians. Ask for asylum from the Americans. I wish I were an American."

Saratov played with the chart on the desk. Off to one side lay the messages. The Japanese had taken Nikolayevsk, Petropavlosk, and Korsakov. The Japanese had parachuted into Ostrov and Okha on Sakhalin Island, where Russian troops were resisting fiercely, according to the Kremlin. The Japanese had attacked Magadan and Gavan—no mention by the Kremlin of Russian resistance. Unconventional warfare teams had taken four emergency submarine resupply bases on the northern shore of the Sea of Okhotsk and in the Kurils—probably less than a dozen well-trained men in each team.

Saratov was certain that all these conquests had been ridiculously easy. The four sub resupply bases didn't even have troops assigned anymore, not since the turn of the century.

The officer who decoded these messages, Bogrov, had whispered the news to two friends, who whispered to friends. Every man on the boat had heard the news by now.

"Bring Svechin to the control room in fifteen minutes."

"Aye aye, sir."

The cramped space of the captain's cabin held only a bunk, a foldout desk, and a chair. It was on this desk that Saratov had the chart spread. He stared at it without seeing it.

The men were defeated. Without firing a shot, they were ready to surrender.

Every man on the boat had grown up on Communist propaganda, that New Communist Man bullshit, an endless diet of crap about how the Party knows best, the moral imperative to care for everyone according to their needs. All that was over, finally, gone forever. Rampant inflation and an ever-expanding population destroyed the bureaucrats' ability to provide. In an age of ever-increasing scarcity of basic necessities, corruption became endemic, crime rampant. Rusted, rotten, and dilapidated, the social framework shuddered one last time in the rising wind, then slowly collapsed. The Soviet Union died in the wreckage, leaving only starving republics without the resources to cope. Seventeen years later, Russia, the largest republic, was ruled by criminals and incompetents interested primarily in lining their own pockets.

The men on this boat were here solely because they had a better chance of eating in the navy than they did out of it. And it was just a chance. For weeks last winter, everyone at the Petropavlosk Naval Base had survived on a diet of beets. Not even bread. Beets three times a day for four and a half weeks. Meanwhile, old babushkas and abandoned children starved in the streets. There were whispers of cannibalism out in the boondocks, but no one knew anything for certain.

The rest of the world is high-teching its way to wealth and fortune, Saratov reflected bitterly. Even Chinese peasants eat better than poor Russians. The Japanese are rich, rich, rich, not to mention the Americans.

And Pavel Saratov drained the alcohol from a torpedo and sold it on the black market to get money to buy food to feed his crew for this cruise! Of course, the torpedoes were not supposed to have alcohol in them. Their fuel was a devil's brew of chemicals that allowed them to run at up to 55 knots, but the torpedo fuel had deteriorated so much over the years while in storage that it was worthless. The armory people fueled the torpedoes now with alcohol, because they had nothing better.

Perhaps he should take the boat to an American port. He had more than enough diesel fuel to make Adak, in the Aleutians. The P-3s were probably patrolling over the Japanese fleet off Vladivostok and Nikolayevsk, guarding the convoys in the Sea of Japan. The way east was wide open.

He wiped his face with his hands, tried to think.

These thoughts were unworthy. Shameful.

He was a Russian officer. Russian officers had led men valiantly and gloriously for hundreds of years, *hundreds.*

Glory. What crap!

For seventy years a fierce, venal oligarchy had ruled the Russian people. Mass murder, starvation, imprisonment, torture, and terror were routinely used to control the population and prevent unrest. And the Russian people had let it happen.

Russians drank guilt with their mother's milk.

They were beaten. Defeated by life. Defeated by their own stupidities and inadequacies.

His men were typical. Most of them just wanted alcohol—vodka or torpedo juice or fermented fruit, whatever. If you gave them alcohol you owned them, body and soul.

We are animals.

Why was he thinking these thoughts?

No one gave a good goddamn about one little diesel/electric submarine or the fifty men inside her. Fifty men, not the sixty-five the ship was supposed to have. Certainly not the brass in Moscow. Those paper-shuffling tubes of fatty Russian sausage sent this submarine to demolish a wreck that had blocked a channel for *ten* years, and they didn't bother asking if the captain had food to feed the crew. Or fuel. Or charts. Or trained men. Just an order from on high: do this, or we will find someone who can.

His eye fell on the Russian Orthodox liturgy book tucked into a cranny in the angle iron above the bunk. The old book had been given to him long, long ago by his mother. The Communists had never allowed religion in the armed forces, a policy that Saratov failed to understand. Banning religion made sense only to Communists. When the navy got rid of its political officers, Saratov began reading services aloud on Sunday mornings at sea and in port. He didn't ask permission; he just did it. At first some of the men grumbled. They soon stopped. They got that essential alcohol occasionally, now and then food, so what did prayers matter?

He could hear the chief in the control room, six paces aft of his door. Bogrov was talking to the XO, then to Svechin, who was loud and sullen, still drunk.

Saratov opened his desk safe and removed his pistol, a 7.62-mm Tokarev. The magazine was full. He inserted it into the handle, jacked the slide to chamber a round. Then he carefully lowered the hammer. The pistol had no safety. He put it into his pocket.

He took the book with him.

Everyone in the packed control room fell silent when he entered. The extra bodies filled the place, took every square inch not taken by the watch team. Even though he was inured to it, the stench of unwashed bodies took Saratov's breath for a moment. He tossed the old book on the chart table.

Svechin was obviously drunk, not at attention. He eyed the captain insolently.

The boat was submerged. Saratov forced himself to check the gauges as everyone stared at him. The boat was four hundred feet down, making three knots to the southeast.

"Drunk again, eh, Svechin?"

"I don't think—"

"Stand at attention when you speak to me," Saratov roared. "All of you. Attention!"

There was a general stiffening all around.

Even Svechin stood a bit straighter. "I—"

"Alcohol from the torpedoes!"

Svechin looked sullen, half-sick. He refused to look at the captain.

"Russia is at war. The torpedoes are our weapons. You are guilty of sabotage, Svechin. In wartime, sabotage is a capital offense."

Svechin blanched. The chief's Adam's apple was in constant motion, up and down, up and down.

"Lieutenant Bogrov discusses classified messages as if they were newspaper articles."

Bogrov was from Moscow, and he believed that gave him some special standing; most of his shipmates came from the provinces, from small squalid villages scattered all over Russia. They had joined the navy to escape all that.

"Captain, I—" Bogrov began.

"Silence, you son of a bitch. I'll deal with you later."

Svechin was pale now, his lips pinched into a thin line.

Saratov could hear them breathing, all of them, above the little noises of the boat running deep. They breathed in and out like blown horses. And he could still smell their stench, which surprised him. Normally his own stink masked that of the other men.

"You men talk of surrender. Of fleeing to a neutral county."

Just the breathing.

"Talk, talk, talk. There isn't a man on this boat! God, what miserable creatures you are!"

Better get it over with.

He pulled the pistol from his pocket, gripped it firmly, and cocked the hammer.

"Do you have anything to say, Svechin, before I carry out the penalty prescribed for sabotage in wartime?"

Svechin's tongue came out. He wet his lips. Perspiration made his face shine. He had thick lips and pimples. "Please, Captain, I didn't mean ... We are all doomed. We're going to die. I—"

Pavel Saratov leveled the pistol and shot Svechin once, in the center of the forehead. The report was a thunderclap in the small space.

Svechin slumped to the floor. His bowels relaxed. The odor of shit nauseated Saratov.

The captain held the pistol pointed toward the overhead, so everyone could see it, while he waited for his ears to stop ringing. He worked his jaw from side to side.

He had an overpowering urge to urinate, but he fought it back, somehow.

"I should shoot you too, Bogrov." That came out like a frog croaking.

He moved so that Bogrov was forced to look into his eyes.

"You hear me?"

"Yes, sir." Bogrov was at rigid attention. He refused to focus his eyes.

Saratov moved to the next man, then the next, staring into the eyes of each in turn.

"Chief, bring the boat to course two three five degrees. One hour after sunset, take the boat to periscope depth and rig the snorkel."

"Aye aye, captain."

"Call me then."

"Aye aye, sir."

"Put Svechin in a torpedo tube. XO, read the funeral service. Then pop him out."

"Aye aye, sir," the XO said.

Saratov used both hands to lower the hammer on the pistol, pocketed it, then went back to his cabin.

He was sitting in his chair with the curtain drawn fifteen minutes later when he heard Bogrov say softly to the chief, "He shoots a man dead, then orders the XO to pray over him. That's one for the books."

"Better shut your mouth, sir." That was one of the steersmen.

"Shut up, both of you," the chief roared, unable to control himself.

The sun was still above the horizon in Moscow at ten o'clock the evening Kalugin entered the Congress of People's Deputies. He came in through the lobby and walked up the aisle, nodding right and left at deputies he knew, but not pausing to shake hands.

He had been a busy man this past week. During the last seventy-two hours he had had almost no sleep, but it didn't show. As he walked down the aisle toward the raised speaker's platform he looked like an aged lion girding himself for his last great battle.

In fact he had already fought the battle and was the victor. Once he believed that Japan really intended to invade Russia, he had moved swiftly to create a political consensus that the nation's survival was at stake. That was the easy part. Then came the crunch: Kalugin demanded that the elected representatives of the people of Russia grant him dictatorial powers to mobilize the nation and save it.

Of course, he had made many enemies through the years. Those he judged to be his worst enemies, he buried. Seven new corpses were now resting in hastily dug graves in the woods outside Moscow. Several dozen deputies who might be brought around if properly persuaded were locked in Lubyanka. Kalugin bought support where required, appointed ministers, and drafted decrees. Tonight, as he walked into the Congress amid the buzz of crisis, with the television cameras of the world watching, he was ready to declare his victory.

Janos Ilin was one of the people in the gallery, packed shoulder-to-shoulder with his fellow FIS officers. He could see the top of Kalugin's balding head as the president moved through the crowd of sycophant deputies.

A dictator. Another dictator. To solve Russia's problems with brute force and hot blood and endless rules and regulations, administered by powerless little men who lived in terror.

Kalugin, the savior.

Kalugin ascended the dais. Now he approached the podium. Massive applause.

Everyone rose to their feet, still applauding.

Finally, Kalugin motioned for his audience to be seated.

"Tonight is a grave hour in the history of Russia. Japanese forces in the far east have captured Vladivostok; Nikolayevsk; Petropavlosk, on the Kamchatka Peninsula; and Sakhalin Island. . . .

"Russia has done nothing to deserve the vicious wounds being inflicted upon her by evil, greedy men, men intent on robbing future Russian generations of their birthright. . . .

"Your leaders have today come to me, asking me to wield the power of the presidency *and the Congress* to save holy Mother Russia."

His voice seemed to grow louder, deeper, to fill the hall, like the thunder of a summer storm on the steppe.

"In the name of the Russian people, I, Aleksandr Ivanovich Kalugin, take up the sword against our enemies."

When Bob Cassidy walked into the lobby of the McGuire Air Force Base Visiting Officers Quarters to register, the first person he saw was Clay Lacy, sitting in the corner looking forlorn.

"Colonel Cassidy, Colonel Cassidy." Lacy rushed over. "I've been waiting for you. I called Washington and they said to come to McGuire, but these people don't have me on their list."

"Uh-huh." Cassidy signed his name on a check-in card as the civilian behind the desk watched.

"I need to see your ID card," the desk clerk said to Cassidy.

"Wearing a colonel's uniform, I look like an illegal immigrant?"

"I just do what I'm told, Colonel."

Cassidy dug out his wallet, extracted the card, and passed it over.

"Didn't get to talk to you after our interview," Lacy was saying, "but I want to go with you. Over there." He nodded his head to the east. Maybe south. He didn't seem to want to say the word *Russia*. "I called Washington and they said to come here, to McGuire, so I did. At my own expense. But when I got here, this man said I wasn't on the list, so he couldn't give me a room."

"Do you really want to go?"

"Oh, yes, sir," Lacy said, glancing at the clerk behind the desk.

"I'll be frank with you, Lacy. You look like a flake to me."

Lacy was offended. "Have you seen my service record?"

"Yeah. You still look like a flake. Think you got the balls for this?"

"Yes, sir." Lacy set his jaw. He looked as if he might cry.

Well, the folks in Air Force Officer Personnel said this guy was one hell of a pilot. Maybe there was some mix-up on the name.

The colonel shrugged. If Lacy couldn't cut the mustard in the air, he would put him in maintenance, or give him a rifle, make a perimeter guard out of him. Surely there was something useful an overgrown teenager like Lacy could do.

Cassidy turned to the clerk. "Where's your list for JCS Special Ops?"

The civilian produced a clipboard from beneath the counter. Cassidy looked over the printed list, then added Lacy's name in ink at the bottom. He handed the clipboard back to the clerk.

"Okay, Lacy. You're on the list."

"Wait a minute, Colonel," the clerk protested. "Base Housing sent this list over—"

"Give Lacy a room, mister. Right now, no arguments or I'll have your job." He said it softly, barely glancing at the desk clerk as he picked up his bags.

The clerk swallowed once, took a deep breath, and watched Cassidy's back as he headed for the elevator. When the elevator door had closed on the colonel, the clerk turned to Lacy. "ID card, driver's license, or something."

———

They gathered that evening in the second-floor television room of the VOQ. Two Air Force policemen sealed the hall.

"For those of you who haven't met me, I'm Colonel Bob Cassidy. My friends call me Hoppy or Butch; you can call me Colonel."

No one smiled. Cassidy sighed, looked at the list.

"Answer up if you're here. Allen, Cassini . . ."

They answered after each name. He knew about half of them, the ones he had recruited and several he had known from years ago.

He put the list down, looked around to see if he had everyone's attention, then began. "Thanks for volunteering. You'll probably regret it before long; that's to be expected. About all I can promise you is an adventure. We are going to Germany in the morning on a C-141. There we'll check out the newest version of the F-22. After a week, two at the most, we'll go to Russia. You pilots will be civilians hired by the Russian government. They may even swear us into the Russian army— we'll see how it goes. The aircraft will be loaned to the Russians by the U.S. Air Force. Although the U.S. markings will be removed, the planes will still be U.S. property, so they will be maintained by active-duty Air Force personnel, who will join us in Germany. Any questions?"

There were none.

"Besides me, I think there is only one other pilot in this room who has ever flown in combat. All of you will be veterans very soon. You undoubtedly have some preconceived notions of what combat will be like. What you cannot know now is how it will feel to have another human being trying his absolute damnedest to kill you. Nor can you know what it feels like to kill another person. All that is ahead."

He looked at their faces, so innocent. Some of them would soon be dead; that was inevitable.

"We all won't be coming back," he said slowly. "If anyone wants out, now is the time to say so. You get a handshake and a free ride home from here, no questions asked."

Nobody said a word. They didn't look at one another, just seemed to focus on places that weren't in the room.

"Okay," said Bob Cassidy. "We are all in this together. From now on, you are under my rules. Not Air Force regulations: *my* rules. Disobey my rules here or in Germany, I'll send you home. Disobey in Russia . . ." He left it hanging.

"No telephone calls, no letters, no E-mail, and no one leaves the building. Those of you I haven't met, I will talk to as soon as possible. I want each of you to know what you are in for. That's all."

Cassidy walked out of the room as someone called the crowd to attention. The people in the room were struggling to snap out of the low lounge chairs as he went through the door. Over his shoulder, he said, "Preacher, come with me."

Preacher was Paul Fain, a tallish man with a square face and a ruddy complexion. When he entered the colonel's room, he closed the door behind him and grinned, displaying perfect white teeth. "Good to see you, Bob."

Cassidy reached for Fain's outstretched hand. "What in the dickens are you doing here, Preach? Of all people, I never expected to see your name on that list."

"Life's an adventure. This sounded like a good one, and when I heard you were in charge, well . . . Here I am!"

"What about Isabelle? What did she say when you broke it to her?"

"She wasn't happy, but she knows me, inside and out. We're stuck with each other."

Fain was the only uniformed ordained minister not in the Chaplain Corps that Cassidy had ever met. He was serving as assistant pastor in his first church when he chucked it all years ago and joined the Air Force. When Cassidy had last seen him, Fain was flying F-22s at Nellis. Isabelle was his long-suffering wife, a woman who thought she married a minister but wound up with a fighter pilot instead.

They chatted for several minutes about old times, and Cassidy made Fain bring him up-to-date on Isabelle and the two children.

Finally, Cassidy said, "Preacher, I want you to think this Russia thing through. The rest of them"—Cassidy nodded toward the television lounge—"are adventurers, rolling dice with their lives. Live or die, they don't really care. They want excitement, to try something new, to bet their lives on their skill and courage. A few of them just want to kill somebody. You aren't like them."

"And you are?"

"Listen to me, Preach. I'm trying to level with you. My wife and kid died years ago. I'm single. I've got nothing in this world. If I get zapped over Russia, no one is going to miss me. No one. The same with that crowd down there. I can order them into combat. When they die I won't lose any sleep over them . . . and no one else will either."

"What makes you think I am different from them?"

Cassidy was embarrassed. "You're different because I know you. And someone *will* miss you—Isabelle, the kids."

Fain didn't reply.

Cassidy growled, "I'll miss you, for Christ's sake. I don't want to take that chance. Go home to Isabelle."

"No. I volunteered for this fight. Somebody has to be willing to lay his precious neck on the line or the ruthless bastards are always going to keep coming out on top. When God wants me, he can take me. That's always been the case, Bob, and Isabelle can live with it. She has faith in me, and faith in God."

Cassidy went over to the window and looked out at the summer evening. Clouds were rolling in. Soon the rain should come.

"I guess I don't have faith," he mused. "Not that kind, anyway. The ruthless, implacable bastards always seem to come out winners." He found this whole discussion irritating. Preacher Fain should have stayed at home. "People live, and then they die. That's the way of the world. I don't want to lose any more friends. I've lost too many people I care about already."

"I have enough faith for both of us, Colonel."

Cassidy didn't know what to say. Fain was cool as ice, as usual. "Okay, Preach. I give up. You want in, you're in. Don't say I didn't warn you. How about sending in Dick Guelich?"

"Thanks, Bob."

"You're my admin officer. We've got a long night of paperwork ahead of us, so get some pencils and paper and a beer from the fridge, then come on back here."

"Okay."

Lee Foy found Aaron Hudek in the entertainment room playing a holographic video game. "Hey, Fur Ball."

Hudek didn't look around. He kept squirting energy balls at alien space fighters, who were addicted to head-on attacks. "Foy Sauce. What are you doing here?"

"Same as you."

Hudek eventually ran out of energy balls. As he fed more coins into the machine, he said, "Couldn't resist a chance at those Jap fighter jocks, eh? Gonna pop a few. If they don't get you first."

"Mr. Personality. Gonna be great having you on this expedition."

"Suck it, Sauce."

"The road might be rocky, but fortunately we have a world-class diplomat along to impress the locals."

Hudek was using both hands on the video game's controls, tapping them, massaging them, caressing them while he moaned with pleasure. The suicidal aliens kept ripping in to get fried, almost too fast for the eye to follow.

Foy giggled. "Still the magic touch with machinery, huh, Fur Ball?"

"Wanta make a bet? A grand to the guy who gets the first kill?" Hudek kept his eyes glued on those incoming alien idiots.

Foy took his time answering. "The difficulty is collecting from a dead man. When I win, you'll probably be long gone to a better, cleaner world."

"God, the camaraderie! The male bonding rituals!" Hudek exclaimed ecstatically. "What a fool I was to think I could live without it."

Hudek shot down several hundred more aliens; then the game ended abruptly, a few points shy of a free game. He studied the score, then muttered, "Damn." He glanced around as he dug in his pocket for more quarters. "You still here? Stay out of my space, Sauce. I don't have time to wet-nurse you."

"You're my executive officer," Bob Cassidy told Dick Guelich. "You got operations," he said to Joe Malan. "We'll land in Germany at the Rhein-Main Air Base. A squadron of F-22s there will transfer all their planes to us and we'll ask for volunteers from the maintenance troops. We should get enough mechanics and specialists to keep the planes flying, at least for a while.

"Our problem is training. I demanded at least a week before we go to Russia. We may get more time, but don't count on it."

"One week. It's nowhere near enough. We don't have time to train them; they are going into combat knowing just what they know now. What we can do is make them think about combat, shake off the peacetime complacency, key them up, get them sharp."

"A week isn't enough time," Guelich said. "Two months, maybe, but a week?"

"We got seven days."

"That'll be enough," Joe Malan said. "I think everybody has trained to combat ready at one time or another. If we put them in the simulator, concentrate on the systems, refresh on tactics, and talk about what they can expect in the air over Siberia, they'll be at seventy-five or eighty percent. The first Zero they see, they'll get pumped the rest of the way."

"That's your job, Joe."

"I have to get transitioned to this plane," Malan objected. "I never flew an F-22."

"Piece of cake," Guelich told him. "We'll put you in the magic box first. It's easier than an F-16 or F-18. Very straightforward airframe. You'll pick up the system quickly."

"What I want to know," Joe Malan said, "is how we are going to do all the paperwork. Air Force squadrons have staffs of clerks and ground-pounders doing this stuff, and we don't."

"What paperwork?"

"A standardization program, evaluations, records; a safety program, lectures, inspections; training records; sexual harassment prevention, counseling, investigations, all of that."

"Who says we have to do that stuff?"

Malan pulled a message from the Air Force chief of staff from the pile waiting for Cassidy's attention. "Right here, in black and white." He began to read from the message.

Bob Cassidy reached for the document, removed it from Malan's hands, and methodically tore it into tiny pieces. He dribbled the pieces into a wastebasket. "Any questions?"

The others laughed.

An hour later, they had hashed out a plan. Cassidy felt relieved— both Guelich and Malan were professionals. Guelich had given his first impression that the job was impossible, yet when told that they were going to do it anyway, he had jumped in with both feet. Malan immediately started planning how to do it.

Cassidy ran them out finally, so he could get some sleep. He was exhausted. When the door closed, he fell into bed still dressed.

CHAPTER TEN

●WHEN HE WAS maneuvering to consolidate his power, Aleksandr Kalugin dwelled for a dark moment on Marshal Ivan Samsonov, the army chief of staff. The two men were opposites in every way. Kalugin loved money above all things, had no scruples that anyone had ever been able to detect, and never told the truth if a lie would serve, even for a little while. Samsonov, on the other hand, had spent his adult life in uniform and seemed to embody the military virtues. He was honest, courageous, patriotic, and, amazingly, embedded as he was in a bureaucracy that fed on half-truths and innuendo, boldly frank. Ivan Samsonov was universally regarded as a soldier's soldier.

Pondering these things, Kalugin decided he would sleep better at night if Samsonov did not have the armed forces at his beck and call. He had Samsonov quietly arrested, shot, and buried.

With that unpleasantness behind him, Kalugin faced his next problem: whom to put in Samsonov's place. The invasion of Siberia had certainly been a grand political opportunity for Kalugin, but he knew that even a dictator must have military victories in order to survive. He needed an accomplished soldier to win those victories, one who could and would save Russia, yet a man in debt to Kalugin for his place. After the nation was saved, well, if necessary, the hero could go into the ground beside Samsonov. Until then . . .

Kalugin pretended to fret the choice for days while the Japanese army marched ever deeper into Siberia. He had already decided to name the man whom Samsonov had replaced, Marshal Oleg Stolypin, but the outpouring of raw patriotism occurring in Russia just then made it seem politic to remain quiet. Since the collapse of communism in 1991, the national scene had too often reflected the public mood: rancor, acrimony, hardball politics, charges and countercharges resulting in political deadlock, which made it impossible for any group to govern. The politicians bickered and postured and clawed at one another while the nation rotted. Until now. At last the Russian people had an enemy they could unite against.

Kalugin thought the moment sublime. He savored it. He was the absolute master of Russia. None opposed him or even dreamed of doing so. All looked to him to save the nation.

Unfortunately, the euphoria would eventually wear off. Sooner or later people would want action. One evening, Kalugin sent a car to Stolypin's dacha in the Lenin Hills to bring the old soldier to the Kremlin.

"I have sent for you," he told the retired officer when he walked into the president's office, "because Russia needs you." Stolypin was escorted by several members of Kalugin's private security force, men he paid personally who did not work for any government agency.

The security people withdrew, reluctantly. They had searched the former soldier from head to toe, looking for weapons, contraband, letters from people in prison, anything. The hallways outside were filled with armed guards, men personally loyal to Kalugin because he had been feeding them and their families for almost twenty years. They were also in the courtyard outside the window, on the roofs across the street. Kalugin was taking no chances.

Now the president offered the old man hot tea. Stolypin had retired from the army before Kalugin won the presidency, so they had never worked together, although they had a nodding acquaintance from parties and official functions.

The marshal was in his early seventies. He had short, white hair and thick peasant's hands. He was stolid, too, like a peasant, and as he sipped his tea, he looked around the president's office vacantly, without interest.

"Tell me frankly," Kalugin said, "what we must do to defeat the Japanese in Siberia."

"I don't know that we can," the old man replied, then sipped more tea. "The draft laws have not been enforced for years; the logistics system has collapsed; weapons procurement has stopped. . . . Baldly, Mr. President, we have no army. . . . No army, no navy, no air force."

"If we spend the summer and fall building an army, can we not win when the Japanese are buried under a Siberian winter?"

"I am not sanguine. Japan is a rich nation. They can supply their forces by air. We will be the ones most hindered by winter."

"Come, come, Marshal," Kalugin scoffed. "The Russian man is tough, able to endure great hardships. Winter is the Russian season."

"In another age, Mr. President, winter was a large battalion. It ruined the French, the Poles, and the Germans. The world has changed since then. Japan is physically closer to the Siberian oil fields than we are. By winter they will be comfortably established, well dug in. Russia will have to mobilize, put the entire economy on a war footing, like we did during World War Two. Even then, we may not win."

"*Enough!*" Kalugin roared. "Enough of this defeatism! I will not hear it. I am the guardian of holy Mother Russia. We will defend her to the very last drop of Russian blood."

Stolypin shifted uncomfortably in his chair. "Mr. President, everything we do must be based on the hard realities. We must work with the world as it is, not as we wish it to be. The bitter truth is that the armed forces are in the same condition as the rest of Russia. It will take time to change that."

Kalugin rapped his knuckles on the desk.

"Ask Samsonov," Stolypin said. "Get his opinion."

"What is your advice?" Kalugin said, his knuckle poised above the desk.

"Negotiate the best deal possible with the Japanese—buy time. Rebuild the army. When we are strong enough, drive them into the sea."

Kalugin made a gesture of dismissal. "That course is politically impossible. By all appearances, we would be compromising with aggression. The people would never stand for it."

"Mr. President, you asked for a professional opinion and I have given it. Building an army will take time."

"Nothing can be done in the interim?"

"We can use small units, bleed the Japanese where we can without excessive cost. However, we must ensure that we do not squander assets that we will need to win the victory later."

"We must do more. More than pinpricks." Kalugin's face had a hard, unyielding look.

Stolypin shifted his feet. He cleared his throat, sipped tea, and sized up the politician in the tailored gray Italian suit seated behind the desk.

"What does Marshal Samsonov say?" he asked finally. "Why isn't he here?"

"He's dead. Tragically. A heart attack, two nights ago. We have not announced it yet.... The people put such faith in him."

Stolypin grimaced. "A good man, the very best. Ah well, death comes for us all." He sighed. After a bit, he asked, "Who is to replace him?"

"You."

Stolypin was genuinely surprised.

"I'm too old, too tired. You need a young man full of fire. He will need to weld together an army, which will not be a small task."

"I am giving you the responsibility, Marshal," Kalugin said crisply. "Your country needs you."

"Can we get foreign help? Military help?"

"We are working on that."

"The military protocol with the United States—will they send troops? Equipment? Fuel? Food? Weapons? God knows, we need everything we can get."

"They are offering a squadron of planes."

"A squadron?" Stolypin thundered. He sprang from his chair with a vigor that surprised Kalugin, then paced back and forth. "A *squadron*! They promised to come to our aid if we destroyed our nuclear weapons. So we did. Fools that we were, we believed their lies."

He stopped in front of a picture of Stalin hanging over a fireplace and stood staring at it. "At least some of the politicians believed them."

"You didn't?"

"Do you have any vodka for this tea?"

"Yes." Kalugin reached into the lower reaches of his desk for a bottle and poured a shot into Stolypin's tea. Stolypin sipped the mixture.

"I didn't believe any of it, Mr. President. The Americans always act in America's best interests, just as we always act in Russia's best interests. They made a promise, just a promise, written on good paper and signed with good ink and worth maybe ten rubles at a curio shop. So I acted in Russia's best interests. I secreted ten warheads, kept them back so they were not destroyed. The last time I saw Samsonov, he said we still have them."

Kalugin couldn't believe his ears. "We still have nuclear weapons?"

"Ten."

"Only ten?"

"Only? We had to lie and cheat to keep ten."

Kalugin was trying to comprehend the enormity of this revelation. "Where are the weapons?" he asked after a bit.

"Mr. President, they are at Trojan Island."

"I am not familiar with the place."

"Trojan Island is an extinct cone-shaped volcano near the Kuril Strait. Although the island is fairly small, the volcano reaches up over two thousand meters, so it is almost always shrouded in clouds, which kept it hidden from satellite photography when we built the base. The nearby waters are deep, ice-free year-round, and there is good access to the Pacific. For these reasons, we built a submarine base there twenty years ago, a base that can only be entered underwater. It is similar to the base at Bolshaya Litsa, on the Kola Peninsula."

"Do the Japanese know of this place?"

"I would be amazed if they did, sir. The base was officially abandoned when the last of the boomer boats were scrapped. We hid the warheads there for just that reason."

"Nuclear weapons," Kalugin mused, his eyelids reducing his eyes to mere slits.

"The use of nuclear weapons involves huge, incalculable risks," Stolypin said. "That road is unknown. We devoted much thought to pondering where it might lead years ago, when we had such weapons in quantity."

"And what were your conclusions?"

"That we would use them only as a last resort, when all else had failed."

Kalugin merely grunted. He was deep in thought.

Stolypin dropped into a chair, helped himself to more vodka and tea.

Kalugin grinned wolfishly. "Marshal Stolypin, let us drink to Russia. You have answered my prayers, and saved your country."

"God saves Russia, Mr. President," Stolypin replied. "He even saved Russia from the Communists, although He took his time with the Reds. Let us pray that He can save Russia one more time."

Several minutes later Kalugin asked, "Are you a believer?"

"I believe in Russia, sir. So does God."

"You are in charge. Fight them. Give me some victories."

"I will use what we have," Stolypin said sourly, "which is very little. If you expect a furious battle that can be filmed for a television spectacle, you had better get someone else, someone who can make an army from street rabble with a snap of his fingers."

Kalugin was thinking about nuclear weapons. When he came out of his reverie, he heard Stolypin saying, "Political posturing is not part of a soldier's job."

Kalugin handed the old marshal an envelope. "Your appointment as chief of staff is in here. I signed it before you arrived. Go to headquarters and take charge. Mobilize our resources, fill the ranks, requisition the guns, clothes, food, fuel, all of it. Do whatever you have to do. Any decrees that you need, draft them and send them to me. Together, we are going to save Russia."

Stolypin reached for the envelope and opened it.

"It is a tragedy that Samsonov is not here," the old soldier said gravely as he read the papers. "He was the most brilliant soldier Russia has produced since Georgi Zhukov."

"I am placing the details in your capable hands, Marshal Stolypin."

"I have given you the same advice that Samsonov would. I wish to God he were here now."

"We will feel his loss keenly," said Kalugin as he walked with Stolypin toward the door.

The sky was growing light in the northeast as Jiro Kimura and three wingmen climbed to 34,000 feet on their way to bomb and strafe the airfield at Khabarovsk, at the great bend of the Amur River. Khabarovsk was a rail, highway, and electrical power nerve center, the strategic key to the far eastern sector. When they held Khabarovsk, the Japanese would own the Russian far east, and not before. The troops were within forty miles now, coming up the railroad and highways from Vladivostok.

For the past two days, Jiro and his squadron mates had flown close air support for the advancing troops, bombing, rocketing, and strafing knots of Russian troops that were preparing positions to delay the Japanese advance. This morning, however, the general had sent this flight to Khabarovsk.

It was going to be a perfect morning. Not a cloud anywhere. To the northeast the rising sun revealed the pure deep blue of the sky and the vastness of the endless green Siberian landscape. From 34,000 feet none of man's engineering projects were visible as the low-angle sunlight flooded the land in starkly contrasting light and shadow. When the sun got a little higher, all one would see from horizon to horizon would be green land under an endless blue sky.

Jiro was flying three or four flights a day, every day. The previous afternoon his plane had needed unexpected maintenance, and he had fallen asleep in the briefing room, after lying down on the floor with his flight gear as a pillow. He was constantly exhausted and always on the verge of sleep.

Some of his comrades were disappointed that the Russians had suddenly withdrawn their airplanes. Jiro had eleven kills when the Russians vanished from the sky, ceding air superiority. One still had to stay alert for possible enemy aircraft, of course, but they just weren't there.

Although the Russians on the ground felt free to shoot like wild men with everything they had, they rarely hit anyone. The Japanese planes stayed out of the light AAA envelope except when actually delivering ordnance. Rear-quarter heat-seekers would also have been a problem if they stayed near the ground for very long, so they didn't.

The Japanese had lost only two Zeroes at this stage of the war. One pilot crashed and died while making an approach to Vladivostok as evening fog rolled in. Another had a total electrical failure and lost his wingmen while he busied himself in the cockpit pulling circuit breakers and trying to reset alternators. He and his flight had been on their way to Nikolayevsk, at the mouth of the Amur, when the failure occurred. The luckless pilot never found the city or the base. He crashed in the boondocks a hundred miles northwest of Nikolayevsk when his fuel was exhausted. Fortunately a satellite picked up the plane's battery-powered emergency beeper after the pilot ejected, and a helicopter rescued him the next day.

Jiro retarded his throttles and began his letdown eighty miles from Khabarovsk. The four war planes drifted apart into a combat spread. Jiro and his wingman, Sasai, were ahead and to the right, Ota and Miura behind and to the left. Ota dropped farther back so that he could swing right and follow the first flight if the ground topography required it.

The shadows on the ground were still dark, impenetrable. Jiro looked at his watch. In eight minutes they would arrive at the target, come out of the rising sun. It would be a splendid tactic, if the sun rose on schedule.

He swung farther east to give God another minute or two with the sun.

"Blue Leader, this is Control." The radio was scrambled, of course, and gave a beep before and after the words.

Jiro pushed his mike button, waited for the beep, then said, "Control, Blue Leader, go ahead."

"We believe a plane has just taken off from your target. It is headed three zero zero degrees, ten miles northwest, climbing. Please intercept."

"Wilco."

Jiro looked around at Sasai. He pointed toward Ota, then jerked his thumb. Sasai nodded vigorously, then slipped aft and away.

Jiro turned left, advanced his throttles, and pulled his machine into a slight climb. He settled on a course of 275, which should allow him to intercept. Now he pushed buttons on the computer display in front of him. When he was satisfied, he tickled the radar. It swept once.

There was the plane. Thirty-four nautical miles away, interception course 278 degrees. He turned to that heading and reset his armament panel. He had been set up to strafe, then shoot rockets. Now he armed the two heat-seeking Sidewinder missiles that the Zero always carried, one on each wingtip.

He tripped the radar sweep again. Thirty-one miles.

The enemy plane was accelerating nicely, headed almost straight away from Jiro, who was now committed to a stern-quarter approach. He eyed his fuel gauges, then pushed the throttle farther forward. The Zero slid through the sonic barrier without a buffet or bump.

With the throttles all the way forward, but without using his afterburners, the Zero quickly accelerated to Mach 1.3.

Jiro decided to risk another sweep. Twenty-four miles.

He was at ten thousand feet now, so he leveled there. He wanted the other plane above him, against the dark background of the western sky. Far below, out to the left, he could see a faint ribbon of light wandering off to the northwest. That would be the Amur River, flowing southeast to Khabarovsk. On the far side was Manchuria. From Khabarovsk, the river flowed northeast to the Sea of Okhotsk. It was always frozen solid in winter.

He was still fifteen miles from the bogey when he first saw it, a spot of silver reflecting the rising sun, against the dark of the fading night.

It's a big plane, he thought. A transport!

He checked his ECM panel as the implications of that fact sunk in. The panel was dark.

Because you never really trust an electronic device, Jiro turned in his seat and looked carefully about him, concentrating on the rear quadrants.

Empty sky, everywhere.

A transport—defenseless.

He heard Ota tell Control that he was attacking the primary target, and he heard Control acknowledge.

Jiro closed quickly on the transport from dead astern. When it was no more than four miles ahead, Jiro retarded his throttles. The gap between the planes continued to close as he coasted up on it.

The bogey was a four-engine transport, very similar to an old Boeing 707, with the engines in pods on the wings, climbing at full power. Just now it was passing through fifteen thousand feet.

Jiro stabilized a few hundred yards aft, directly behind, well below the transport's wash.

He sat looking at it for what seemed like a long, long time, unsure of what to do. Actually the time was less than a minute, but it seemed longer to Jiro. He slid out to the right, so he could see the side of the plane and the tail, illuminated by the rising sun. Then he dropped back into trail.

Finally he keyed the mike. After the beep, he spoke. The hoarseness of his voice surprised him.

"Control, Blue Leader."

"Go ahead, Blue Leader."

"This bogey you wanted investigated. It's an airliner—four-engines, silver. Lots of windows. Aeroflot markings."

"Wait."

Silence, broken only by Jiro sucking on his oxygen, with the background hum of the engines. He eased up and under the transport; the roar of the Russian's engines became audible. He could just feel a bit of the rumble of the air disturbed by the big plane's passage, its wash.

He dropped down a bit; the ride smoothed and the Russian's engine noise faded.

"Ah, Blue Leader," Control said. "Destroy the bogey and RTB."

Jiro sat looking at the airliner. They were climbing through twenty thousand feet now.

"Blue Leader, this is Control. Did you copy? Destroy the bogey and return to base." The mission controller was in Japan, in a basement at the defense ministry probably, staring at his computer screens. The reason his voice sounded so clear and strong on the radio was because the radio signal was directed at a satellite, which rebroadcast it.

Jiro's eyes flicked around the cockpit, taking in the various displays and switches.

He took off his oxygen mask and rubbed his face furiously, then put the mask back on.

"Blue Leader, Control . . ."

Well, there was nothing to be gained by prolonging this. "Control, Blue Leader."

"Did you copy, Blue Leader?"

"Understand you want me to destroy this airliner and return to base."

"Destroy the bogey, Blue Leader. Report bogey destroyed."

"Control, this thing's an airliner. Tell me that you understand that this bogey is an Aeroflot airliner."

Silence. He was being grossly insubordinate. He could just imagine the clenched jaws of the senior officers.

Well, hell, if they didn't like it, they could cashier him, send him back to Japan.

"Blue Leader, Control. We understand the bogey has Aeroflot markings. You are hereby ordered to destroy it. Acknowledge."

"I copy."

He retarded the throttle, let the airliner pull ahead. The distance began to grow: five hundred yards, a thousand, fifteen hundred.

Jiro flicked a switch on the throttle to select the left Sidewinder. He pulled the nose up, put the dot in the center of the HUD directly on the airliner. The Sidewinder growled: It had locked on one of the big plane's engines.

Jiro squeezed the trigger on the stick. The Sidewinder leapt off the rail and shot forward. Straight as a bullet it flew across the gap toward the four-engined monster.

A puff of smoke. A hit: the inboard left engine.

He sat there watching as the airliner's engine began trailing smoke. Now the big silver plane began to move back toward him, which was an optical illusion. Actually, it was slowing and he was creeping up on it. He retarded his throttles, cracked the speed brakes.

"Fuck." Jiro said the word in English.

"Fuck!" Now he screamed it.

Furious, he selected the right Sidewinder, got the tone, then squeezed it off.

It impacted one of the transport's right engines: another little flash.

The huge silver plane wasn't climbing anymore. Its left wing came down, twenty . . . now thirty degrees; the nose dropped. It began a turn back toward Khabarovsk.

"Fall, you Russian bastard," Jiro whispered. He opened his speed brakes to the stops and dropped his left wing, cutting across the turn, closing the distance. He was out to the left now, in plain view of the pilots if they only took the time to look this way.

The airliner's left engine was visibly on fire. No, the wing was burning. Shrapnel from the missile's warhead must have punctured the wing tank, and jet fuel was burning in the slipstream.

The big silver plane's angle of bank was at least sixty degrees now, its nose down ten degrees.

It was then that Jiro realized that the big plane was out of control.

Perhaps the controls had been damaged by the missile shrapnel or the fire.

He pulled away, got his nose level, and watched the silver plane spiral down into the early-morning gloom.

Down, down, down . . . miles to fall . . .

Time seemed to stand still. The airliner got smaller and smaller.

The Russian plane was just a tiny silver dot, almost lost from view, when its flight ended in a flash, a tiny smear of fire amid the morning shadows.

That was all. A splash of fire, and they were gone.

Jiro pointed the nose of his plane south, toward Vladivostok. He pushed the throttles forward and let the nose rise into a climb.

"Control, Blue Leader . . ."

"Blue Leader, Control, go ahead with your report."

After an evening of cogitation, Aleksandr Kalugin decided to deliver an ultimatum to Japan threatening nuclear holocaust. Since he had bombs and Japan didn't, he could see no good reason why he should not put the bombs in play. He was not committing himself to any specific course of action, merely threatening one.

He called in Danilov, the foreign minister, and had him draft the ultimatum. Two hours later, he looked the document over carefully as Danilov sat on the edge of his seat, his hands folded in his lap.

Danilov was nearly seventy years old. He had spent his adult life as a professional diplomat. Never had he seen a Soviet or Russian government seriously weigh the use of nuclear weapons. Now, to his horror, Kalugin was threatening their use without even discussing the matter with his ministers. Is this where perestroika and democracy lead? To nuclear war?

"Sir, Japan may not withdraw from Siberia."

Kalugin finished the paragraph he was reading before he looked at Danilov. "They might not."

"They may not believe this ultimatum."

"What is your point?"

"We have repeatedly assured the world that our nuclear weapons were destroyed. Now, by implication, we are admitting that those statements were not true."

Kalugin said nothing. He merely stared at the foreign minister, who felt his skin crawl.

"Japan may believe that we do not have any weapons remaining," the minister observed, "in which case they will disregard this ultimatum."

Kalugin went back to the draft document. A sunbeam peeped into the room between the drapes on the high window behind the president, who sat reading, his head lowered.

He might nuke the Japanese, Danilov thought, suddenly sure that the ultimatum was not an idle threat. If they don't pull out of Siberia, Kalugin might really do it.

CHAPTER ELEVEN

● ANOTHER CLEAR, HOT day. Plumes of diesel exhaust and dust rose into the warm, dry air behind the Japanese army trucks—all forty-seven of them—and gently tailed off to the east. The convoy was on a paved road beside the Amur River—a paved road with a lot of wind-blown dirt on it—rolling northwest at about twenty miles per hour. They were a day northwest of Khabarovsk, in a wide river valley defined by low hills or mountains to the northeast and southwest. The river, a mile to the left, formed the border with China, but no fences or guard towers marked it.

Forty of the trucks carried supplies for Japanese forces a hundred miles ahead. Eight of the vehicles held soldiers, and the fuel, food, water, and cooking supplies necessary to keep the convoy rolling.

The road wasn't much—just a crowned two-laned paved road in a wide, treeless valley. It followed the natural contours of the land in a serpentine way along the path of least resistance. Although there were no signposts to proclaim it, the road was merely an improvement of an ancient trail. There were some culverts, occasionally a bridge, but in many places water routinely washed over the road. Dry now, many of the low places would be impassable in winter.

From the road one could occasionally see sheep or goats cropping the sparse grass, here and there a shack or yurt, once in a great while a rattletrap civilian truck going somewhere or other, trailing its own dust plume. Occasionally, a dirt road led off from the main road. A few of these led to open pit mines in the hills, where manganese or some other ore was extracted from the earth with obsolete, well-worn equipment, sweat, and a lot of hard work.

There were few people in this land. The natives shrank instinctively from the Japanese soldiers, who ignored them. Children in the doors of shacks watched the trucks approach, then retreated to the dark interior as the lead vehicle, a truck with a multibarreled antiaircraft gun mounted on the flatbed, drew near.

The Japanese ate dust and watched the sky. Some of them were wishing the Russian soldiers hadn't destroyed the railroad trestles and bridges as they retreated. If the railroad had remained intact, these soldiers would be riding a train west instead of jolting around in trucks.

The shimmering, brassy sky seemed to reflect the earth's heat back to it. High and far to the west a thin layer of cirrus clouds would diffuse the sun this afternoon, but that was many hours away.

The brilliant sun was hard to look at. When the curves of the road allowed, the older drivers looked anyway, almost against their will, holding up a hand or thumb to block the burning rays and searching the sky while they fought the wheel to keep their trucks on the highly crowned road.

The eagles didn't come from the sun's direction. They came from the northwest, straight down the valley, over this road, swiftly and silently, just a few hundred feet above the ground.

The driver of the lead truck saw them first, less than a mile away, two Sukhoi-27s, streaking in like guided missiles.

He cranked the wheel over and swung the truck on two wheels off the road. The men in back, the gun crew, almost fell out.

He was just quick enough to save their lives.

The cannon shells impacted on the road behind the lead truck and walked straight into the next vehicle, where they lingered for a fraction of a second as the pilot of the lead plane dipped his nose expertly. This truck exploded under the hammering.

As the fireball blossomed, the pilot was already shooting at another truck halfway down the convoy. The truck did not explode; it merely disintegrated as a dozen 30-mm cannon shells impacted in two brief seconds.

The pilot released the trigger and selected a third target, toward the end of the column. Still racing along at five hundred knots, he squirted a burst at that truck but missed.

He glanced left to ensure his wingman was where he should be, then dropped the right wing for a hard turn. After ninety degrees of heading change, he rolled left into a sixty-degree angle of bank. After 270 degrees of turn, he rolled out heading northwest, back toward the column of trucks. His wingman was still with him, out to the left.

Both pilots selected targets as they raced once again toward the trucks, whose drivers were frantically trying to get them off the road on either side. Not that it mattered.

With just the gentlest nudges of their rudders and caresses of their sticks, the pilots pointed their planes at targets chosen at random and squirted bursts from their internal GSh-30-1 guns. Four trucks exploded on that pass. One, which contained artillery ammunition, detonated with an earsplitting crash.

The gun crew in the lead truck was still trying to get the restraining straps off the antiaircraft gun so they could point it when the Su-27s swept overhead and disappeared into the brassy sky in the direction from whence they had come, northwest.

It took the convoy commander an hour to get the undamaged trucks back on the road and rolling. Nine trucks had been destroyed or damaged too badly to continue. One of the nine had not been touched by the strafing aircraft; the panic-stricken driver had tried to drive over several large rocks, which shattered the transmission and tore the rear axle loose from the truck's frame.

Fourteen men were dead, ten wounded. One of the wounded was horribly burned; a sergeant shot him to put him out of his misery.

The soldiers placed the dead men in a row near the road, amid the burned-out trucks. Someone else would have to bury them later. The officer in charge had his orders.

The soldiers got back in the trucks and resumed their journey northwest.

On the third mission of the day, Major Yan Chernov led his wingman, Major Vasily Pervushin, back to the truck convoy on the river road from Khabarovsk. Chernov was the commander of the 556th Fighter Squadron based at Zeya. He and his wingman were flying the only two operational aircraft. The enlisted men had been laboring for days to drain the water from the fuel-storage tanks, then transfer the remaining fuel by hand into the planes. There was no electricity at the base, so the job was herculean, involving hand pumps, fifty-five-gallon drums, and lots of muscle.

Chernov did not think there were any cluster bombs on the base, but while he was airborne on the first strike, his ordnance NCO found some in an ammo bunker that was supposed to be empty. The bombs were at least twenty years old. Still, they were all the Russians had for ground attack, so they were loaded on the planes.

Just now, he and Pervushin, his second in command, raced southeast a hundred feet or so above the ground. Chernov was watching for vehicles off to the left, along the river road.

The two Sukhois were indicating 525 knots, .85 Mach, which was

about as fast as it was safe to carry the bombs—they were not supersonic shapes. The treeless plain raced under the Sukhois, almost as if
the fighters were motionless in space and the earth was spinning madly
beneath them. The illusion was very pleasant.

There, at ten o'clock, on the horizon: a plume of dust.

This morning they had made two passes over the target convoy, the
first from the northwest, the second from the southeast. This time Chernov and Pervushin had planned to approach from the southeast and
drop the bombs on the first pass. Since they had the ammo in the guns,
they wanted to make a second pass, quickly, and the quickest way was
a hard turn, then back down the trucks from the northwest to the
southeast.

Chernov pointed to the dust, made sure Pervushin nodded his understanding. This convoy was farther northwest than the one they had
attacked that morning.

The ECM gear was silent. Not a peep of an enemy radar.

These Japanese, running truck convoys without air cover ...

There *could* be air cover, of course, running high with their radars
off. Chernov glanced up into the afternoon haze, looking for tiny black
spots against the high cloud.

Nothing.

Not seeing them didn't mean they weren't there. It simply meant
you hadn't seen them.

The dust was passing behind his left wing when he motioned for
Pervushin to drift out farther.

Satisfied, he began a shallow turn. He wanted to be wings-level over
the road for several miles before he reached the convoy to give himself
and Pervushin time to pick out targets.

Turn, watch the ground racing by just beneath the plane, keep the
wings at no more than ten degrees of bank, and glance up occasionally,
look for enemy fighters. *Watch the nose attitude, Chernov! Don't fly into
the ground.*

He reached for the armament panel. Bombs selected. Fusing set.
Interval set. Master armament switch on.

Wings level, Pervushin was well out to the right, dropping aft. He
would follow Chernov in a loose trail formation.

Five hundred twenty-five knots ... Chernov let his plane drift up
until he was about three hundred feet above the ground. After the
clamshell fuselage of the cluster bomb opened, the bomblets needed to
fall far enough to disperse properly.

Trucks. A row of them. They appeared to be racing toward him, but he was the one in flight. As Tail-end Charlie disappeared under the nose, Chernov mashed the pickle button on the stick. He could feel the thumps as the bombs were kicked off, all six of them in about a second and a half.

Chernov held the heading for another three seconds, then rolled into an eighty-degree angle of bank with G on and held it for ninety degrees of heading change. Now he rolled the other way and turned for 270 degrees.

He watched the gyro swing, concentrated on keeping the nose above the horizon. With his left hand, he flipped switches on the armament panel, enabling the gun.

Wings level again, the Russian pilot was almost lined up on the trucks, four of which were obviously on fire. He stabbed the rudder and jammed the stick forward, pointing the nose, then eased the stick back ever so slightly.

Squeeze the trigger, squint against the muzzle flashes as the vibration reaches him through the seat and stick, walk the shells through the target truck. Then another.

In four seconds his shooting pass was done, enough time to aim at two trucks; then Chernov was pulling G to get the nose above the horizon and rolling hard right to avoid ricochets. With a positive rate of climb, in a right turn, he raised the nose a smidgen more, twisted in his seat and glanced back over his right shoulder.

Horror swept over him.

A gun, on a truck, shooting, a death ray of tracers . . . Pervushin, on fire, rolling hard left, nose dropping . . .

A tremendous explosion of yellow fire as Pervushin's Sukhoi fighter flew into the ground.

No parachute visible.

Yan Chernov tore his eyes away and checked his nose attitude. He was still climbing.

Damnation!

"Sir, where's Major Pervushin?" the NCO asked Yan Chernov after he raised the canopy and shut down his engines at the Zeya Air Base.

"Dead."

"Fighters?"

"A gun. One gun. On a truck."

"Could he have . . ."

"No."

"His wife is at Dispersal, sir. The trucks carrying the families won't leave for a while, so she came here to wait for him."

Chernov sat in the cockpit letting the wind dry his face and hair. He was exhausted. Finally he made himself look in the direction of the dispersal shack, a large one-room wooden-frame building on the edge of the concrete. She was standing outside, shading her eyes against the sun, looking this way. The wind was whipping at her dress.

Chernov couldn't do it. It was his duty, but he couldn't.

"Sergeant."

"Yes, Major."

"Go tell her."

"Yes, sir."

The Zero pulled hard to bring his nose around, setting up a head-on pass. Dixie Elitch horsed her airplane to meet him head-on, trying to minimize the separation and give her opponent as small an angle advantage as possible. Alas, the Japanese pilot's nose lit up; cannon shells reached for her in a stream, as if they were squirted from a garden hose.

"These guys got fangs and will bite you good if you let them," said the male voice in her earphones. That was Joe Malan, who was back there with the simulator operator, no doubt enjoying himself immensely.

Dixie put on the G to escape the shells. She fully intended to pull right into the vertical, but Malan read her mind. "If this guy follows you up, you're going to give him another shot. You really don't want to be out in front of one of these people. Are you suicidal?"

By the time he finished speaking, she had unloaded the plane and rolled it 270 degrees. Now she laid the G on. Smoothly back on the stick, right up to nine G's on the HUD. In a real F-22, her full-body G suit would be fully inflated, but the simulator didn't pull G's. It did roll and pitch in a sickeningly realistic manner, however, so the cockpit smelled faintly of stale vomit. So did real cockpits.

She came around hard, turning at thirty-two degrees per second with the help of vectored thrust. No other plane in the world could turn like that, even the Zero.

Unfortunately the Zero had not been standing still or plodding along straight while he waited for her to finish her turn. She craned her head, looking for it.

"No, damn it," Malan said in her headphones. "Look at your displays. The infrared sensors are keeping track of this guy. What does your computer tell you?"

"He's high and right. I'm in his left-rear quarter."

"Pull up and shoot."

Dixie kept the nose coming. The missile-capability circle came into view on the HUD. As the red dot centered in the circle, she heard a tone, almost a buzz, indicating the heat-seeking Sidewinder missile had locked on. She squeezed off the missile, which roared away from her right wingtip.

A flash.

"Got 'im."

She relaxed the G.

"Okay, let's go back to base, shoot an instrument approach. Remember, in combat you *must* let the computer help you. The computer is your edge. The computer will keep you alive."

She wiped the sweat from her face and grunted.

"The computer is the brain of the plane. You're just the loose nut on the stick."

"Yeah."

When the session was over and she was standing on the floor under the simulator, Joe Malan replayed her mission on a videotape. He had just started the tape when Bob Cassidy came in, stood behind Dixie, and watched silently.

"He came in so fast from the front I couldn't get a missile shot."

"He was inside the envelope," Malan said. "Did you try to switch to the gun?"

"Never occurred to me," she admitted.

"I don't think you could have gotten the nose over quickly enough for a shot. You had only about three-quarters of a second, maybe a second. You must ensure you don't cross his nose, give him a shot at you. That is critical."

"Yes, sir," Dixie Elitch said.

"Even in a no-radar environment, this guy is making a lot of heat. Your IR sensors will pick him up; the computer will identify him, track him, show you his position at all times. Don't go lollygagging, cranking your head around to try to track him visually. Keep focused on those displays, keep flying, and take a shot when you get one. While you're engaged with this guy, somebody else might be sneaking up to put a knife into you, so kill him as quickly as possible."

"Okay."

"Go get some rest. See you back here at eleven tonight. Tonight, we'll do two bogeys at a time."

"Terrific."

As Dixie went through the classroom area, Aaron Hudek passed her on his way to the simulator. "Stick around, babe," he said, "and see how it's done."

"Watching people get zapped in that thing nauseates me," she shot back.

At the instructor's console of the simulator, Bob Cassidy asked Joe Malan, "How is she doing?"

"Pretty good. Picks it up quick. All these kids do. The speed with which they absorb this stuff amazes me."

"Video games. A lifetime of video games."

"All life is a video game to this generation. Hudek is next, then you."

Aaron Hudek was standing beside them. "Make yourself comfortable, Colonel. I'll show you how it's done." The humble one grinned.

Cassidy snorted.

"I can talk it and walk it, Colonel."

"I hope."

"Just watch." Hudek went up the ladder toward the cockpit, which stood almost ten feet off the floor on massive hydraulically actuated arms.

"I like Fur Ball's brass," Malan muttered.

"I'll like it too, *if* he can fly."

Hudek could. Malan started with in-flight emergencies and Hudek handled them expeditiously, by the book. Interceptions were no problem, nor were dogfights where he bounced his opponent. After three of those, he was bounced by a single opponent. He quickly went from defensive to offensive and shot the opponent down. The second opponent was wiser, more wily, but Hudek was patient, working his plane, taking what the opponent gave him, waiting for his enemy to make a mistake.

"He's damned good," Malan told Bob Cassidy, who was watching

Hudek's cockpit displays on the control panel in front of Malan. "Maybe the best we have."

A simulator was not a real airplane, nor were the scenarios very realistic. They were merely designed to sharpen the pilots' skills. "The problem," Cassidy told Malan, "is going to be getting close enough to the Zero to have a chance at it. In close, with smart skin and infrared sensors, the F-22 has the edge. Getting there is going to be the trick."

"I thought you said the F-22's electronic countermeasures would allow us to detect the Zero before it could see us on radar?"

"Theoretically, yes. Say it works—you know the enemy is there, but his Athena protects him from your radar. You can't shoot an AM-RAAM—it won't guide. How do you get in to Sidewinder range?"

"I don't know."

"We'd better figure that out or we'll be ducks in a shooting gallery."

The following day was even more frustrating for Yan Chernov than the previous one. Everything that could go wrong did. Electricity to the base was off; fueling had to be done by hand; only three airplanes were flyable—three out of thirty-six. The others had mechanical problems that the men were trying to fix, or had been scavenged for parts to keep the other planes flying. One of the three was fueled and armed. Chernov intended to use it to give the Japanese some grief.

The 30-mm cartridges for the cannon were so old that some of them had swelled; these defective cartridges would jam the gun when they were chambered, so all the cartridges had to be checked by hand with a micrometer, the defective ones thrown away, then the good ones loaded by hand into the linkages that made them into a belt. At last, the belt went into Chernov's plane.

After all that, four AA-10 missiles were loaded onto the missile racks. Chernov suited up, strapped in, then tried to start the engines. The left engine wouldn't crank.

Another hour was wasted while mechanics changed the starter drive.

Chernov went back to the dispersal shack and tried once again to call regional military headquarters. At least the telephones worked. But no one answered the ringing phone at regional HQ. The phone just refused to ring at the GCI site in this sector. Maybe the lines were down somewhere . . . or perhaps the Japanese had fired a beam-rider antiradiation missile at the radar to knock it off the air.

Chernov went out onto the concrete ramp and sat down in the shade of a wing so he could watch the mechanics work. He had a lot of things on his mind: antiradiation missiles, telephones that didn't work, Japanese soldiers, and a dead pilot.

To resist a Japanese attack on the base with a few dozen men would be suicidal. He had ordered the base personnel to leave, taking all the military families with them. In the absence of orders from higher authority, the responsibility was his.

Oh well, he would probably be dead in about an hour, so what did it matter what the Moscow bureaucrats thought when they got around to wondering why the antiaircraft guns at the Zeya Air Base were not manned.

He was nervous. Maybe a little scared. He had never been in combat before yesterday. The action then hadn't taken the edge off. His stomach was nervous, his hands sweaty. He was having trouble sitting still.

Today, he knew, there would be Zeros. There should have been Zeros yesterday.

He could do it, though. He told himself that over and over. He was a professional. He had a good airplane; he knew how to use it.

The odds were against him. One plane against . . . how many? An air force. Their ECM gear would pick up his radar. . . .

He would leave it off, he decided. Eyeball-to-eyeball would be his best chance.

Maybe his only chance.

"Major, what if the Japanese attack?"

One of the mechanics was standing in front of him, holding a wrench, examining his face with searching eyes. "You're sitting under the biggest target on the base, the only armed fighter."

"All these planes look good from the air," he replied, gesturing toward rows of Sukhois and MiGs parked in revetments.

The mechanic rejoined the others. Chernov stretched out, using his survival vest for a pillow, and watched the sky. The sun was shining through a high cirrus layer. There were scattered clouds at the middle altitudes. The clouds subdued the light, made the sky look soft, gauzy.

Yan Chernov took a deep breath, tried to force himself to relax.

Finally the mechanics came to him. "We're finished, sir."

"Good. Very good."

"It should work."

"Yes," he said.

"What do you want to do, Major?" the crew chief asked.

"Help me strap in. Have the men work on getting another plane fueled. Arm it. Check the ammo, load four missiles. If there is time this evening, I will take it up." If he was alive this evening, that is.

"Some of the other pilots want to fly."

"No."

Chernov had no orders to launch strikes on the Japanese. He had already lost one man. Russia might need these men later. No sense wasting them.

This time the left engine started, as did the right.

When the ordnance men and mechanics were satisfied, Chernov gave the signal for the linesmen to pull the chocks. They did so, and he taxied.

He made no radio calls. He didn't turn on the radar or the radio. The ECM panel received careful attention, however, and he tuned the volume so he could hear the sound of any enemy radar the black boxes detected.

He taxied onto the runway, stopped, and quickly ran through his preflight checks. Satisfied, he released the brakes as he smoothly advanced the throttles to the stops, then lit the afterburners.

The heavy Sukhoi accelerated quickly. Just seconds after the plane broke ground, Chernov came out of burner to save fuel.

Airborne, with the gear up and flaps in, Yan Chernov pointed the fighter southeast, down the Amur valley. He leveled at twenty thousand feet and retarded the throttles to cruise at .8 Mach.

The afternoon was getting late. The rolling plain below looked golden in the summer haze, like something from a fairy tale. Here and there were clumps of trees, pioneers from the boreal forest to the north, trying to make it in low places on the prairie. Occasionally a road could be discerned through the haze, but no villages or towns. The haze hid them.

Chernov turned on his handheld GPS, a battery-powered Bendix-King unit made in America and sold there for use in light civilian airplanes. Within seconds, his position came up on the unit. He keyed in the lat-long coordinates of the Svobodny airfield and waited for a direction and distance. There!

One hundred and twenty miles from Svobodny, Chernov's ECM picked up the chirp of a Japanese search radar. He was probably too far out for the operator to receive an echo, which was good. Chernov turned ninety degrees to the left and began flying a circle with a 120-mile radius, with Svobodny at the center. The GPS made it easy.

Yan Chernov concentrated on searching the afternoon sky and listening intently to the ECM.

Not another aircraft in sight.

That was certainly not surprising. Acquiring another aircraft visually was difficult at best beyond a few miles. At the speeds at which modern aircraft flew, when you finally saw it, you might not even have enough time to avoid it. And in combat, the performance envelope of air-to-air missiles was so large that if you saw the enemy, either you or the other pilot had made a serious mistake, perhaps a fatal one. Still, Chernov kept his eyes moving back and forth, searching the sky in sectors, level with the horizon, above it, and below it. He was alone, which was not the way modern fighters are designed to fight.

The radar that his GCI controller normally used was off the air. Perhaps it had been damaged by a Japanese beam-riding missile. Perhaps the power company had turned off the electricity. Maybe the GCI people had piled into trucks and fled west to escape the Japanese. No one was answering the telephone there, so who knew? Perhaps it didn't matter much one way or the other.

And this was an old plane, an obsolete fighter. Once, not many years ago, the Sukhoi-27 had been the best fighter in the world, bar none. But after the collapse of communism in '91, development of new fighters in the new Russia dried up from lack of money. The nation couldn't even afford to buy fuel for the fighters it had; everything was tired, worn, not properly cared for.

Amazingly, Japan had plenty of planes that performed equal to or better than this one. As Russia rusted, the Japanese built a highly capable aircraft industry.

And here Chernov was, in an obsolete, worn-out plane that hadn't flown—according to the logbook—in nine months and three days, hunting Japanese planes with his naked eyes.

Out here asking for some Japanese fighter pilot to kill him quick.

Begging for it. Kill me, kill me, kill me. . . .

According to an intel officer hiding in the city of Svobodny whom he had spoken to on the telephone that morning, the Japanese were flying supplies in from Khabarovsk and bases in Japan.

He thought he saw a plane, and he changed his heading to check.

No. Dirt on the canopy.

He checked his fuel, checked the GPS. . . . He wasn't going to be able to stay out here for very long, not if he expected to get back to base flying this airplane.

He was coming up on the Bureya River when he saw it, a speck running high and conning. The guy must be 36,000 or 38,000 feet, headed northwest.

Chernov turned to let the other plane pass off his right wing on a reciprocal heading. If it was a Japanese transport—and all the planes in these skies just now were Japanese—it must be going to Svobodny. Right heading, right altitude . . .

If it was a transport going to Svobodny, there were fighters.

The Russian major glanced at his ECM, listened intently. Not a peep, not a chirp or click.

Well, damnit, there must be fighters, not using their radars. They must be below the transport, below the conning layer, and too small to be visible at this distance.

Thank God he had his radar off, or they would have picked up the emissions and be setting a trap right this minute.

His heart was pounding. Sweat stung his eyes, ran down his neck . . .

He checked his switches—missiles selected, stations armed, master arm on.

The transport was still eight or ten miles away when it went by Chernov's right wingtip. He laid the Sukhoi into a sixty-degree angle of bank and stuffed the nose down while he lit the afterburners, shoved the throttles on through to stage four.

The heavy jet slid through the sonic barrier and accelerated quickly: Mach 1.5, 1.7 . . . 1.9.

Passing Mach 2 he raised the nose into a climb, kept the turn in.

The AA-10 was a fire-and-forget missile with active radar homing. When its radar came on, the Japanese were going to get a heady surprise.

So was Chernov if the Japanese had a couple of fighters fifteen miles in trail behind the transport. He looked left, then right, scanning the sky hurriedly. The sky looked empty. Which meant nothing. They could be there.

The transport was just a dot, a flyspeck in the great vastness, still well above him and conning beautifully. About ten miles, he figured, but he couldn't afford to turn on the radar to verify that. He was closing from fifteen degrees right of dead astern.

He centered the dot in the gunsight, squeezed off a missile. It shot forward off the rail trailing smoke. He lowered the nose, aimed a little left, and fired a second missile. A hard right turn, fifteen degrees of heading change, and a third missile was in the air. Total elapsed time, about six seconds. If there were Japanese fighters there, the missiles would find them.

The third missile had just disappeared into the haze when the ECM squealed in his ears.

The AA light was flashing, and a red light on the instrument panel just below his gunsight: "*Missile!*"

Yan Chernov slammed the stick sideways and pulled. The plane flicked over on its side and he laid the G on. A target decoy was automatically kicked out by the countermeasures gear.

Five . . . six . . . seven G.

A missile flashed over his right wing and detonated. A miss. The Missile warning light went out, but the ECM continued to chirp and flash direction lights. The Japanese were on the air now.

Ten years ago nothing on the planet could turn with a Su-27. It could still out-turn missiles, so Yan Chernov was still alive.

He came out of burner, retarded the throttles as quickly as he dared—he certainly didn't want to flame out just now—and let the G bleed off his airspeed. He got the nose up to the horizon.

A Japanese fighter overshot above him.

There might be two of them . . .

His skin felt like ice as he slammed the stick right and rolled hard to reverse his turn. The ECM was singing.

The Japanese pilot was turning left, beginning to roll back upright.

Chernov pulled with all his might to raise the nose.

As the enemy fighter streaked across from right to left, Chernov had his thumb on the 30-mm cannon, which vomited out a river of fire. The finger of God.

The flaming river of shells passed through the wing of the Japanese fighter.

Chernov rolled upside down, pulled as he lit his burners. There had to be someone else out there: the ECM was chirping madly.

The earth filled the windscreen. Going straight down, accelerating . . . *Only 23,000 feet, fool.* He rolled the plane and scanned quickly. Nothing. Now the ECM was silent.

He began to pull. Pull pull pull at seven G's, fight to stay conscious. . . . The sweat stung his eyes, and his vision began to gray.

He was screaming now, watching the yellow earth rushing up at him, trying to stay conscious.

He was going to make it.

Yes!

Relax the stick, drop to a hundred feet or two, just above the earth, and let the old girl accelerate.

The ECM stayed silent.

He twisted his head, looked behind. Right. Left.

Nothing.

Two planes falling way off the right. On fire—one of them large enough to appear as a black dot against the yellow cirrus layer.

When Yan Chernov taxied into the hard stand at Zeya, his flight suit and gear were soaked. The sweat was still running off him in rivulets, even though he had the canopy open. On the instrument panel, the needle on the G meter that recorded the maximum G pulled that flight rested on 9.

Nine G's with only a stomach-and-legs G suit. The wings might have come off under that much overstress. He would have to have the mechanics carefully inspect the plane.

Chernov waited until the linemen had the chocks in place, then secured the engines.

"Water," he said. The senior NCO passed up a bottle.

"How did it go, Major?" one of the junior pilots asked after he finished drinking. There were four of them standing there, gazing at the empty missile racks and the gun port with the tape shot away.

"I got two, I think. Maybe three. One of them almost took my scalp."

"Very good."

"Luck. Pure luck. They just happened to come along, and I just happened to see them before they saw me." He shook his head, filled with wonder that he was still alive.

"They are good?"

"Good enough." He tossed his helmet down, then climbed down from the cockpit. When he was on the ground, he drank more of the water. "Do you have another plane ready?"

"Yes, Major," said the senior NCO.

"Two?"

"Just one, sir. We hope to get three more flyable tonight by cannibalizing parts from the down birds. And the fueling takes forever."

"Any word from Moscow?"

"No, sir. They haven't called."

"We will fly the planes west in the morning, as many as we have fuel for. As many as we can get started."

Damn Moscow. With almost no fuel, no spare parts, little food, one-third of the mechanics the squadron was supposed to have, and an inoperative GCI site, he couldn't do much more, even if Kalugin wrote the order in blood. He was being realistic. He had flown a stupid solo mission, almost gotten killed, affected the course of the war not at all, and now it was time to face facts: Russia was defenseless.

"I'll bet Zambia has a better air force than we have," one of the junior officers muttered.

Chernov took off his flight gear and sat down by a main tire with the water bottle and waved them away.

"Let me rest awhile."

His mind was still going a thousand miles an hour, replaying the missile shots and the Japanese fighter slashing across in front of his gun. The emotional highs and lows—amazing! He would never have believed that he could feel so much elation, then, five seconds later, so much terror. He was wrung out, like a sponge squeezed to millimeter thickness in a hydraulic press.

Five minutes later one of the NCOs came for him from the dispersal shack.

"Sir, Moscow is on the line. Someone very senior."

"How senior?"

"He says he's a general, sir. I never heard of him."

Chernov walked across the ramp and entered the dispersal building, a single room with a naked bulb in the ceiling—not burning, of course; the only light came from the dirty windows. A large potbellied wood-stove stood in the center of the room. The four or five enlisted men in the room fell silent when Chernov walked in and reached for the phone.

"Major Chernov, sir."

"Major, this is General Kokovtsov, aide to Marshal Stolypin."

"In Moscow?"

"Headquarters."

"I've been trying to telephone regional headquarters and Moscow since the Japanese invaded. You are the first senior officer I've spoken to."

The desk soldier had other things on his mind. "I asked to speak to the commanding officer. Are you in command of the base?"

"Apparently so, General."

"A fighter base should have a brigadier general in command."

"Our general retired four years ago and was never replaced. Two of our squadrons were transferred three years ago and took their airplanes with them. The other squadron was decommissioned: The people left, but the airplanes stayed, parked in revetments. My squadron, the Five hundred fifty-sixth, is the last."

"And you are a major?"

"That is correct, sir. Major Chernov. We used to have a colonel. This spring, he and some of the other officers took several vehicles and left. We haven't seen them since. They said they were going to Irkutsk, near Lake Baikal. To find work. The colonel had relatives in Moscow, I believe. He talked of the city often, so he may have gone there."

"He had orders?"

"No."

"He deserted!"

"Call it what you like."

"Desertion."

"The colonel drove out of here in broad daylight. The others too. They were owed over eighteen months' pay. They hadn't seen a ruble in six months."

Silence from Moscow. Finally, the general said, "Why are you still there?"

"My wife left me five years ago, General. I'm alone. This place is as good as any other."

"You are loyal."

"To what? What I am is stupid. The government owes me almost two years' pay. I haven't been paid anything since the colonel was, nine months ago. Neither have these enlisted men. We're selling small arms and ammunition on the black market to get money for food. When we don't have any money, we ask for credit. When we can't get credit, we steal. But enough of this social chitchat—what did you call me to talk about?"

"I'm sorry."

"Believe me, so am I."

"Marshal Stolypin wants you to harass the Japanese. Just that. Launch a few sections a day, try to shoot down a transport or two, force them to maximum effort to protect their resources."

"I thought Stolypin retired years ago. Samsonov is—"

"Samsonov is dead. Stolypin has come out of retirement to lead us against the Japanese."

"Maybe he can work a miracle."

"Don't be insubordinate, Major."

"I'm trying, sir."

"So what have you done, if anything, to fight the war?"

"I went up awhile ago. One plane. They shot at me; I shot at them."

"One sortie?" he asked, disbelief apparent in his voice.

"Three today. We flew six yesterday, four the day before."

"Only thirteen?"

The jerk! Chernov had dealt with asshole superiors all his adult life. He kept his voice absolutely calm, without even a trace of emotion. "We can launch one more sortie this evening. We have fuel for perhaps eight more; then we're done."

"We'll have fuel delivered."

"The electricity has been off here for a month. No one has paid the power company, so they shut it off. We have to pump the fuel from the tanks to the planes by hand, which takes a lot of time and effort."

"President Kalugin has signed a decree. The electricity will be turned back on."

"Terrific. War by decree." Yan Chernov couldn't help himself. He was losing his composure. Maybe it was adrenaline aftershock.

"We want you to launch some sections to harass the enemy," the general said from the safety of Moscow. "Don't be too aggressive, you understand. Inflict just enough pain to annoy them. That is the order of Marshal Stolypin."

Chernov lost it completely. "You fool! We worked for four days to get six sorties out yesterday. Two sorties a day on a sustained basis is all we could possibly launch, even if World War Three is declared. My executive officer was killed this morning. We have no food, no fuel, no electricity, no spare parts, no GCI site, no intelligence support, no staff. . . . *We have nothing!* Have I made it clear? Do you comprehend?"

"I am a general, Major. Watch your tongue."

"Get your head out of your ass, General. We can't defend this base. We should be flying these planes west to save them. It's just a matter of time before the Japanese attack. It's a miracle they haven't already. I can only assume you and Stolypin *want* the Japanese to attack us, because you are taking no steps to prevent it. When we're dead, you idiots in Moscow won't have to ever feed us or pay us or—"

The headquarters general hung up before the major completed the last sentence. When Chernov realized the line was dead, he quit talking and slammed down the telephone.

Everyone in the room was staring at him.

"Everything that can fly goes west at dawn," Chernov shouted, spittle flying from his lips. "Work everyone all night."

"Yes, sir."

Chernov turned to face the junior officers who had trickled in while he was on the telephone.

"Get the trucks we have left. Fuel them. Have the men load the tools and all the food we have. They may take their clothes. Nothing else. No furniture or televisions or any of that other crap."

He was roaring at the top of his lungs, unable to help himself. "We will drive west, all the way to Moscow. If we get there before the Japanese, we will drag the generals from their comfortable offices and hang them by the balls."

Yan Chernov stomped out to pee in the grass.

Delivery of the Russian ultimatum to the Japanese was a chore that fell to Ambassador Stanley P. Hanratty. The Russian diplomats had all left Tokyo the day after the invasion, turning out the lights and locking the door of the embassy as they left. The U.S. government offered to assist the Russians diplomatically in the Japanese capital until relations were restored, an offer that Kalugin seized upon. Delivery of the ultimatum was Ambassador Hanratty's first chore for the Russians. Of course, he and the U.S. government were privy to the contents of the note.

Hanratty returned the following morning to the Japanese foreign ministry to receive the Japanese reply. "We find it difficult to believe, in this day and age," the Japanese foreign minister said as he handed over the written reply, "that any government on the planet would threaten another with nuclear war. Still, in anticipation of just such an event, Japan has developed its own nuclear arsenal. Should Russia attempt to launch a first strike upon Japan, the Japanese government will, with profound regret, order a massive retaliatory strike upon Russia."

It was late in the day in Moscow when Kalugin received the Japanese answer from Danilov. He read the reply carefully, then handed the paper back without a word.

CHAPTER TWELVE

●By working throughout the long evening and short night, the officers and enlisted men of Major Chernov's squadron at the Zeya Air Base got six planes into flyable condition. The planes were ready a half hour before the true dawn. Chernov had the best one armed with cannon shells and four AA-10 missiles.

Chernov had ordered five of his pilots, the five most senior, to fly to Chita, five hundred nautical miles west, well beyond range of the Zeros. Now he slapped them on the back, watched them strap in, start engines, and taxi. They took off one by one, white-hot exhausts accelerating faster and faster and faster. The roar of their engines filled the night with a deep, rolling thunder.

The fighters kept their exterior lights off and did not bother to rendezvous. They retracted their wheels as they came out of burner and turned west. Still, it was several minutes before the roar of the last plane had faded.

Yan Chernov stood beside the sixth plane and listened until even the background moan was gone and all he could hear were the insects chirping and singing, as they had done on this steppe every summer since the world was young.

The senior warrant officer came over. They shook hands. "Roll the trucks now," Chernov said. "Get the men to Chita, if possible. If not, go as far west as you can. The Japanese may attack at dawn, hoping to catch us sleeping." He glanced at his watch. The night at these latitudes was only two hours long.

"Do you really think so, Major?"

"There is a chance they'll strike as soon as there is light enough."

"Why today?"

"I hurt them yesterday. They should have hit us days ago. Now they will."

"I suppose."

Chernov shrugged. "This morning or soon."

"I've already sent the other trucks on. I'll wait and go with your linesmen."

Chernov held out his hand. The warrant office took it.

The major smoked the last of his cigarettes as he eyed the northeastern sky, waiting for the first glow of dawn. He had been rationing himself, to make the cigarettes last. When these were gone ... well, without money ...

The night was not really dark. At this latitude summer night could accurately be described as a deep twilight. He could see stars, so the sky was clear and visibility good. Chernov had grown up in a village dozens of miles from the nearest town, far from urban light pollution, so stars were old friends.

He had finished his last cigarette and was strolling around the airplane, touching it, caressing it, trying to stay calm and focused, when the stars in the east began to fade.

He climbed to the cockpit and the senior linesman helped him strap in. "Take care of yourself, sir."

"Peace and friendship, Sergeant," the pilot said, repeating the traditional phrase.

He sat alone in the cockpit, watching the sky turn pale. He had no fuel to waste, yet if he delayed his takeoff too long, the Japanese would catch him on the ground. If they came.

He could wait no longer. He gave the signal to the linesman.

Seven minutes later, sitting on the end of the runway, he ran through his takeoff checklist. Everything looked good. The radio didn't work, so he didn't turn it on. The ECM gear did work. He watched the telltale lights intently, listened with the volume turned up to maximum. And he saw and heard nothing.

Maybe the Japanese weren't coming. Maybe he would be shot for cowardice in the face of the enemy. Be shot by that officious desk general who had called yesterday wanting the brigadier. A sick joke, that.

The stars were going fast.

Yan Chernov released the brakes and smoothly shoved the throttles forward to the stops. Pressures good, fuel flow fine, rpm and tailpipe temperatures coming up nicely. . . .

Now he lit the burners. The white light of the afterburners split the darkness like newborn stars.

The acceleration pushed him back into the seat. Despite the fact the

Sukhoi-27 was a big plane, weighing about 44,000 pounds this morning, it accelerated quickly. Soon the trim lifted the nosewheel off the pavement. He steadied her there, flew her off.

Gear up, then out of burner as soon as possible. When everything was up and in, he turned to the southwest. The most probable direction for an approach by enemy attackers was southeast. If he could make another side attack before they spotted him, he might be able to . . .

He leveled at ten thousand feet and let the speed build to .8 Mach. At this low altitude, fuel flow was high. Nervous, he glanced again at his watch. He had been airborne for six minutes.

After ten minutes of flight, he began a long, slow 180-degree turn. His head was on a swivel, searching the early-morning sky in every direction, especially to the south and east. He was tempted to tap his radar for one sweep, just to see, but he decided it was too dangerous.

The sky to the northeast was a pale blue. Visibility excellent, easily fifty miles. It's just that small airplanes more than a few miles away are exceedingly difficult to see in the great vastness of the sky, he thought. And this early, with the earth below still dark, the task was almost impossible—unless the planes were in that northeast quadrant, silhouetted against the growing light.

He tried to resist the temptation to stare toward the northeast. They would probably approach the base from the southwest, from the darkness!

He searched futilely in all directions.

Nothing.

Maybe the Japanese aren't coming.

What a fucked-up war! *It's every man for himself, comrades. We have fucked up our country so badly that we have nothing to sustain our soldiers with. It's poor, polluted, filled with starving people and radioactive waste.*

Chernov did a 360-degree circle, then another one.

He was sweating.

Well, this idea was stupid. Stupid, stupid, stupid. He should have gone with the others to Chita, talked to the people at headquarters from a telephone there, set up a liaison with a tanker squadron. Su-27s should be operated from a secure, well-defended base, one properly supplied with fuel and ordnance and spare parts, one beyond the range of the Japanese. Then, with the help of airborne tankers, the fighters could be launched on combat missions against the enemy here at Zeya or even at Khabarovsk.

Why dawn? Why did he think they would come at dawn?

He admitted to himself that he didn't know the answer to that question. He just sensed it. A dawn attack seemed to fit.

He glanced at his fuel guage. Then his watch.

Keep the eyes moving, look at that sky, look for the tiniest speck that isn't supposed to be there.

His ECM chirped. Just a chirp and a flash of light. He eyed the panel, waiting for the light to flash again, waiting for a strobe to indicate direction. Nothing. He looked outside. He couldn't maintain a watch on the damned panel.

Maybe a Japanese pilot had given in to the temptation that Chernov had resisted—maybe he had tickled his radar, let it sweep once, just to verify that . . . to verify . . .

Three tiny specks, way out there, against the blue of the dawn. The sun was just ready to pop over the earth's rim, and above the growing light in the sky he could see moving black specks. Three. No, four. Five. Six. Moving to the west. They would pass well north of Chernov's position.

So.

Six. Damn! Why did there have to be so many?

He turned to the southwest. If he came out of the darkest part of the sky while they were working over the base, he would be difficult to acquire visually.

They would turn their radars on as soon as they suspected he was around. Still, if he got first shot . . .

Yan Chernov eased the throttles forward, right against the stops. He wasn't ready for afterburner yet. Full power without the burners gave him .95 Mach.

Now the ECM panel lit up. The Zeros were looking for planes over Zeya.

He eased the nose into a descent, let the plane accelerate, retrimming constantly. Mach 1, now 1.1, now 1.2. Still at full military power.

He made the turn to go back toward the base, checked the handheld GPS.

Master armament switch on.

Four missiles selected, lights red. They were armed and ready. Each squeeze of the trigger on the stick would fire one.

He leveled at five hundred feet, just above the earth. Down to Mach 1.1, decelerating because the engines could not hold him supersonic without the thrust of the afterburners. If only he had a modern plane, like an F-22. Or even a Zero.

Fifteen miles. Fourteen. Thirteen—a nautical mile every six seconds.

He glanced again at the ECM panel. All ahead, nothing behind. *Nothing behind that is radiating.* He took a ragged breath, tried to calm himself. His heart felt like a trip-hammer in his chest.

Ten miles. Nine. Eight . . .

At seven miles he pulled the nose up five degrees and squeezed off an AA-10 missile. Then a second, third, and fourth, as fast as he could pull the trigger. These fire-and-forget missiles had active radar homing. With luck, two or three of them would find targets.

He opened the afterburners full. The acceleration pushed him back into his seat. His fingers flicked the switches to select "Gun" on the armament panel.

The Japanese must have picked up the radar emissions of the in-bound missiles.

Now he flipped the switch that caused his radar to transmit.

The scope blossomed.

He was still looking outside, through the gunsight, when he saw the first flash—a missile hit. Now another. And a third.

The fourth missile must have missed.

Yan Chernov glanced at the radar scope, quickly turned one of the knobs to adjust the gain.

A plane on the left, heading slightly away.

He looked through the gunsight. There! At eleven o'clock.

A *transport*! Parachutes in the air! Paratroops. The Japanese were taking the field. All that registered in Chernov's mind without conscious thought. He was concentrating on the transport.

He was going to get a deflection shot. He was doing Mach 1.4; the other plane, probably two hundred knots max.

He jabbed at the rudder, adjusted the stick with both hands to get the nose where he wanted it. He squeezed the trigger, and the gun erupted, hosing fire.

It was over in two seconds. The stream of white-hot lead was in front of the enemy transport, then, with the gentlest touch on the right rudder, stitched it from nose to tail. The four engine turboprop blew up and Chernov shot just behind the expanding fireball, still accelerating. Mach 1.7 now, all the Sukhoi would give him in this thick air. His eyes registered the sight of more parachutes, but he was busy flying. The enemy radars were emitting in his rear quadrant now. He let the nose sag in order to get down against the earth.

As the seconds ticked by, he felt his shoulder blades tighten. Sure enough, the Missile light under the gunsight began to flash.

Level thirty meters above the ground, Chernov punched out chaff, rolled the plane ninety degrees to the left, and pulled the stick into his gut until the meter read 7 G's. Sweat stung his eyes. The horizon was right there, a line through his gunsight. He fought the temptation to look over his left shoulder, concentrated instead on keeping the horizon below the dot in the gunsight that represented his flight path. If that dot dropped below the horizon, he would be into the ground in seconds, and very, very dead.

A missile went over his right shoulder, exploded harmlessly after it was by.

The next one went off just under the plane, a sickening thud that slammed the plane hard.

He rolled right, through level, into a right turn. Less G now, because the Missile light was off. So was the ECM panel. It shouldn't be. The Japanese were still back there, perhaps trying to catch him. If he could keep his speed up, they never would. He needed to extend out.

For the first time, he glanced at his system gauges, the gauges that told him of his steed's health.

Uh-oh. Hydraulic pressure was dropping; he had three yellow warning lights and a red. The red was a generator.

Oh, God! The ECM panel was silent because it lost power when one of the generators dropped off the line.

Just then another missile exploded above him: a flash, a pop, followed by a rattle of shrapnel against the fuselage.

He leveled the wings. Despite the low altitude, he risked a look aft.

Nothing visible behind. Still Mach 1.6 on the airspeed indicator.

Fuel trailing away behind the right wing. He could just see the fuel boiling off the wing in the rearview mirror. A glance at the gauge for fuel in the right wing. Almost empty.

Another gentle left turn. He consulted the GPS. Fifteen miles from the base, going northeast.

Yan Chernov kept the left wing down about ten degrees, let the nose slowly come toward the north, then the northwest. It seemed as if the wing was almost in the grass of the steppe. The sensation of speed was overpowering, sublime; he was orbiting the planet at a distance of five meters. He watched intently ahead, focused with all his being, tugging the plane over rises and rolling hills. If the wing kissed the earth now, he would never know it: He would be dead before the sensation registered.

He leveled the wings, heading west.

Are the Zeros chasing? They must not have the fuel to chase.

Oil pressure to the right engine was dropping quickly.

Chernov came out of burner. When he did, the right rpm began dropping. He pulled the throttle to idle cutoff, secured the fuel flow.

He still had one engine, one generator.

At fifty miles from the base, he took off his oxygen mask and swabbed the sweat from his eyes and face.

He checked the fuel again. Must be another leak somewhere. He had enough for thirty more minutes of flight, if he didn't have any fuel leaks. With leaks, less. But he was alive.

Pavel Saratov walked the periscope around slowly. The attack scope protruded just inches above the surface of the sea, which fortunately was calm today. Still, a wave occasionally washed over the glass. When it did he paused until he could see again, then continued his sweep. Visibility was about ten miles, he estimated.

There were three ships in view, two going into Tokyo Bay, one leaving. Container ships, one about thirty thousand tons, the other two larger.

Not a warship in sight. Not even a patrol boat.

He flipped the handle so that he could scan the sky. Overcast in all directions. No airplanes.

Back to the ships. Two going northeast, up the channel into the Uraga Strait entrance to Tokyo Bay, one coming out.

The ship nearest the land was too far away and opening the distance, but if he hurried, he could probably get firing solutions on the other two and send them to the bottom. Now.

He had ten torpedoes. He should have had a dozen, which would have been a full load, but there had been only eleven fueled torpedoes in the naval armory, and he had drained the fuel from one to sell for food. These were not new, modern torpedoes—they were the old 53–65 antiship, wake-homing torpedoes, the first of the Soviet wake-homers.

Saratov had loaded the ten torpedoes aboard *Admiral Kolchak* because naval regulations required that the boat be armed whenever it went to sea. Not that anyone gave a damn. Saratov loaded the torpedoes anyway. It seemed to him that if he didn't obey naval regulations, he had no right to demand obedience from the men.

He had always feared the implications if he and the men one day just chose not to obey. Would they then be merely a bunch of bums looking for a meal ... seagoing bums? Pirates?

He pulled his head back from the scope. The members of the attack team were looking at him expectantly, waiting for him to call ranges and bearings that they could put into the attack computer.

"No warships," he told Askold, the executive officer.

Askold was from the Ukraine, but he had chosen the Russian navy seventeen years ago, when the union collapsed. The Ukrainian navy looked like a good place to starve. He grinned at Saratov now. "Let's blast away and get the hell out."

"There should be warships," Saratov said, turning his attention back to the periscope. "The entrance to Tokyo Bay, for God's sake."

"Are you sure there are no submarines about?" Askold asked the sonar operator, who shook his head no. He looked insulted. If he had heard anything that might be a submarine amid the cacophony of screw noises around the entrance to this bay, he would have said so.

"Give me another few turns on the motors, Chief," Saratov ordered. The boat was going so slowly that the bow and stern planes were ineffective, which caused the submarine to bob up and down, making the scope rise too far out of the water and then dip under.

"Aye aye, sir."

After one more complete look around, Saratov ordered the scope lowered. He turned to the chart on the table. "There should be patrol boats, destroyers, an airplane, something."

Had he lucked into an interlude when the pickets guarding the entrance to the bay were off watch? If so, he should strike quickly and make his escape.

Askold stood beside him, staring at the chart. "Ten torpedoes... What are we going to do afterward?" He asked the question softly, actually in a whisper.

"I don't know," Saratov murmured.

"Assuming we survive the afterward."

"They've left Tokyo Bay unguarded."

Askold pinched his nose. "There must be an antisubmarine net across the entrance. That at the very least."

"There are no picket boats to open and close it. Two freighters are going in now, one coming out. It's wide open."

"How arrogant are these people?"

"We had four diesel/electric boats at sea in the Pacific when the war started. All the nuke boats are junk. If you were Japanese, wouldn't you put your antisubmarine forces around your invasion fleet?"

"Hmm, the invasion fleet. That *is* the target we were assigned," Askold said, pretending to be thinking aloud.

"I wonder if headquarters assigned all four of our boats to Vlad?"

"Perhaps," Askold said slowly. "Do you think—"

"I only know that there are no antisubmarine forces here," Saratov interrupted. "Not even a rowboat."

Saratov motioned for the periscope. When it was up, he made another complete sweep, then turned so that he was looking at the entrance to Tokyo Bay. The entrance was several miles wide. The bay was huge, over a hundred square miles.

One thing was certain: The Japanese would never expect a Russian sub to go in there. Hell, they weren't even expecting an enemy sub here at the entrance.

There was a huge refinery on the west side of the bay at Yokosuka, near the naval base. North, up the west coast of the bay, was Yokohama, the commercial shipping port. The main anchorage at Yokohama would be full of tankers, bulk freighters, container ships.

Ten torpedoes—six were in the tubes, all of which were in the bow. This class of boat had no stern tubes.

He also had four shoulder-fired RPG-9 antitank rockets that he had obtained in a trade a few years back. The rockets had two-kilo warheads, which would punch a hole in any tank on earth, but they weren't ship killers.

The boat had no deck gun, of course. There hadn't been a deck gun on a Soviet submarine since the last one was removed in the early 1950s. Deck guns made too much noise when the submarine was submerged and were of limited utility when surfaced. Still, in a crowded anchorage, with the sailors taking their time, aiming at big, well-lit, stationary targets at point-blank range, a gun certainly would be nice.

This boat was equipped with tubes to launch four surface-to-air missiles. The tubes were in the sail, and they were empty. Saratov hadn't seen a missile in years.

The two demolition experts and their plastique—he had forgotten about them.

"Down scope."

The captain surveyed the expectant faces . . . so eager, so trusting! The faith of these fools!

Saratov turned back to the chart. After studying it for a moment, he pointed with a finger. "XO, let's head eastward at slow speed. After dark, we'll surface and recharge the batteries."

"Yes, sir." Askold reached for the parallel ruler.

"Sonar, I want you to listen carefully this afternoon. Listen for destroyers, patrol boats, anything that isn't a freighter or fishing smack. Let's see what tonight brings."

He looked at his watch. Two in the afternoon.

"At three, I want to see all officers in the wardroom."

The army truck came along the paved highway at a good rate of speed. There wasn't much traffic, only a few trucks, and almost all of them going west to escape the invaders.

Yan Chernov sat on a rock beside the highway, watching the trucks come and go. He had been bleeding from a cut on his arm, but he had torn a strip off his undershirt and bound it up, and now the bleeding seemed to have stopped. Somehow he had also strained his right shoulder in the ejection, although nothing seemed to be broken or ripped. The shoulder ached fiercely; he moved it anyway, trying to work out the soreness.

God, he was tired. He was tempted to stretch out beside the road and sleep.

A bleak landscape. The breeze from the west carried clouds. The clouds obscured the sun now and the air was cool.

He was walking around to keep warm when one of the trucks flying by slammed on its brakes and stopped a hundred meters beyond him.

Yan Chernov picked up his helmet and survival vest and walked toward the truck.

His senior warrant officer got down from the cab, trotted toward Chernov. He stopped, saluted, then pounded Chernov on the back.

CHAPTER THIRTEEN

● "GENTLEMEN, THERE IS no Russian-held territory for us to return to," Pavel Saratov said to his department heads.

"There may be a few fishing villages too small for the Japanese to bother with," the youngest one said. He was no more than twenty-three or twenty-four. "We could abandon the boat and swim ashore."

"You wish to fish, do you, Krasin?"

The others pretended to chuckle. They were tightly crammed in around the small wardroom table.

Captain Saratov continued: "Tokyo Bay is the largest port in Asia, perhaps in the world. We have ten torpedoes, four RPG-9s, and a hundred kilos of plastique. I propose to enter the bay, reconnoiter, then hit them where it hurts the most."

"Captain, why don't we just sink three or four ships out here and be done with it?"

Saratov looked from face to face. Finally he said, "The question is, What can we do that will hurt them the most?"

"Sir," the engineer began, "I don't think it is reasonable to ask the men to risk their lives to kick the Japanese. The fact is, Russia is in no position to oppose Japan. We no longer have the military capability to fight a war in the Moscow suburbs, much less in the western Pacific. The men know all this. What will we gain?"

Pavel Saratov stared at the young officer, stunned. He had never heard such a comment from a junior officer. In the old days when political officers rode the ships, such a comment would have meant the immediate termination of a naval career. He tried to keep his face under control. Finally he said, "I am not asking the men to do anything. I give orders and they obey."

They said nothing to that. The execution was too fresh.

"XO?"

"You make the decision, Captain. I am with you wherever you go." That was an old, old joke. No one laughed. Askold had a weakness for terrible jokes.

"Thank you for that thought, XO. Should we go in? Your candid opinion, please."

Askold took out a pack of cigarettes, offered them around the table. Even Saratov took one. When they were smoking, the XO said, "We can hurt them worse inside. Sinking a big tanker in the harbor at Yokohama will have political implications in Japan that we can't begin to calculate. They'll probably get us before too long, no matter what we do. Let's kick them in the balls while we have a leg to swing."

"What about afterward?" the engineer asked.

Pavel Saratov didn't answer. The young officer reddened.

"I don't know," the captain said finally.

"There probably won't be an afterward," one of them said crossly to the offender. "Do you wanted it written out and signed?"

No one else had anything to say.

"Back to your duties," the captain said.

"Sir, what should I put into the evening report to Moscow?" the com officer asked.

"Nothing. There will be no evening report. There will be no radio transmissions at all unless I give a direct order."

"But, sir, we didn't make an evening report last night or the night before. Moscow may think we're dead."

"The Japanese may think that, too. Let's hope so."

Bogrov lingered after the others left. He was from Moscow, a naval academy graduate. When he and Saratov were alone, he said, "You didn't have to shoot Svechin."

"Oh, you precious little bastard, you think not, do you?"

Bogrov came to attention to deliver the riposte. He must have been thinking about it all day. "I think that—"

"Shut up! Fool! They *must* understand—all of them. I am master of this vessel. I swore an oath, and *that oath means something to me.* I will fight this boat. Every man will do his duty. I will execute any man who doesn't. No one has a choice—not me, not you, not any of them."

Bogrov said nothing.

"Everyone whines about conditions at home." The captain made a gesture of irritation. "None of that is relevant."

Pavel Saratov crossed his hands on the table in front of him and lowered his eyes to them. His voice was very low.

"If you say one negative or disrespectful word in front of the men, Bogrov, just one, I will put a bullet into that putrefying mass of gray shit you use for brains. You will obey orders to your last breath, your last drop of blood, or I'll personally stuff your corpse into a torpedo tube."

Cassidy and his pilots quickly settled into a routine at Rhein-Main Air Force Base in Germany. Every day each pilot spent at least two hours in one of the simulators running intercepts, dogfighting, handling emergencies. Another two hours were spent at the instructor's station watching a comrade fly the box, as the simulator was known. The rest of the working day they studied the manual on the aircraft and took written tests designed to reinforce what they already knew and to find any areas that needed refreshing.

The second evening in Germany, Bob Cassidy got them together as a group in a classroom near the simulator.

"I've been told that some of you want to post mail on the net. Is that right?"

"Yes, sir," three or four of them muttered.

"Okay, you may do so, but each letter must be censored by another officer. Pick your own censor. Any disputes that can't be resolved amicably by the writer and censor go to Preacher Fain for resolution. All the letters must be encrypted before posting."

Nods and smiles all around. Four or five of them looked around the room, obviously considering whom they might ask to censor their mail. Bob Cassidy continued:

"Everything we discuss in this room for the rest of the evening is classified. *Everything*."

All the faces were directed toward him again.

"We are going to Russia this weekend. We're going to be here for four more days, and we'll fly each of those days. We'll go in flights of four, with myself or Dick Guelich leading. We'll keep doing the simulators, but we want to see each of you in the air, see how you handle the plane.

"Sunday, we will fly the planes to Chita Air Base in Siberia. Tankers will escort us there, refuel us en route. We'll go armed, ready to fight our way in.

"The F-22 squadron commanders here in Germany have been more than cooperative. The enlisted technicians that we must have to maintain the planes have volunteered en masse. So have the maintenance and staff officers. I was in the unique position of having more volunteers than we could use, so, after consulting with the squadron COs, I took the very best people available. The Air Force will lift these folks and their equipment to Chita tomorrow.

"As we speak, Sentinel missile batteries are on their way to Russia. The new Russian chief of staff, Marshal Stolypin, has agreed to place these batteries in the positions where the American technicians believe they will be the most effective.

"The Russians view this squadron and the Sentinel missile batteries as tangible proof that America is willing to come to their aid. They are doing everything in their power to help us help them. The burden, quite simply, is on us to perform.

"The time has come to lay the cards on the table, to speak the bald, unvarnished truth. I don't know why you came with me—I have never tried selling before—I doubt if I'll try it again. Regardless of why you are here, you need to know that the odds are excellent that you will die in combat within the next few weeks.

"I want each of you to ask yourself, Is this what I want? Am I willing to kill other human beings? Am I willing to die to help Russia?

"You are volunteers. Tonight is the last night I will send you home with a handshake and a thank-you. There will be no recriminations, no regrets if you come to me tonight and tell me you have reconsidered and want to go home. I understand. Tomorrow is a different deal. Tomorrow you will be in the Russian Air Army. Tomorrow I can promise nothing."

They looked at each other, trying to see what the people on their right and left thought. Everyone was wearing his poker face and checking to see how well the others wore theirs.

"I can tell you, some of us will die. How many, I don't know. Only God knows. But some of us *will* die. I don't know who. Maybe all. I have no crystal ball. The fighting will be desperate. No quarter will be asked, none given. There are no rules in knife fights or aerial combat.

"We are going to be flying and fighting over some of the most godforsaken real estate on the planet. If you eject, no helicopter will come looking for you. No rescue brigade is going to saddle up to drag your ass out of the bush. The CIA says they will try to help, but I wouldn't hold my breath. If you can't take care of yourself, you are going to die out there a million miles from civilization. I doubt if anyone will ever find your corpse. Siberia is huge beyond comprehension.

"Think about it this evening. I'll be in my room if anyone wants to talk."

Bob Cassidy left then. Before he went to his room, he went to the base communications office and put in a secure call via the satellite phone to General Tuck's aide in the Pentagon, Colonel John Eatherly. He called each evening, told Eatherly everything. Tonight they discussed the pilots.

"Will any of them quit?"

"Lacy might. I don't know. We'll see."

"What about Hudek?" Eatherly asked. "I almost dropped my teeth when I saw his file. I think maybe you're taking a big chance with him."

"He's a killer, a psychopath."

"Hmmm . . ."

"Some of the best aces have been crazy as bed bugs. Guys like Albert Ball, the Red Baron . . ."

"A dozen or two I could name," Eatherly agreed.

"So I brought the guy. I hope I don't live to regret it."

"Well, if he gets too weird, you can shoot him yourself. The Russian regs are a bit more liberal than the UCMJ." The UCMJ was the Uniform Code of Military Justice, which governed discipline in the U.S. armed forces.

Cassidy laughed at that.

"At least you can laugh," Eatherly said.

"That's because I don't know how many are going to quit on me. I'd better go find out."

Bob Cassidy said good night and walked back to the VOQ. In his room he worked on paperwork undisturbed until midnight, then turned out his lights and went to bed. No one even tapped on the door.

After dark, the Russian submarine *Admiral Kolchak* raised its snorkel and started its diesel engines. The boat was twenty miles east of the island of Oshima, outside the entrance of Tokyo Bay. Saratov or the XO kept a constant watch through the periscope. After observing the lights of several freighters, Saratov concluded that visibility was down to about three miles in light rain. Every ship up there was radar-equipped, and the Japanese probably had shore-based radar to help keep track of shipping, so surfacing was out of the question.

He worried about the destroyers that he couldn't see. Was it carelessness, arrogance, hubris that caused the Japanese to leave the door to Tokyo Bay unguarded? Or had they set a trap, a trap to catch a fool?

Saratov had no combat experience, of course. The Soviet/Russian navy had not fired a shot since 1945, before the captain was born. He felt as green as grass, completely out of his element.

Had he assessed this situation correctly, or was there something that he was missing?

Right now a little experience would be a comfort. He consoled himself with the thought that the Japanese didn't have any more experience than he did.

His neck and arms began to ache. He kept his eyes glued to the scope, kept it moving.

Two hours later, he was still at it. He wanted as much of a charge on the batteries as possible before he secured the diesel engines and lowered the snorkel.

If only this were his old nuclear-powered *Alfa* boat! He could stay on the bottom of Tokyo Bay until the food ran out. Not so with this diesel/electric museum artifact; *Admiral Kolchak* could remain submerged for about seven days with the electric motors barely turning over. Even with the engines off, lying on the bottom, seven days was about the limit—the air would be so foul that the men would be in danger of death by asphyxiation.

Every hour he was in the bay the chances of remaining undetected diminished. He had no time to waste. He must either attack the Japanese or sneak away out to sea.

He worked his way toward the entrance, waiting for a ship to come along that was going in. If the Japanese had passive listening devices—hydrophones—at the entrance, the sound of a freighter rumbling through might hide the sound of this boat.

He had to play it like the Japs were listening, because they might be. The damned fools *should be,* anyway.

Midnight passed, then one o'clock. The XO relieved Saratov at the scope for fifteen minutes while he relieved himself, looked at the chart, and drank a hot cup of tea.

It was past two when he saw a big container ship, over fifty thousand tons, steaming along the channel to enter the bay. It was bearing down on the sub, making about ten knots. He was tempted to torpedo it then and there.

No. We can do more damage inside.

He got out of the container ship's way, then muttered to the officer of the deck, "This one. We go in with this one."

He kept the snorkel up. Running at ten knots on the battery would quickly drain it, and he couldn't afford that. On the other hand, the boat made a lot more noise with the diesels running than it did on the battery. If the Japs had hydrophones at the entrance to the bay, the odds were good that they would hear the sub.

Even if the Japanese hear it, Pavel Saratov thought, they may not recognize the sound for what it is. Or they may ignore it. He needed a nearly full charge on the battery going in. Tomorrow night he would have little time to put a charge on, and he might need every amp to evade antisubmarine forces. He thought the problem through and made his choice.

He turned the boat and fell in about five hundred meters behind the freighter. It was huge, and lit up like a small city.

With the scope magnification turned up, he could read the words on the stern: LINDA SUE, MONROVIA. There were actually two little spotlights on the stern rail that illuminated the name.

He had spent the evening studying the chart of the bay. He recognized the turn in the channel off Uraga Point and the naval anchorage. He stayed with *Linda Sue* as she steamed slowly and majestically along the channel that would take her to the container piers at Yokohama or Tokyo. There were numerous small craft in the bay, despite the limited visibility and rain—launches, fishing boats, police cruisers.

Several small fishing craft were silhouetted against the city lights on the western shore of the bay, which ran from horizon to horizon. Then he saw a boat anchored just outside the shipping channel. Reluctantly, he ordered the diesel secured and the snorkel lowered. The sound of the diesel exhausting through the snorkel was loud if one was on the surface listening, so Saratov decided to play it safe.

He cruised up to Yokohama and examined the hundred or so ships waiting to get to the piers for loading and unloading. A forest of ships from nations all over the world—all except Russia. Well, they were all fair game as far as he was concerned, discharging and taking on cargo in a belligerent port.

It took five hours to cruise up the bay, then back south, where he picked a spot to settle into the bottom mud a kilometer offshore from a refinery on the northern edge of Yokosuka, north of the naval base. A pier led from the refinery out into the water about a half kilometer. Two conventional tankers were moored to it, but at the very end rested a liquid natural gas—LNG—tanker, with a huge pressure vessel amidships.

He had a splitting headache. He stood in the control room massaging his neck, rubbing his eyes.

No one had much else to say. When they did want to communicate, they whispered, as if the Japanese were in the next room with a glass against the wall. Perhaps they sensed they were on the edge of something, something large and fierce and infinitely dangerous.

Saratov smiled to himself, went to his tiny stateroom, and stretched out on the bunk. Although the men didn't know it, the boat was probably safer in the mud of Tokyo Bay than it had been at any time since the start of hostilities.

Tonight. They would roll the dice tonight.

In the meantime, he had to sleep.

The two navy enlisted demolition divers sat across from Pavel Saratov in the wardroom, sipping tea. It was late afternoon. Dirty dishes were stacked to one side of the table.

The demolition men were magnificent physical specimens. Of medium height, they didn't have five pounds of fat between them. With thick necks, bulging biceps, and heavily veined weight lifter's arms, these two certainly didn't look like sailors.

"Where did the navy get you guys?" Saratov asked.

"We were Spetsnaz, Captain," one of them said. His name was stenciled on his shirt: Martos. The other was named Filimonov. "They disestablished our unit, discharged everybody. We had a choice—a gang of truck hijackers or the seagoing navy."

"Hmmm," the captain said, sipping tea.

Filimonov explained. "The hijackers were the better deal. Less work, more money. Unfortunately, they liked to brag and throw money around. We thought they would not be with us long. Last we heard only a few are still alive, hiding in the forest."

"Capitalism is a hard life."

"Very competitive, sir."

"I want you to destroy a refinery. Could you do that?"

"A refinery! With the plastique?"

"I thought you might go out through the air lock in the torpedo room, swim ashore—the distance is about a kilometer—plant the explosives, then swim back to us."

They looked at each other. "It would be possible, sir. When?"

"Tonight. As soon as it's dark. How long would it take?"

"The longer we have, the better job we can make of it."

"I want to start fires they can't easily extinguish, do maximum damage."

"Ahh, maximum damage." Martos grinned at the captain, then at Filimonov. Half his teeth were gray steel.

Filimonov's face twisted into a grimace. It occurred to Saratov that this was his grin.

"Give us six hours and we will start the biggest fire Tokyo has ever seen."

"Six hours," Filimonov agreed. "Maximum damage."

"Okay," Pavel Saratov said. "Six hours from the moment you exit the air lock."

"We do not have our usual equipment aboard, Captain. Without some kind of homer, we will have difficulty finding the boat on our return."

"Any suggestions?"

"We could make a small float, perhaps, anchor it to the air-lock hatch."

"What if the submarine is on the surface?"

"That would be best for us, sir."

Saratov made his decision. "We'll take the risk. We will surface at oh-three-thirty."

"We'll find the boat, sir."

"After we surface, we will wait fifteen minutes for you. If you do not return during those fifteen minutes, we will leave without you."

"If we do not return, Captain, we will be dead."

Pavel Saratov went to the torpedo room to watch Martos and Filimonov exit through the air lock. Both men had on black wet suits and scuba gear. The plastique, fuses, and detonators were contained in two waterproof bags, one for each man. Two sailors could barely lift each bag.

Both swimmers had knives strapped to their wrists. Saratov wished he had guns to give them, but he didn't. The Spetsnaz had waterproof guns and ammo for their frogmen, but navy divers weren't so equipped.

"Don't fret it, Captain. The knives are quite enough. We are competent, and very careful."

They went into the air lock one at a time. Martos was first. He climbed the ladder into the lock, donned his flippers, then with one hand pulled the bag of explosives that the sailors held up into the lock. The sailors dogged the hatch behind him.

Five minutes later, it was Filimonov's turn. He, too, had no trouble pulling the bag of explosives the last three feet into the lock. He gave the sailors a thumbs-up as they closed the hatch.

When he heard the outside hatch close for the second time, Pavel Saratov looked at his watch. It was 21:35. At 03:30, he would surface the boat, twenty-four hours after he had secured the snorkel.

Saratov went back to the control room. The XO and the chief were there. "They are gone. At oh-three-thirty we will rise to periscope depth, take a look around, then surface. I want two men on deck to help get the Spetsnaz swimmers aboard. I want two more men in the forward torpedo room to stand by with the rocket-propelled grenades. If we see a target for the grenades, they can go topside and shoot them. When we get the swimmers aboard and the refinery goes up, we will go to Yokohama and fire our torpedoes into that tea party."

The faces in the control room were tense, strained.

"We will give a good account of ourselves, men. We will do maximum damage. Then we are going to squirt this boat out through the bay's asshole and run like hell."

Two or three of them grinned. Most just looked worried. They have too much time on their hands, the captain thought. Too much time to sit idly thinking of Russia's problems, and of girlfriends or wives and children caught in a Japanese invasion. If they are not given something to do soon, they will be unable to do anything.

"I expect every man to do his job precisely the way he has been trained. We will be shooting torpedoes and shoulder-fired rockets. Enemy warships may detect us. Things will be hectic. Just concentrate on doing your job, whatever it is."

"Aye aye, sir," the XO, Askold, said.

"Chief, visit every compartment. Tell everyone the plan, repeat what I just said. Every single man must do his job. Go over every man's job with him."

"Aye aye, Captain."

"XO, I want another meal served at oh-one hundred. The best we can do. Would you see to it, please?" All this activity would use precious oxygen—the air was already foul—but Saratov felt the morale boost would be worth it. Using oxygen and energy that would be required later if the Japanese found them before they surfaced was a calculated risk. Life is a calculated risk, he told himself. "Better break out the carbon-dioxide absorbers, too."

"Yes, sir."

"Bogrov, send this message to Moscow when we surface." He passed a sheet of paper to the communications officer. "I want the navy and the Russian nation to know what these men have done, to know that each and every one of them has done his duty as a Russian sailor."

"I'll encode it now, sir," Bogrov said. "Have it ready."

"Fine."

When the Russian sailors aboard *Admiral Kolchak* cleaned up after the postmidnight meal, they had nothing to do but wait. They had had all day and all evening to prepare for action. All loose gear was stowed and the equipment had been checked and rechecked. Every man was properly dressed, red lights were on throughout the boat in preparation for surfacing, each man was at his post.

So they waited, watching the clock, each man sweating, thinking of home or the action to come, wishing for . . . well, for it to be over. The uncertainty was unnerving. No one knew how it would go, if the Japanese would find and attack them, if they would make it to the open sea, if a P-3 or destroyer would pin them, if they would live or die.

Many had girls or wives in Petropavlosk, so there was a lot of letter writing. They thought of home, of Russia in the summer, the long, languid days, the insects humming, the steppe covered with grain, girls smiling, kissing in the dark. . . . It was amazing how dear home and family became when you realized that you might never see them again.

There was a scuffle in the engine room between two young sailors, and the chief handled that. They called for him and whispers went around; Pavel Saratov pretended not to notice.

He lounged on a small pull-out stool, with his head resting against the chart table. He kept his eyes closed. Several of the men thought he was asleep, but he wasn't. He was forcing himself to keep his eyes closed so that he would not look again at his watch or the chronometer on the bulkhead, not be mesmerized by the sweeping of the second hand, not watch the minute hand creep agonizingly along.

The Spetsnaz divers were out there now, planting charges. The refinery was supposed to go up at 03:45. If it didn't, there was nothing he could do about it. Oh, he could squirt a few grenades that way, but the damage they could do was minimal.

It was possible that the Japanese had captured the Spetsnaz divers and were right this minute organizing a search for the submarine that had delivered them. Possible, though improbable. That men capable of taking Martos or Filimonov alive were guarding this particular refinery was highly unlikely.

What if the Japanese spotted the sub from the air?

Someone in a plane, looking down, might have seen the shape of the submarine through the muddy brown water. They might be waiting in the refinery. They might have antisubmarine forces gathered, be waiting for the boat to move before they sprung the trap.

They may have killed Martos and Filimonov. They might be dead now. If they are, I would never know, Saratov thought. They would just not return, and the refinery would not explode.

Someone was fidgeting with a pencil, tapping it.

Saratov frowned. The tapping stopped.

Getting the sub out of the mud of this shallow bay would be a trick. It would probably broach. Well, as long as no one was nearby.... But he would have to be ready to go, keep her on the surface, take her by the Yokohama anchorage shooting torpedoes.... He and the XO had the headings and times worked out, and the XO would keep constant track of their position, so Saratov wouldn't be distracted by navigation at a critical moment.

He took a deep breath. Soon. Very soon . . .

All refineries are essentially alike: industrial facilities designed to heat crude oil under pressure, converting it to usable products. When Martos and Filimonov emerged from the water of Tokyo Bay carrying their bags of explosives, they scurried to cover and paused to look for refinery workers or guards. There were a few workers about, but only a few. Of guards, they saw not one.

Almost invisible in their black wet suits, the two Russian frogmen moved like cats through the facility, pausing in shadows and crouching in corners. Satisfied that they were unobserved and would remain that way for a few moments, they began assessing what they were seeing. Years ago, training for just such a day in the unforeseeable future, they had learned a good deal about refineries.

Now they pointed out various features of this facility to each other. They said nothing, merely pointed.

The absence of guards bothered Martos, who began to suspect a trap. He looked carefully for remote surveillance cameras, or infrared or motion detectors. He removed a small set of binoculars from his bag and stripped away the waterproof cover. With these he scanned the towers and pipelines, the walls and windows. Nothing. Not a single camera. This offended him, somehow. Japan was at war, a refinery was a vital industrial facility, a certain target for a belligerent enemy, and there were no guards! They thought so little of Russia's military ability they didn't bother to post guards. Amazing.

The two frogmen separated.

They took their time selecting the position for the charges and setting them, working carefully, painstakingly, while maintaining a vigilant lookout. Several times, they had to take cover while a worker proceeded through the area in which they happened to be.

Martos had allowed plenty of time for the work that had to be done. Still, with so few people about, it went more quickly than he thought it would.

A little more than an hour after he and Filimonov came ashore, he had his last charge set and the timer ticking away. He went looking for Filimonov, whom he had last seen going toward a huge field of several dozen large white storage tanks that stood beside the refinery.

He was moving carefully, keeping under cover as much as possible and pausing frequently to scan for people, when he first saw the guard.

The guard was wearing some kind of uniform, and a waterproof rain jacket and hat. He had arrived in a small car with a beacon on the roof. When Martos first saw him he was standing beside the car looking idly around, tugging and pulling on his rain gear, adjusting it against the gently falling mist. He reached back inside the car for a clipboard and flashlight.

Now he strolled along the edge of the tank farm, looking at this and that, in no particular hurry.

Did someone mention a war?

Martos scurried across the road into the safety of the shadows of the huge round tanks. He moved as quickly as prudence would allow.

Where was Filimonov?

A large pipeline, maybe a half a meter in diameter, came out of the refinery and ran in among the tanks, with branches off to each tank. Lots of valves.

Filimonov liked pipelines. A ridiculously small explosive charge could ruin a safety shutoff valve and fracture the line.

Martos retraced his steps, looking for his partner. He could just go back to the water's edge and wait, of course, but if he found Filimonov and helped set a charge or two, they would be finished sooner. And it just wasn't good practice to leave a man working on his own without a lookout.

He eased his head around a tank and glimpsed the small beam of light from a flashlight. The guard!

Around the tank, moving carefully in the darkness, feeling his way ... He waited a few seconds before he looked again. There, now the guard had passed him, walking slowly, looking. . . . Had the guard seen something? Or was he just—

A shape blacker than the surrounding darkness materialized behind the guard and merged with him. The flashlight fell and went out.

Now the guard was dragged out of sight between the tanks.

Martos went that way.

He found Filimonov sitting beside the guard, holding his head in his hands. Even in that dim light, Martos could see the unnatural angle of the guard's head, the glistening blood covering the front of the rain jacket. A glance was enough—Filimonov had cut the guard's throat, almost severed his head.

But why was Filimonov sitting here like this?

"Let's go, Viktor."

Filimonov's shoulders shook.

God, the man was crying! "Viktor, let's go. What is this?"

"It's a girl!"

"What?"

"The guard is a *woman*! Look for yourself."

"Well ..."

"A *woman* guard! Of all the stupid ..."

"Let's go, Viktor. Let's finish and get out of here."

"A *woman* ..." Filimonov stared at the corpse. He didn't move.

A tinny radio voice squawked, jabbering a phrase or two in Japanese, then ended with a high interrogative tone. The guard must be wearing a radio!

Martos found the bag. Checked inside. One charge left. Working quickly, he affixed it to the base of a nearby tank, out of sight of the guard's body. He inserted a detonator into the plastique and wired it to a timer. He checked the timer with his pencil flash. It was ticking nicely, apparently keeping perfect time.

He took Filimonov's arm and pulled him to his feet.

"We have no time for this. She is dead. We cannot bring her back."

The radio on the guard's belt clicked and jabbered.

"A *woman*. I never killed a ... Not even in Afghanistan. I didn't know—"

"Viktor Grigorovich—"

"Never!"

Martos hit him then, in the face. That was the only way. Filimonov offered no resistance.

He seized Filimonov's arm and shoved him toward the bay.

"They are going to come looking for her," said Martos.

"She doesn't weigh forty kilos," Filimonov muttered softly, still trying to understand.

When Jiro Kimura wrote to his wife, Shizuko, he didn't know when she would get the letter, if ever. All mail to Japan was censored. This letter would certainly not pass the censor, a nonflying lieutenant colonel whose sole function in life was to write reports for senior officers to sign and to read other people's mail.

Jiro wrote the letter anyway. He began by telling Shizuko that he loved and missed her, then told her about the flight to Khabarovsk, during which he had shot down an airliner.

His commanding officer and the air wing commander had tried to humiliate him when he returned. They were outraged that he had questioned Control.

"The prime minister might have been there. He is personally directing the military effort. He may have given the order for you to shoot down that airplane."

Jiro hadn't been very contrite. He had just killed an unknown number of defenseless people and he hadn't come to grips with that. He stood with his head bowed slightly. It was a polite bow at best. No doubt that contributed to the colonels' ire. The wing commander thundered:

"You have sworn to obey orders, Kimura. You have no choice, none whatsoever. The Bushido code demands complete, total, unthinking, unquestioning obedience. You dishonor us all when you question the orders of your honorable superiors."

Kimura said nothing.

His skipper said, loudly, "An enemy airplane in the war zone is a legitimate target, Kimura. Destruction of enemy airplanes is your job. The nation has provided you with an expensive jet fighter in order that you might do your job. You dishonor your nation and yourself when you fail to obey every order instantly, whether the matter be large or small. You dishonor me! I will not have you dishonoring me and this unit. You will obey! Do you understand?"

Jiro wrote this diatribe in the letter, just as he remembered it. He had felt shame wash over him as the two colonels ranted. His cheeks colored slightly, which infuriated him. His commanding officer misinterpreted his emotions and decided he had had enough of the verbal hiding, so he fell silent. The wing commander also stopped soon after.

Jiro Kimura felt ashamed of himself and his comrades, these Japanese soldiers, with their Bushido code and their delicate sense of honor which required the death of everyone on an airliner *leaving* the battle zone because someone, somewhere gave an order.

They were frightened, little men. Little in every sense of the word, Jiro reflected, and wrote that in his letter to his wife.

He was ashamed of himself because he lacked the moral courage to disobey an order that he thought both illegal and obscene. This also he confessed to Shizuko.

As he paused in his writing and sat thinking, he felt the shame wash over him again. The problem was that he was not a pure Japanese. Those damned Americans and their Air Force Academy! He had absorbed more than just the classroom subjects. The ethics of that foreign place were torturing him here.

The Japanese said he had dishonored his superiors and comrades by his failure to obey. The Americans would say he dishonored himself because he obeyed an illegal, immoral order. The only thing everyone would agree upon was the dishonor.

An American would call a reporter and make a huge stink. Maybe he should do that.

He felt like shit. He wasn't Japanese enough to kill himself or American enough to ruin his superiors. That left him writing a letter to Shizuko.

"Dearest wife . . ."

He loved her desperately. As he wrote, he wondered if he would ever see her again.

CHAPTER FOURTEEN

●THEY SAT IN the mud near the hole in the chain-link fence that they had cut going in. Martos arranged his scuba gear so that he could slip it on in seconds. Filimonov, on the other hand, sat morosely by his gear, staring out at the blackness of the bay.

Martos checked the fluorescent hands of his watch: 01:12.

They had finished sooner than he thought they would.

The submarine would not rise off the floor of the bay until 03:30. Visibility in the muddy water was limited to a few feet, so their flash-lights would be of little use finding the submarine underwater. He knew roughly where it was, a kilometer beyond that liquid natural gas tanker at the end of the tanker pier. Still, he would never find it sub-merged. They would have to wait for the sub to surface.

Nor was it wise to swim out into the bay now, then spend two hours fighting the currents and tide, drifting God knows where.

Although the refinery was well lit, the two men were nearly invisible on this mud flat between the water and the fence. Black wet suits, a black night, dark mud, rain misting down . . . The tanker pier looked like a bridge to nowhere, with lights every yard or two, stretching out across the black water to the anchored LNG carrier. Now that was a weird-looking ship, with that giant pressure vessel amidships.

Martos eyed his partner.

"Viktor, it wasn't your fault."

Filimonov had reacted to a perceived threat without thinking. He saw a guard, wearing rain gear, possibly armed, so he had acted auto-matically.

The other guards would come looking for the woman soon. When she failed to check in on the radio, they would probably assume that the radio had failed, perhaps a dead battery. They would wait a rea-sonable amount of time, then expect her to check in on her car radio. Finally, they would come looking.

Damn! Things had been going so well.

Even if the security force found some of the demolition charges, they would not find them all. Not before they blew. Yet every one they found was one less to explode, that much less damage to the installation.

"We must expect the unexpected. Everything doesn't always go as planned."

"I was setting a charge," Filimonov muttered. "She surprised me."

"See, it wasn't your fault. You didn't know the guard was a woman. You are not the Japanese son of a whore who hired this woman, put her in a uniform, and sent her to guard a valuable national asset in wartime."

Filimonov sighed. He laid down on his back in the mud. He stretched his arms out as if he were on a cross.

"No one in Russia would be so stupid," Martos said.

Filimonov didn't say anything. This withdrawal bothered Martos.

"You *must* forget this, Viktor. I am your friend. You must *listen*."

The minutes passed in silence. There was only the lapping of the tiny waves at the water's edge and the faint, distant hooting of a foghorn. Martos could feel the feathery caress of the mist on his face, and the miserable, slithery cold of the wet suit, which he had learned to tolerate years and years ago.

A guard car came down the street, turned the corner, and disappeared in the direction of the tanks. In moments they would find the dead guard's vehicle.

Martos looked at his watch: 01:47.

Ten minutes. Within ten minutes, they would find the body, call for help.

He toyed with the idea of going back to kill these men. Or women. Unfortunately, they would probably call in the alarm to their office, wherever that was, before he could kill them both. Even if he did eliminate them, someone else would come looking.

Martos pulled the top of the wet suit over his head and arranged it around his face. "Let's get ready, Viktor."

Filimonov didn't move.

Martos kicked his partner in the side—hard. "Enough! Get ready. I order you. Put on your gear."

Filimonov still didn't move.

"You want to stay here? Do you want me to kill you, Viktor Grigorovich? Dead is the only way you can stay on this beach."

Filimonov turned his head.

"You are my friend, Viktor. My best friend. I know you did not mean to kill a woman—this woman, any woman. I know that God forgives you, Viktor. I know that somewhere in heaven this very minute your mother forgives you. She knows you did not intend to kill a woman. She knows what was in your heart."

Another guard car came racing down the street, squealed its brakes on the turn, and disappeared, going toward the tanks.

"They have found her, Viktor. They are doing for her what must be done. It is time for us to leave. We have responsibilities, too. The captain will be waiting."

He tugged at Viktor's arm. "There are fifty men on that submarine. They will keep the faith. They will be vulnerable there on the surface, waiting for us. We must keep faith with them."

Nothing.

Martos donned his flippers, put on the scuba tanks, arranged the mask on his face. He tested the regulator, took a breath from the mouthpiece.

"Okay, you bastard. Lie here and get captured. Betray your country. Betray your shipmates. Over a dead guard. You stupid bastard. Your mother was a slut. A whore. She was sucking cocks the night some drunk stuck his—"

Filimonov came for him. Martos dashed for the water.

He moved as fast as he could in the tanks and flippers. Unburdened by gear, Filimonov was quicker. He dragged Martos off his feet in the shallows and went for his throat.

God, he was strong. Fingers like steel bands.

Martos was at a severe disadvantage. He wanted to use just enough force to cause Filimonov to cease and desist; Filimonov wanted to kill.

Martos kneed him in the balls. Filimonov kept coming, got fingers around Martos's throat, began to squeeze.

Martos was under six inches of water, but he didn't have the mouthpiece in. Not that he could have breathed, with Filimonov squeezing his neck. He pounded on Filimonov's head with his fist, tried to get a thumb in his eye.

He was losing strength. The vise around his neck tightened relentlessly.

He pulled his knife and swung at Filimonov's head—once, twice, three times—and felt the pressure on his neck ease. He swung the butt of the knife again with all his strength.

Filimonov lost his grip on Martos's neck.

One last mighty smash of the butt end of the knife into his head caused Filimonov to lose consciousness.

The faceplate of his mask was shattered. Martos discarded it.

Lights. A spotlight! A car, driving along the fence, the driver inspecting the wire with a spotlight.

Martos got a firm grip on the headpiece of Filimonov's wet suit, turned him face up, and dragged him into deeper water. When the water reached his waist he inserted the scuba mouthpiece in his mouth and started swimming, towing Filimonov.

The tide was strong and the night was black. Martos swam with one hand, towing Filimonov with the other, looking over his shoulder at the refinery and trying to swim straight away from it. The salt spray stung his eyes.

Why didn't Filimonov regain consciousness?

He concentrated on swimming, on breathing rhythmically, on maintaining a smooth, sustainable pace. Occasionally he glanced over his shoulder.

Filimonov didn't try to help, didn't move. A concussion?

Two cars were at the fence, near the hole, their headlights pointing over the water. A spotlight played across the water. It went by the swimming men. They were too far out to be seen from the shore.

The Japanese would find Filimonov's flippers and scuba tanks soon, if they hadn't already. They would call in an alarm.

Damn, damn, damn.

If another P-3 caught the submarine in this shallow bay, they were all dead men.

Hell, we're all going to die. We're all condemned. That is the truth that this fool Filimonov doesn't understand.

"Mr. Krasin, take the boat up to periscope depth."

"Aye aye, Captain."

Krasin was the OOD. He began giving orders.

Everyone was at their post. Everyone was ready. For the last hour no one had said much. They had watched the clock, chewed fingernails, fretted silently. Now the waiting was over. Live or die, it was time to get to it.

The submarine refused to come out of the mud on the floor of the bay. Without way on, the only means of lifting the boat was positive buoyancy. More and more air was forced into the tanks, forcing out the water that held the submarine below the surface.

The keel of the sub was eighty feet down, just below periscope depth. She's going to go up like a cork, the captain thought, resigned.

Seconds later the submarine broke free of the mud's grasp and rose quickly, too quickly.

"All ahead flank," the captain ordered. "Full down on the bow planes."

The submarine broached anyway, broke the surface. Then the water pouring back into the tanks took effect, and the boat got enough way on for the bow and stern planes to get a grip on the water. They helped pull her back under.

"Watch it, Chief," the captain said sharply, well aware that if they lost control now and drove the sub's bow into the mud, they would probably have to abandon ship.

The chief knew his boat. He got her stabilized and let her sink to periscope depth.

"Up scope," Pavel Saratov ordered, as if nothing out of the ordinary had happened.

After a quick 360-degree sweep, the captain said, almost as an afterthought, "Perhaps we should stop engines, Mr. Krasin, wait for the Spetsnaz divers. They will not be pleased if we leave without them."

The XO winked the OOD.

"Stop engines."

Saratov walked the scope around again, taking his time, looking carefully.

Well, he could see the lights of the refinery, the tankers at the tanker pier, the LNG carrier. Yokohama glowed in the misty darkness. Several dozen anchored ships were in view. The lights of Tokyo farther north were invisible in the misting rain and fog. He saw no ships or boats anchored close by.

Saratov backed off from the scope and gestured with his palm for it to be lowered. "Gentlemen, I suggest we surface and collect our swimmers."

The OOD gave the necessary orders, and the submarine rose slowly from the sea.

Martos was very tired. Filimonov had not moved since he knocked him out, and the current was running toward the entrance of the bay, which meant Martos had to swim north constantly in order to remain more or less in one place.

He had not managed to remain in that one place. When the submarine surfaced, he was at least a half mile south of it, swimming toward it while towing Filimonov.

He spit out the mouthpiece. "It wouldn't hurt"—he took a breath—"for you to help . . . swim a little . . . you large piece . . . of horse's dung."

Filimonov remained motionless. Martos knew he had just dinged his friend four or five times with the butt end of his knife, hardly enough to stun a mouse. This hardheaded ox had been hit harder than that in barracks brawls and never even blinked.

He heard the submarine break water. Heard the splash of a large object and heard the sucking sound as it went back under.

He didn't hear it surface the second time, but he heard the metallic clanging of the conning tower hatch being thrown open. He was already swimming in that direction, dragging Filimonov.

"You foolish . . . simple . . . son of a bitch! Help me."

Finally he stopped. Ensuring that Filimonov's head didn't go under, he shouted, "Hey! Over here."

They would never hear him. He had a flashlight on his belt, so he reached for it. Gone, probably in the fight.

Filimonov's light . . . still there.

Something unnatural about the big man. Martos turned the flashlight on and waved it in the general direction of the sub.

"Viktor, speak to me. Say something, my friend."

He shined the flashlight in Viktor's face. The glare of the light on the white skin took getting used to. It was several seconds before Martos's eyes could focus.

Filimonov's eyes were open, unfocused. They did not track the light. The pupils did not respond. Viktor Filimonov was dead.

What? How . . .

"Viktor, you . . . you . . ."

The sub glided up. The wash pushed him away from it. Two men on deck threw a line. Keeping a firm grip on Filimonov's wet suit, Martos wrapped the line once around his wrist and called, "Pull us aboard."

"What's wrong with him?"

"Grab him. Pull him aboard."

After they pulled Filimonov from the water, they dragged Martos onto the slimy steel deck. He was so tired he could barely summon strength to stand.

"What's wrong with him?"

"He's dead. Get him below."

The sailors lowered Filimonov's body through the torpedo reloading hatch. Martos was still on deck when one of the large storage tanks at the refinery exploded. At this distance the noise was just a pop, but the rising fireball looked spectacular, even against the background lights of Yokosuka.

"The captain wants to see you, on the bridge," someone told him.

Filimonov's body lay on the deck walkway, between the racks holding the spare torpedoes. The corpsman was examining it. Martos made his way aft.

From the control room he climbed into the conning tower, then on up the ladder onto the tiny bridge, or cockpit, atop the sail. Pavel Saratov was watching the receding refinery through his binoculars.

"Sir."

"How did it go?"

"We set the charges. Filimonov killed a guard—a woman. Cut her throat. He became morose. We fought. I thought I knocked him out. Apparently, I killed him."

Saratov shifted his attention from the fires of the refinery, which was receding behind, to the lights of a ship far ahead, off the port bow. "Come right ten degrees," he said to the sailor beside him, who was wearing a sound-powered telephone headset.

The sailor repeated the order into the headset, then confirmed, "Right ten, sir."

Martos wanted to get it off his chest. "When he was a boy, maybe seven or eight, Viktor Filimonov's mother was killed. In Odessa. Some sailor slashed her. She was a whore. The sailor sliced her eighty-nine times. She bled to death."

"So . . ." the captain said.

"The authorities took Viktor to identify his mother's body. I don't think he ever forgot how she looked, sliced to ribbons, her entrails coming out, blood everywhere. . . . Sometimes he talked about it."

"I want to hear about this, later," the captain said. "You did a good job on the refinery. It is burning nicely. I wanted you to know."

"Yes, sir."

"Did you mean to kill your partner?"

"No, sir. Absolutely not."

"We'll talk later. You may go below."

Martos went.

The captain studied the ship off the port bow. It looked small, about fifteen thousand tons. Not worth a torpedo. They could do much better.

"Not this one," he said to the talker standing beside him. "All ahead two-thirds." The talker repeated the order, and in seconds Pavel Saratov felt the diesels respond.

Too bad about the swimmer.

Several miles behind another fireball rose out of the refinery complex.

The wind in his hair felt good. Saratov inhaled deeply, savoring the musky aroma of tidal flats and salty sea air and the tang of the land.

Martos was in the tiny galley eating bread when the corpsman found him. The diesel engines made the surfaced boat throb. There was just enough swell inside the bay to make it pitch and roll a bit.

"Look at this," the corpsman said. He opened his hand. "He had this between his teeth."

It was a red plastic capsule, waterproof, but ruptured.

"Poison," Martos whispered.

"Poison?"

"A suicide pill. He must have had it in his mouth."

"Why would . . ."

"He must have been thinking about it," Martos said slowly. "Maybe he accidently bit it when I whacked him on the head. You bite it, death is nearly instantaneous."

The corpsman looked at Martos strangely, then turned away.

"An accident," Martos murmured to himself. "He must have put it in his mouth as we sat there waiting. . . .

"Oh damn!"

The reporter's name was Christine something. She looked like a caricature. Her hair was immaculately coiffed and lacquered so heavily that it reflected the television lights. She wore some kind of horrible safari jacket, something discount stores sell for two-thirds off the day after Christmas.

Her makeup was heavily layered to cover the deep lines that radiated around her eyes. Caked, gaudy lipstick made her mouth look like an open wound. She glanced once at the camera, then stood staring at Bob Cassidy, waiting. She was the pool reporter, chosen by her colleagues to ask the questions because Cassidy had been willing to subject his pilots to only one interview.

The television lights were hot. A trickle of sweat ran down Cassidy's face. He wiped it away.

Someone must have said something to the reporter through her earphone, because she started talking.

"Colonel, I understand you are leading the Americans hired to fly the F-22s?"

He nodded, once.

"If I may ask, why you?"

They were looking for a bastard without a family, and they found me. He didn't say that, of course. "I volunteered."

"Why?"

"Why not?"

"How many Americans are with you?"

"About one hundred and fifty."

"When do you plan to go to Russia?"

"Soon."

"You aren't very talkative, are you, Colonel?"

"That wasn't one of the qualifications for the job."

"How much are the Russians paying you?"

"You'll have to ask the State Department that question. Or the Russians."

"Rumor has it that you get a bonus for every plane you shoot down. Is that true?"

"Ask the Russians. They sign the checks."

"Isn't that blood money?"

"If they pay it, I assume the money would be for the plane, not the pilot. A plane doesn't bleed, does it?"

"What do you hope to accomplish in Russia?"

"Shoot down Japanese planes."

She made a sign to the cameraman, and the red light on the camera went out.

"You are being uncooperative, Colonel."

"This isn't the NFL. I'm here only because the State Department said to make myself available. I am available."

"I asked to shoot these interviews with an F-22 as background. You refused. Why is that?"

"They aren't my airplanes, ma'am."

"We asked to talk to the African-American pilot. Which one is he?" She glanced at her list.

" '*The* African-American.' That is really grotesque. I'll pretend you didn't say it."

"You do have a black pilot, don't you?"

"Alas, no."

"Why not?"

"I don't know. It just happened. I'm politically incorrect. Rip me to shreds."

"Couldn't you say something about Russia? Perhaps you had a Russian grandparent . . . something about aiding in the fight for freedom, something like that?"

Cassidy looked grim. "You say it," he told her, then took off his mike and got out of the hot seat.

Of course, the person the reporters were most interested in interviewing was Lee Foy, but he was having none of it. He was nowhere to be found. Cassidy asked Preacher Fain where Foy was, and was told, "Foy said something about finding a whorehouse. I'm to say that to this reporter if she asks."

"Okay."

Apparently the reporters didn't know he was an ordained minister, so Christine didn't ask all those juicy questions that Fain feared she would. Fain tried to play it straight. He was here to help keep peace in the world, doing his duty, fighting for victims of aggression, defending an American ally, et cetera.

After fifteen minutes, Preacher looked greatly relieved as he got out of the chair.

Most of the pilots gave Christine more of the same, until she got to Clay Lacy. When asked why he was here, he said, "The fighter-pilot ethos has a compelling purity, a rare strain of selflessness and self-sacrifice that too often we lose sight of in modern life. I find it"—he searched for words—"almost religious. Don't you agree?"

Christine made a noise.

Lacy continued. "I want to see how I will face a competent, couragous, dedicated warrior who seeks to kill me. Will I have enough courage? Will I be bold? Will I fight with honor, and die with honor if that is required? These are serious questions that bedevil many people in this perverted age. I'm sure you've thought about these things at length. Haven't you?"

Christine sat staring, her mouth open. Lacy waited politely. "I see," she finally managed.

"I'm delighted that you do," he told her warmly. "Most of these pilots"—he flipped his hand disdainfully—"are merely flying assassins, out to kill and be paid for it. They have no ideas, no insight, no intellectual life. I am not like them. I explore the inner man."

When Lacy went over to the colonel after his interview, he asked, still deadly serious, "How did I do, sir?"

"Fine, Lacy. Fine. You are now the unit public affairs officer."

Aaron Hudek gave a performance that was the equal of Lacy's, or perhaps even better. When asked why he had volunteered, he told Christine, "This is the only war we have."

"How do you think you will feel, killing a fellow human being?"

"It'll be glorious." Hudek gave Christine a wolfish grin. "I can't wait. I'll blow those yellow Jap bastards to kingdom come so goddamn fast they'll never know what hit 'em. Just you watch."

Stunned, Christine recovered quickly. "How do you know that you won't be the one who falls?"

"Oh, it ain't gonna be me, lady. I'm too good. I'm the best in the business. The F-22 Raptor is good iron. I can fly that fucking airplane. I'm gonna go through those goddamn Japs like shit through a fan. Can't stand Japs. I guess it's personal with me, something about Pearl Harbor and all that damned so-sorry fake politeness—but I won't let that interfere with what I have to do. I'm going to stay cool and kill those polite little sons of bitches."

Christine didn't know what to say.

Hudek smiled at the camera, unhooked his vest mike, got up, and walked out, right by Dixie Elitch, who averted her gaze as he passed her.

Dixie sat down in the interview chair and smiled sweetly as one of the technicians hooked up her mike.

"Ms. Elitch," Christine began.

"Captain Elitch, please. That is my rank in the Russian Air Army. I am *very* proud of it."

She managed to say that with just the faintest hint of a Russian accent. Watching from behind the camera, Bob Cassidy covered his face with his hands.

"*Captain* Elitch," said Christine, smiling brittlely.

"All my life I have loved Russian things—furs, vodka, Tolstoy,

Tchaikovsky, Chekhov, Pavlov..." Dixie's recall of things Russian failed her here. She waved airily and motored on:

"I am *so* thrilled to have this opportunity to actually *go* to Russia, to succor her people in their hour of need, to serve this magnificent yet tragic nation in my own small way, and, just perhaps, make a contribution to the betterment of the downtrodden proletariat. And even—dare I say it?—the bourgeoisie."

"Are all of you people assholes?" Christine snarled.

"Unfortunately, I believe so," replied Dixie Elitch. She looked straight into the camera and flashed her absolute best "I'm available tonight" smile.

When he went to bed that night, Bob Cassidy found himself thinking of Dixie. This annoyed him. He had ten thousand things on his mind, and now he was thinking about a woman, one who was off-limits to him. Oh, he knew the engraved-in-stone rule of the modern, sexually integrated armed forces: no fucking the troops. And no flirting, sighing, dating, kissing, marrying, or loving—none of that male-female stuff.

In the brave new Air Force middle-aged colonels who got to thinking night thoughts about sweet young things were usually gone quickly. The "grab your hat, don't let the door hit you in the ass on your way out" kind of gone.

Bob Cassidy had spent his adult life in uniform, around women now and then, and he had never before gone to bed thinking about one.

Except Sweet Sabrina. He'd thought of her every night when she was alive, and many, many nights since she died. He often dreamed of her, dreamed of touching her again, of kissing her just once more, of somehow reaching across the great gulf that separated them. Robbie was sometimes in those dreams too, sitting on Sabrina's lap, running across a lawn or through the house or laughing while diving into piles of fall leaves.

These dreams used to wake him up, drive the sleep from him. He would walk the empty house, so utterly alone.

Thinking of anyone but Sabrina seemed disloyal somehow.

He tried to conjure up her image to replace the grinning face of Dixie Elitch.

He was thinking of Sabrina—or was it Dixie?—when he finally drifted off.

CHAPTER FIFTEEN

● PAVEL SARATOV KNEW there were a lot of ships anchored off Yokohama, but he didn't know how many until he was within the anchorage, which extended for miles. Over a hundred, easily, he estimated.

He reduced the boat's speed to six knots. "The big freighter fifteen degrees right of the bow, about two thousand meters. Containers four deep on her deck. She is our first target." Saratov was wearing the sound-powered headset. He had sent the talker below. The only other person on the bridge was the second officer, who was scanning behind and to both sides for enemy planes or warships.

"We have her, sir."

Down below, they were using the radar. All the skipper had to do was designate a target. He had already given orders that they would shoot one torpedo at a time, at targets he picked. He wanted to do all the damage possible.

The torpedoes were huge—twenty-one inches in diameter, twenty-seven feet long—and carried warheads containing 1,250 pounds of high explosive, enough to sink most ships.

Twenty seconds later the first torpedo was on its way. A minute after that they fired another torpedo at a laden bulk carrier. The first one hit the container ship with a dull thud that carried well through the water and was clearly audible aboard the submarine. The bulk carrier and the third target, another container ship, were hit in turn. The fourth torpedo was expended on yet another container ship, a huge one festooned with lights.

Still moving at six knots, the sub was deep inside the anchorage, completely surrounded by ships, when the crew fired the fifth torpedo at a monstrous freighter riding deep in the water. It was close, almost too close, but the torpedo warhead exploded with a boom that sounded quite satisfying to Pavel Saratov. Slowly, almost imperceptibly, the freighter began to sag in the middle. The torpedo broke her back. Yes!

Saratov turned to exit the anchorage to the east. One tube was still loaded. In the torpedo room the crew began the reloading process. It would take about an hour to get one of the huge torpedoes into a tube.

Well, he had given the Japanese something to think about. No doubt they were alerting their antisubmarine forces right now. The sooner he got this boat out of Tokyo Bay, the better.

"Flank speed," he told the people below. "Give me every turn you've got."

Sushi called Toshihiko Ayukawa at home on the scrambled telephone. "Sir, I thought I should call you immediately. We intercepted a transmission from a Russian submarine. He says he is in Tokyo Bay."

"What?" Ayukawa sounded wide-awake now.

"It's right off the computer, sir. I thought you should be informed." The raw, encrypted signal was picked up by a satellite and directed to a dish antenna on top of the building. From there, it went to a computer, which decoded it, translated the Russian into Japanese, and sent it to a printer. The whole sequence took thirty-five seconds—the paper took thirty seconds to go through the printer—if the Russians were using one of the four codes the Japanese had cracked, and if they had encoded their message properly. Sometimes they didn't.

"Read it to me," Ayukawa said.

Sushi did so. When he had finished Ayukawa spent several seconds digesting it, then asked, "Have you alerted the Self-Defense Force?"

"Yes, sir," Sushi said blandly, managing to hide his irritation. Ayukawa's question implied that Sushi was incompetent. Apparently Ayukawa thought he had no time to be polite, to observe the simplest courtesies. In any event he didn't try.

"The explosive charges in the refinery mentioned in the message began exploding twenty minutes ago, sir. The Lotus Blossom refinery at Yokosuka. And a freighter in the Yokohama anchorage has just radioed in, saying it was torpedoed.

"How long have we had the submarine's message?"

"It came in only minutes ago, sir. I called the Self-Defense Force, alerted harbor security and the Yokosuka Fire District. Then I telephoned you."

"Very well." Ten seconds of silence. "A submarine!"

Ayukawa was appalled. Those military fools told the prime minister that they had sunk all the operational Russian subs that were under way when the war broke out at Vladivostok and Sakhalin Island. They refused to tie up scarce military assets guarding ports in the home islands when every ship was needed to conquer an empire. After all, what could you expect of Russians?

Exploding refineries and sinking ships would prove the military men miscalculated, embarrass everybody, cause the government to lose face. Another disaster caused by overweening pride and shortsightedness. Atsuko Abe, take note.

"I had better call the minister," Ayukawa said to no one in particular. He hung up the telephone without saying good-bye.

Sushi cradled his instrument and made a face.

The guided-missile destroyer *Hatakaze* was three hundred yards away from a berth at Yokosuka Naval Base pier when the communications officer buzzed the bridge on the squawk box. A flash-priority message from headquarters had just come out of the computer printer: "Russian submarine attacking ships Yokohama. Intercept."

Hatakaze's captain was no slouch. He ordered his crew to general quarters, waved away the tug, and steamed out into the bay, working up speed as quickly as the engineering plant would allow.

Hatakaze had been continuously at sea for two weeks. She participated in the destruction of the Russian fleet rusting in Golden Horn Bay and helped shell troops on the Vladivostok neck that were trying to impede advancing Japanese forces. During all that shooting, her forward 127-mm Mk-42 deck gun had overheated, which caused a round to explode prematurely, killing two men and injuring four more. Her aft gun was working just fine. As soon as she could be spared, the force commander sent *Hatakaze* home for repairs. Due to the shortage of ammunition, most of *Hatakaze*'s remaining 127-mm ammo was transferred to other ships, yet she still had a dozen rounds on the trays for the aft gun.

Hatakaze was making twenty knots when the radar operators picked *Admiral Kolchak* from among the clutter of ships, small boats, and surface return. The Russian submarine was making fifteen knots southwestward toward the refinery. That merely made her a suspicious blip; her beaconing S-band radar made the identification certain.

Although the submarine lacked the excellent radar of the Japanese destroyer, the destroyer was a bigger, easier target. The operator of the sub's radar saw the blip of a possible warship—a fairly small high-speed surface target coming out of the Yokosuka Naval Base area—and reported it to Captain Saratov as such.

Pavel Saratov pointed his binoculars to the south, the direction named by the radar operator below.

The rain had stopped; visibility was up, maybe to ten miles.

There was the destroyer, with its masthead and running lights illuminated. After all, these were Japanese home waters.

Saratov pounded the bridge rail in frustration.

The destroyer would soon open fire with its deck gun. If the sub submerged, the destroyer would pin it easily, kill it with antisubmarine rockets—ASROC.

He had known it would end like this. Entering the bay had been a huge gamble right from the start. A suicidal gamble, really.

He looked southwest, at the blazing refinery and the LNG tanker moored at the end of the pier. He had been intending to use the sixth torpedo on that tanker. A maneuverable destroyer, bow-on, would be a difficult target.

Another glance at the destroyer. "What is the range to the destroyer?" he demanded of the watch below.

"Twelve thousand meters, Captain, and closing. He has turned toward us, speed a little over thirty knots."

"And the tanker?"

"Two thousand five hundred meters, sir."

"Give me an attack solution on the destroyer. Set the torpedo for acoustic homing."

"Aye aye, sir."

"And keep me informed of the ranges, goddamnit!"

"Yes, captain."

Submerging in this shallow bay would be suicidal. Saratov dismissed that possibility.

He looked longingly at the LNG tanker, a target of a lifetime. She was low in the water, a fact he had noted as he entered the bay and steamed by her. She was full of the stuff.

"We'll run in against the tanker and cut our motors." The Japanese destroyer captain wouldn't be fool enough to risk putting a shell into that thing.

With the tanker at our back, Saratov thought, maybe we have a chance. At least he could get his men off the sub and into the water.

"Aye aye, sir."

"Come thirty degrees right, slow to all ahead two-thirds."

He heard the order being repeated in the control room, felt the bow of the sub swinging.

"Destroyer at eleven thousand meters, sir."

Saratov looked back at the oncoming destroyer. *Why doesn't he shoot?*

The refinery was blazing merrily. At the base of the fire, he could just make out the silhouettes of fire trucks. The Spetsnaz divers certainly had done an excellent job.

Saratov swung the glasses to the tanker pier. Several fire trucks with their flashing emergency lights were visible there. He wondered why they were on the pier; then his mind turned to other things. He checked the destroyer again. Why didn't he shoot? They most certainly were in range.

"Twelve hundred meters to the tanker, Captain."

The captain of the *Hatakaze* could see the burning refinery with his binoculars. He could not see the black sail of the Russian submarine that his radar people assured him was there, but he could see the blip on the radar repeater scope just in front of his chair on the bridge. And he could see the return of the tanker pier and the tankers moored to it. The range to the sub was about nine thousand meters.

ASROC was out of the question, even though the target was well within range. The rocket would carry the Mk-46 torpedo out several kilometers and put it in the water, but the torpedo might home on one of the tankers.

Captain Kama elected to engage the submarine with the stern 127-mm gun. Not that he had a lot of choice. He was already within gun range, but he would have to turn *Hatakaze* about seventy degrees away from the submarine to uncover the gun. Of course, if the gun overshot, one of the shells might hit a tanker. If the LNG tanker went up, the results would be catastrophic.

He decided to wait. Wait a few moments, and pray the submarine didn't shoot a torpedo.

"Prepare to fire the torpedo decoys," he ordered. "And watch for small boats. Tell Sonar to listen carefully." Listen for torpedoes, he meant.

What a place to fight a war!

The refinery fire was as bad as it looked. The conflagration lit up the clouds and illuminated the tanker pier with a ghastly flickering glow. Numerous small explosions sent fireballs puffing into the night sky. These explosions were caused when fire reached free pools or clouds of petroleum products that had leaked from ruptured tanks or pipes.

The firefighters had no chance. There was too much damage in too many places.

As the fires grew hotter and larger, the glow cast even more light on the sea.

The submarine approached the LNG tanker, which was limned by the fire behind it. Saratov could see people moving about on the decks, probably trying desperately to get under way. He imagined the tanker skipper was beside himself.

"All stop," he told the control room.

The submarine glided toward the tanker, losing way. Two hundred meters separated the two ships.

"Left full rudder."

The nose began to swing.

"Looks like another destroyer, sir. Coming out of Yokosuka. Bearing one nine five, range thirty-two thousand meters."

"Keep the boat moving, Chief, at about two knots."

"Aye aye, sir. Two knots."

The deck of the submarine was barely out of the water. He had never ordered the tanks completely blown. "Secure the diesels. Switch to battery power."

"Battery power, aye."

Saratov kept his binoculars focused on the Japanese destroyer, which was closing the range at about a kilometer per minute.

The throb of the diesels died away. He could hear the rush of air and the crackling of the refinery fire. Somewhere, over the refinery probably, was a helicopter. He could hear the distinctive whopping of the rotors in the exhaust.

"We have the first destroyer on sonar," the XO reported.

"Be ready to fire tube six at the destroyer at any time."

"Aye, Captain. We're doing that now. Destroyer at seven thousand meters."

"How long until the first reload is ready?"

"Another twenty minutes, Captain."

Terrific! We have exactly one shot. If we miss . . .

He must have seen us! "You ready to shoot?"

"Yes, sir."

Saratov waited, his eyes on the destroyer. He wasn't shooting, which Saratov thought was because the tanker lay just behind. He could hear voices, shouts, in a foreign language that Saratov thought might be English. It certainly didn't sound like Japanese, and it sure as hell wasn't Russian.

"Six thousand meters, and he's slowing."

Saratov had been waiting for that. The Japanese skipper wouldn't hear much on his sonar at thirty-two knots, yet the high speed was an edge in outmaneuvering the torpedo.

"Tube Six, fire!"

The boat jerked as the torpedo went out, expelled by compressed air.

Aboard *Hatakaze,* the captain was watching the tiny radar blip that was the submarine's sail. If only he would submerge, clear away from that tanker!

The destroyer's speed caused too much turbulence and noise for the bow-mounted sonar, so he had ordered the ship slowed. Way was falling off now.

"Torpedo in the water!"

The call from the sonar operator galvanized everyone. "Right full rudder, all ahead flank," Captain Kama ordered. "Come to a new heading zero nine zero. Deploy the torpedo decoys. Have the after turret open fire when their gun bears."

The deck tilted steeply as the destroyer answered the helm.

"He's turning eastward, Captain," the attack team told Saratov, who was still on the bridge, his binoculars glued to his eyes.

"I see that, goddamnit. What's his speed?"

"Fourteen knots. His engines are really thrashing. I think he is accelerating."

The destroyer was almost beam-on now. Flashes from the gun on the afterdeck! Even with that tanker directly behind the submarine, he is shooting!

"Dive, dive, dive. Let's go down."

Saratov unplugged his headset. Hanecki was already going through the hatch. The deck was tilting. Saratov clamored through the hatch and pulled it down after him just as the first of the five-inch shells hit the water . . . right beside the sail.

"Periscope depth!"

"Periscope depth, aye."

They could hear the shells splashing into the water. Damn, the shooting was accurate.

"Running time on the first fish?"

"Thirty more seconds, sir."

"Give me a ninety-degree right turn. Tell the torpedo officer to get a tube loaded with all possible speed."

"Aye aye, sir."

"Thank you, XO."

They were just flat running out of options. He wasn't ready to tell them yet, but if the last torpedo missed, he was going to surface the boat alongside the tanker and abandon her. He wasn't going to let his men die in this sardine can when they had nothing left to fight with.

He was thinking about this, watching the heading change as the boat turned, waiting for the boat to sink the last five feet to periscope depth, when he heard the explosion. The torpedo! It hit something. But what?

The men cheered. A roar of exultation.

"Quiet!"

"Keep the turn in, Chief, make it a full three hundred and sixty degrees. All ahead one-third. Raise the big scope."

He glued his eye to the large scope when it came out of the well. The small attack scope was nearly useless at night.

The destroyer was still moving. At least the front half was. The stern . . . Jesus! The torpedo had blown it off.

"The torpedo blew the ass off the destroyer," Saratov said to the control room crew. "Pass the word. It is on fire and sinking."

When the whispers and buzzing died away, Saratov asked, "Sonar, what do you hear?"

"Not much, Captain. The LNG tanker has started its engines. It will be getting under way soon, I think."

"Let's get out of here, Captain, while we are still alive."

The second officer said that. He looked pale as a ghost.

Saratov looked from face to face. Several men averted their gaze; one chewed on his lip. Most met his gaze, however. The second officer couldn't stop swallowing—he was probably going to puke.

Saratov took the microphone for the boat's PA system off its hook, flipped the switch on, adjusted the volume.

"This is the captain. You men have done well. We have hit the enemy hard. We have destroyed a huge refinery, sunk three ships at least and damaged two more. We have just killed a destroyer that was trying to kill us. I am proud of each and every one of you. It is an honor to be your captain."

He paused, took a deep breath, thought about what he wanted to say. "We are going to surface in a few moments, see if we can set this LNG tanker on fire; then we are going to get out of this bay, run for the open sea."

The second officer lost it, vomiting into his hat.

"Do your job. Do what you were trained to do. That is our best chance."

He put the microphone back into its bracket.

"There's another destroyer up there, Captain."

"I am aware of that." Saratov looked at the XO, lowered his voice. "Let's leave the radar off. Without the radar beaconing, we are just another tiny blip."

"As long as we keep our speed down," Askold muttered.

"Sonar, what's the position on that second destroyer?"

"I estimate twenty thousand meters, Captain. It's hard to tell for sure, with all the noise in the water."

"Keep listening."

"Do you want to finish reloading one of the bow tubes before we surface, Captain?" Askold asked.

"The Japanese will put the time to better use than we can. Every gray boat they have will be strung across the bay's entrance if we give them time enough."

He raised his voice. "Sonar, leave the radar secured. No emissions."

"Aye aye, sir."

"Have the forward torpedo room break out the rockets. We will surface, blow the bow tanks. Pop the hatch and put a man on deck with an RPG-9. We might as well try them."

If the rockets failed—and they probably wouldn't even fire: He'd had them for six, no, seven years—he would just call it a day and run for it. The torpedomen would get a tube reloaded soon, and boy, it would be nice to have a loaded fish when he went down the bay.

"Up scope."

He walked it around while the XO talked to the forward torpedo room on the squawk box. *Hatakaze*'s bow was on fire, dead in the water. The stern seemed to have sunk. The LNG tanker was still against the pier, the fire in the refinery visible behind it. The second destroyer was not in sight. If that skipper had any sense, he would station himself in the entrance of the bay and wait for the submarine to come to him.

He gave the chief a new heading, to the northeast, so the LNG tanker would be off the port side. *Hatakaze* was three or four kilometers southeast, so that wreck wouldn't be a factor.

In an hour, the sky would be light with the coming dawn, and there would probably be four destroyers waiting.

Pavel Saratov lowered the periscope and gave the order to surface.

Saratov opened the hatch and went up the ladder to the tiny cockpit on top of the sail. The second officer followed, taking up his usual station looking aft and to both sides. The tanker was on the port bow, about eight hundred meters away.

If anything, the refinery fire was more intense, brighter, than it had been fifteen or twenty minutes ago. Several areas that had not been burning before were ablaze now. He could hear the roar of the flames here, almost a kilometer away. The firestorm sounded like rain and wind on a wild night at sea.

Even the clouds seemed to be on fire. They were shot through with sulfurous reds, oranges, and yellows, lighting the surface of the black water with a hellish glare.

The submarine lay inert on the oily sea. Belowdecks, the crew was blowing water from the forward tanks to lift the deck so that it was no longer awash. Saratov and the second officer scanned the surface of the bay for the destroyer they knew was about, somewhere. The bottom of the burning clouds was about a thousand feet above the water and visibility was good, maybe ten miles.

"Who is the shooter?" Saratov asked on the sound-powered headset.

"Senka. He knows all about it."

"Get him on deck. We haven't got all damned night."

He shouldn't have said that. Shouldn't have let the men know the tension was getting to him.

Where in hell is that destroyer?

When he put the binoculars down there was a man on deck, reaching down into the hatch. When the man straightened he was holding an ungainly tube in his hands. He put it on his right shoulder.

The batteries in those grenade launchers were probably as dead as Lenin.

Senka didn't waste much time. He braced himself, aimed for the tanker, and fired.

The batteries worked. The rocket-propelled grenade raced away in a gout of fire that split the night open. Straight as a bullet it flew across the water, straight for the giant steel ball that contained liquid natural gas.

A flash. That was it. Two kilos of warhead in a flash, then nothing.

"Try another one. Give him another one."

At least the rocket reached the target, which Saratov had feared was a bit out of range. The shaped charge must have hit a girder or something, Saratov thought, examining the tanker through his glasses. He could just see the feathery lines of the gridwork of girders that supported the pressure vessel. If the grenade didn't actually reach the pressure vessel, the warhead would never damage it.

Senka didn't waste time. Apparently he knew what he was about. He put the launcher on his shoulder; then he was examining it, then he threw it into the water. He reached down into the hatch for the third one.

Senka fired again. The missile ignited and raced across the black water toward the tanker. Another flash on impact. Then nothing.

"Try the last one; then we are out of here."

"Five more minutes on the torpedo, Captain."

Saratov acknowledged.

Where is that second destroyer?

A flash from the right.

Saratov looked. He saw a destroyer, bow-on, headed this way. Another flash from the bow gun.

A shell hit the water just beyond the sub.

Saratov was about to yell "Dive," but he saw Senka face the LNG tanker and raise the launcher to his shoulder.

Saratov opened his mouth just as a shell hit the aft top corner of the sail and exploded. A piece of shrapnel caught the captain in the side of the head and knocked him unconscious. The shrapnel disemboweled the second officer, killing him instantly.

The XO reached up through the hatch and grabbed Saratov by the ankles. He had a firm grip on the skipper and was pulling him into the hatch when Senka, on deck, fired the last RPG-9.

This time the rocket went through the gridwork that supported the pressure vessel and vented its shaped explosive charge into the vessel itself, puncturing it.

The intense pressure on the liquefied natural gas inside the vessel caused it to vent out the hole in a supersonic stream that made a high-pitched, earsplitting whistle. Several people on the tanker heard it. That was the last thing they would ever hear. In less than a second, a large cloud of natural gas had formed outside the hole, which was still molten hot from the explosive. The gas ignited.

The fireball from this explosion grew and grew; then the pressure vessel split. A thousandth of a second later, six thousand tons of liquefied natural gas detonated.

The explosion was the worst in Japan since the atomic bombing of Nagasaki, and almost as violent. The LNG tanker was vaporized in the fireball, as was much of the tanker pier. One of the tankers still moored there had been taking on gasoline, and it too detonated, adding to the force of the explosion. The other tanker, off-loading crude oil, was split open by the blast like a watermelon dropped on concrete. Its cargo spontaneously ignited.

The concussion and thermal pulse of the initial blast leveled the remaining structures at the refinery. The petroleum products that had not yet been consumed merely enhanced the force of the expanding fireball. Of course, the people on the tankers and pier and fighting the fires in the refinery were instantly cremated.

When the concussion reached the submarine eight hundred meters away, *Michman* Senka, who had fired the final PRG-9, was swept overboard. It didn't matter to Senka, because he was already dead, fried by the thermal pulse of the explosion. The pulse instantly heated the black steel hull of the boat and sent the water droplets and rivulets that had been on the deck wafting away as steam. A tenth of a second later the concussion arrived, denting the submarine's sail, smashing loose dozens of the anechoic tiles that covered the boat's skin and pushing it so hard that the sub went momentarily over on her beam.

Pavel Saratov knew nothing of all this, because he was unconscious. Somehow as the boat went over, the XO managed to pull him through the hatch. A ton or so of water came in before the boat righted itself. Water also poured through the hatch in the forward torpedo room and would have flooded the boat had the sub stayed on its side any longer.

Miraculously, the submarine righted itself, and the men in the forward torpedo room managed to get the hatch closed and secured. In the sail, the men there wrestled with the hatch and dogged it down just as the second concussion and the bay surge from the explosion pushed the boat over on her beam a second time.

When the captain of the destroyer *Shimakaze,* charging for the Russian submarine, saw the fireball growing and expanding, his first thought was that one of the shells from his deck gun had hit the tanker, just exactly the calamity he had warned the gunners against in the event they got a chance to shoot.

The thermal pulse ignited the destroyer's paint. The concussion smashed out the bridge windows and dented the sheet metal as if had been pounded by Thor's hammer. Since the destroyer was almost bow-on to the blast, it rode through the first concussion with only heavy damage to its superstructure, its radar and antennas and stack. The helmsman was killed by flying glass. He went down with a death grip on the helm. Still making over twenty knots, the destroyer went into a turn. When the second concussion arrived, the ship heeled hard, then righted herself. The bay surge that followed, however, put her over on her beam. Unlike the submarine, she did not come up again.

The fireball from the LNG tank expanded and grew hotter and hotter, brighter and brighter. The temperature inside the submarine rose dramatically—until the men were being parbroiled inside a 150-degree oven. Then the temperature fell, though not as fast as it had risen.

Minutes later, the temperature in the boat almost back to normal, the XO climbed to the bridge to assess the damage. Angry black water roiled over the place where the tanker and pier had been. All the small boats that had dotted the waters of the bay were gone. In three or four places the water appeared to be on fire, but it was gasoline and raw crude burning.

The shore . . . the city was aflame for five miles in both directions. The thermal pulses and concussions had done their work. The surges of air into and away from the fireball had done the rest.

The main periscope was bent, the glass smashed. Whether from the five-inch shell of the destroyer or the blast, Askold couldn't tell. There was no trace of the second officer, whose corpse, like Senka's, had gone to a sailor's grave.

The XO called down a heading change, and more speed. With the main periscope out of action, he kept the boat on the surface.

With her diesels driving her at twenty knots, *Admiral Kolchak* went southward down the bay, charging the batteries as she went. When the first light of dawn appeared in the eastern sky she was rolling in the Pacific swells.

Askold took her under. She was a tiny little boat, swimming through a great vast ocean, so when she disappeared beneath the surface it was as if she had never been.

CHAPTER SIXTEEN

●THE WEEKS FOLLOWING the disaster in Tokyo Bay wore heavily on Prime Minister Atsuko Abe. At least 155,000 people died in the explosions and fires that raged out of control for two days in Yokosuka. Emergency workers estimated that 100,000 were injured; at least half the injuries were burns.

Obeying standing orders, when the Yokosuka refinery fire was reported, the duty officer in the war room in the basement of the defense ministry called both Prime Minister Abe and the chief of staff of the Japanese Self-Defense Force at their homes. Both Abe and the general were in the war room when the LNG tanker exploded.

They sat there saying little as the reports came in. A television station quickly launched its helicopter. Soon the stunning visual panorama played endlessly from large-screen televisions mounted in strategic places throughout the room.

Garish, ghastly fires everywhere, a sea of flame and destruction— these were the images burned into the minds of the men watching in the war room, and of the Japanese public, because these scenes were also playing live on nationwide television.

Although Abe did not want the public to witness this calamity, he was powerless to prevent the television stations from showing what they pleased unless he wished to declare martial law, and he didn't. He wasn't about to admit that the situation in metropolitan Tokyo was beyond the control of the civilian government. Not yet, anyway.

The prime minister's first instinct was to blame the catastrophe on an earthquake. A tremor caused fatal damage to the refinery, which finally blew up disastrously. This would have been a good story and certainly plausible, but unfortunately the videotape from the television helicopter proved conclusively that the fire had started in several different places, as many as eight, and spread at least a half hour before the explosion that flattened the refinery and several square miles of nearby city.

Worse, the cameraman in the helicopter managed to get footage of the Russian submarine several minutes before the fatal detonation. She was lying on the surface near the LNG tanker, a recognizable black shape quite prominent against the reflection of the fire in the black water.

When the LNG tanker blew, the helicopter was dashed to earth and shattered as if it were a toy in the hands of some horrible Japanese movie monster. Of course, the television station made a tape of the video feed; they played the footage of the submarine over and over and over. The boat looked evil lying there in the darkness, its decks awash, its silhouette an ominous black shape amid the reflected glare of the holocaust.

The public mood, somber enough after the invasion of Siberia was announced, turned even more gloomy. The racial memory of the B-29 firebombings of World War II was too fresh. Television pictures of burning cities, with the nation again at war, mesmerized the Japanese. The business of the nation ground to a halt as they watched in horror.

Who was responsible?

"Atsuko Abe is responsible for every dead Japanese and every scarred, mutilated survivor."

A senior member of an opposition party voiced this obvious truth; that sound bite was also carried nationwide by the television stations.

Another senior politician added soberly, "It appears that our leaders have underestimated the Russians' military capacity."

Abe's reaction to this criticism was to cast about for ways to end the public's unhealthy fascination with the submarine raid, the burned-out city, and the victims. He demanded legislation to censor the press, to put a stop to the public airing of negative comments. His party had a sufficient majority in the Diet to carry the day. At his insistence, the television went back to baseball and dramas; the newspapers avoided all mention of the war except when running news released by the defense ministry, which they published without comment.

While he got his way, Abe was enough of a politician to realize that he had expended valuable political capital that he might need later, but he saw no alternative. If the public lost faith in the war effort now, before the conquest was assured, he and everything he had tried to achieve would be doomed.

The one bright spot in the censorship fiasco was the removal of the daily list of casualties from Siberia from the nation's front pages. Troops were encountering unexpectedly heavy opposition from ill-equipped Russian units, units that could almost be categorized as guerilla irregulars. Even without the daily butcher's lists, however, the public seemed to sense that all was not going well.

"Where will the Russians strike next?"

All over Japan, people asked that question. There were, of course, no answers. Abe supporters accused the doubters of being unpatriotic. The mood grew even uglier.

Part of the problem was the economy. Japan's stock market was quickly closed by the Abe administration when war broke out. In the real economy, things went rapidly to hell. Demand for Japanese goods in the United States, Japan's largest foreign market, dropped dramatically. After the submarine disaster, shipowners refused to transport the raw materials and manufactured goods that kept the factories running and people eating. Idled factories laid off workers in huge numbers.

Atsuko Abe wrestled with these problems, too. He and General Yamashita, the military chief of staff, believed that the military should take over the nation's factories and shipping assets. This step was bitterly resisted by key members of Abe's party, who pointed out that the war was supposed to stimulate the economy, not kill it.

"Why is it," Abe demanded of his party's senior members, "that everyone is a patriot when patriotism is free, yet when it has a price, it has no friends?"

In western Russia life had become even more severe than it was before the Japanese invasion. Great masses of people were still hungry, factories still idle, and civilian construction projects stalled. Everyone was being squeezed as the military slowly and inexorably took control of every aspect of the nation's life. Every man between the ages of eighteen and twenty-five who could pass a physical was being drafted and sent to recruit depots, there to wait for arms and equipment from obsolete, worn-out factories that were being restarted by decree. Everything—food, fuel, clothing, housing, everything—was being rationed. The censored media printed only propaganda. A people with little hope could see that their country had gone from bad to worse.

The news of the devastation in Tokyo Bay caused by a Russian submarine hit this Russia with a stupendous impact. Pictures of *Admiral Kolchak* and a file photo of Pavel Saratov in his dress uniform were printed in the newspapers, made into posters, and displayed endlessly on television. The meager facts of Saratov's life from his navy personnel file were expanded into a ten-thousand word biography that was printed in every newspaper in Russia west of the Urals. The loss of innocent life in Japan was horrific, frightening, but the image of a few brave men in a small submarine sneaking into the Japanese stronghold to cripple the arrogant, swaggering bully struck a deep chord in Russian hearts starved for good news. The press in Europe, in North and South America, and in Australia picked up the stories and broadcast them worldwide. Within four days of the disaster Pavel Saratov was the best-known Russian alive.

During this orgy of patriotism Marshal Oleg Stolypin was trying to find the wherewithal to defend the nation. As he lay in bed at night trying to sleep, Stolypin had visions of Japanese armored columns following the railroad west all the way to Moscow. He would awaken with the nightmare of Japanese tanks in Red Square fresh in his mind. There weren't enough troops to stop the Japanese if they really made up their minds to do it.

Apparently the Japanese weren't bold enough to risk everything on one wild lunge westward. Or foolish enough. Going blindly where little was known did not appeal to Stolypin's military mind, either. The old gray marshal did not believe in luck. Unlike the late Marshal Ivan Samsonov, Stolypin was not a brilliant man. He was smart enough, but he had to look situations over carefully, weigh all the risks, ponder the possibilities. Once he was sure he was right, however, he was an irresistible force.

Stolypin had quickly assembled and put to work an experienced staff that knew the true state of the Russian army. Armed with presidential decrees and newly printed money, military arms and equipment were broken out of storage and issued to the troops and new recruits, new equipment was rushed into production, and the transportation system was drastically and ruthlessly overhauled.

The marshal concentrated on building his military strength. Any plans he made were going to hinge on the forces at his disposal. Increasing those forces was his first priority.

His second priority was augmenting those forces in Siberia that could hurt the Japanese now. Men, weapons, ammo, and food were sent east by truck, train, and airplane. The marshal well knew that the meager forces in Siberia could not defeat the Japanese, but for the sake of the nation's soul, they had to fight.

One day Stolypin called on Aleksandr Kalugin to discuss the military situation. He found the president sifting through newspaper clippings and watching three televisions simultaneously.

"Saratov has united the Russian people," Kalugin muttered, waving a fistful of clippings. "They adore him."

A few minutes later, apropos of nothing, the president remarked, "The man who crushes Japan will hold Russia in the palm of his hand."

He listened distractedly to Stolypin's report.

"We're losing, aren't we?" he demanded at one point.

"Sir, the Japanese are setting up military defenses in depth to protect the oil fields around Yakutsk and Sakhalin Island. They are digging in to stay around Khabarovsk and stockpiling men and equipment for a push up the Amur valley. My staff and I believe they intend to advance as far west as Lake Baikal before winter sets in, set up their first line of defense there."

During most of this, Kalugin was shaking his head from side to side, slowly, with his eyes closed. "Questions are being asked in the congress," he said. "The deputies want to see progress toward military victory. Our present small-unit actions merely harass the Japanese. Surrendering half of Siberia is not one of our options."

"Mr. President, we do not have the forces to—"

"The people demand action! The deputies *demand* action! *I demand it of you!*"

Stolypin didn't know what to say. He didn't panic—panic wasn't in him. He repeated the truth to the president. "We are doing all we can. Every day we grow stronger; every day we are one day closer to victory."

Kalugin rose from his chair, shouting, "Lies, lies, lies! Every day the Japanese army advances deeper into Russia. I have listened to your lying promises long enough."

He spun on the aging marshal, confronted him. "We must seize the moment. This moment in history is a gift; we must face it with bold resolve. We must not shrink from our duty." Kalugin lifted his hand before his face and stared at it. "We must strike with all the might and power we possess. The man who strikes first will conquer."

He smashed his fist down on a glass table, which shattered into a thousand pieces.

"The prize is Russia, all of Russia. The man who refuses to be reasonable will triumph. That is the way of war. Atsuko Abe knows that. He is also a student of Genghis Khan."

"Mr. President, we are striking the Japanese with all our strength."

"No! No, Marshal Stolypin, we are not. We have ten nuclear weapons. When these weapons are exploding on Japan, then . . ." Kalugin drew a ragged breath. "*Then* will the victory be ours. We must apply overwhelming military force. Weakness merely tempts them, sir. I have studied these things. I know I am right. We must annihilate our enemies. *Then Russia will be mine.*"

One of the people Stolypin made time for every day was Janos Ilin. Ilin briefed him on the extent of the Japanese penetration of Siberia. Ilin was remarkably well informed. Extraordinarily so. He had the names of the Japanese units, how many men, how much equipment, even the names of the commanders. He used all of this to annotate tactical maps for the marshal, who spent spare moments studying them.

Once the marshal questioned Ilin. "Where does all this information come from? I never realized the Foreign Intelligence Service was such a font of knowledge. I can't even communicate with my units on a timely basis, yet you seem to be getting these maps from Tokyo every morning."

"Sir, you know full well I cannot answer that question. If I start telling secrets, I soon won't have any."

"You are much better informed than the GRU." The GRU was the army general staff's intelligence arm.

"We work different sides of the street."

That was the last time the marshal brought up the subject.

When the business of the day was over, Ilin usually lingered a few moments to chat. He was, of course, younger than the marshal and had never worked with him before.

"Are you one of those," Ilin asked, "who longs for the old days of glory?"

"Alas, no. The old days were not glorious. Corruption, selfishness, incompetence, blighted, drunken lives, universal poverty, pollution, wastage . . . Believe me, those days are best behind us."

"But the army? It was huge, capable, the pride of every Russian."

"The Kremlin gave us plenty of money and we shook our fists in the world's face. The world trembled, yet the real truth was that the Soviet Union was never able to do more than defend itself. The nation was always poor. Our forces were designed for defense, not offense. For example, we had no ability to mount an invasion of the United States, although the Americans thought we could. Invading Afghanistan was the limit of our capability, and we lost there because we couldn't force a quick decision."

"So what is Russia's destiny?"

"Destiny?" The old man snorted.

"Our future."

"After we defeat Japan? The great days for Russia all lie ahead. Without the paranoia of the Cold War, the psychotic babble of the Communists, and the expense of a huge military establishment, Russia will bloom as she has never bloomed before. You may live to see it, Ilin."

A day or so later, as Ilin put away his charts and notes after a briefing, he said, "Too bad Samsonov is not here. He was brilliant."

"That he was," the marshal agreed. "He was my prodigy. I know genius when I see it, and I saw it in him. He was the best we had. Just when we needed him most, he is gone. Sometimes I wonder if God still loves Russia."

"God had nothing to do with Samsonov's death," Ilin said, his eyes carefully searching the old man's face.

"What are you saying?"

"I want to know if I speak in confidence."

"Do you think I have a loose tongue?"

"I think you are an honorable man, but if I am wrong we are both doomed."

"I have no time for this."

Ilin's eyes didn't miss a single muscle twitch in Stolypin's face. "Kalugin had Samsonov executed. Kalugin's personal bodyguard killed him. They buried him in the forest thirty miles north of the city."

The old man's face turned gray. "How do you know this?"

"My business is to know things. I have spies everywhere. My God, man, this is still Russia."

"You have proof?"

From his jacket pocket Ilin produced a small photograph and passed it to the marshal. Samsonov's head lay on a mound of dirt. There was a large bullet hole in his forehead. His eyes were open.

"The hole in his forehead was the exit hole. He was shot from behind."

Stolypin handed over the photo.

Ilin took out a match, struck it, applied it to the corner of the celluloid. He dropped the flaming picture in an ashtray.

"Why did you tell me this?"

"Kalugin has his men checking out the nuclear weapons at Trojan Island. They took the top experts in Russia with them."

Marshal Stolypin took a deep breath, then exhaled slowly. He kept his eyes on the residue of the photograph in the ashtray. A wisp of smoke danced delicately in the eddies of air.

Stolypin met Ilin's eyes.

Ilin continued: "I am told that when Kalugin's men are sent to kill someone, they ask the victim to sit in the front passenger seat. As the car rolls along, they talk of inconsequential things. When the victim is relaxed, off his guard, he is shot in the back of the head. It is quite painless, I believe."

"So you have warned me."

Ilin nodded. After a bit, he spoke again, softly. "Aleksandr Kalugin is another Joseph Stalin. He is paranoid and has no scruples, none whatever."

"He is insane," Marshal Stolypin said slowly, remembering his discussion with Kalugin several days before, during which the president smashed a glass table with his fist.

The Russians named the outfit American Squadron and ran stories on television and in newspapers to improve public morale. The capabilities of the F-22 Raptor were extolled to the skies. The Russian reporters called it a "superplane," the best in the world. Flown by these ace American pilots, all of whom had volunteered to fly and fight for the Russian Republic, the F-22 would sweep the Japanese criminals from the skies in short order.

Street kiosks sold posters showing the American volunteers standing around an F-22 with the flag of old Russia painted on the fuselage. No one outside the squadron was told that the flag had been painted on with water-based paint. After the photographers left, the linesmen carefully washed the still-damp paint from the aircraft's smart skin.

Col. Bob Cassidy was appalled when the military situation was explained to him at headquarters in Moscow. The Russians were not yet ready to resist the Japanese on the ground with conventional warfare tactics.

When he was taken to meet Marshal Stolypin after the briefing, he kept his opinions to himself. The old man's face revealed nothing. He listened to the translator, nodded, examined Cassidy as if he were looking at a department-store dummy.

Bob Cassidy sat at attention. He felt as if he were back in the Air Force Academy for doolie summer. The old man had that effect.

Now the Russian marshal commented.

"We are doing what we can for Russia, Colonel. I am sure your president would say that he also is doing what he can. I expect you to do likewise."

"Yes, sir," Cassidy said, blushing slightly when he had heard the translation.

The marshal continued, absolutely impassive.

"I would like for the American Squadron to attack the Japanese air force. Win air superiority. Once you have it, or while you are winning it, shoot down their transports, prevent them from repairing the railroads. If the Japanese are dependent on ground transportation, we will defeat them this winter."

"May I ask, Marshal, how much pressure you want us to put on enemy truck convoys?"

"Use your discretion, Colonel. I am of a mind to give the Japanese all of Siberia they wish to take. It is a very big place. On the other hand, if you can create in them a burning desire to return to Japan, you will save many lives."

The thought occurred to Bob Cassidy that Stolypin must play a hell of a game of poker. "This winter, your army will attack?"

"This winter," said Marshal Stolypin, "we will kill every Japanese soldier in Siberia. Every last one."

When the aerial wagon train arrived at the air base in Chita, the C-5 transports landed first. The base consisted of two runways, almost parallel, about seven thousand feet long. There wasn't much room for error. The transports landed and taxied off the runway into the parking area while Col. Bob Cassidy kept his flight of six F-22s high overhead. Two other airports, each with two runways, lay a few miles to the southwest. These were old military bases and had not been maintained, so the concrete was crumbling. An emergency landing there would probably ruin jet engines.

Cassidy was keeping a close eye on his tac display. A Washington colonel, Evan Register, had given Cassidy and the pilots accompanying him to Chita a brief last night, before the beer bust.

"The Athena device in the new Zeros will keep them hidden from your radar. And shooting an AMRAAM at a Zero is a waste of a good missile—Athena will never let the darn thing find its target. Leave your radar off. Radiating will make you a beacon for the Zeros—they will come like a moth to light.

"Sky Eye is your edge. The radars in the satellites have doppler capability. While they cannot see the Zeros, they can see the wakes they make in the air, especially when they are supersonic. A supersonic shock wave is quite distinctive."

"Wait a minute," one of the junior pilots said, wanting to believe but not quite ready to. "What's the catch?"

In the back of the room, Cassidy tilted his chair back and grinned. Stanford Tuck had not let him down.

"Well, of course there are some technical limitations," the Washington wizard admitted. "This *is* cutting-edge technology. Detecting aircraft wakes with doppler works best in calm air. Summer turbulence, thunderstorms, rain, hail—all such conditions degrade the capability. The computer can sort it out to some extent, but remember the satellites are whizzing along, so the picture is constantly changing, and there is a lot of computing involved. We've been watching the wakes of Zeros for several weeks now. As long as the weather doesn't change, we'll be okay."

Cassidy looked at his troops and shrugged. What could you do?

At 25,000 feet over Chita, Bob Cassidy wondered how effective Sky Eye was today. The air at this altitude seemed smooth enough. The sun was diffused by a high, thin layer of cirrus, which cut the glare somewhat.

The land below looked uninviting. Chita was a small town on the upper reaches of the Amur River, backed up against a snow-covered mountain range, with another to the south. The arid land reminded Cassidy of Nevada or central Oregon. The runways below looked like bright strips on the yellow-brown earth. From this altitude the aircraft parking mats and a few buildings, probably hangars, were also visible.

Fifteen hundred miles from the sea, the Amur River was a seasonal stream now carrying water from melting snow. Two bridges crossed the river, one for the Trans-Siberian Railroad and one for trucks. Just before the snows came, the river would cease to flow. Any water trapped in it would freeze solid.

Khabarovsk lay a thousand miles downstream. From there, the river flowed northwest another five hundred miles to the Sea of Okhotsk.

The tac display showed empty sky around the F-22 formation. He punched the display to take in all the territory between Chita and Zeya, five hundred nautical miles east. Five hundred nautical miles, the distance between Boston and Detroit. The distances in Siberia were going to take some getting used to. The land was vast beyond imagination. Man had barely made an imprint here.

Cassidy wondered about Jiro Kimura. Was he still alive? And if so, where was he?

Jiro was on his mind a lot lately, just when he should be thinking of something else, concentrating on the job at hand. Cassidy growled at himself and tried to think of other things.

Not a single bogey on the tac display, neither toward Khabarovsk nor Nikolayevsk. That bothered Cassidy. It would be nice if the satellite saw one or two . . . but it didn't. Apparently. Subject, of course, to the inevitable high-tech glitches.

Cassidy glanced down at the transports on the airfield. They were quite plain at this altitude. If all was going as planned, the crews were unloading the Sentinel batteries, which were mounted on trailers. The aircraft also brought four Humvees, which would pull the trailers. A Sentinel unit was being spotted on each side of the runway and turned on. The others would be towed away from the base that afternoon and evening, set up in a pattern on local roads in the area. As soon as the units were off-loaded, the two C-5s would take off and head back over the pole toward Alaska. Tankers were supposed to meet them several hours out.

Tankers had been crucial to the success of this operation, moving airplanes and equipment a third of the way around the globe and arriving ready to fight. Finding a tanker in the vastness of the sky had always been a challenge, a real tightrope act when one was low on fuel. GPS now made the rendezvous phase routine, which was fine by everyone.

Now Cassidy eyed his fuel gauges. The fighters had tanked an hour ago, so they were fat, but Cassidy didn't know how much longer he could remain strapped to this ejection seat. He'd been sitting in this cockpit over six hours. He itched and ached. He squirmed in the seat, trying to give his numb butt some relief.

Another half hour passed. One of the C-5s taxied to the end of the runway, sat there for five minutes, then began to roll. The other was taxiing as the first one lifted off.

Cassidy waited until the C-5s were ten minutes north, then pulled the throttles back and started down.

The first problem the Americans faced was parking their planes. The base was beyond the tactical range of Zeros flying from Khabarovsk, which was cold comfort since the Japanese now had planes at Zeya. And if they used a tanker, they could strike this base anytime they wished from almost anywhere, including Japan.

With that in mind, the F-22s were dispersed all over the field. The revetments were full of obviously abandoned fighters, some of them old MiG-19s and MiG-21s. Some of these antiques had flat tires, oil leaks, sand and bird's nests in the intakes. The Americans pushed and pulled the Russian iron out of the revetments and put the F-22s in. Then they rigged camouflage nets.

Some of the best spots, concrete revetments completely hidden by large trees, were already taken by Sukhoi-27s, which looked ready to fly. The Sukhois were attended by grubby, skinny Russians who smelled bad and didn't speak English. The Americans passed out candy bars and soon made friends. While the candy was eaten eagerly, the Russians really wanted cigarettes, which the Americans didn't have.

Now that he was on the ground, Cassidy thought the Chita area was a bit like Colorado. The base and the small town huddled around the railroad station a few miles away were in a basin, surrounded by snow-covered mountains to the north, west, and south. The air was crystal-clear. From here, it was a long way to anywhere.

At least the communications were first-rate: The Americans had brought their own com gear, portable radios that bounced their signals off a satellite, which meant that the operators could talk to anyone on the planet.

Cassidy got on the horn immediately. He used the cryptological encoder, set it up based on the date and time in Greenwich, then waited until it phased in. When he got a dial tone, he called the Air Force command center in the Cheyenne Mountain bunker in Colorado Springs.

"All quiet, Colonel. They haven't stirred much today."

Bob Cassidy breathed a sigh of relief. By the following morning, the defenses here would be ready, but not quite yet.

Everything was a problem, from berthing to bathrooms. The pilots got an empty ramshackle barracks and the enlisted got two. The bathrooms were appalling. Each building had one solitary toilet without a seat to serve the needs of the eighty people who would be bunked in that building.

"If my mother saw this, she'd faint dead away. She always wanted me to join the Navy, live like a gentleman," Bob Cassidy told a little knot of junior officers he found staring into a dark, filthy barracks bathroom.

"Why didn't you?"

"I used to get seasick taking a bath."

"You've certainly come to the right place, Colonel. You won't have to take baths here."

"Fur Ball, you and Foy Sauce go dig a hole for an outhouse. Scheer, you take these others and tear down that old shack across the road for wood. Get some tools from the mechanics and watch out for rusty nails. And build one for the enlisted troops, too."

When Cassidy disappeared, Hudek said disgustedly, "Outhouses! We've come halfway around the world to build outhouses."

"Glamour," Foy Sauce muttered. "High adventure, fame . . . I am so goddamn underwhelmed, I could cry."

That evening everyone ate in an abandoned mess hall. The stoves used wood from the nearby forest. The doctor who had accompanied the group from Germany refused to allow anyone to drink the water from the taps, so bottled water was served with the MREs—meals, ready to eat. The MREs were opened, warmed somewhat on the stoves, and served.

Later that evening, Maj. Yan Chernov came looking for the commanding officer. He had a translator in tow. After the introductions, he told Cassidy, "My men need food. We came here from Zeya two weeks ago. The base people have no extra food."

"How many of you are there?"

"Sixty-five."

Cassidy didn't hesitate. "We'll share, Major." He caught the supply officer's eye and called him over. After a brief conversation, he told the translator, "Dinner for your people will be in twenty minutes."

"We have no money. Nothing with which to pay."

"Zeya is down the valley, isn't it?"

"Yes. East. The Japanese attacked. I shot down a few."

"With Su-27s?"

"Yes, good plane."

"My first name is Bob." Cassidy held out his hand.

"Yan Chernov."

"Let's have a long talk while you eat. I want to know everything you know about the Japanese."

The sea was calm, with just the faintest hint of a swell. The boat rocked ever so gently as it ghosted along on its electric engines. Fog limited visibility and clouds blocked out the night sky. A gentle drizzle massaged Pavel Saratov's cheeks as he stood in *Admiral Kolchak*'s tiny cockpit atop the sail. He took a deep breath, savoring the tang of the sea air, a welcome contrast from the stink of the boat.

Alive. Ah, how good it was. Unconsciously he fingered the lumpy new scar on his forehead, a jagged purple thing that came out of his hairline and ran across above his left eye, then disappeared into his hair over his left ear. The fragments of the Japanese shell that struck the bridge had torn off half his scalp.

The corpsman had sewn the huge flap of skin back in place, and fortunately it seemed to have healed. The scar was oozing in several places—an infection, the corpsman said. He smeared ointment on the infected places twice a day. Every morning he used a dull needle to give Saratov an injection of an antibiotic as the crew in the control room watched with open mouths. Saratov always winced as if the needle hurt mightily. He had inspected the bottle of penicillin before the first injection. The stuff was grossly out of date, but since it was all they had, he passed the bottle back to the corpsman without comment and submitted to the jabs.

An hour before midnight. Here under the clouds, amid the fog, it was almost dark, but not quite. A pleasant twilight. At these latitudes at this time of year the night would not get much darker. At least the clouds shielded the boat from American satellites. He wondered if the Americans were passing satellite data to the Japanese. Perhaps, he decided. Saratov didn't trust the Americans.

Behind Saratov, the lookout had the binoculars to his eyes, sweeping the fog. "Keep an eye peeled," Saratov told him. "If the Japanese know we are here, we will have little warning."

As his wound healed, Saratov had ordered the boat northward, keeping it well out to sea. He lay in his bunk staring at the overhead and eating moldy bread, turning over his options.

He refused to make a radio transmission on any frequency. The danger of being pinpointed by radio direction finders was just too great. One evening the boat copied a message from Moscow. After it was decoded, Askold delivered it to the captain, who read it and passed it back.

"Captain, Moscow says to go to Trojan Island. I have never heard of it."

"Umm," Saratov grunted.

"It's not on the charts."

"It is a submarine base, inside an extinct volcano, near the Kuril Strait. It was a base for boomers. Abandoned years ago."

"What will we do, Captain?"

"Hold your present course and speed. Let me think for a while."

Trojan Island. After several days of thought, Saratov decided to try it, because the other options were worse.

Now he spoke into the sound-powered telephone on his chest. "XO, will you come up, please?"

When the executive officer was standing beside Saratov in the cockpit, he said, "The island is dead ahead, Captain. Four miles, if our navigation is right."

"I haven't been here in twelve years," Saratov muttered. "I hope I haven't forgotten how to get in."

"Amazing," the XO said. "A sub base so secret that I never heard about it."

"You weren't in nuclear-powered submarines."

"What if there is nothing there anymore?"

"I don't know, Askold. I just don't know. It's a miracle the P-3s haven't found us yet. Sooner or later they will. I thought about stopping a freighter, putting all the men aboard and scuttling the boat. We have an obsolete submarine, the periscope is damaged, we're running low on fuel and food, and we have only four torpedos left. We've done about all the damage we can do."

"Yes, sir."

The XO concentrated on searching the fog with binoculars.

They heard the slap of breakers on rocks before they saw anything. Probing the fog with a portable searchlight, Saratov closed warily on the rocky coast at two knots. At least the sea was calm here in the lee of this island.

He finally found rocks, rising sheer from the sea.

It took Saratov another hour to find the landmarks he wanted, mere fading gobs of paint smeared on several rocks. He was unsure of one of the marks—there wasn't much paint left—but he kept his doubts to himself. After taking several deep breaths, Saratov turned the boat, got on the heading he wanted, then ordered the boat submerged.

In the control room, he ordered the *michman* to take the boat to a hundred feet, then level off. While this was going on, he studied the chart he had worked on for an hour earlier that day.

"I want you to go forward on this course at three knots for exactly five minutes, then make a ninety-degree right turn. If we go slower, the current will push us out of the channel."

"Aye aye, Captain."

"If we hit some rocks at three knots we'll hole the hull," one of the junior officers said, trying to keep it casual.

"This is a dangerous place to get into," the captain replied, trying to keep the censure from his voice. Now didn't seem the time to put junior officers in their place. "Sonar, start pinging. Give me the forward image on the oscilloscope."

As the submerged boat approached the island, the hole in the rock became visible on the scope. Pinging, afraid of going slower, Saratov aimed for the tunnel.

Around Saratov, everyone in the control room was sweating. "This is worse than Tokyo Bay," the XO remarked. No one said a word. All eyes were on the oscilloscope.

As the sub entered the hole, Saratov ordered the speed dropped to a knot. He crept forward for a hundred yards, watching the scope as the sonar pinged regularly. The chamber ended just ahead.

With the screws stopped, the chief began venting air into the tanks. The sub rose very slowly, inching up.

When the boat reached the surface, Saratov cranked open the hatch dogs, flung back the hatch, and climbed into the cockpit.

The boat lay in a black lagoon inside a huge cavern. That much he had expected. What Saratov had not expected were the electric lights that shone brightly from overhead. A pier lay thirty meters or so to port. Standing on the pier were a group of armed men in uniform: Russian naval infantry. Saratov gaped in astonishment.

One of the men on the pier cupped his hands to his mouth and called, "Welcome, Captain Saratov. We have been waiting for you."

CHAPTER SEVENTEEN

⬤ SEVERAL OF THE armed naval infantrymen, Russian marines, on the pier were officers. As the submarine was secured to the pier, Saratov saw that one officer wore the uniform of a general. When the soldiers had pushed over a gangplank, the general skipped lightly across like a highly trained athlete. He didn't bother to return the sailors' salutes.

Saratov didn't salute, either. The general didn't seem to notice. He stood on the deck, looking up at the dents and scars on the sail and the twisted periscope.

"How long will it take to fix this?" he asked, directing his question at Saratov.

"If we had the proper tools, perhaps two days for this damage. The missing tiles will take several weeks to repair, and the new ones may come off again the first time we dive."

The general climbed the handholds to the small bridge. "My name is Esenin."

"Saratov."

"Shouldn't you be saluting or something?"

"Should I?"

"I think so. We will observe the courtesies. The military hierarchy is the proper framework for our relationship, I believe."

Saratov saluted. Esenin returned it.

"Now, General, if you will be so kind, I need to see your identity papers."

"We'll get to that. You received an order directing your boat to this base?"

Saratov nodded.

The general produced a sheet of paper bearing the crest of the Russian Republic. The note was handwritten, an order to General Esenin to proceed to Trojan Island and take command of all forces there. The signature at the bottom was that of President Aleksandr Kalugin.

"And your identity papers. Proving you're General Esenin."

"Alas, you have only my honest face for a reference."

"Oh, come on! A letter that may or may not be genuine, a uniform you could acquire anywhere? Do I look like a fool?"

"We also have weapons, Captain. As you see, I am armed and so are my men. If you will be so kind as to observe, they have your sailors under their guns as we speak."

The soldiers were pointing their weapons at the sailors, who were busy securing the loose ends of the lines. "All personnel at this base are subject to my authority, including you and your men," General Esenin concluded.

"I didn't know there were any personnel here."

"There are now."

Saratov handed the letter back. He leaned forward, with his elbows on the edge of the combing.

"I congratulate you on your victory in Japan, Captain. You have done very well."

Saratov nodded.

"By order of President Kalugin, you have been promoted to captain first class."

"My men are owed five or six months' pay. Can you pay them? Most of them have families to support."

"Alas, no one will be mailing letters from Trojan Island."

Saratov turned his head so that the general could not see his disgust. "How long will it take to ready your boat for sea?"

"The periscope . . . if there is another in the stores here, that will take several days. The radar is out of action. We have several cracked batteries. If the people here have the parts and tools and food and fuel and torpedoes, perhaps a week."

The general nodded abruptly. "We will repair your boat as speedily as possible, refuel and reprovision it; then you and your crew will take me and a special warfare team back to Tokyo."

Saratov tried not to smile.

"You look amused, Captain."

"Let's be honest, 'General.' This boat will never get into Tokyo Bay a second time."

"I know it will be difficult."

Saratov snorted. "For reasons we can only speculate about, the Japanese left the door open the first time. We grossly embarrassed them. I assume you know the Asian mind? They lost a great deal of face. They will go to extraordinary lengths to ensure that we do not succeed in embarrassing them again. By now they have welded the door shut."

"No doubt you are correct, but I have my orders from President Kalugin. You have your orders from me."

"Yes, sir."

"Just so that we understand each other, Captain, let me state the situation more plainly: this boat is going back to Tokyo Bay. If you do not wish to take it there under my orders, we will give you a quick funeral and your executive officer will have his chance at glory."

Saratov bit his lip to keep his face under control. Esenin glanced his way and smiled.

"You find me distasteful, Captain. A common reaction. I have an abrasive personality, and I apologize." His smile widened. "Then again, perhaps *distasteful* is an understatement. Perhaps, Saratov, like so many others before you, you wish to watch me die. Who knows, you may get lucky."

Esenin flashed white teeth.

Saratov tried to keep his face deadpan. "I hope you are a tough man," he told Esenin. "When they weren't expecting us, the Japanese almost killed us. Next time, they'll be ready. Dying in one of these steel sewer pipes won't be pleasant. There is just no good way to do it. You can be crushed when the boat goes too deep and implodes, maybe die slowly of asphyxiation when the air goes bad. If we get stuck on the bottom, unable to surface, you'll probably wish to God you had drowned."

Esenin's smile was gone.

"We might die together, Saratov," he said. "Or perhaps I shall watch you die. We will see how the game goes."

The general climbed down the rungs welded to the sail to the deck. He paused and looked up at Saratov. "You have five days and nights to get ready for sea. Make the most of them."

The next day Bob Cassidy took off leading a flight of four. He had slept for exactly two hours. According to the people at Space Command in Colorado Springs, two Zeros had their engines running at Zeya, five hundred miles east. Ready or not, the Americans could wait no longer.

This morning Paul Scheer flew on Cassidy's wing. The second section consisted of Dick Gvelich and Foy Sauce.

Cassidy swung into a gentle climbing turn to allow the three fighters following him to catch up. Joined together in a tight formation, the four F-22s kept climbing in a circle over the field. They entered a solid overcast layer at eight thousand feet and didn't leave it until they passed twenty thousand.

In the clear on top, they spread out so that they could safely devote some time to the computer displays in their cockpits. The first order of business was checking out the electronics.

The F-22 acquired its information about distant targets from its own onboard radar, from data link from other airplanes, or via satellite from the computers at Space Command in Colorado Springs. In addition, the planes contained sensors that detected any electronic emissions from the enemy, as well as infrared sensors exquisitely sensitive to heat. The information from all these sources was compiled by the main tactical computer and presented to the pilot on a tactical situation display.

The airplanes shared data among themselves by the use of data-link laser beams, which were automatically aimed based on the relative position of the planes as derived from infrared sensors. Each plane fired a laser beam at the other and updated the derived errors in nanoseconds, allowing the computers to fix the relative position of both planes to within an inch. In clouds or bad weather, the data-link transfer was conducted via a focused, super-high-frequency radio beam.

Each pilot knew exactly where the others were because his computer, the brain of the airplane, presented the tactical situation in a three-dimensional holographic display on the MFD, or multifunction display, in the center of the instrument panel. On his left, another MFD presented information about the engines, fuel state, and weapons. On his right, a third MFD depicted God's view, the planes as they would look from directly overhead while flying over a map of the earth.

The pilot selected the presentations and functions he wanted by manipulating a cursor control on the right or inboard throttle with his left hand. The aircraft's control stick, on the side of the cockpit under his right hand, was also festooned with buttons, so without moving his hands from stick and throttles, the pilot could choose among a wide variety of options that in earlier generations of fighters would have required lifting an arm and mechanically throwing a switch or pushing a button.

The current state of the art in fighter planes, the F-22 Raptor was a computer that flew, capable of a top speed of about Mach 2.5 and maneuvering at over 9 G's. The semi-stealthy design was intended to enable the pilot to detect the enemy before he was himself detected. Alas, the Athena capability of the Zero gave it the edge. In modern war any pretense of airborne chivalry had been completely jettisoned:

the pilot who shot first and escaped before the victim's friends could do anything about it would be the victor.

Level at thirty thousand feet, the Raptors accelerated in basic engine to supercruise at Mach 1.3. The pilots flipped a switch to turn on the chameleon skin of their planes. The planes faded from view as their skin color changed electronically to blend them into the summer sky.

As briefed, Scheer turned left five degrees and held the heading until the gap between him and the leader had widened to five miles, then he turned back to parallel Cassidy's course. The second section moved right and spread out in a similar manner. With his four planes spread over twenty miles of sky, Cassidy hoped to optimize his chances of getting one plane into Sidewinder range on any Zero they chanced to meet. If one plane was detected, the others could circle in behind the attacking Zero while it was engaged with its intended victim. That was the plan, anyway, carefully explained and diagrammed.

As the cloud deck under them feathered out, the land below became visible under scattered cumulus clouds that were growing as the sun warmed the atmosphere.

The planes flew east. Cassidy began hearing the deep bass beep of a search radar probing the sky on a regular scan. The beep made Cassidy fidgety. Of course, the stealthy shape of the F-22 prevented the operator from getting enough of a return to see the American fighters—he knew that for a fact—but still . . .

The visibility today was excellent. On the left, a huge range of mountains wearing crowns of snow stretched away to the horizon. On the right, another range ran off haphazardly into the great emptiness toward Manchuria. The land was so big, so empty. A pilot who ejected into this trackless wilderness was doomed to die of exposure or starvation. At Cassidy's insistence, the following day the U.S. Air Force would fly in a Cessna 185 on tundra tires, with long-range tanks, to use as a search and rescue plane if the need arose.

To fly the plane and operate the computers—there were actually five of them: three flight-control computers, an air-data/navigation computer, and a tactical computer—the Raptor pilot had to concentrate intently on the torrent of information being presented graphically on his HUD and the three MFDs. There was no time for sight-seeing, for trying to spot the enemy with the human eye. The pilot was merely the F-22's central processing unit.

This thought went through Bob Cassidy's mind as he forced himself to concentrate on the displays in front of him.

The miles rolled by swiftly at Mach 1.3. Not much longer . . .

Clad in a full-body G suit and a helmet that covered his entire head, Cassidy couldn't even scratch his nose. Sweat trickled down his face. Since he couldn't do anything about it, he ignored it.

Cassidy was nervous. He shook his head once to clear the sweat from his eyes, toyed with the idea of raising the Plexiglas face shield on his helmet so he could get his fingers to his face and wipe the sweat away. That would take maybe fifteen seconds, while the plane would traverse almost three and a half miles of sky.

Not yet.

Cassidy took a few seconds to stare at the spot in space where the computer said Scheer had to be. Nothing. The chameleon skin had blended the fighter into the sky so completely it was invisible to the naked eye.

Today, of course, the F-22s had their radars secured, the tac display no longer blank. The Sky Eye had located the enemy and the satellite was beaming down the information. Two Zeros were in the air over Zeya. These must be the two that were on the ground with their engines running an hour ago.

As the range decreased and Cassidy shrank the scale of the display, he realized that the Zeros were on some kind of training mission. They were not in formation. They flew aimlessly back and forth over the base, did some turns, just wandered about. Perhaps the pilots were flying post–maintenance check flights.

At fifty miles, Cassidy and Scheer began their letdown. The transports bringing bombs to Chita would not arrive until tomorrow, so today all the F-22s could do was strafe.

Gvelich and Foy stayed high and together. They would go for the airborne Zeros.

Cassidy could hear the baritone beep of a search radar sweeping past his plane. The beeps were quite regular, which made him believe that the operator did not see him. Too little energy was being reflected from the stealthy shape of the F-22 to create a blip on the operator's screen. Finally, as the range closed, the returning energy would be sufficient to create a blip, and the operator would see him. Cassidy wondered how close that would be.

He acquired the airfield at fifteen miles. The afternoon sun was behind him and slightly to his right, so he and Scheer would be essentially invisible as they came over.

Throttling back more, Cassidy let his speed drop to Mach 1. He wanted every second he could to shoot, but he wanted to arrive with minimum warning.

Down to three thousand feet, ten miles, lined up on the ramp, Cassidy pulled the throttles back even farther. Scheer was already separated out to the left, looking for his own targets. The other plane had faded from view. Cassidy had to check the tac display to make sure where Scheer was.

The routine beeps of the enemy radar changed drastically. Now the operator was sweeping the beam back and forth over the two F-22s repeatedly. Nine miles. They had made it in to nine miles before being picked up.

Bob Cassidy was down to five hundred knots when he saw the enemy fighters. There were five of them, parked in a row on the ramp. At least he hoped they were Zeros. They might have been Russian iron, but he didn't have time to make sure. Cassidy turned hard to get lined up, checked to make sure he had the ball in the center, and glanced at the altimeter.

The row of fighters was coming at him fast. And Paul Scheer appeared out of nowhere in his left-frontal quadrant, no more than fifty feet away. Paul was going to strafe these guys, too.

Cassidy throttled back still more. He was down to three hundred knots now.

Scheer opened fire, walked a stream of shells across the parked planes, and broke left. Smoke poured from one of the planes.

Cassidy walked his shells across the planes, too, and broke right.

"Make a pass at the hangars, Paul, and we're out of here. I'll join on you."

"Yes, sir."

Cassidy circled to the south as Scheer shot up the hangars. The pilot could see several missile batteries sitting in plain sight. He snapped four fast pictures of the base area with a digital camera. When he got back to Chita, he could plug the camera into a computer and print out the pictures: instant aerial photos.

Paul headed west after his second strafing pass and Cassidy joined on him. They lit burners and climbed away.

No one had fired a shot at the Americans.

Dick Gvelich was ten miles behind his intended victim and closing at Mach 1.8 when the bogey dot on the HUD moved left. The guy must be turning, he thought.

He dropped his left wing to compensate and centered the dot.

There, he could see him, just a speck slightly above the horizon, turning left. Five miles, four, now the Sidewinder tone . . . and Dick Gvelich squeezed off the missile. It leapt off the rail in a fiery streak and disappeared into the blue sky, chasing that turning airplane ahead.

A flash on the enemy airplane! Got him.

Hudek pulled off right and watched the Zero. It rolled upside down, its nose dropped, and then the ejection seat came out.

Lee Foy's Zero was potting along straight and level. Foy's ECM was picking up enemy radar transmissions, but the Zero was pointed in the wrong direction to see the F-22s. Precisely what the Japanese pilot was doing, Foy couldn't imagine. He just prayed that the enemy aviator kept doing it for a few more seconds. At four miles with the enemy in sight, Foy was closing fast, overtaking him with maybe three hundred knots of closure.

Half a world away from the warehouse, Foy decided not to waste a missile. He clicked the cursor on the gun symbol on his main MFD and pulled off a gob of power.

His speed bled down quickly. The enemy pilot kept flying straight and level.

Foy checked his tac display. Nobody around except Gvelich, stalking his victim six miles to the west. Because he didn't have religious faith in these gadgets, Foy checked over both shoulders to ensure the sky was clear.

The Zero was still potting along like an airliner going to Newark. One mile away, a hundred knots of closure.

A half mile, seventy knots.

Now, Foy reduced power, put the crosshairs in the bull's-eye made by the horizontal and vertical stabilizers. The center of the bull's-eye was the exhaust pipe.

Foy was coming up from dead astern. *Whump*—he entered his victim's wash and began bouncing around.

Closer still, no more than three hundred yards.

Still closer . . .

At a hundred yards, Foy stabilized. Although his plane was bumping along in the Zero's wash, the crosshairs in the heads-up display were skittering around on the enemy plane's tailpipe.

I should have used a Sidewinder! This isn't aerial combat—this is murder.

Unable to pull the trigger, he sat there staring at the Zero. At ninety yards, he could wait no longer.

The Gatling gun hammered at the enemy plane, which seemed to disintegrate under the weight of steel and explosive that was smashing through the fuselage from end to end.

As the Zero faded in a haze of fuel, an alarm went off in Lee Foy's head. He released the trigger as he pulled back hard on the stick. The F-22 responded instantly, climbing away from the gasoline haze just as the Zero caught fire.

The fire ignited the vapor trail, which became a flame a hundred yards long. Then the Zero blew up.

Lee Foy bit his lip, glanced at his tac display to see where Hudek was, then turned that way.

For a moment there, he had flown with his heart, not his head, and he had almost paid the price. He had come very close to dying with the Zero pilot.

"Sorry, pal," Foy Sauce whispered.

Cassidy, Gvelich, and their wingmen were fueling from a bladder on the ground at Chita when four Zeros came hunting late in the summer evening. The Zeros were radiating, searching for airborne bogeys. The F-22 raid on Zeya had caused a seismic shock in the war room in Tokyo.

Two sergeants had just finished setting up a Sentinel battery twenty miles east of Chita on a dirt road that ran through the forest. It had taken every minute of two hours to make that journey over the ruts of a terrible road. They feared the Sentinel would be damaged from all the bumps and jolts.

Finally, the GPS said they were twenty miles east, so they stopped, disconnected the trailer from the Humvee, and activated the unit. First the solar panels had to be turned to the south, then five switches thrown and a key removed, so the unit could not be turned off by anyone wandering by. The whole deal took about a minute, and most of that involved setting the solar panels.

The sergeants had just gotten back into the Humvee and were trying to get it turned around when the first missile leapt upward from the battery, spouting fire. With a soul-shattering roar, the rocket engine accelerated the missile upward too fast for the eye to follow. By the time the sergeants were looking up, all they could see was the fiery plume of the receding missile exhaust.

Even as they craned their necks, too awed to move, the second missile ignited.

As the thunder faded, the sergeant behind the wheel gunned the Humvee's engine and popped the clutch. He careened past the battery, still on its trailer, and shot off down the rutted road toward Chita.

The pilot of the Zero that took the first missile never even saw the thing coming. He was checking his displays, scanning the sky, and keeping an eye on his flight lead when the missile detonated just a foot away from the nose cone of his aircraft. The shrapnel sliced through the side of the plane, sprayed the nose area where the radar was housed, and shattered the canopy. Shrapnel cut through the pilot's helmet into his skull, killing him instantly. He never even knew he'd been hit.

The second Sentinel missile had been tracking the same radar as the first missile, and when the radar ceased transmitting, the second Sentinel tried to shift targets. It sensed other radars emitting on the proper frequency and selected the strongest signal. The canards went over and the missile began its turn . . . far too late. The flight leader was looking toward his doomed wingman, the flash of the detonating warhead having caught his eye, when the second missile streaked harmlessly between the two planes.

"Missiles coming in!" He said it over the air.

"What kind of missile?" That was Control.

"I don't know. One just struck my wingman, though, and the plane appears to be out of control. He is going down now. Eject, Muto! Eject! Get out while you can!"

Muto was past caring.

The three remaining Zeros were trying to get it sorted out when a Sentinel missile struck another Zero. The pilot lived through the warhead detonation, but his plane was badly crippled. He pulled the throttles to idle to get it slowed while he turned back toward Khabarovsk, where these planes were based.

The flight leader was mighty quick. He turned off his radar and ordered the surviving wingman to do the same. Few pilots would have correctly diagnosed the problem in the few seconds he devoted to it.

Three seconds later, another missile went sailing past a mile away, out of control.

"Beam-riders," the leader told Control.

He initiated a turn to the east, intending to make a 180-degree turn and head for home.

Halfway through the turn, Dixie Elitch and Fur Ball Hudek came roaring in with their guns blazing. The wingman lost a wing on the first pass.

The leader rolled upside down and pointed his nose at the earth. He had his head swiveling wildly when he caught a brief glimpse of afterburner flame coming from a barely discernible airplane; then the plane was gone.

He had no idea how many planes he faced, and he correctly concluded that the time had come to boogie. He punched out chaff and decoy flares as the Zero rocketed straight toward the center of the home planet.

One of the flares saved his life. Hudek triggered a Sidewinder, which went for a flare.

"Let's not waste fuel," Dixie said over the air, calling Hudek off.

"Gimme a break, baby. Let me kill this Jap."

"You heard me, Fur Ball. Break it off."

Hudek could see the Zero pulling out far below. "And to think I could be selling used cars in Hoboken." He flipped on his radar, tried to get a firing solution for an AMRAAM. Ahh ... there it was! The radar was looking right at it. *Should I or shouldn't I?*

"Get off the radio, Fur Ball."

"You bet, sweet thing. I'll get my CDs going again."

"Muto and Sugita were hit by missiles. I think they were guiding on our radar beams. When I turned the radar off, several missiles went by, striking nothing. Then we were jumped by fighters. I do not know how many. I think they killed Tashiro then. I ran for my life."

"Do not be ashamed, Miura. You are still alive to fight again."

"Colonel, I have not yet told you the most unbelievable part. Do not think I am crazy. Believe that I tell you the truth."

"Captain Miura, give us your report."

"I could not see the enemy fighters. They were invisible."

The colonel looked shocked. Whatever he had been expecting, that was not it.

"Are you sure, Miura? It is often difficult to see other airplanes in a dogfight. Light and shadow, cloud, indistinct backgrounds . . ."

"I am positive, sir. I got a glimpse of one, saw the afterburner plume. The plane was shimmering against the evening sky, barely visible. It was there and yet it wasn't. Then the angle or the light changed and I lost it. The enemy fighter was there, *but I couldn't see it.*"

In the silence that followed this declaration, Jiro Kimura spoke up. "That would not be impossible, Colonel. I have read of American research to change the color of metal using electrical charges."

The colonel was not convinced. "I have heard of no such research by the Russians."

"I doubt if the Russians could afford it, sir," Jiro answered. "These may be planes from the American Squadron that we have heard about. If so, they are American F-22 Raptors."

"Write up your report, Miura," the colonel said. "I will forward it to Tokyo immediately."

In the ready room the other pilots had a tape going on the VCR, a tape of a broadcast on an American cable channel. Jiro merely glanced at the television as he walked by . . . and found himself looking at Bob Cassidy.

He stopped and stared. Cassidy's voice in English was barely audible, overridden by a male translator.

Cassidy! Oh my God!

"Hey, bitch! You cost me a kill. I could have got that Jap."

"You call me a bitch again, Fur Ball, and you'd better have a pistol in your hand, because I'm going to pull mine and start shooting."

Aaron Hudek's face was red. He shouted, "Don't ever pull another stunt like that on me again. Got it?"

"As long as I'm the flight leader," Dixie Elitch said heatedly, "you're going to obey my orders, Hudek. In my professional opinion, we didn't have the fuel to waste chasing that guy. We had another hour of flying to do before we could land to refuel. You knew that as well as I did. At any time during that hour we could have been forced to engage again if more Zeros had come along."

"All I had to do was squeeze the trigger. I had a radar lockup."

"Then you should have fired."

"*You* said not to." Hudek's voice went up an octave.

"Well, what's done is done. You should have potted him, then joined on me."

"Aah, sweet thing, I'll bet you didn't want me to shoot the little bastard in the back. Not very sporting."

"Second-guess me all you like, Hudek, but in the sky, you'd better do what you're told."

"Or what? You gonna waste some gas shooting me down?"

"No," Bob Cassidy snapped as he walked over. "She won't have to do that. Everyone in this outfit is going to obey orders, you included. Disobey an order and your flying days are over. You'll be walking home from here. I guarantee it."

"Okay, Colonel. You're the boss."

"You got that right," Cassidy shot back.

"I was ready to squeeze it off," Hudek continued. He held up a thumb and forefinger half an inch apart. "I was that close." He sighed heavily. "We're gonna regret letting that last Jap scamper away to tell what he knew. I regret it right now."

"You had a radar lock-up?" Cassidy asked sharply.

"As the guy was getting out of Dodge."

"Perhaps the Athena gear wasn't working," Cassidy mused.

"Maybe. I dunno."

"You should have pulled the trigger, Hudek. Dixie didn't want you to waste gas. Next time, pull the damned trigger."

Dixie blew Hudek a kiss.

Fur Ball grimaced, then wandered away looking for something cold to drink. His first combat, and he had let one get away. *Augh!*

Alas, all he would find to drink was water.

There was, he reflected, one tiny spot of light in this purée of incompetence, stupidity, and lost opportunities—Foy Sauce had refused his offer of a bet on the first Zero. Forking over a grand would have really hurt. At least he got half the credit for the guns kill with Dixie. That was something, though, Lord knows, not much.

No doubt the Chink would rag him unmercifully anyway. Double *augh!*

CHAPTER EIGHTEEN

● WORKING IN SHIFTS around the clock, the men of *Admiral Kolchak* took three days to ship a new periscope and radar antenna. They also took on a full load of torpedoes and diesel fuel, provisioned the ship with canned vegetables and meat, refilled the freshwater tanks, washed their clothes, and took baths. The cracked batteries took more time. There was no way to replace the missing anechoic tiles on the boat's hull, so they didn't try.

It was in the shower that the XO, Askold, approached Pavel Saratov, who was standing in the hot water with his eyes closed, letting it massage his back and head.

"Captain, we've found four missiles for the sail."

"Are you sure they are the right ones?"

"Twenty years old if they are a day, but I've already loaded one. It fits."

"Very good, Askold."

"Sir, where does General Esenin want us to go?"

"Back to Tokyo Bay," Saratov said after a bit. No doubt Askold picked the shower for his questions because with all this water noise a microphone couldn't overhear their conversation.

"The men are very unhappy."

"Umm." Saratov opened his eyes and reached for the soap.

"They'll be ready for us this time."

"He has written orders, signed by President Kalugin. We don't have any choice."

Askold concentrated on scrubbing.

"Look at the provisions," Saratov said. "Food, torpedoes, diesel fuel—they must have flown this stuff in here over the Pole. Somebody somewhere gave these people a hell of a priority."

"It's crazy. A diesel/electric boat? A few torpedoes? We can win the war for Russia?"

"Russia's only operational submarine in the Pacific is *Admiral Kolchak*. Our other three were sunk attacking the Japs off Vladivostok."

"So what are we going to do in Tokyo Bay?"

"Esenin has a mission. He just hasn't bothered to tell us serfs what it is."

"Captain, the men—"

"XO, the officers and *michmen* and enlisted men of *Admiral Kolchak* are going to obey orders. They are going to do as they are told. They swore an oath to obey, and by all that's holy, they will."

"Yes, sir."

"Esenin will shoot anyone who fails to obey orders. If he doesn't, I will. You'd better tell them."

"Aye aye, sir."

"This is bigger than all of us, Askold. We have no choice. None at all."

"I understand, Captain."

That was the way he put the fear in Askold, who refused to look at him.

When the executive officer left the locker room, still buttoning his shirt, Saratov sat heavily on the bench. He found himself fingering the scar on his forehead.

He should have died in Tokyo Bay. Askold saved his life, and Saratov almost wished he hadn't.

"He intends to nuke Japan," Janos Ilin told Marshal Stolypin. The old man stared at him stonily, which unnerved Ilin a little. One could never tell what the old bastard was thinking, or if he was. Talking to him was like talking to a portrait.

"He isn't that stupid," Stolypin said finally.

"He *is* that stupid. Believe me. He thinks if he nukes Tokyo, Japan will collapse and he will be the new czar of Russia. His position will be unassailable."

Stolypin shook his head from side to side like an old bear. "We can win without nukes. We are bleeding them with hit-and-run raids. The Americans are in position to fight the Zeros toe-to-toe. This winter, we will unleash an army of half a million men against them. We *can* win, on the battlefield."

"Kalugin will not wait. He wants to save Russia now."

"When I saved those weapons, I was thinking of possible conflicts with former Soviet states. Ahh... The Japanese have earned their doom."

"No doubt," Janos Ilin said crisply, "but while the Japanese government is collapsing, the military might retaliate with their own nuclear weapons. They have warheads for their satellite-launch missiles, developed in secret. They might launch them at Russia."

Stolypin goggled. "Those are the first words I have ever heard about Japanese nuclear weapons. How good is your information?"

"Absolutely reliable. In fact, Kalugin knows the Japanese have nuclear warheads mounted on missiles. He sent them an ultimatum, which they rejected. Prime Minister Abe told him that if he uses nuclear weapons on the Japanese, they will retaliate."

"I know of no ultimatum."

"Obviously, Kalugin doesn't believe Prime Minister Abe. And he's willing to bet Russia that Abe is lying."

"This changes everything," Stolypin mumbled, and leaned back in his chair.

The old soldier looked out the window, then played with the letter opener on his desk. That and a pen were the only items visible. Stolypin's bureaucratic tidiness bothered Ilin. It was his experience that neatniks were neurotic.

"All these years," Stolypin muttered, "the balance of nuclear terror kept anyone from pulling the trigger. Until now . . . How do I know you are telling me the truth?"

"I would make this up? For what reason?"

"You come to me with a tale. The president is a madman bent on pulling the nuclear trigger. Perhaps he sent you here to see if I was loyal."

"Spoken like a true peasant. Your paranoia becomes you, Marshal."

"If you want to sneer at me, Ilin, do it somewhere else," the marshal said, his face as calm as a clear summer sky. "I don't have time for it."

"I have only the whispered words of men I trust."

"Whispered words of men I don't know will not move me, Ilin. I want proof. Bring me proof or don't come back."

Janos Ilin rose from his seat and left the room.

The four F-22s topped the cloud layer in a spread formation. None of the F-22s were transmitting with their radar.

Today Aaron Hudek was Cassidy's wingman, flying five miles out to the leader's left. Dixie Elitch led the second section; she was five miles away to the right, and Clay Lacy was five miles beyond her.

Their heading was slightly north of east. The late afternoon sun shone over their left shoulders. The clouds below were thickening and the gaps looked ragged and gloomy. To the north, east, and south Cassidy could see massive thunderstorms, which were growing out of the turbulent clouds below.

The ECM was silent.

Cassidy still didn't completely trust all this high-tech gadgetry, so he pushed the ECM self-test button. The lights on the ECM panel flashed in a test pattern and the audio beeped and honked. The concert and light show lasted sixty seconds, by which time Cassidy heartily wished he hadn't played with the darn thing. He had tested it on the ground an hour ago.

The autopilot flew the plane nicely. Sitting in the generous cockpit, Cassidy thought the fighter rode like a 747 crossing the Pacific. Not a hint of turbulence. Solid, tight, smooth as silk. Where was the stew with the drinks?

Idly, Cassidy mused about the strange twists of fortune that had brought him here, to a foreign war where the only person on earth who might be considered one of his family was flying a fighter on the other side.

Life is bizarre at times, he decided. Totally unpredictable.

Dixie was a little too far away, but Cassidy didn't want to break radio silence to tell her to tighten up.

Two hundred miles to Zeya. The F-22s would be there in fifteen minutes.

Cassidy twiddled his computer cursor, told the magic box to attack the target he had programmed while still on the ground. The National Security Agency selected the targets by studying satellite reconnaissance photos. They converted latitude and longitude coordinates into code by use of map overlays, then passed the coded coordinates by scrambled satellite data link. The coded coordinates were plotted on maps brought from the States and reconverted to latitude and longitude; the resulting lat/long numbers were handed to the pilots to be programmed into the aircraft's attack computer.

The pilots were given only coordinates: They didn't know what they were bombing. It was a curious disconnect—if you didn't know, you wouldn't feel guilty. *I'm not responsible—the people in Washington told me to push the button and I pushed it.*

Hanging in Cassidy's small internal weapons bay were two one-thousand-pound green bombs. On the nose of each bomb was a GPS receiver, a computer, and a set of four small movable canards, or wings. The target coordinates were fed to the bomb's computer by the aircraft's computer, which also determined where the bomb should be dropped based on the known wind at altitude. As the unpowered bomb fell, the GPS receiver located the bomb in three-dimensional space and fed that data to the computer, which calculated a course to get the bomb where it was supposed to go and positioned the canards to steer it there. The accuracy of the system was phenomenal. Half the bombs dropped from above thirty thousand feet would hit within three meters—about ten feet—of the center of the programmed lat/long bull's-eye.

Today as Cassidy flew toward the Zeya airfield at 34,000 feet at Mach 1.3, the computer figured an attack solution and presented steering commands to the pilot. The plane's autopilot followed the commands with no input from the pilot.

Everything is automated, he thought. The machine does everything for you but die.

Due to the fact that the weapons could steer themselves, at this altitude the window into which they must be dropped was a large oval, or basket. Any bomb put into the basket would have the energy to steer itself to the desired target, if, of course, the computer and GPS receiver in the nose functioned properly. Just in case, the approved procedure was to drop two bombs on each target.

The symbology in the HUD was alive, moving predictably and gracefully as Bob Cassidy threaded his way between thunderstorms to make his supersonic bomb run five miles above the earth. When he was within the basket, he released the first weapon by pushing once on the pickle on the joystick. He felt just the slightest jolt as the first bomb was jettisoned from the weapons bay. Another push sent the second bomb after the first. Behind Cassidy, bombs were falling from the other planes, each of which was running its own attack.

The sonic booms arrived at the Zeya airfield before the bombs did. Four of them in less than a second, like an incoming artillery barrage.

The bombs startled Jiro Kimura, who scanned the cloudy sky. He had been walking toward the headquarters building to report to the base commander, but upon hearing the booms, he spent two seconds looking for enemy airplanes. Then he remembered the Zeros he and his wingman had flown in just an hour ago from Khabarovsk, and he started running back toward the parking mat.

Now he heard the roar of the engines, quite audible five miles under the speeding planes.

Jiro looked up again. He was searching the cloud-studded sky when the first bomb hit the ammunition storage depot on the edge of the base, two miles away. The resulting explosion leveled trees in every direction for a thousand yards. The explosion was so large that the detonation of the second bomb in the middle of the mess went completely unnoticed.

Jiro was facedown in the weed-studded dirt before the concussion of that explosion reached him.

A nearby hangar being used to store rations took two bombs in two seconds, those dropped by Aaron Hudek. After the bombs detonated, the hanger roof rose fifty feet in the air before it began falling. The walls of the building collapsed outward.

The pair of bombs dropped by Dixie Elitch fell on the fuel farm, two miles away from headquarters on the other side of the base. These bombs ignited two fuel fires, which quickly sent enormous columns of black smoke into the darkening evening clouds.

The last set of bombs, those dropped by Clay Lacy, was targeted on the headquarters building behind Jiro. The first bomb hit the northwest corner of the building, causing a fourth of the building to collapse in a pile of rubble. The second missed the building on the east side by ten feet; the explosion fired the brick masonry of the wall like shrapnel through the remaining structure.

The concussion of the two bombs pummeled Jiro Kimura as he lay facedown in the dirt a hundred feet away. Miraculously, the flying debris caused by the two bombs only dusted him with mortar and powdered brick.

When the air cleared, he picked himself up, wiped the dust and dirt from his eyes, and brushed the worst of it from the front of his uniform.

His thoughts began to clear. The people inside the building . . .

Jiro jerked open the door of the headquarters building and rushed inside.

The dust in the air was so thick he could barely see. The electric lights were off. He groped his way down the hall and into the war room. The air was opaque.

Holding a handkerchief in front of his mouth and nose so that he could breathe, Jiro groped his way into the room. Something hit his legs. He bent down, blinking furiously, trying to see. It was a body. Half a body—from the waist down.

The floor was covered with thousands of pieces of bricks.

The air was clearing.

More bodies, and pieces of bodies, arms at odd angles, severed heads . . .

He looked up. As the swirling dust cleared, he could see patches of dark clouds through the gaping hole where the northwest corner of the building had stood. And he could hear the roar of jet engines.

The Americans had just released their bombs when Zero fighters surprised them. Suddenly, the ECM was wailing and the displays showed yellow fighter symbols, Zeros, out to the left and closing rapidly. Then one of the Zeros put a missile into the air and all hell broke loose.

The Americans slammed their throttles into full afterburner and broke hard to avoid the oncoming missile. Cassidy turned into the missile at eight G's, the massive titanium nozzle behind the afterburners tilting the fire cones up to help the jet turn faster. His full-body G suit automatically inflated to keep him from passing out.

The HUD showed targets everywhere. Unfortunately, the computer displayed the targets' positions in real time, not where they would be after Cassidy pointed his plane so that the targets were within the missile's performance envelope when he managed to get a firing solution. Solving that four-dimensional problem by looking at the computer displays while in danger of losing your life was the art of the supersonic dogfight. Some pilots could do it; others flew transports and helicopters.

Cassidy flipped the weapons selector to "Missiles" while in an eighty-degree bank pulling four G's. A Zero was almost head-on when the aircraft vector dot came rapidly into the missile-capable circle, so he pulled the trigger. An AMRAAM missile roared away in a gout of fire.

The AMRAAM didn't guide! Of course not, stupid! It can't see the Athena-protected Zero.

Cassidy didn't have time to fret his mistake. Another missile streaked across his nose, not a hundred feet away, from left to right.

He had a target down and to his right, so he rolled hard and pulled toward it. The plane was turning away, so if he could outturn it, he could get a high-percentage stern shot. The G's pressed down on him and he felt the G suit squeezing viciously. He fought to inhale against the massive weight on his chest.

Now he had Sidewinders selected on the MFD. The enemy fighter was close, almost too close, but when he got a locked-on tone from the missile, Cassidy fired. Two seconds later he saw an explosion out of the corner of his eye. *Did I get him?*

He was diving now toward the earth, pulling three G's. He relaxed the G, leveled his wings, reapplied G. Nose coming up, more G, lower the left wing because a Zero was behind and left and high and the missile light on the instrument panel was flashing as the ECM wailed. . . . Pull, pull, pull!

Another explosion off to the right.

A plane flashed in front, a Zero, and Cassidy slammed the wing down to follow.

Clay Lacy saw the missile that killed him. It was fired by a Zero just two miles away at his four o'clock low, and tracked toward him straight as a laser. Lacy's computer was displaying two possible targets in front of him, recommending the one to the right, when out of the corner of his eye he saw the missile coming. To his surprise, he now realized the Missile warning light was flashing and the aural warning tone wailing at full cry. The missile was less that a second from impact when he saw it, and Clay Lacy knew he had had the stroke.

"Shit," he said, and pulled into a nine-G grunt.

It wasn't enough. The missile went off just under the belly of the aircraft, blasting shrapnel into the wing fuel tanks and shredding the airplane's belly. Shrapnel coming through the floor of the cockpit killed Clay Lacy less than a second before the aircraft blew up. As the fireball expanded, fed by the aircraft's fuel, two long cylinders—the aircraft's engines—shot out of the explosion and fell in a ballistic trajectory toward the earth five miles below.

The disappearance of one of the three other friendly green fighter symbols from his tac display registered on Bob Cassidy. He was too busy to wonder who had been hit.

He was solidly in the clouds, flying as if he were in the simulator back in Germany.

He rocketed down, doing almost Mach 2, checking the tac display for enemies who might be locking him up for a missile shot. He came out of burner and cracked his speed brakes a few inches to help him slow.

Uh-oh, ten miles off to the right—another Zero, shifting to a high radar PRF (pulse repetition frequency) for a shot. *Now* it was on the display—why hadn't Sky Eye seen the Zeroes when the F-22s were inbound to the base?

He racked the F-22 into a hard right turn, nine G's, over twenty degrees heading change per second at this speed. He saw the streak on the MFD as the enemy fighter launched a missile.

Cassidy flipped his fighter over on its back, pulled the nose thirty degrees down, and lit the afterburners. His plane was automatically pumping out chaff and decoys—they would save him or they wouldn't.

He elected to go under the enemy fighter, too fast for the Zero to get his nose down for another shot.

That was the way it worked out. The enemy's missile didn't guide. Cassidy came out of burner and pulled up to turn in behind the Zero, which was also turning hard to get on his tail, a fatal mistake. Nothing in the sky could turn with a Raptor.

Cassidy selected his gun.

He was going to get a shot, a blind, in-the-cloud shot. He was outturning the Zero. He kept the G on, fought against it as he tried to pull the aircraft vector dot through the target symbol on the HUD so that the two dots would cross at less than a mile.

Now!

He squeezed the trigger and held it down. Fire poured from his Gatling gun.

In the Zero, the Japanese pilot had lost the American on his tactical display. He was turning hard, trying to reacquire the F-22 on radar so that he could fire another missile. He never knew what killed him. The first of the cannon shells from the F-22 passed behind the Zero and he never saw them. Then the river of high explosive swept across his plane.

Several of the shells passed through the left horizontal stabilator; then four shells smashed the left engine to bits. Five shells shredded the main fuel cell behind the cockpit. Three of the shells struck the pilot, killing him instantly. Another two shells went through the nose of the aircraft, smashing the radar. The damage was done in a third of a second; then the stream of shells passed on ahead of the aircraft.

The Zero flew on for three more seconds before fuel hit the hot engine parts and the aircraft exploded.

"Yankees check in."

"Two's up." That was Hudek.

"Three." Dixie.

Four should have sung out here, but he didn't.

"Four, are you there?" Cassidy asked. He was at full throttle, racing west from Zeya.

No answer from Lacy.

"Yankees, stay with me. Lacy, where are you, son?"

"I think he bit the big one, skipper." That was Hudek.

"Lacy, you flaky bastard, answer me, son. Where are you?"

When they landed back at Chita, night had fallen. The three fighters taxied to their respective revetments and shut down.

In the office they used as a ready room, they put the video discs into the postcombat computer and played the mission again. The computer took the information from all three of the surviving planes, merged it, and presented it as a three-dimensional holograph. They saw the American aircraft and the Zeros, the maneuvering, the missiles flying—all of it was right there for everyone to watch. Every brilliant maneuver and every mistake was there for all to see.

"We fired fifteen missiles and killed six Zeros. One gun kill. We lost a plane and pilot."

"Too bad about Lacy."

"God, that's tough."

"You wasted that AMRAAM when you squirted it at that Zero, Colonel. That Athena gear they have really works."

"We never picked them up on the ECM. They didn't turn on their radars until we were on top of them."

"That was their mistake."

"The satellite never saw these guys until they were on us."

"Late-afternoon build-ups, lots of thermals . . ."

"Cost us a man."

"Lacy screwed up, skipper," Fur Ball Hudek said flatly. "Look at this sequence." He pointed at two planes in the holographic display. "This villain passes behind Flake at a right angle, turns hard into him to get a firing solution. Flake is busy chasing these two over here. See that? Flake had target fixation; he lost the bubble. Clay Lacy's dead because he fucked up."

That was the nub of it. In this business errors were fatal.

"Okay, let's recap. The Zeros got into us before we knew they were around. Lacy screwed up and got hammered. But the Japs screwed up too. If they had sat fifty miles out squirting missiles at us, we couldn't have touched them. They'll learn from this. Just you watch."

Cassidy got on the satellite telephone to Washington. He wound up with Colonel Eatherly at home. After Cassidy finished explaining the mission, Eatherly said, "We have satellites over that area most of the time. Sometimes they can see airplanes. I can't say more than that. I'll talk to General Tuck tomorrow. Maybe he'll eat some ass. But I can tell you right now, Space Command is doing all they can with the technology."

"I understand."

"Sorry about your pilot."

"If the wizards know Zeros are airborne, maybe they could call us on the sat phone. Back up all this techno-crap. Our duty officer could call out traffic over the base radio."

"We'll do it."

Cassidy was exhausted. He had no appetite. He wandered off to the lower bunk he called home.

He lay there staring at the ceiling. He had pulled the trigger repeatedly today. What if one of those Japanese pilots had been Jiro? What would Sabrina say?

If he had killed Jiro . . .

A wave of revulsion washed over him. He was too tired to sit up, yet he couldn't sleep.

He lay in the bunk with his eyes open, staring into the darkness.

CHAPTER NINETEEN

● PAVEL SARATOV WAS in *Admiral Kolchak*'s control room studying charts of Japanese waters when the XO called down from the sail
cockpit.

"Better come up here, Captain, and take a look."

Saratov put down his pencil and compass and climbed the ladder.

"Look, Captain." Askold pointed.

On the pier, General Esenin and his troops were milling smartly
around a truck carrying four metal containers. A crowd of civilians was
unloading welding equipment from another truck.

"What is this, Captain?"

"I don't know."

"Those look like jet-engine shipping containers. Doesn't make
sense."

"Ummm."

"Those are the sloppiest naval infantrymen I've ever seen," Askold
grumped. "They don't wear their uniforms properly. They don't know
how to care for their equipment. They have little respect for superior
officers. . . ." He trailed off when he saw that Saratov had no intention
of replying.

After a few minutes, Esenin came across the gangway and called up
to the officers on the bridge. "Come down, Captain, please."

Saratov descended the ladder. Askold was right behind him.

"I need your technical expertise, Captain Saratov. I wish to weld
these four containers to the submarine. Where would you suggest?"

Saratov was dumbfounded. "Outside the pressure hull? Our speed
will be drastically affected."

"No doubt."

"Worse, the water swirling around the containers will make noise."

Esenin frowned.

"What is in the containers, anyway?"

"We will discuss that later. Suffice it to say, I have been ordered to attach these containers to the hull of this ship and I intend to do so. The only question is where."

"They are going to be in place when we submerge? While we are underwater?"

"Yes."

"The noise—"

"Explain." Esenin flicked his eyes across Saratov's face.

"The more noise we make underwater, the easier we are to detect."

"The easier we are to detect," Askold added, "the easier we are to kill."

Esenin shot Askold a withering look. "Don't patronize me, little man. My bite is worse than my bark."

"What is in the containers, General?" Saratov asked again.

"Each contains a nuclear weapon. They have been carefully water-proofed, packed, and so on. The job was cleverly done, believe me. The containers allow water to flow in and out so they will not be crushed when the submarine goes deep. Our job is to deliver these weapons."

"Deliver?" Saratov murmured, his voice a mere whisper.

"These are old warheads from ICBMs, from the days when our missiles were not very accurate. To ensure the target would be destroyed even if the missile missed by a few miles, the designers heavily enriched the warheads. Each of these weapons yields one hundred megatons."

"One hundred million tons of TNT equivalent..." said Askold, staring at the containers.

Saratov scrutinized the general's face. The man was mad. Or a damned fool.

"You have never been on a diesel/electric submarine, have you?"

"No," Esenin admitted.

"Any submarine?" Saratov bored in. "Have you ever been on any submarine?"

"No."

Saratov tried to collect his thoughts. "General, I don't know who made this decision, but it was misinformed. A diesel/electric submarine is an anachronism, an artifact from a bygone age. Every decision the captain makes, all of them, revolves around keeping the battery charged."

Esenin looked unimpressed.

"These boats don't really go anywhere," Saratov explained. "They merely occupy a position. They can hide, but they can't run. When discovered, they are so immobile that they can easily be destroyed. Do you understand that?"

"You made it to Tokyo Bay."

"Indeed. And a heroic feat it was! All the Japanese antisubmarine forces were on the other side of the island, in the Sea of Japan."

"We will have to be smarter than the Japanese."

"Smarter? When this boat runs at three knots, it must snorkel one hour out of every twenty-four. At six knots, it must snorkel eight hours out of twenty-four. If we cannot get the snorkel up, we are down to one or two knots, just steerageway." Saratov felt his voice rise. "I have been pinned before by American ASW forces. In peacetime. You cannot imagine what it is like, knowing they have you, knowing they can kill you if they wish, anytime they wish. My God, man! I've had dummy depth charges knock tiles off the sub's skin."

"I think you are a coward."

Saratov took two deep breaths. "That may be the case, sir. But coward or not, I think you are a fool."

"This boat is the only submarine we have in the Pacific," Esenin said, shrugging. "It will have to do."

"We are on a fool's errand, a suicide mission. A competent antisubmarine force will quickly locate and kill us." Pavel Saratov pointed at the deck. "Don't you understand? This steel tube will be your coffin."

"This boat will have to do."

Saratov couldn't believe it. "Why don't you go alone, in a rowboat? You will have the same chance of success, and sixty other men won't die with you."

"Enough of this," Esenin snarled.

"So if by some miracle we get to Tokyo, we find an empty pier and tie up alongside. Your men steal a truck and you haul the warheads over to the rotunda of the Diet?"

The corner of Esenin's mouth twitched.

"Better weld them to the deck, here in front of the sail," Saratov said. He walked forward to the open hatch leading into the torpedo room. The men were loading torpedoes this morning. Four were already in. He stood with his back to Esenin, watching the men work the hoist and manhandle the ungainly fish.

The morning was warm, with little wind. Last year's autumn leaves were crunchy underfoot.

Janos Ilin stood on a small hill amid the trees smoking a cigarette. His suit coat was open. Leaning against a tree was a rocket-propelled grenade (RPG) launcher. At the foot of the hill, thirty meters from where Ilin stood, was a paved road.

The road was one of the feeders into the Lenin Hills, north of Moscow. Aleksandr Kalugin had a dacha three kilometers farther north. He would be coming along this road soon, as he did every morning, on his way to the Kremlin with his bodyguards. Kalugin had an apartment in the Kremlin, of course, which he used whenever he did not wish to spend an evening at home with his wife. For reasons unknown to Ilin, last night Kalugin had gone home. He was there now.

Kalugin's armored Mercedes would soon be along. Two other vehicles would accompany it, both large black Mercedes, one in front of Kalugin's vehicle, one behind. Each of the guard cars contained five heavily armed bodyguards who normally wore bulletproof vests. These men were competent, ruthless, and very dangerous. Janos Ilin had but himself and four other men. He intended to kill the bodyguards before they could get out of their cars. If he failed, the bodyguards would kill him.

Ilin had picked this spot with care.

Only a short stretch of road was visible here. The cars would come around a curve fifty meters away. The road was banked and wooded on either side here, so the cars could not leave the road. If the road was blocked, the cars would be trapped.

This whole setup gave Ilin a bad feeling, but he could not afford to spend time finding a better one. Unfortunately, Kalugin was paranoid— with good reason one had to admit—and his security force was top-notch. So far, the president's loyal ones had not caught wind of Ilin's intentions, a situation that could not last forever. Ilin was well aware of the security dynamics: he must strike soon or not at all.

Smoking the cigarette and enjoying the warmth of the morning air, Ilin wished he had more men. He had considered asking Marshal Stolypin for a few, then decided the gain would not be worth the risk. He had spent five years with the men he had now; trust was something that did not grow overnight. And trustworthy or not, every additional person admitted to the conspiracy increased the likelihood that it would be discovered. Janos Ilin, spymaster, well knew about conspiracies, the building blocks of Russian history.

The day before, he had gone to see Marshal Stolypin with a cassette player and a tape. On the tape was a conversation between Kalugin and one of his lieutenants, who at the time was in Gorky.

Stolypin had said nothing as he listened to the two men discussing the nuclear destruction of Tokyo. They debated the American response, discussed the probability that the Japanese might retaliate, and then got down to it.

"Unless we use extraordinary measures, Japan will inevitably win the war," Kalugin told his confederate. "Our nation is too poor to finance the effort it will take to win with a conventional army and air force. The gap is too great."

"You must seize absolute power. Destroy all who oppose you."

"That would take time, and there is many a pitfall along the way. I have thought long about Russia. No one can take Russia back to where it used to be. No one. And if we try, the deputies will rescind their grants of power. Either the government will fall or Russia will face civil war again."

"I, too, hear these things."

"We *must* defeat the Japanese," Kalugin said. "Victory or death—those are our alternatives. You understand?"

"I do. Have you seen the genuine affection the people have for Captain Saratov? Crowds chanting his name, resolutions demanding that he be promoted, decorated, his picture plastered all over Moscow . . ."

Stolypin listened to the rest of it, then shoved the cassette recorder back across the table toward Ilin.

"If we want our country, we will have to fight for it," Ilin said. "Again."

The old man rubbed his hair with a hand, looking at nothing.

"He is sending a submarine to Tokyo. Nuclear weapons will be aboard. The plan is to put the weapons in a fault on the seafloor. There is a fanatic aboard, a man named Esenin. He swore an oath to Kalugin. If threatened with destruction, he will detonate the weapons in the mouth of Tokyo Bay."

"Will he do it?"

"By reputation, he is a patriotic zealot. He was an assassin for the GRU."

"Yuri Esenin?"

"That's right."

"I thought he was dead."

This morning Janos Ilin finished another cigarette without tasting it, then glanced at his watch. It was a few minutes past seven. He stamped his feet impatiently.

The radio came to life. "Car."

Fifteen seconds later, a black Mercedes came around the curve and into view. Nope. One of the ministers. Three of them lived near Kalugin along this road. After the car passed the small knoll where Ilin stood, it went by a truck with a high-lift basket and another truck carrying a power pole, then went around the next curve. In the fully extended lift, a man was working on a transformer mounted near the top of a pole. A flagman stood on the road near the lift truck.

"Here they come. Three cars."

Ilin crushed out his new cigarette on a tree as the second truck, the one with the power pole on it, pulled completely across the road, blocking it. The man in the cab jumped down. He had an assault rifle in his hands.

Janos Ilin knelt. He picked up the rocket-propelled grenade launcher and flicked the safety off.

The first car came around the curve and braked as the flagman waved his red flag. The second and third cars were right behind. Kalugin was in the second car. The first and third cars were full of loyal ones.

Ilin leveled the grenade launcher at the first car, which was now almost stopped, exhaled, and pulled the trigger.

The *whoosh* of the rocket was loud.

The grenade impacted the first car at the passenger's side door. The car jumped forward, a dead foot on the accelerator, the engine roaring. It crashed into the side of the truck blocking the road. Although the car was jammed firmly against the truck, the engine revved higher and higher as the tires squalled and smoked against the pavement.

As Ilin worked feverishly to reload the launcher, the driver of the second car slewed the rear end of his car around in a power slide. Smoke poured from the tires. Over the screeching of the tires, Ilin could hear a machine gun hammering.

Ilin got his grenade loaded as the third car slid to a complete stop. The doors of the car were opening as he pulled the trigger. The rocket struck the engine compartment and the shaped charge exploded inward. Men leaping from the car were cut down by machine-gun bullets, which were being fired from the lift basket above.

Meanwhile, Kalugin's car had completed its turn. At least one of

Ilin's men was pouring bullets at it. The bullets made tiny sparks, flashes, where they struck the armor and were deflected.

Kalugin's car shot by the third car on the far side with its tires squalling madly as Ilin slammed another grenade into the launcher. He pointed the weapon at the rapidly accelerating car and pulled the trigger.

The grenade smacked into a tree trunk thirty feet in front of Ilin. The charge severed the trunk and the tree began to topple.

Ilin grabbed his radio. "He's coming back north."

"I can't get the goddamn engine started." The man there was supposed to drive another power-line repair truck across the road.

"Shoot at the tires! Shoot at the tires! Don't let him get away."

With the grenade launcher in one hand and the radio in the other, Ilin ran down the hill and sprinted for the curve. He heard three short bursts of automatic-weapon fire, then silence. As he rounded the curve, he saw Kalugin's car rounding the far curve, three hundred meters on.

Ilin turned and walked back to the ambush site. One of the men lying on the road by the closest car, the trailer, was still moaning. Ilin drew a pistol and shot him in the head as he went by. The other four men who had been in the car were lying on the pavement in various positions, perforated by machine-gun bullets.

The engine in the car against the truck had stalled. The five men inside were apparently dead.

The flagman was taking no chances. He fired a shot into every head.

"Do the ones in the other car, too," Ilin told him.

The man who had driven the truck across the road came over to Ilin. As the single shots sounded, he said apologetically, "We almost pulled it off."

Ilin shouted at the man in the lift basket, who was on his way down. He had an air-cooled light machine gun cradled in his arms. "Did you shoot at Kalugin?"

"I got off just one burst. I saw sparks where the bullets were striking the armor. I'm sorry."

"We blew it," Ilin said with a grimace.

"Maybe we should get the hell out of here."

"That is probably a good idea."

As the limo shot along the two-lane road, Aleksandr Kalugin hung on to the strap in the backseat and shouted at the driver. Still shaken from the assassination attempt, he had already concluded that there was a good chance that his bodyguards, or one of them—perhaps his driver?—had betrayed him. Now he was telling the driver which way to go as they approached each intersection.

It was too dangerous to return to the dacha, so he gave the driver directions for an alternate route into Moscow.

Kalugin pulled the telephone from its storage bracket and dialed an operator. He kept his eyes on the road ahead. He removed his pistol from a pocket and laid it in his lap.

If the driver took a wrong turn, he, Kalugin, would personally put a bullet in the man's brain. He fingered the automatic as if it were a set of worry beads.

An aide in his office answered. Kalugin told him about the ambush in as few words as possible, keeping strictly to the facts. The aide would know what to do with the information.

In odd moments Kalugin made lists of his enemies. The A list included political opponents and rivals in the Congress, bureaucrats who had publicly opposed him in the past, and candidates who had run against him in past elections. The B list included critics, newspaper editors who had printed damaging editorials or news stories, bureaucrats who didn't jump when he growled, businessmen who refused to go along with his suggestions—basically carpers and footdraggers. The C list, the longest, contained everybody else that Kalugin thought less than enthusiastic about his leadership of the nation. Some persons had managed to get on this list by avoiding a handshake at parties or receptions. Several were husbands of women Kalugin thought attractive; some were there simply because he had seen their name in a report or in print and thought that person might someday be dangerous.

He had discussed threats to his power with his top aides on several occasions in the past, developed contingency plans, delegated power to men he trusted, men who owed him for their status, their place, the bread they ate.

Even now, as his car raced along, the aides would be ordering everyone on the A list arrested and interrogated. Perhaps the police would discover the culprits before Kalugin's internal security apparatus did, and if so, fine. Kalugin would proceed on both fronts regardless.

Perhaps something good would come out of this crime against his person. Maybe he could use this event as an excuse to crush some of his most vocal enemies. Their downfall would be a lesson for all the rest.

———

Three of Kalugin's men were waiting in his office when Janos Ilin arrived for work that morning. The secretary in the outer office gave him the news.

"What do they want?"

"They didn't say, sir. They had a presidential pass, so I put them in your anteroom. They went into the office without my permission."

When you screw up an assassination, this is what happens, he thought. You walk into rooms wondering if you are about to be arrested and tortured or if they want your help chasing assassins.

Janos Ilin didn't turn a hair. He walked across the anteroom to his office door and opened it. He walked in and stopped. One of them was sitting in his chair, trying to jimmy the locks on the desk drawers. Another was using a pick on the file cabinet's locks.

"What the hell is this?"

"Ah, the man with the keys. Sit down, Comrade Ilin. Sit down. And I'll trouble you for your keys."

Ilin remained standing.

"Someone tried to assassinate President Kalugin a short time ago. We are investigating."

"Did they harm the president?"

"No."

"Why are you investigating here?"

"Sit, Ilin. Sit. The keys, please."

They worked for over an hour, flipping through files, reading notebooks, looking at every sheet of paper they could find. All the while, Ilin sat and watched, apparently unconcerned. The only things that he didn't want these thugs to see were the files on agents in place in foreign countries. Fortunately, those files were in the agency's central records depository, under continuous armed guard.

"When did this assassination attempt take place?"

"This morning. The president was on his way to the Kremlin."

"Have you made any arrests?"

"We are trying to decide if we should arrest you."

Ilin snorted.

"Your sangfroid is quite commendable."

"I have nothing to hide. I have not lifted a finger against anyone. You can read those files until doomsday and that fact won't change."

When the leader was finished, he seated himself again behind the desk, in Ilin's chair. From his pocket he produced a list. "You will arrest these men. Jail them in the cells downstairs, begin their interrogations. Tape every interrogation. These instructions are from the president."

When they departed, they left one man, who now parked himself beside Ilin's chair. Ilin began making telephone calls as he examined the list. The leaders of opposition political parties, judges, public men ... Marshal Stolypin was not on this list. That meant nothing. He might be on another list.

Kalugin was wasting no time. This list had not been typed this morning.

Ilin called in his deputies, gave instructions.

The Japanese air commander in Siberia, Matsuo Handa, spent a tense night huddled with his top subordinates. The American Squadron was costing them planes and pilots. The missiles that sought out the Zero radar, the invisible F-22s—there was a lot on the plate.

One thing that the Japanese commander knew was that he could not sit idly on the defensive waiting for the Americans' next move. Fighting defensively went against all of his samurai instincts. Attack was the policy that best fit the Japanese spirit, he believed. The men wanted to attack and so did he. The only question was how.

Jiro Kimura's squadron commander took his young ace with him to the headquarters conference. He remembered Jiro's comment about the technical feasibility of electronically changing the color of an aircraft's skin, and he wanted the air commander to hear it, too.

"Sir, I do not understand how the American fighters found the Zeros over Zeya," Jiro Kimura said to Colonel Handa. "The surviving pilot states that at no time did he receive an ECM warning that American planes were in the area. A postflight check of his electronic countermeasures equipment showed that it was functioning properly. Apparently the Americans were not using radar. How did they find our planes?"

"They must have visually acquired the Zeros," Colonel Handa said. Most of the senior brass seemed to share this opinion. Jiro didn't believe it.

"Sir, if I may express my opinion," Jiro said. "Waiting in ambush with radars off, relying on the ECM to inform us of the enemy's presence, is the wrong way to employ the Zero. This airplane was designed as an offensive weapon. We must search with radar, find the enemy before he can find us, and launch our missiles first. Closing to short range with F-22s is a fatal error."

"We waited in ambush with our radars off because the F-22 can detect our radar emissions before we can detect the F-22."

"I understand, sir. Our challenge is to make the Americans fight our fight. We must lure them to a place where we can engage at long range."

"That's a wonderful proposal, Kimura," Handa said. "But it isn't practical. We have not been aggressive enough. That is why we find ourselves in this deplorable situation."

The conference, Jiro thought, went downhill from that point.

After a discussion of possible options, Colonel Handa decided to lead a daytime strike on Chita. Half the planes would go in low, on the deck, to drop cluster bombs and strafe. The other half would go in high, use their radars for a few seconds out of each minute, and attempt to engage the American fighters while the low planes struck the base. The flight would launch from Khabarovsk, so it would need tankers coming and going.

"Colonel Handa," Jiro suggested, "perhaps we should try a night attack first, to further feel out the American capabilities."

"The planes strafing and dropping cluster weapons need daylight and decent weather to be effective," the colonel answered. "We are facing a capable, aggressive enemy who has drawn first blood. We must attack, force him to parry our blows or he will seize the initiative and we will find ourselves on the defensive."

"We must strike first," the squadron commanders agreed. Like Colonel Handa, their hearts and minds were geared to the offensive.

When Jiro left the meeting at midnight, he was profoundly discouraged. The colonel was playing right into the Americans' hands, he thought. The enemy expected the Japanese to attack Chita, he argued, so they should not. The colonel's mind was made up. Cassidy already had Handa on the defensive, and Handa didn't want to admit it.

Jiro wandered over to the most dilapidated hangar on the base, where one of his friends, a helicopter pilot, was quartered. "Tell me, Shoichi, do you people have any of those infrared headsets, the kind you wear when you fly at night?"

"Yes, we have four of them. They are helmets, with earphones, visors, and so on. They will not take an oxygen mask, however."

"May I borrow one tomorrow?"

"Why?"

"I want to fly with it. I have a theory and wish to test it."

"For you, Jiro, of course. Here, have a beer."

When the chief of Asian intelligence at the Japanese Intelligency Agency, Toshihiko Ayukawa, received agent Ju's message, it had already been decoded and translated. It now rested in a new red file folder. He opened the folder and perused the short, neat columns of Japanese characters. The message read:

> *Russia has ten atomic warheads.*
> *Kalugin has ordered contingency planning for their use against Japan.*
> *At least four of the warheads will be delivered by submarine, target unknown.*

Ayukawa felt the hairs on the back of his neck tingling. Good ol' Agent Ju. He was the one who said Russia had destroyed the last of its nuclear weapons. Only a fool would bet on that as gospel truth, but no doubt that message had been a factor, one of many, in the Abe government's decision to invade Siberia.

Now Ju had changed his tune. Was he lying then or lying now?

Pavel Saratov was the last man to leave the cockpit on top of *Admiral Kolchak*'s sail. He took a final look at the four containers welded to the deck, ensured the boat was stationary in the middle of the small lagoon, pointed at the underwater entrance, then went down the hatch and dogged it after him.

Esenin was in the control room. He seemed a bit less imperious than he usually was, or perhaps it was Saratov's imagination.

"This is the tricky part," Saratov said to the chief, who nodded. "We must get steerageway on the boat before it drifts. Let's dive."

The chief gave the order while Saratov examined the sonar image on the oscilloscope.

Esenin's executive officer was a major, or at least he wore a major's uniform. He looked pale, Saratov thought, as air gurgled from the tanks and seawater rushed in.

Saratov shook his head in annoyance. He should ignore these two and concentrate on the task at hand, which was getting this boat safely out of the mountain.

A half hour later the boat had cleared the tunnel and the shallow water. It was dark up there, and overcast, so Saratov took the boat to snorkel depth and started the diesels.

Two hours later when he went to his tiny cabin, Esenin was already there, sitting in the one chair.

"Ah, Captain, come in. And please close the door."

The compartment was very small. Saratov squeezed by the chair and sat on the bunk.

"I thought this a good time to discuss our mission, Captain."

Esenin picked up the rolled-up chart from the desk, removed the string that held it, and spread it out. Saratov looked over his shoulder.

"You know Tokyo Bay? The sound to the south of it?"

"I recognize it."

"As you can see, marked on this chart in red are a number of major geological faults. You can see where they run." His finger traced several of the longest. "The fault in which we are interested is this one." His finger came to rest. "It will not be necessary to tie up to a pier and steal a truck."

Saratov didn't bother to reply.

"I have a recommendation from Revel, a leading geologist in Moscow, who studies these sorts of things with international groups," Esenin continued. "He thinks the most unstable fault is this one, at the entrance to Tokyo Bay. It has not moved in at least three hundred years, and it is very ready.

"Our task is to place our four weapons in a row atop this fault, two miles apart. When the weapons detonate, the concussion should break the eastern plate free, causing it to rise significantly."

"How significantly?" Pavel Saratov couldn't take his eyes from the chart.

"The geologist thinks the potential is there for a movement on the order of ten feet. Of course, explosions of this magnitude will vaporize an extraordinary amount of water, so the sea will rush in to fill the void. Movement of the plate will merely speed the water along."

"I see."

"The tidal wave should be quite extraordinary. A tsunami, I believe the Japanese call it. If the professor's calculations are correct, the tidal wave should be two hundred feet high when it washes over Tokyo."

"Only four warheads?"

"We will explode two simultaneously. The second set will be timed to blow exactly three minutes later. Professor Revel believes the earth should be moving down at that moment, on a long oscillation cycle, so the second set of explosions should reinforce that movement. True, we constructed the scenario hurriedly, but we have great faith in Professor Revel's computer models. It should work. It *will* work."

"All we have to do," Saratov said heavily, "is get over the fault, toss off the weapons, and sail away."

"I leave it in your capable hands, Captain."

"I will do all I can, General. Alas, any chance of success lies in the hands of the Japanese. They will be hunting us, and the odds are on their side."

CHAPTER TWENTY

● PUFFY CLOUDS FLOATING in a calm summer sky greeted the Japanese pilots as they climbed out of Khabarovsk headed for their tanker rendezvous. There were sixteen Zeros divided into two gaggles of eight. Colonel Handa led the eight planes of the high echelon. He had allowed his senior commanders to choose where they wished to fly, and they all wished to fly high, with him. The glory was in shooting down enemy planes in combat, not strafing hangars and barracks.

Still, the commanders put their very best subordinates in the eight airplanes that were going to strike the base.

Colonel Handa had intended to exhort his pilots at the briefing to do their best for the honor of Japan and the Zero pilot corps, but then he thought better of it. I have watched too many American movies, he told himself.

"They're coming," Lee Foy shouted as he slammed down the telephone. "Headed this way. Over a dozen. Took off ten minutes ago."

The American pilots went into the dispersal shack—an old hen coop that they had commandeered, cleaned, and moved to the parking mat—for their final briefing. Everyone was checking his watch. The pilots managed to avoid one another's eyes.

Bob Cassidy was glad the Japanese were on their way. The suspense was over. He had known the Japanese would attack eventually; he just hadn't known it would come so soon.

His people were ready. He had just six planes available, so he divided them into three flights. He would take Paul Scheer north of the base and wait until the Sentinel missiles had forced the Zero pilots to shut off their radars. Then he and Scheer would go in among them.

Dixie and Aaron Hudek were going out to the northwest of the base, Preacher Fain and Lee Foy to the southwest. They would come in when Cassidy called them.

Each plane carried eight Sidewinders and a full load of ammo for the gun. Cassidy had ordered the AMRAAMs left behind. He was betting that the Sky Eye data link would work. If it didn't, this fight was going to be a disaster.

He was also betting that the Japanese would avoid Chinese airspace and come in from the east, the most direct route from Khabarovsk after avoiding China. If the Zeros circled and came in from another direction, they might find a pair of F-22s with their radar and drop them both.

Every choice involves risks. Life involves risk. Breathing is a risk, Cassidy thought.

He and his pilots needed some luck. If they got a little of the sweet stuff, they could smash the Zeros right here, today, once and for all. And if luck ran the wrong way . . . well, you only had to die once.

Cassidy stood in front of the blackboard. He already had all the freqs, altitudes, and call signs written there from the planning session. "Okay, people. They are on their way. They'll hit the tankers and motor over our way, we hope. Let's go over the whole thing one more time, then suit up. We'll man up an hour and a half before they are expected, and take off an hour prior."

No one asked a single question. Eyes kept straying to wrist watches. When the brief was over, Cassidy walked outside, went around behind the shack, and peed in the grass. Finally, he suited up, taking his time.

He was standing outside the shack, looking at the airplanes, thinking about Sweet Sabrina and little Robbie and Jiro Kimura when he heard the satellite phone ring. Lee Foy answered. Fifteen seconds went by; then Foy shouted, "Sixteen Zeros. They've finished tanking and are on their way here. ETA is an hour and twenty-eight minutes from right now."

"Let's do it!"

"Let's go."

They grabbed gear and helmets and began jogging for their planes.

When the planes were level at altitude after tanking, Jiro Kimura slid away from the other flight of four Zeros that was assigned to the ground attack mission. He was wearing the night-vision helmet that he had borrowed from the helo pilots, but he didn't have it turned on. He wanted to try that now.

First, he checked his three charges, Ota, Miura, and Sasai. They were precisely in position, as if he had welded them there. They were good pilots, great comrades.

Satisfied, Jiro engaged the autopilot and began fiddling with the helmet. Before takeoff he had turned the gain setting to its lowest reading, as the helo pilot had advised. Now he lowered the hinged goggles down over his eyes. The battery was on, so the goggles were working, or should be.

His eyes slowly adjusted to the reduced light levels. Oh yes, there was the other flight, out there to the right.

He turned his head from side to side, taking in the view. The view to both sides was limited, and he couldn't read the instruments on his panel, but in combat, he wouldn't need to: he could find every dial and switch blindfolded.

The real disadvantage to the helmet was weight. In a helicopter a twelve-pound helmet on a healthy man was no big deal if he didn't have to wear it too long, but in a fighter, pulling G's, the story would be much different. At five G's, the darn thing would weigh sixty pounds, which would be a nice test of Jiro's neck muscles. Ten G's might be enough to snap his neck like a twig.

It just stood to reason that if the Americans had figured out a way to cancel visible light waves, their airplanes still might be visible in the infrared portion of the spectrum.

Jiro's oxygen mask was lying in his lap. The helo helmet had no fittings to accept the mask. The Zero's cockpit was partially pressurized with a maximum three psi differential, so even though the plane was at 25,000 feet, the cockpit was only at 9,000. If the canopy was damaged or lost, Jiro would have to hold the mask to his face with his left hand while he flew with the other.

The F-22s took off in pairs, Cassidy and Scheer first, then Dixie and Hudek, then Fain and Foy. The enlisted troops stood on the ramp watching the planes get airborne, basking in the thunder of the engines. As the wheels came into the wells, the pilots turned on their aircrafts' smart skin. The noise of the engines continued to rumble for minutes after the planes disappeared from view.

After the noise had faded, the senior NCO told the troops to get in the trenches, freshly dug by a backhoe that was sitting near the dispersal shack. They could safely stay out of the trenches for a while but the NCO was too keyed up to wait. Better safe than sorry.

The Zero symbols appeared on Bob Cassidy's tactical display at a range of two hundred miles. He was fifty miles north of the base at twenty thousand feet, cruising at max conserve airspeed, about .72 Mach. Scheer was on his left wing, out about a hundred yards. The symbols were so bunched together, Cassidy couldn't tell exactly how many bogeys were there.

The main problem with Sky Eye was that at long ranges the symbols were grossly compressed, and at short ranges they were unreliable. The gadget seemed to give the best presentation when the bogeys were from five to fifty miles away. Inside five miles, he would be forced to rely upon the F-22s' infrared sensors; the data from all the F-22s was shared, so the computers could arrive at a fairly complete tactical picture.

At least he had dodged the first bullet today: the Zeros were coming in from the east, right up the threat axis.

Cassidy checked the position of the other two flights of F-22s. He thought Preacher Fain was too close to the base.

"Preacher, this is Hoppy. A few more miles south, please."

Preacher acknowledged.

Cassidy checked everything: the intensity of the HUD displays, master armament switch on, the proper displays on the proper MFDs, cabin altitude, engine gauges. . . . He was ready.

Preacher Fain tightened his shoulder harness and ensured the inertial take-up reel was locked, so that he would not be thrown about the cockpit. He adjusted his oxygen mask, wiped a gloved hand across his dark helmet visor, and checked the armament panel.

Fain glanced at his tac display: Lee Foy was right where Fain wanted him, about five hundred feet out and completely behind his leader. With Foy well aft and off to one side, Fain was free to maneuver left, right, whatever, without worrying about a midair collision. And the wingman was free to follow the fight and keep the bad guys off Fain's tail while the leader engaged.

The high Zeros were only forty miles from the base. The low ones were thirty miles out. Eight in each flight. Fain eyeballed the rate of progress of the top group and tightened his turn radius. He wanted to come slicing in behind them just after they got into the Sentinel zone, when they were certain to have their radars off. He wanted to knock as many down as possible in the first pass, then dive to engage the lower ones. The Zeros down low were going to be juicy, pinned against the deck as the invisible F-22s came down on them from above. Oh boy!

The heart of the Sentinel missile system was its computer, which contained a sophisticated program designed to prevent an enemy from causing all the missiles in the battery to be launched by merely sweeping his radar once, shutting down, then repeating the cycle. The program required that the target radar sweep repeatedly and be progressing into the missile's performance envelope at a rate of speed sufficient to enable it to get into range by the time the missile arrived. If these parameters were met, the computer would fire two missiles, one after the other, then sit inactive for a brief period of time before the system would again listen for the proper signals.

The guidance system in the missiles was more sophisticated than the computer in the battery. As the missile flew toward its target, the computer memorized the target's relative position, course, and speed, so in the event the target radar ceased radiating, the computer could still issue guidance signals to the missile. Of course, the probability of a hit decreased dramatically the longer the target radar was off the air. If the target radiated again while the missile was still in flight, the computer would update the target's trajectory and refine its directives to the guidance system.

The system worked best when the missile was fired at an airplane that was flying directly at the Sentinel battery. Due to the geometry of the problem and the speeds of the target and missile, the missile's performance became degraded if it wound up in a tail chase.

As Colonel Handa flew toward the Chita Air Base, he was flipping his radar from standby to transmit, then back again, over and over. He had instructed all the other pilots to leave their radars in the standby position—which meant the radar had power but was not transmitting—but he was scanning with his to see if he could detect any enemy planes aloft, or induce the Americans to fire one of their antiradiation missiles. Handa didn't know that the missiles were fired from automated batteries; indeed, the possibility had never even occurred to him.

The eight strike airplanes had left the upper formation a hundred miles back. They were down on the deck now, five hundred feet above the treetops, flying at a bit over Mach 1.

Handa kept waiting for his ECM warning devices to indicate that he was being looked at by enemy radar, but the devices didn't peep. There seemed to be no enemy radar on the air. Or, thought Handa ominously, no radar that his ECM devices could detect. Perhaps the Americans had taken another technological leap of faith and were using frequencies that this device could not receive. Or perhaps their radars were in a receive-only mode, merely picking up the beacon of his radar when it was on the air. If only he...

He dropped that line of thought when the first Sentinel missile shot by his aircraft at a distance of no more than one hundred feet. The brilliant plume of the rocket motor made a streak on the retina of his eye. Handa's heart went into overdrive.

As he scanned the sky for more missiles—the visibility was excellent—he forgot to flip the switch of his radar back to standby. That was when another Sentinel missile, launched automatically almost sixty seconds before, slammed into the nose cone of his fighter.

The thirty-pound missile was traveling at Mach 3 when it pierced the nose cone and target radar in a perfect bull's-eye. Handa's plane was traveling at Mach 1.28 in almost the opposite direction. The combined energy of the impact ripped the Zero fighter into something in excess of two million tiny pieces. The expanding cloud of pieces hit the wall as each individual fragment of metal, plastic, flesh, cloth, and shoe leather tried to penetrate its own shock wave, and failed.

The other Zeros continued on toward the Chita Air Base as the pieces of Handa's fighter began to fall earthward at different rates, depending on their shape. The fuel droplets fell like rain in the cool summer sky, but the motes of metal and flesh behaved more like dust, or heavy snow.

After Colonel Handa's Zero disintegrated, the other seven planes in his flight continued straight ahead. Several seconds elapsed before the remaining pilots realized what had happened. During that time, the planes traversed almost a mile of sky.

Without their radars, the pilots were essentially blind. At these speeds, they couldn't see far enough with their eyes. At that very moment, Bob Cassidy and Paul Scheer were ten miles away, at two o'clock, on a collision course at Mach 2.15. The two American fighters were two hundred yards apart, abreast of each other, with Scheer on the left.

"We'll shoot two each, Paul, then yo-yo high and come down behind them."

"Gotcha, Hoppy."

The seekers in Sidewinders had come a long way in the forty years the missile had been in service. The primary advantage of the missile was its passive nature: it didn't radiate, so it didn't advertise its presence. The short range of the weapon was more than compensated for by its head-on capability.

At five miles, Bob Cassidy got a growl and let the first missile go. He still had not acquired the Zeros visually, and of course the Zero pilots had not seen him. He fired the second missile two seconds later, at a range of three miles. With both missiles gone, Bob Cassidy pulled the nose of his fighter into an eighty-degree climb, half-rolled and came out of burner, then pulled the nose down hard as the plane decelerated. He finally saw the Zeros below him, going in the opposite direction, toward the base.

Scheer had fired two Sidewinders almost simultaneously and was also soaring toward heaven and pulling the nose around.

One of the American missiles missed its target due to the rapidly changing aspect angle. It passed the target aircraft too far away to trigger the proximity fuse.

The other three missiles were hits. One went down the left intake of a Zero and detonated in the compressor section of the engine, ripping the plane to bits. Another missed the target aircraft by six inches; its proximity fuse exploded adjacent to the cockpit and killed the pilot instantly.

The warhead of the fourth missile detonated above the left wing of the Zero it was homing on, puncturing the wing with a hundred small holes. Fuel boiled out into the atmosphere.

The pilot felt the strike, saw his flight leader's airplane dissolving into a metal cloud, then saw fuel erupting from his own wing. He had not glimpsed an enemy aircraft and already two Zeros were destroyed, one was falling out of control, and he was badly damaged. He began a hard left turn to clear the area.

Cassidy saw this plane turning and shoved forward on his stick, which, since he was inverted, stopped his nose from coming down. He rolled right ninety degrees onto knife edge and let the nose fall.

The Zero below him continued its turn.

This was going to work out nicely—Cassidy was going to drop right onto the enemy pilot's tail. Cassidy would use the gun.

Dropping in, rolling the wings level, he pushed the thumb button as the enemy plane slid into the gunsight. The plane vibrated, muzzle flashes appearing in front of the windscreen, and the Zero was on fire, with the left horizontal stabilator separating from the aircraft.

Now Cassidy rolled into a ninety-degree bank and pulled smoothly right up to nine G's. He wanted to get around in a hurry to rejoin the fight. For the first time, he took a second to check his tac display for the position of the other five F-22s.

Only he and Scheer were still upstairs. The other two sections were descending in a curving arc.

Dixie Elitch and Aaron Hudek each fired a Sidewinder as they came roaring down on the flight of four Zeros from the northwest. The missiles tracked nicely. Dixie squeezed off another, and a third.

Her first missile converted the target Zero to a fireball, and the second went into the fireball and exploded. Her third missile took out another Zero, just as the pilot flying the third plane, the one struck by Hudek's first missile, ejected.

She was less than two miles from the last Zero and trying to get a missile lock-on tone when Hudek sliced in front, his tailpipes just beyond her windscreen.

Dixie pulled power and popped her boards to prevent a collision.

Hudek didn't bother with a missile. He intended to use his gun. He closed relentlessly on the sole remaining Zero of the flight of four.

Preacher Fain led Lee Foy down on Jiro Kimura's flight. They squeezed off two Sidewinders, one each, and both missiles tracked.

Still wearing the night-vision helmet, Kimura was craning his neck, trying to see what was happening. The Zeros exploding on his right certainly got his attention. He half-turned in his seat, using the handhold on the canopy bow to turn himself around.

And he saw the F-22s, coming down on the Zeros from behind at a thirty-degree angle.

"Break left," he screamed into his oxygen mask. He was holding the mask with his left hand. Now he dropped the mask and used that hand to hold the helmet steady as he used his right to slam the stick over and pull hard.

Fain's missile couldn't hack the turn. It went streaking into the ground.

Miura wasn't quick enough. Foy Sauce's 'winder went up his right tailpipe and exploded against the turbine section of that engine. Pieces of the engine were flung off as the compressor/turbine, now badly out of balance, continued to rotate at maximum rpm.

Miura felt the explosion, saw the right engine temp gauge swing toward the peg, and knew he was in big trouble. He pulled both engines to idle cutoff as the right engine fire light illuminated and honked on five G's to help slow down. As the plane dropped below five hundred knots, he pulled the ejection handle. Three seconds later the parachute opened, just as his jet exploded.

At this point, the fight was one minute old.

Holding the heavy night-vision helmet and goggles with his left hand, Jiro Kimura turned a square corner. Only he, of all the Japanese pilots, could see the American fighters descending upon them. At one point the G meter recorded eight G's, and Kimura was not wearing a full-body G suit, as the Americans were. He was flexed to the max, screaming against the G to stay conscious, as he honked his mount around.

It was then that Lee Foy made a fatal mistake. Perhaps he didn't see Jiro turning, perhaps he had fixated on his intended next victim, Sasai, or perhaps he was checking the position of his wingman on his tac display. In any event, he didn't react quickly enough to Jiro's turn in his direction, and once Jiro triggered a Sidewinder at point-blank range, he had no more time. The American-designed, Japanese-made missile punctured the F-22's fuselage just behind the cockpit and exploded in the main fuel cell, rupturing it by forcing fuel outward under tremendous pressure. When the fuel met oxygen, it ignited explosively.

Lee Foy had just enough time to inhale deeply and scream into his radio microphone before he was cremated alive.

Aaron Hudek saw the explosion out of the corner of his eye as he was dispatching the last of the Blue Flight Zeros with his cannon. He recognized Foy's voice on the radio.

"Sauce?"

Every F-22 pilot heard Hudek's call.

Jiro Kimura had already fired a second missile. While the first one was in the air, he got a growl on an F-22 four miles away, one turning

272 • STEPHEN COONTS

hard after a Zero. He squeezed it off. Then he turned ten degrees toward an F-22 in burner that was coming at him head-on.

This was Fur Ball Hudek.

The F-22 was shooting. A river of fire, almost like a searchlight, was vomiting from the nose of the American fighter. The finger of God reached for him.

Just how he avoided it, Jiro could never explain. He slammed the stick over and smashed on the rudder and his plane slewed sideways, almost out of control. At that moment, he mashed his thumb down on the gun button.

The shells poured from the cannon in his right wing root.

He wiggled the rudder just as Hudek flashed through the steel stream with his gun still blazing.

Aaron Hudek felt the hammer blows. His left engine fire light went on, the temp went into the red, and the rpm started dropping. He glanced in the rearview mirror and saw fire streaming along the side of the plane.

He started to reach for the ejection handle, but there was another Zero in front of him, this one flown by Jiro's wingman, Ota. At these speeds there was no time to think, but even if there had been, perhaps Aaron Hudek's decision would have been the same. With a flick of his wrist he brought the two fighters together almost head-on.

Jiro's second Sidewinder sprayed the belly of Dixie Elitch's fighter with shrapnel. The plane continued to respond to the controls and the engines seemed okay, but horrible pounding and ripping noises reached Dixie in the cockpit. It sounded as if the slipstream was ripping pieces off.

Automatically, she retarded her throttles, deployed her speed brakes, and pulled the nose skyward to convert airspeed into altitude.

After Cassidy and Scheer fired the last of their Sidewinders, only two of the eight high Zeroes were still under their pilots' control. Still in loose formation, these two nosed down steeply and went to full afterburner. They didn't turn or weave, just kept descending until they were within thirty feet of the valley floor. Their sonic shock waves raised a dust cloud behind them.

Cassidy leveled at ten thousand feet and came out of burner. He didn't want to use all his fuel chasing these two.

"Can you get 'em, Paul?"

"I think so."

Scheer was gaining on the fleeing pair when Cassidy turned back toward the low fight, which was still being waged near the base.

Preacher Fain was ninety degrees off Jiro's heading and a mile behind him when the Japanese pilot saw him with the infrared goggles. Jiro knew most of his comrades were dead, and if he continued to fight he soon would be, but to ignore this F-22 in his rear quarter would be suicide. Kimura pitched up hard and rolled toward Fain.

Fain was surprised. This was the only Zero that engaged the F-22s.

This guy must see me, he thought. Perhaps the chameleon gear is not working. . . . He too pitched up, committing himself to a vertical scissors.

Corkscrewing around each other, the two fighters went straight up, each trying for an angular advantage and each failing to get it.

Jiro was beside himself. He was 950 miles from home base, surrounded by enemies, and time was running out. Time was on his opponent's side. He had to end this quickly.

He pulled the throttles to idle, popped the speed brakes. Going straight up, the Zero slowed as if it had hit a wall.

Preacher Fain squirted out in front.

Jiro rammed the throttles forward and thumbed in the boards as he pushed the nose toward Fain.

Sensing his danger, Fain pulled back on the stick with all his strength. The F-22 came over on its back and dipped its nose toward the earth as bursts of cannon shells squirted past.

The shells were going by his belly. Fain continued to pull.

Then he realized the ground was rushing toward him. He was descending inverted, seventy degrees nose-down, in burner, passing eight thousand feet.

Preacher Fain flicked the F-22 upright and pulled until he thought the wings would come off. The G meter read twelve G's when his fighter struck the earth at Mach 1.2.

Dixie Elitch ejected when her airspeed dropped to 250 knots. The airplane was burning by then. She had shut down the left engine when the Left Fire warning light came on, but now the flames were visible in the mirror behind her.

"Dixie's bailing out," she said over the radio.

She took a deep breath and pulled the handle between her legs with both hands.

The fight had lasted just two minutes.

The maintenance troops at the base saw someone descending in a parachute, but they had no idea it was Dixie. Four of them went after her in a Humvee. The hardest part was finding her, a mile out in the forest from the nearest road. She was hung up in a tree. It took them twenty minutes to get her down, which they accomplished by chopping down the tree. Although shaken, she was none the worse for wear. An hour and a half after her ejection, Dixie and her rescuers walked out of the woods.

Jiro Kimura taxied into the revetment at Khabarovsk, opened the canopy, and shut down. The plane captain installed the ladder while Jiro unstrapped, then scampered up. "Sir, where are the others?"

"Dead. Or out in the forest. I don't know."

The plane captain couldn't believe it. He thought Jiro was joking.

As he walked across the ramp with the night-vision helmet and his flight bag, Jiro met his squadron executive officer. "Where are they, Kimura?"

"They were shot down, sir. All of them. I am the only one left."

"Including the wing commander?"

"He died first, I think. My flight was well below him then, but I think his aircraft was struck by a missile and disintegrated. Then the Americans jumped us. It was over quickly."

"F-22s?"

"They never saw them, Colonel. Their airplanes are invisible. Without radar, the others had no chance. I had this." Jiro held up the helmet. "I borrowed it from the helicopter squadron. I could see them only in infrared, not regular light."

"Fifteen aircraft!" The colonel was incredulous.

"Yes, sir."

"How many enemy aircraft were there?"

"Six or eight. I am not sure. No more than eight, I think."

The exec reeled. He caught himself. "Did we get *any* of them?"

"I got one, I think, sir. Another F-22 flew into the ground trying to evade me. If anyone else scored, I do not know about it."

"I want a complete written report, Kimura, as soon as possible. I will send it to Tokyo." The colonel turned his back so that Jiro couldn't see his face.

Jiro walked on toward the dispersal shack.

They couldn't all be dead. Surely some of them had ejected safely. Sasai, Ota, Miura . . .

As he walked, Jiro Kimura wiped away tears.

When Cassidy and Elitch got back to the squadron, Paul Scheer was sitting with his feet up on the duty desk, smoking a cigar. He gave them a beatific smile.

"Hear anything from the others?" Cassidy snapped.

"Nope. I watched the discs from your plane and mine. I'm pretty sure they're dead."

"You look awful damned crushed about it."

Scheer refused to be flustered. He puffed on the cigar a few times, then took a long drag and exhaled.

"Colonel, it's like this: If I were dead and Fur Ball were sitting here instead of me, I would want him to have a cigar. I would want him to savor this sublime moment. If I could, I would light the cigar for him."

Scheer stretched out his arms and yawned. "Best goddamned two minutes of my life. The very best." He sighed. "The sad thing is that it's all downhill from here. What could possibly equal that?"

Scheer slowly got to his feet. As cigar smoke swirled around his head, he hitched up his gun belt, reached into his unzipped G suit and scratched, then helped himself to a swallow of water from a small bottle. Opening the desk drawer, he extracted two cigars and held them out.

"One each. This was our stash, Hudek's and mine. When you smoke them, think of Fur Ball and Foy Sauce and the Preacher. Three damned good men."

Cassidy and Elitch each took the offered cigars.

Paul Scheer strolled out of the room, trailing smoke.

When he was lying in his bunk that evening, Jiro Kimura could not sleep. The morning fight kept swirling through his mind. After a while, he got out his flashlight, pulled the blanket over his head, and wrote a letter to his wife.

Dear Shizuko,

Today we had a big fight with the American fighters, the American Squadron that you have been hearing about. Bob Cassidy is their commanding officer!

Ota, Miura, and Sasai are missing in action and presumed dead. By the time you receive this letter, their families will have been notified.

As you know, I have been very concerned about meeting Cassidy in the sky. Today I must have done so. He was probably there. Beloved wife, you will be proud to know that I did not hesitate to do my duty. I did my very best, which is the only reason I am still alive. Still, I have worried so about the possibility of shooting at Cassidy that I now feel guilty that my comrades are dead. Strange how even secret sins return to haunt you. That is a very un-Japanese thought, but the Americans always assured me it was so. Secret sins are the worst, they said.

I have promised myself to think no more of Bob Cassidy. I will be cold-blooded about this murderous business. I will fight with a tiger's resolve.

I write of these things to you because I may not see you again in this life. It is probable that I shall soon join my friends in death, which is not a prospect I fear, as you know. Still, the thought of my death fills me with despair that you will be left to go on alone, that we will not live long lives together, which was, we always believed, our destiny.

If I die before you, I will be waiting for you in whatever comes after this life. When you are old and full of years, you will rejoin the husband of your youth, who will be waiting with a heart full of love. Know that in the days to come.

Jiro

CHAPTER TWENTY-ONE

●THE TRAIN WAS barely an hour north of Vladivostok when it derailed. Isamu Iwakuro felt the engine and cars lurch. He had spent his adult life working as a locomotive repair specialist, and he knew.

The car he was in, the second behind the last locomotive, went over on its side and the lights went out. The car skidded for what seemed to be a long time before it came to rest.

Inside the car, civilians and soldiers and their baggage were hopelessly jumbled. Someone was screaming.

Iwakuro managed to get upright and clamber over several seats toward the door, all the while shouting for everyone to remain quiet and not panic.

Then the explosions began. Steel and smoke ripped through the shattered railroad car.

Antitank grenades!

The explosions popped like firecrackers. All up and down the train, he could hear the hammering of the grenades. And he could hear machine guns, long, ripping bursts.

Something smashed into his shoulder and he went down. Another explosion near his head knocked him unconscious.

When Iwakuro came to, he could see nothing. Night had fallen, although he didn't know it. At first, he thought he was blind. His shoulder was bleeding and hurt horribly, so he knew he was alive. He felt his way over bodies, searching for a way out of the railroad car. He saw a bit of light, finally, just a glimmer from a distant fire.

Somehow, he managed to crawl through a hole in the floor of the railroad car, which was still on its side.

To his right, away from the engine, he saw that one of the freight cars was burning.

Iwakuro crawled directly away from the train. When he had gone at least fifty meters, he sat and tried to bind his coat around his shoulder.

He was sitting in the grass, moaning ever so slightly, when someone shot him in the back.

Rough hands rolled him over. A flashlight shown on his face.

Now someone grabbed him by the hair and rammed a knife into his neck. Isamu Iwakuro filled his lungs to scream, but he was dead before the sound came out.

The man who had shot Iwakuro finished cutting off his head. He dropped it into a bag with six others. His orders were to decapitate every body he found.

Two hundred miles east of Honshu *Admiral Kolchak* was at periscope depth, running at six knots on a course of 195 degrees magnetic. Through the main scope Pavel Saratov could see an empty, wind-whipped sea and sky.

After a careful, 360-degree transit with the scope, Saratov ordered it lowered. The navigator was bent over the chart table when Saratov joined him.

"How fast do you want to go, Captain?" As was usual aboard *Admiral Kolchak*, the navigator asked the question in a low, subdued voice.

"I want to keep a good charge on the batteries at all times," Saratov answered, automatically making his voice match the navigator's. "We must be able to go deep and stay there to have any chance against the Jap patrols."

"We are in the Japanese current, bucking it. We would make better time if we got out of it to the southeast, then headed southwest."

"Stay in it, right in the middle. We're in no hurry."

"Do you really think they are looking for us?"

"You can bet your life on it."

Askold leaned over the table. "How do you plan to go in, Captain?"

"I have no plans. We must see what develops."

"Getting out?"

"God knows. We will see."

"What will you see, Saratov?" The voice boomed in the little room. Esenin was right behind them. As usual, he was wearing the box, a gray metal box about three inches wide, five inches long, and an inch deep. It hung on a strap around his neck. Since the boat had submerged at Trojan Island, he had never been without the box.

"We will see if we can get out of Japanese waters alive," Saratov said.

"Don't be such a pessimist. This is an opportunity of a lifetime to do something important for your country."

"For you, General, perhaps. These men have already struck a stupendous blow for Russia."

"Don't be insubordinate," Esenin snapped. "You are in a leadership position."

"I'm in command of this vessel, and I won't forget it."

Esenin looked into the faces of the men in the control room. Then he turned to Saratov and whispered, "Don't push me."

A P-3 came that night. The sonar operator heard it first. The watch officer called Saratov, who was lying down in his stateroom, trying to sleep.

The plane went by about two miles to the south, flying east.

"He's flying a search pattern," the navigator said.

"Probably," Saratov said, "but the question is, Are we inside the pattern or outside of it?"

The sound of the plane disappeared. After a few minutes the watch team relaxed, smiled at one another, and went back to checking gauges, filling out logs, reading, and scratching themselves. Esenin had stationed one of his armed naval infantrymen in the control room. The man was trying to stay out of the way, but in a compartment that crowded, it was impossible. He had to move whenever anyone else moved.

Saratov eyed the man. He was in his mid-twenties, said almost nothing, obviously understood little of what went on around him. Was he a real naval infantryman? Or was he something else? Apparently, he had never before been to sea, or had he?

The P-3 returned. It went behind the submarine a mile or so to the north, headed west.

"We're in his pattern," the navigator said.

"Hold this heading. In about ten minutes, we'll cross his original flight path. He'll search behind us."

That was the way it worked out. Still, the XO and the navigator looked worried.

At midnight, when the captain gave the order to snorkel, the XO wanted to discuss it. "Sir, the P-3s can pick up the snorkel head on radar."

"We must charge the batteries, Askold. If we cannot do it here, we will never get into the mouth of the bay and back out."

Askold bit his lip, then repeated the snorkel order to the chief.

As luck would have it, within thirty minutes the sub entered a line of squalls. Heavy swells and rain in sheets hid the snorkel head. The rocking motion of the boat, just under the surface, made the sailors smile. They knew how rough it was up there.

Saratov drank a cup of tea in the wardroom while Esenin and his number two, the major, silently watched. Then Saratov went to his cabin and stretched out on the bunk.

He couldn't sleep. In his mind's eye he saw airplanes and destroyers hunting, searching, back and forth, back and forth . . .

The sonar operator called the P-3 sixty seconds before it went directly over the submarine. The duty officer immediately ordered snorkeling stopped and the electric motors started. The plane went by, fifteen seconds passed, then it began a turn.

"He's got us," the watch officer said. "Call the captain."

Saratov heard that order as he came along the passageway. "Take it down to a forty meters," Pavel Saratov said after the chief reported the diesel engines secured. "Left full rudder to one zero zero degrees."

"Left full rudder, aye. New course one zero zero."

Esenin came to the control room. A moment later the major arrived, just in time to hear the sonar operator call, "Sonobuoys in the water." He began calling the bearings and estimated ranges of the splashes as the navigator plotted them.

"Let's get the boat as quiet as we can, Chief."

"Aye, Captain. Slow speed?"

"Three knots. No more. And go deeper. Seventy meters."

"Down on the bow planes. Up on the stern planes," the chief ordered. The *michman* on the planes complied.

Saratov looked at his watch. The time was a bit after 0300.

"P-3 is coming in for another run, Captain. He sounds like he's going to go right over us."

"Keep me advised."

"Steady on new course one zero zero."

"Keep going down, Chief. One hundred meters. Somebody watch the water-temp gauge. Let me know if we hit an inversion."

"There should be an inversion," the duty officer muttered, more to himself that anyone else. "This *is* the Japanese current."

"P-3's going right over our heads."

"Come left to new course zero four five."

Out of the corner of his eye, Saratov noted Esenin's facial expression, which was tense. The major, standing beside Esenin, looked worried.

"One hundred meters, Captain."

"Make it a hundred and fifty."

"One fifty, aye."

"How deep is the water here?" the major asked the navigator, who didn't even check the chart before he answered.

"Six miles. We're over the Japanese trench."

"So what happens if we can't lose this airplane?"

"He puts a homing torpedo in the water." The navigator looked at the major and grinned. "Then we die."

"Two hundred meters, Chief," the captain said.

Passing through 170 meters, the temperature of the water began to rise. The duty officer saw it and sang out.

"Just how deep can this boat go?" the major asked the XO.

"Two hundred meters is our design depth."

The captain missed this exchange. He was wearing a set of sonar headphones, listening with his eyes shut.

At this depth the boat creaked a bit, probably from the temperature change, or the pressure. Saratov heard none of it. He was concentrating with all his being on the hisses and gurgles of the living sea. Ah yes . . . there was the beat of the plane's props. He opened his eyes, glanced at the sonar indicator, which was pointing in the direction of the largest regular, man-made sound. The enemy airplane was almost overhead . . . now passing. . . .

Splash! A sonobuoy. Or a torpedo.

"Deeper, Chief. Down another fifty meters."

"Aye, Captain."

More sonobuoys. Going away. Well, at least the P-3 didn't have the sub bracketed. The crew was searching for something they had, then lost.

"I think they have lost us, Chief. Now they'll try to find us again. Hold this depth, heading, and speed."

A wave of visible relief swept through the men in the control room.

Saratov took off one of the sonar earphones and asked Esenin, "Those shells we welded to the deck—how much pressure are they built to withstand?"

"I don't know."

"We'll find out, eh," said Pavel Saratov. "You can tell them when you get home," he added, and rearranged the earphones.

Atsuko Abe read the message from Agent Ju and snorted in disbelief. "How can we believe this?"

"We cannot afford to ignore it," said Cho, the foreign minister, speaking carefully. "If there is one chance in a thousand that Ju is correct, that is an unacceptable risk."

"Don't talk to me of unacceptable risk," Abe snarled. Cho had been one of the most vocal proponents of taking the Siberian oil fields. Today they were in the prime minister's office off the main floor of the Diet. He normally used this office to confer with members of his party.

Abe shook the paper with the message on it at Cho. "We lost fifteen Zeros to the American Squadron two days ago. The generals believe we will be able to hold our own from now on, but that is probably just wishful thinking. The essential military precondition to the invasion of Siberia was local air supremacy. It has been taken from us."

Cho said nothing.

"Last night two hundred civilians and thirty soldiers were killed in a railroad ambush a mere fifty kilometers north of Vladivostok. Guerillas murdered a whole trainload of people in an area that is supposed to be secure, an area that is practically in our backyard."

Abe straighted his tie and jacket. "This morning in Vladivostok, the heads were dumped on the street in front of Japanese military headquarters." Abe looked Cho straight in the eye. "I can prevent the news being published, but I cannot stop whispers. Corporate executives know their employees are being slaughtered. No Japanese is safe anywhere in Siberia. The executives are demanding that we do *something*, prevent future occurrences."

Cho gave a prefunctory bow.

"The United Nations is moving by fits and starts to condemn Japanese aggression. When that fails to deter us, someone will suggest an economic boycott. The Russians are very active in the UN—they are shaking hands and smiling and preparing to nuke us. They are willing to do whatever it takes to win. I ask you, Cho, are you willing? Cho?"

"Mr. Prime Minister, I advocated invasion. I firmly believe that possession of Siberia's oil fields will allow this people to survive and flourish in the centuries to come. That oil is our lifeblood. It is worth more to us than it is to any other nation."

Atsuko Abe placed his hands flat on his desk. "Without air supremacy we will be unable to resupply our people in Siberia this winter. Air supremacy is absolutely critical. Everything flows from that."

"I see that, Mr. Prime Minister." Cho's head bobbed.

"The American Squadron at Chita must be eliminated. The generals tell me there is only one way to ensure that all the planes, people, equipment, and spare parts are neutralized: we must strike with a nuclear weapon."

Cho blanched.

"*This* is the crisis," Abe roared. "We are committed! We must conquer or die. There is no other way out. We have bet everything—*everything*—our government, our nation, our lives. Do you have the courage to see it through?"

"This course will be completely unacceptable to the Japanese public," Cho sputtered.

"Damn the public." Abe slapped his hands on the desk. "The public wants the benefits of owning Siberia. A prize this rich cannot be had on the cheap. We must pay for it. Nuking Chita is the price. We cannot get Siberia for one yen less."

"The Japanese people will not pay *that* price."

Abe waved Ju's message. "I am not suggesting that we nuke Moscow! Open your eyes, man. The Russians are trying to nuke us!"

"It is the use of nuclear weapons that is the evil, Mr. Prime Minister. You know that as well as I. Once we attack Chita, we may be forced to launch missiles at other targets, including Moscow. Once it starts, where will it stop, Mr. Prime Minister?"

Abe brushed aside Cho's words, pretended that he hadn't heard. "Military necessity requires the destruction of the American Squadron. The squadron is Russia's responsibility; Russia must bear the consequences."

"With respect, the decision is not that easy." Cho groped for words. "In 1945 the Americans used the atomic bomb on Japan and blamed Japan for making it necessary. You have just agreed that the Americans were correct all those years ago."

"I am not going to argue metaphysics, Cho. If Tokyo goes up in a mushroom cloud, will you be willing to use nuclear weapons then?"

"No! Never. The Japanese people will never be willing to use nuclear weapons on anyone. Mr. Prime Minister, *you* were the one who demanded that the development of these weapons be kept a state secret, that the public never be informed."

"Who will tell them that we used them?"

Silence followed this question.

Abe busied himself rearranging items on his desk. Finally, he said:

"A small bomb, eight or ten kilotons, should do the job nicely. We will attack with airplanes, so the rocket people will know nothing. The American Squadron at Chita will be wiped off the face of the earth. The Russians will see that further resistance is hopeless. Siberia will be ours. The United Nations will be forced to recognize a fait accompli. No more Japanese soldiers will die; oil will go to Japanese refineries; natural resources will supply our industries. Our nation, *our people,* will flourish."

"I tell you now that it will not be so easy."

"This is the only choice we have," Abe thundered. "We must have that oil!"

Cho refused to yield. "Japan will never forgive us," he said obstinately.

Atsuko Abe forced himself to relax in his padded armchair.

"Victors write the history books," he said when he had recovered his composure. "The Russians are about to have a nuclear accident at Chita. They've had such accidents before, at other places. According to Ju, they have hidden nuclear weapons from international arms-control commissions, thus violating treaties they willingly signed—they are plotting to use these weapons on Japan. These are truths waiting to be discovered by anyone who asks enough questions in the right places."

Abe pointed at Cho. "You know that we tried—repeatedly—to settle this matter diplomatically. Kalugin refused to enter discussions. Categorically refused. The Russians are gloating over the Tokyo Bay incident, applauding the catastrophic loss of innocent life, rejoicing at our embarrassment, and the Japanese people are furious."

He used a finger to nudge the message from Ju lying on the desk in front of him.

"The time has come to give the bastards a taste of their own medicine."

"What airplane will deliver the weapon?"

"Zeros."

"The Zeros haven't been doing very well lately. That is the whole problem. What if they fail to get through?"

"Then we will try again with something else. *We will do what must be done.*"

At the morning briefing, Jack Innes told President David Herbert Hood about a note that had been handed to one of the CIA operatives the day before in Moscow by a street sweeper, one of the old women who swept trash and dirt from public places with a long twig broom.

Then he handed Hood a translation of the note.

The Russian government has ordered nuclear attacks on Japan. A submarine is presently attempting to deliver four high-yield nuclear weapons to the sea floor near Tokyo, where they will be detonated to create an earthquake and tidal wave. If for any reason the submarine attack fails, Kalugin is prepared to launch a nuclear attack via air against Tokyo.

"Is this credible?" the president asked.

"We believe so, Mr. President. As you will recall, several senior Russian specialists insisted that Russia had not destroyed all their nuclear weapons."

"I never thought they would, either," Hood admitted. "But even if they cheated, every weapon destroyed was one less."

"The note implies that the submarine is at sea now, so last night we tried to find it with satellite imagery." Innes flicked off the lights and displayed a large image on the screen behind him. "This is a computer-generated image of a section of the northern Pacific created from radar and infrared inputs." Innes used a small flashlight to put a red dot on the screen. "Here, we believe, is the signature of a snorkeling diesel/electric submarine."

"Surely the Russians would use a nuclear-powered sub for a mission like that."

"If they had one, sir, I'm sure they would. The Tokyo Bay attack was carried out with a conventional diesel/electric boat."

"Where is that sub?" Hood gestured toward the screen.

"When this was put together last night, the boat was about one hundred and eighty miles off Honshu, heading southwest. It's very near the main shipping lanes."

"Is that the only submarine out there?" the president asked.

"No, sir. The Japanese have two currently at sea. At least we believe they are Japanese." Innes flipped to a map display and used the pointer. "One is patrolling in Sagami Bay, the other near the northern entrance to the Inland Sea. All Japan's submarines are diesel/electric boats."

"Where are our boats?"

Innes projected an overlay on the screen. "Here, Mr. President."

Hood massaged his forehead for a moment. Finally, he said, "Normally I'd want some more confirmation before we did anything. This is very tenuous. And yet, Kalugin is capable of this. He would push the button."

"Remember the report we received last week from the U.S. military attaché in Moscow? He had an interview with Marshal Stolypin. The marshal said the Russians were just trying to get into the fight."

"A negotiated settlement with the Japanese would not wash in Russia just now," Hood agreed. "Still, the evidence for nuclear escalation is damned thin."

The president smacked the table with his fist. "That asshole Abe! Nuclear war. Well, we'd better tell the Japanese about all this. Maybe they can sink that sub."

"Yes, sir."

"Then get the Japanese and Russian ambassadors over here. Today. At the same time. Demand that they come. I'd better have another chat with those two. And notify the Joint Chiefs—see if they have any ideas."

"Are you considering military cooperation with the Japanese to thwart any attacks?"

"I am. In the interim, I want to see what the Space Command people can make those satellites do. See if they can come up with some independent verification of that note."

Hood stood, then took another look at the satellite view of the Russian submarine's snorkel signature, which Innes had returned to the wall screen.

"I have a really bad feeling about helping the Japanese," Hood said. "They have sown the wind and now the hurricane is almost upon them. Yet I don't see any other way. If the nuclear genie pops out of the bottle, I don't know what the world will look like afterward. Neither does anyone else. And I don't want to find out."

At Chita, Yan Chernov, with translator in tow, went looking for Bob Cassidy. He found him in the ready room poring over satellite photos that had been encrypted and transmitted via radio from Colorado.

Chernov glanced at the photos, labeled "SECRET NOFORN" then turned his attention to the American. "Colonel Cassidy, I wish to thank you for feeding me and my men."

"You are leaving?"

"Yes. We have been ordered to shift bases to Irkutsk, on Lake Baikal. We are flying the planes there today. The ground troops will leave tomorrow."

"We enjoyed having you in the mess."

"Americans eat better than anyone on earth, except, of course, the French. For years I refused to believe that. Now I am convinced."

Cassidy laughed. They talked for several minutes of inconsequential things, then bid each other good-bye. With a feeling of genuine regret, Cassidy watched the Russian leave. Major Chernov, he thought, would be a credit to any air force.

As he sat back down to study the satellite photos, he wondered why the Sukhoi squadron was being withdrawn. True, the Zero was more than a match for the Su-27, but with F-22s to keep the Zeros occupied, the Sukhois would be useful in the ground-attack role.

Well, no one had asked his opinion. He should probably tend to his end of the war. His end involved an attack on the Zero base at Khabarovsk this evening, in the twilight hour before dark. He went back to plotting run-in lines.

Janos Ilin took two of his men with him when he visited the gadget room, or, as some called it, "the James Bond room," in the old KGB headquarters on Dzerzhinsky Square in Moscow. Here the instruments of espionage were stored, issued, and returned after use. Of course, the man who ran it was known as Q. Unlike the suave British civil servant of the movies, this Q was fat, waddled when he walked, and spent most of his time poring over his records. Dust rested in every corner of the place, undisturbed from year to year.

Q had settled into this sinecure years ago. Like many Russian peasants, a little place to call his own was all Q wanted from life, and this was it. Today he scowled at Ilin and the two men following him as they walked between benches covered with listening devices and tape recorders to the little corner desk where Q did business.

"Good morning, Q," Janos Ilin said, pleasantly enough.

"Sir." Q was sullen.

"Some information. You know of the assassination attempt on the president?"

Q looked surprised. "I had absolutely nothing to do with it, sir. You can't seriously think—"

"We don't think anything. We are here to ask some questions. Where are the records of equipment issues for the last six months?"

"Why, right here. In this book." Q almost wagged his tail trying to be helpful. He displayed the book, opened it to a random page. "You see, my method of record keeping is simplicity itself. I put the item in this column—"

"Where are your keys?"

"You can't have the keys. I suppose I could show you anything you want to see, but you can't—"

"The keys." Ilin held out his hand. He kept his face deadpan. The men behind him moved out to each side, where they could see Q and he could see them.

Q opened a desk drawer. It contained a handful of key rings, each with several dozen keys.

"The inventory, please."

"What inventory?"

"Don't play the fool with me, man," Ilin snarled. He could really snarl when aroused. "I haven't the time or temper for it. I'll ask you again: Where is the inventory of the equipment you have in this department?"

"But . . . The inventory is old, sir. It's not completely up-to-date. It's—"

"Surely you have an inventory, Q, because regulations require you to have one. I checked. If you don't, I'm afraid I shall have to place you under arrest."

Q almost fainted. "Those black binders on the shelf." He pointed. "I don't let people browse through them, you understand. The equipment the service owns is a state secret."

"I understand completely. Now, if you will go with these gentlemen. They have some questions to ask you."

Q's panic returned. He was really quite pathetic. "What if someone comes with a requisition while I am away?"

"This office is closed until you return. Go on." One of the men reached out and put his hand on Q's arm.

When they were out of the room, Ilin locked the door behind them.

Ilin had, of course, been in this room from time to time over the years, but he had never really looked through the place. He didn't know what Q had here, much less where he kept it. Ilin sat down at the desk with the inventories. As he suspected, they were worthless. They hadn't been updated in twenty years. Still, there was a match between some of the letters and numbers in the inventory list and the numbers in Q's logbook.

Each item in the logbook had a one- or two-word description, a letter and a number, followed by signatures, times, dates, et cetera.

Ilin studied the descriptions. He examined the keys. Ah, the keys were arranged by letter. Here was the A ring, the B ring, and so on.

Ilin began looking around. Q had most of this end of a floor for his collection, eleven rooms filled with cabinets and cases and closets—all locked. The place was almost like a museum's basement, a place to store all the artifacts not on display upstairs.

Ilin inspected the bins and cabinets as he walked from room to room with the logbook in hand. Q had never inventoried this material because he didn't want anyone else to know what was here. He was the indispensable man.

Weapons filled two rooms. So did listening devices. Who would have believed that so many types of bugs existed?

It took Janos Ilin an hour to find what he wanted. There were six of them in a little drawer in an antique highboy from the early Romanov era. The polished wood was three hundred years old if it was a day.

He checked the logbook. None of these items were listed. Ilin examined the half dozen. They had tags on them bearing dates. He selected the one with the latest date. It would have to do.

Back at Q's desk, he put the logbook back on the shelf and returned all the keys to the desk drawer. He stirred them around so that none were in their original position.

Could he safely leave Q alive?

That was a serious question and he regarded it seriously. If the man talked to the wrong people . . .

Perhaps the thing to do was just arrest him. Hundreds of people were in the cells now. One more would make no difference. When this was over Q could go back to his job none the worse for wear, as, one prays, would all the others. There was a risk, of course, but it seemed small, and Ilin would not have any more blood on his hands. The blood was becoming harder and harder to wash off.

How much blood is Kalugin worth?

Ilin left the James Bond department, turning the lights out and locking the door behind him. He rode the elevator up to his floor, then went into a suite of offices adjacent to his. His men were there with Q.

"Put him in the cells. Hold for questioning."

Q collapsed. One of the agents tossed the last inch of a glass of water into his face.

When Ilin left the room, the man was sobbing.

It was one of those rare summer evenings when the clouds boil higher and higher and yet don't become thunderstorms. Hanging just above the western horizon, the sun fired the cloudy towers and buttes with reds, oranges, pinks, and yellows as the land below grew dark.

Bob Cassidy led his flight of four F-22s south, up the Amur valley, toward the Japanese air base at Khabarovsk. They were low, about a thousand feet above the river, flying at just over the speed of sound. To the east and west, gloomy purple mountains crowned with clouds were just visible in the gathering darkness.

Two F-22s carrying antiradiation missiles to shoot at any radar that came on the air were approaching Khabarovsk from the west. Farther behind were two more F-22s. Joe Malan was leading this flight, which was charged with finding and attacking airborne enemy airplanes.

Earlier that evening Cassidy had vomited so violently he didn't think he could fly. He had started thinking about Jiro and Sweet Sabrina again, and gotten physically ill. The doctor had given him something to settle his stomach. "I think your problem is psychological," the doctor had remarked, which brought forth a nasty reply from Cassidy, one he instantly regretted. He apologized, put his clothes on, and went to fly.

The mission had gone like clockwork. Two tankers flying from Adak, in the Aleutians, rendezvoused with the fighters precisely on time a hundred miles north of Zeya. If all went well, they would be at the same rendezvous in sixty-four minutes, when the eight strike airplanes needed fuel to make Chita. If they weren't, well, eight fighter pilots were going to have a long walk home.

As usual, Cassidy was keyed up. He was as ready as a man can be. The wingmen were in position, the data link from the satellite was presenting the tactical picture, and the plane was flying well, smart skin on, master armament switch on, all warning lights extinguished.

And there wasn't a single enemy airplane in the sky. Not one.

The satellite downlink must be screwed up. Again.

"Keep your eyes peeled, people," Cassidy said over the encrypted radio circuit. Perhaps he shouldn't have, but he needed to.

Should he use his radar? Take a peek? If the enemy still didn't know he was coming, they would certainly get the message when his radar energy lit up their countermeasures equipment.

Twenty-five miles. The planes in his flight spread out, angling for their assigned run-in lines. The targets this evening were the enemy aircraft and their fueling facilities: the trucks, bladders, and pumping units.

Where were the Japanese?

Had they caught them on the ground?

His fighter was bumping in mild chop as Bob Cassidy came rocketing toward the air base at 650 knots, almost eleven miles per minute. His targets were a row of Zeros that two days ago had been parked in front of the one large hangar on the base.

There was the hangar! He slammed the stick over, corrected his heading a few degrees. His finger tightened around the trigger, but in vain: The Zeros weren't there.

The ramp was empty when he roared across it five hundred feet in the air, still doing 650 knots.

"There are no Zeros," somebody said over the air.

Was this an ambush? Were the Zeros lurking nearby to bounce the F-22s? Perhaps the Zeros were on their way to Chita—right now!

"Shoot up the hangars and fueling facilities," Cassidy told the other members of his flight. "Watch for flak and SAMs."

He made a wide looping turn and headed for the city of Khabarovsk. The railroad tracks pointed like arrows toward the railroad station.

Train in the station!

Squeeze the trigger . . . walk the stream of shells the length of it.

God, there are people, soldiers in uniform, running, scattering, the engine vomiting fire and oily black smoke . . .

He made another wide loop, still searching nervously for flak, and came down the river. He found another train, this time heading south toward Vladivostok. He attacked it from the rear, slamming shells into every car.

The entire plane vibrated—in the gloomy evening half-light the beam of fire from the gun flicked out like a searchlight. Flashes twinkled amid a cloud of dust and debris as the shells slammed into the train, fifty a second. Then he was off the trigger and zooming up and around for another pass.

With the throttle back, the airspeed down to less than three hundred, he emptied the gun at the train. He watched with satisfaction as two of the cars exploded and one of the engines derailed.

Climbing over the town, he called on the radio for his wingmen to join for the trip back to Chita.

Where are the Zeros?

CHAPTER TWENTY-TWO

● *ADMIRAL KOLCHAK* WAS running slow, two hundred meters deep, making for the entrance to Sagami Bay, the sound that led to Tokyo Bay. Pavel Saratov sat in the control room with the second set of sonar earphones on his head. About every half hour or so he would hear the faint beat of turboprop engines: P-3s, hunting his boat. Of that, Saratov had no doubt.

Esenin came and went from the control room. Apparently he was wandering through the boat, checking on his people, all of whom wore sidearms and carried a rifle with them. As if they could employ such weapons in this steel coffin. Still, the sailors got the message: the naval infantrymen were there to ensure the navy did Esenin's bidding. Saratov got the message before the sailors did.

Esenin had his little box with him, of course, hanging on the strap around his neck. Now, as he listened for planes and warships, Saratov speculated about what was in the box.

When he had examined that topic from every angle, he began wondering what the sailors were thinking. He could look at their faces and try to overhear their whispers, but that was about it. The crowded condition of the boat did not allow for private conversations, even with his officers. And no doubt Esenin wanted it that way, because he kept his people spread out, with at least one man in every compartment of the boat at all times.

Everyone knew where the boat was going and why. The first day at sea, Saratov had told them on the boat's loudspeaker system.

Now they were chewing their lips and fingernails, picking at their faces, thinking of other places, other things. The absence of laughter, jokes, and good-natured ribbing did not escape Saratov. Nor did he miss the way the sailors glanced at the naval infantrymen out of the corners of their eyes, checking, measuring, wondering. . . .

This evening Askold brought Saratov a metal plate containing a chunk of bread, a potato, and some sliced beets cooked in sour cream.

As he ate, Askold showed him the chart. "We are here, Captain, fifty miles from the entrance to the bay."

Saratov nodded and forked more potato.

"Do you wish to snorkel tonight?"

Saratov nodded yes. When he had swallowed, he said, "We must snorkel one more time for several hours, before we go in. We are taking a long chance. It's like a harbor up there, ships and planes . . ."

"Can't we go in on the battery charge we have?"

"Not if we expect to come out alive."

"When?"

"Tonight."

"We have been lucky. The thermal layer—"

"Lucky, ummm . . ."

"When we leave the Japanese current—"

"The thermal layer will run out."

"Yes," Askold murmured, and glanced at his hands. He watched his captain chew a few more bites, then went away.

Jack Innes reported to President Hood in his bedroom at the White House. The president was donning a tux.

"Another disease luncheon," Hood said gloomily as he adjusted the cummerbund over his belly. "I'd like to have a dollar for every one of these I've sat through in the last thirty years."

"The Japanese have sent everything they have after that sub."

"Where is it now?"

"We don't know."

Hood looked a question.

"Unless he comes up to periscope depth, we can't see him with the satellite sensors. And there are some storms over the ocean off Japan— he may be under one."

"How long can an electric boat like that stay under?"

"I asked the experts, Mr. President. One hundred and seventy-five hours at a speed of two knots."

"More than *seven* days?"

"Yes, sir. But the boat must go so slowly that it is essentially immobile. Once the hunters get a general idea where a conventional sub is, it is easily avoided and ceases to be a threat. Speaking of Russians, they deny that the boat in the satellite photo is one of theirs."

Hood was working on his cuff links. "Is it?"

"We think so, sir. But it could be Japanese."

"Or Chinese, Korean, Egyptian, Iranian. . . . Seems like everybody has a fleet of those damned things."

"The Russian response to yesterday's conference is being evaluated at the State Department. The Kremlin denies any intent to use nuclear weapons. On Japan or anyone else. They say there's been some mistake."

"I hope they don't make one," Hood said fervently.

"The real question is what the Japanese are up to. They withdrew their Zeros from Khabarovsk to Vladivostok. Space Command doesn't know why."

"It's a damned good thing the Japs don't have nuclear weapons," the president said, glancing at Innes.

"The director of the CIA says they don't."

"Well, Abe told Kalugin that Japan had nukes when he answered Kalugin's ultimatum. Either Abe is the world's finest poker player or the director of the CIA is just flat wrong."

"Abe doesn't strike me as the bluffing type."

"Didn't I see an intelligence summary a while back that said the Japanese might have developed a nuclear capability?"

"One of the analysts thought that was a possibility. The CIA brass vehemently disagreed."

"Have the White House switchboard find the analyst. Have him come to the hotel where they are holding this lunch. When he gets here, come get me."

"Yes, sir."

Admiral Kolchak took an hour to rise from two hundred meters to periscope depth. Glancing through the attack scope, Saratov thought, My God, it is raining! Heavily. A squall. Nothing in sight or on the sonar. Who says there is no God?

The crew ran up the snorkel and started the diesel engines, which throbbed sensuously as they drove the boat along at ten knots. The swells overhead gave the submarine a gentle rocking motion. Sitting with his eyes closed, Pavel Saratov savored the sensation.

"They are going to get us this time, Captain," the sonarman said softly, almost a whisper.

Saratov tried to think of something upbeat to say, but he couldn't.

He pretended he didn't hear the *michman*'s comment, which mercifully the man didn't repeat.

"The technological superiority that the Americans have given the Russians must be eliminated, in the air and on the ground. The F-22 squadron base at Chita will be destroyed and the F-22s eliminated as a threat."

The Japanese officer who made this pronouncement was a two-star general. His short dark hair was flecked with gray. He was impeccably uniformed and looked quite distinguished.

Three of the four Zero pilots sitting around the table nodded their concurrence. The fourth one, Jiro Kimura, did not nod. Despite his fierce resolve, he immediately thought of Bob Cassidy when the general mentioned the F-22 squadron base.

The general didn't seem to notice Jiro's preoccupation, nor did any of the colonels and majors who filled the other seats in the room.

"I have just come from a briefing at the highest levels in the defense ministry in Tokyo. Let me correct that and say the very highest level. As everyone in this room is aware, air supremacy over Siberia is absolutely essential to enable us to supply our military forces and the civilian engineering and construction teams this winter. Without it . . . well, without it, quite simply, we must begin withdrawing our forces or they will starve and freeze in the months ahead. In fact, without air supremacy, it is questionable if we can get the people out that we have there now.

"Frankly, if Japan cannot neutralize the technological edge the Americans gave the Russians, Japan will lose the war. The consequences of such an event on the Japanese people are too terrible to imagine.

"Gentlemen, the survival of our nation is at stake," the general continued. "Consequently, the decision has been made at the very highest level to use a nuclear weapon on Chita."

The room was so deadly quiet that Jiro Kimura could hear his heart beating. He didn't know Japan had nuclear weapons. Never even dreamed it. From the looks of the frozen faces around the room, the fact was news to most of the people here.

"I must caution you that the very existence of these weapons is a state secret," the general said, albeit quite superfluously.

"The weapons we will use will be of a low yield, about ten kilotons, we believe, although we have never actually been able to verify that yield by testing one of these devices."

One of the pilots sitting at the table held up his hand. The general recognized him. "Sir, my father's parents died when the Americans bombed Nagasaki. I cannot and will not drop a nuclear weapon on anyone, for any reason. I took an oath to this effect before I joined the military. My father demanded it of me."

The general gave a slight bow in the pilot's direction, then said, "You may be excused from the room."

The general looked at the colonels. The senior Zero pilot, Colonel Nishimura, rose from his chair against the wall and reseated himself beside Jiro at the table.

Jiro Kimura didn't know what to do. His mouth was dry; he was unable to speak. He was hearing what was said and seeing the people, but he was frozen, overcome by the horror of being here, being a part of this.

The two-star droned on, then used a pointer on the map hanging behind him. Four planes, four bombs, one must get through. The senior man, now Colonel Nishimura, was in charge of tactical and flight planning.

Then it was over and Jiro was walking down the hallway with his fellow pilots, feeling his legs move, seeing the doorway to the building coming toward him, going down the outside stairs, walking across the lawn, and vomiting in the grass.

When he first heard it, Saratov wasn't sure. He pressed the earphones against his head and listened intently. The night had come and gone, he had snatched a couple of hours of sleep, and he was back in the control room, watching the sonarman play with the data on his computer screen and listening to raw sound on his own set of earphones.

A P-3 was up there, somewhere, and the beat of its propellers was insistent. Embedded in that throb . . . Yes. Pinging. Very faint. Far away.

"Captain . . ." said the sonarman, who was in his tiny compartment a few feet away.

"I hear it, too," Saratov muttered.

He listened for a while, then got off his stool and looked at the chart. "Where are we, exactly?" he asked the navigator.

"Here, Captain." The navigator pointed.

"If we stay on this course, we go in the main channel?"

"Yes, sir."

"General Esenin—ask him to come to the control room."

Despite the fact that Esenin hadn't had a bath in days, he looked like a Moscow politician, clean-shaven and spotless.

Saratov took off the headphones and handed them to the general. "Listen."

After a bit, Esenin said, "I hear ... humming."

"That is a P-3, looking for us. Do you hear a chime?"

After a moment, Esenin said, "I believe so. Very faintly. Like a bell."

"That is a destroyer, probably near the entrance to the main channel. He is echo-ranging his sonar. Pinging. Sending out a sound that echoes off solid objects, like submarines."

"But we hear the noise and can avoid him."

"If you will, please look at the chart. The destroyer is roughly here, pinging away. Somewhere closer to the mainland will be a Japanese submarine. They will be listening for the sonar ping to echo off our submarine, yet they will be too far away from the emitter for us to hear the echo from their boat. Do you understand?"

"Yes." Esenin handed the earphones back. "What do you suggest?"

"I am wondering just how secret your little mission to flood half of Japan really is."

"Are you suggesting that there has been a security leak?"

"I suggest nothing. I merely observe that the Japanese seem well prepared for our arrival, almost as if someone told them we were coming."

"I fail to see the relevance of that observation."

"Perhaps it isn't relevant."

"We have our orders. We will obey. Now, how do you propose to get us in there?"

"I don't know."

"Think of something, Captain. Keep us alive to do our duty."

Saratov put the earphones back on and retreated to his stool. He listened to the pinging and stared at the navigator's chart, which lay on the table a few feet away.

Other people were also talking of duty.

"Colonel Nishimura, I do not think I have the warrior's spirit that will be necessary to complete this mission."

"Kimura, no sane man *wants* to drop a nuclear weapon. We will do it because it is our duty to our nation."

"I understand, Colonel. But we all have a similar duty. Someone else can fly this mission and fulfill his duty."

"I cannot believe you said that, Kimura. The comment is offensive."

"I do not mean to offend."

"You are a Japanese officer. You have been chosen for this mission because you have had the most success against F-22s. Your experience cannot be replaced."

"It is true, I am still alive when others are dead. And it is true, I successfully shot down several F-22s. Both these feats happened because I wore a helicopter night-vision helmet to see the enemy. I was the only pilot to do so. I suggested it to others, including Colonel Handa, who refused because higher authority had not sanctioned it."

"Ah, yes, good Colonel Handa, a bureaucrat to the backbone. That sounds like him."

"I survived only because I wore the helmet."

"Everyone will wear such a device on this mission," Nishimura replied. "We have altered them to attach to our regular helmets so that we can also wear our oxygen masks."

"Then you don't need me," Jiro rejoined. "I wish to pass the honor of striking this blow for the nation to one of my colleagues."

The colonel struggled against his temper. "You have the experience. Only you. I want to hear no more of this. Honor and duty require this service of you. The future of your country is at stake."

"Saito was excused. This is also his country. Extend to me the same courtesy that was extended to him."

"Have you taken an oath, like Saito?"

Kimura lowered his head. "No, sir," he admitted.

"All that you are," the colonel said thoughtfully, "you owe to Japan, to the Japanese people, who gave you life, nurtured you and educated you and made you the man you are. Your obligation cannot be erased or made smaller."

"I owe other obligations too," Kimura murmured.

"I do not wish to discuss this further," the colonel said. "We will speak of it no more."

"Gentleman, this is the situation." Pavel Saratov looked around the packed control room at his officers, and, of course, at General Esenin. "Above us, P-3s are searching. They cannot find us because we are under an inversion layer, a layer we will probably leave in a few miles. Still, we are deep, traveling slowly, and they would have to go right over us to get a reading on their magnetic gear."

Saratov certainly had their attention. "Ahead of us about thirty miles is an enemy warship, pinging regularly. That warship is probably a large destroyer or frigate, carrying one or two helicopters equipped with dipping sonar. We will hear the helicopters as we get closer. Somewhere near that warship is probably one, perhaps even two or more submarines. They are lying deep and quiet, listening for us. I suspect one is on the far side of the destroyer, but it could be anywhere.

"I have considered all our options. If we go in under a freighter, the echo ranging will detect us. No doubt that is why they are doing it.

"We face the classic battery-boat dilemma. If we go in quickly, we will prematurely drain our batteries and need to snorkel in Sagami Bay, which would be suicidal. If we go in slowly, trying to save battery energy, we will expend lots of time and we'll be at the mercy of the tides. Three knots will just hold us in place; then when the tide pushes us, we will get a mere six knots. Alas, that will have to do.

"Our only choice is to be bold. When the tide turns in two hours, we will close the destroyer and shoot two torpedoes set to home on noise. They will probably put decoys in the water. We may get a hit; then again, we may not. Regardless, the confusion factor will be high. That, I hope, will give us an opportunity to slip into Sagami Bay."

"You really have no plan," Esenin said, frowning in disapproval.

"You may say that, sir," Saratov admitted. "We can only take advantage of opportunities that come our way. The enemy must positively identify every target before they shoot. We have no such handicap. Everyone we hear is the enemy. On the other hand, we can only do what the battery lets us do."

No one said anything.

"We go so slowly, yet time is critical," Saratov said. "We must get into the bay before other antisubmarine forces arrive and join the search. Once inside, we must find our fault and settle onto the bottom.

"Are there any questions?"

They stared at him with drawn, dirty, haggard faces dripping sweat, although the temperature was not warm. Whatever they had been expecting, this wasn't it.

"General Esenin."

"What if you fail to torpedo the destroyer?"

"Then, sir, we will both get to experience our very first depth charging. I hear that it is a religious experience."

"You have balls, Saratov. I'll say that for you."

The *michmen* and naval officers exchanged glances, trying to keep their faces deadpan. Saratov thought he knew what they were thinking, but with Esenin standing there . . .

"Do you intend to go up and use the periscope, Captain?"

"We must shoot from this depth."

He bent over the chart table with the XO and navigator beside him. "Our torpedoes have a range of ten miles. We must get within that range to shoot, but not so close that we are detected. With the destroyer's screw noises and bearing change, we should be able to get an idea of his course and speed, and therefore his relative position and range. Navigator, you and Sonar start a plot. What I think he is doing is circling in a racetrack pattern. I suspect our best maneuver will be to approach that pattern from the seaward side and shoot when the torpedoes have the shortest distance to run.

"XO, let's flood four of the tubes and open the outer doors. The doors make a bit of noise coming open."

"Aye aye, Captain."

Saratov donned the sonar earphones and got back on his stool. He checked the clock.

"Mr. President, the intel analyst is in the limo outside."

David Herbert Hood made his excuses, shook hands with the important people at the head table, and headed for the hotel lobby. He shook some more hands there, then got into the limo for the ride to the White House.

The analyst turned out to be a young woman, and she was obviously flustered. She was wearing jeans and tennis shoes. "Mr. President."

"This is Deborah Buell, Mr. President."

"Glad to meet you. Sorry to call you away from a Saturday at home."

The analyst assured him there was no problem.

"A while back, you wrote a summary that said that Japan may have nuclear weapons. Do you remember that?"

"Oh, yes, sir. That was several months ago."

"Why did you think that was a possibility?"

"My section does economic analyses of foreign economies. It seemed to me that a significant percentage of Japan's government spending could not be accounted for in the normal ways. Basically, I thought they were spending a lot of money off-budget. So I began looking at other sectors of the economy where the money could be going. The high-tech engineering firms have been doing very well in Japan for years, and it's hard to see why—the civilian products that they should be producing don't seem to be there. Anyway, to make a long story short, it seemed to me that Japan might have several major black weapons programs. They have the technical wherewithal to make bombs, if they wanted them. So I wrote in the summary that they may have these weapons." A black program was one so secret the government did not acknowledge its existence.

"What did your superiors think of your reasoning?"

"They thought there was not enough evidence. Still, they reluctantly agreed to let me put it in the summary, labeled as a possibility."

"Surely you've thought more about this since then?"

"Yes, sir. And I've done more research. I still can't prove it."

"But you stand by your assertion. It's a possibility."

"In my opinion, it is."

"Ms. Buell, I appreciate you taking your time to chat about this. After the limo drops me, it can take you back to your car."

She laughed nervously. "I'm glad someone reads those summaries, Mr. President. The people at the office think they go to the great file cabinet in the sky."

"No doubt they do, Ms. Buell. But I read them first."

"Mr. President, I don't want to talk out of school, but there was an unsubstantiated rumor going around in the intelligence community earlier this summer that the Japanese had operational nukes. It was never more than a rumor and no one could ever verify who started it. Shortly after that, Japan invaded Siberia. It seems possible, to me anyway, that the Japanese started the rumor to discourage any thoughts the Russians might have about using nuclear weapons to defend themselves."

The president gave the woman a long, hard look as he got out of the car. "Thank you," he told her.

As they walked the corridors of the White House, the president asked Innes, "What are the Japanese doing about that sub?"

"They have at least four airplanes and six surface ships hunting for it between its last known position and the entrance to Tokyo Bay. One of the naval types over there told our people that the Japanese are afraid of a Yokosuka refinery repeat. They don't want another disaster like that on their hands."

"What if it isn't going to Tokyo Bay?"

"That's what has them worried. They have everything they own in the water east of the Japanese islands looking for this sub. The submarine could be a red herring. The Russians could be about to do something spectacular off Vladivostok."

"What does Abe say about this development?"

"He remarked to Ambassador Hanratty that if Russia still has nuclear weapons, they have lied to everyone for years."

"That's news?"

"He wants the United Nations to step in. Pass some sort of resolution promising the use of armed force against anyone who uses nuclear weapons."

"Uh-huh."

"And he wants the UN involved in Siberia. Basically, he repeated his demand that the UN give Japan a mandate to act as guardian of the native people, develop the place, and sell Siberian resources for world-market prices."

"He'll never get that," the president said as he plopped into his chair behind his desk in the Oval Office.

"He probably knows that. He's just making his position clear."

"So what do you think?"

"I think both Russia and Japan are up against the wall. The war is out of control. Something is going to happen in the very near future."

Four hours after the conference in the control room *Admiral Kolchak* was in position. Barely making steerageway, about a knot, just enough to keep the planes effective, she was headed northwest toward the strait that led to Sagami Bay. Five ships had gone overhead, freighters from the sound, going to and from the bay. War or no war, the wheels of commerce continued to turn.

From his stool outside the sonar shack, Pavel Saratov could see the chart. Actually, he was looking almost over the navigator's shoulder, so he could also see the measurements, the lines, the tiny triangles.

The sub was actually approaching the destroyer's racetrack from a forty-five-degree angle. The screw noise would be the loudest when the destroyer was going away from the sub. The torpedo would home on that noise. One hit with these giant ship-killers should be enough. The trick was to get the hit.

Saratov had been sitting on this stool, listening to the sounds, trying to hear another submarine, for the last five hours. Amazingly, he wasn't a bit tired. He was too keyed up.

He had to have a plan for every contingency. Askold had briefed the torpedomen and engineers, ensured everyone knew what was expected and was ready to do it without hesitation.

Sometime during this hustle and bustle, *Michman* Martos eased his head into the control room, looked around, made eye contact with the captain, then left.

Two hours ago, Saratov had conferred with Esenin. "How accurate is the GPS?" Esenin asked.

"For the best accuracy, we should surface and let the equipment get a position update from the satellites. It is within a few meters now, however."

"That will have to do," Esenin said with a frown.

"Yes."

"When we get to the fault, I will have my men ready."

"Are they experienced divers?"

"They know what they have to do, believe me. I am going out first."

"Whatever."

"You have a Spetsnaz diver aboard."

"We do. *Michman* Martos."

"I have had a talk with him. I do not think he is politically reliable."

"It's been a few years since I heard that phrase."

"You know what I mean. I need men I can trust."

"To the best of my knowledge, he didn't volunteer. I do not want any clouds on the man's professional ability, General. He is highly trained, experienced, and up for a medal for his service during the Yokosuka refinery attack. He deserves the honor."

"No doubt he does," Esenin said, then went on to another subject.

Now that conversation seemed as if it had taken place in another lifetime. Now there was only the boat, swimming gently forward amid the screw noises and the sounds of the sea. And the pinging: *ping . . . ping . . . ping* . . . Saratov sat with his eyes closed, listening intently to the orchestra.

There were other submarines nearby. Saratov could feel them.

"We shoot in five minutes, Captain," said the XO.

Esenin was rolling dice with the lives of every man on the boat. He wanted to set off four nuclear devices, to murder tens of millions of people. Even if the four blasts were insufficient to create a tsunami, the fireballs would broach the surface, fry coastal villages, create horrible tides that would inundate vast areas. Detonating these devices near the mouth of Tokyo Bay—perhaps Esenin would get a tidal race going back up the bay after the initial surge out of the bay, toward the blast area.

"Three minutes, Captain."

He could hear the destroyer, powerful screws, turning. . . . This was the closest point of approach, four miles. If it didn't detect *Admiral Kolchak* now, the submarine would get its shot.

Esenin didn't seem to understand that if you nuke *them,* you have made it easier for someone to nuke *you*. Probably he thought that aspect of the matter was Kalugin's problem. The people in Moscow. In the Kremlin. Those people.

The destroyer was still turning. The pitch of the screw noises changed as the aspect angle changed.

"Two minutes."

"Are we ready?"

"Yessir."

"Sonar, have you heard anything?"

"No, sir."

"One minute."

The destroyer was steady on its new course, angling away from *Admiral Kolchak*. It was doing about ten knots, making a mile every six minutes. The submarine was making one nautical mile per hour, so it was essentially dead in the water, screws barely turning over, every nonessential electrical unit off. Even the boat's ventilation fans were off.

"Fire tube one."

Saratov heard the blast of compressed air that ejected the torpedo from the tube and then heard its screws bite into the sea.

He had taken the precaution of turning down the volume on his earphones, which was a good thing. The torpedo was not quiet.

As the screw noises faded, he slowly twisted the volume knob back to maximum sensitivity.

The running time for this fish was six and a half minutes. Presumably the sonar operator aboard the destroyer would pick up the sound of the inbound torpedo and report it to the captain, who would probably order the launch of acoustic decoys. If the ship's company was competent, the decoys would be in the water in plenty of time. In fact, they might even be launched early.

Saratov took off the sonar headset, eyed the clock as the second hand ticked off a full minute since the first fish went into the water.

"Fire tube two."

Perhaps the second torpedo would arrive unexpectedly.

After the second fish was launched, he fought the urge to kick the boat to flank speed and go charging past this destroyer, which he hoped would soon be very busy. The risk was too great. Saratov did, however, order up five knots and changed course sixty degrees to the right to clear the area where the torpedoes were launched. A competent antisubmarine commander would have a helicopter in this area dipping a sonar as soon as possible.

Saratov turned sixty degrees to starboard after launching his torpedoes because that course was the most direct one into Sagami Bay. What
he didn't know was that this course, chosen for good reason, pointed
Admiral Kolchak directly at the Japanese submarine *Akashi.*

The sonar operator aboard *Akashi* heard the torpedoes and reported
them. "High-speed screws, two one zero degrees relative."

"How far?"

"Several miles, sir," the operator said.

Unfortunately, there was no way he or his captain could instantly
determine the target of the torpedoes. Given enough time, any right or
left drift in the relative bearing would become apparent. If there was
none, the torpedoes were on a collision course.

Time was what was needed, and the captain didn't have any to
spare. If torpedoes were aimed at him, he should locate the enemy
with active sonar, fire a torpedo in reply, launch decoys, and try to
evade the incoming fish. If, on the other hand, the torpedoes were
aimed at the beacon destroyer, giving away his submarine's position by
the use of active sonar was not immediately necessary. Nor was it ad-
visable.

The captain was well aware of the long-range capabilities of Russian
twenty-one-inch torpedoes, and this factor helped tilt the decision. The
shooting had started—his ship was in harm's way—he didn't want to
waste time waiting for bearing drift that he thought probably was not
there. On the other hand, there were two freighters on the surface
nearby. The government refused to close this area to civilian shipping.
Before he launched a torpedo the captain had to be sure of his target.

"Start pinging," he told the sonar operator. "Flood tubes one and
two and open the outer doors." To the officer of the day, he said,
"Come left sixty degrees and give me flank speed."

The ping of the active sonar raced through the water, and just behind it the noise of the submarine's twin screws thrashing as they bit
into the water to accelerate the submarine.

Aboard *Admiral Kolchak,* Saratov and the sonarman both heard the
ping and screw noises.

"Quick," Saratov said to the sonarman. "A bearing."

"Zero one zero relative, Captain. A submarine."

"Set tube three on acoustic homing."

"Tube three set acoustic."

"Ten degrees right bearing."

"Ten degrees right bearing set."

"Fire tube three."

"Tube three fired, Captain."

Both the sonar operators aboard *Harukaze*, the Japanese destroyer manning the picket station between Oshima Island and the Tateyama Peninsula, the eastern entrance of Sagami Bay, heard the unmistakable sound of small high-speed screws when the first of *Admiral Kolchak*'s torpedoes was still four minutes away from the destroyer. Their computers verified what their ears were telling them: torpedoes. They immediately reported the screw noises and the bearing to their superior, the tactical action officer in Combat, who reported it to the bridge on the squawk box.

The captain ordered the acoustic decoys deployed. Within sixty seconds, three of the four ready decoys were in the water. One of the decoys, the decoy that should have been ejected the farthest to starboard, was not launched due to a short circuit in the launcher.

While a small knot of sailors and petty officers worked frantically to remedy this glitch, the captain had a decision to make. Should he continue on this course, turn left, or turn right? He elected to turn right, to starboard, for a perfectly logical reason—there was a Japanese submarine to starboard, in the mouth of the bay, and drawing the enemy in that direction seemed like a good idea.

The captain had already turned his ship and was steady on the new course when the OOD reported that one of the acoustic decoys had failed to deploy.

The captain had only seconds to consider this news when Saratov's first torpedo hit an acoustic decoy, destroying it without exploding, and went roaring past the ship about a hundred yards to port.

Harukaze's sonar operators were listening to the decoys and the screw noises. The loss of one decoy changed the pitch of the cacophony. In addition, the sound of the first torpedo dropped in volume and pitch as it receded. The computer displayed a graphic of the torpedo's track. It had missed by only a hundred yards!

The two grinned at each other and shouted congratulations. Tight sphincters relaxed somewhat.

The junior operator was the first to get back to business. He was amazed to hear high-speed screw noises very near, and getting louder. He couldn't believe what he was hearing and stared at his computer screen. Another torpedo!

This is no drill. These are real torpedoes!

"Torpedo," he shouted as he stared at the bearing presentation on the screen and tried to concentrate so that he could repeat the number to the tactical action officer.

The big Russian ship-killer smashed into the stern of *Harukaze*.

Water being essentially incompressible, most of the force of the explosion was directed into the structure of the ship. The explosion ripped off *Harukaze*'s rudder and both screws, bent the shafts, and smashed a huge hole in the after end of the ship. Water poured into both engine rooms, drowning the engineers who had survived the initial blast concussion.

The ship drifted to a stop and began sinking at the stern.

The echoes from the pings were very faint when they returned to *Asashi*. The Russian submarine was almost bow-on, three miles away, and four hundred feet deeper than *Asashi*. Sounds echoing off the rising seafloor were causing havoc with the computer. In addition, the sonar operator was also trying to determine the bearing drift on the torpedo noises that he was hearing. He was getting a positive drift when the acoustic decoys from *Harukaze* went into the water and complicated the problem. Then the explosion from *Harukaze* reached him, quite loud, water being an excellent conductor of sound. All this input, much of it extraneous, was giving the computer fits.

He reported the explosion and the bearing, relieved and sick at the same time. Relieved because his boat was not the target, and sick because the bearing was to *Harukaze,* which he had been listening to for hours.

He was startled when he heard more screw noises amid the horrifying sounds of ripping metal and bulkheads collapsing. Automatically, he checked the bearing.

"Another torpedo, Captain. Bearing two one zero relative."

The relative bearing was the same as the first torpedo he heard, but not the magnetic bearing, because *Asashi* had turned sixty degrees.

"Screw noises getting louder, Captain. Little bearing drift apparent."

"Launch the acoustic decoys," the captain barked.

"Screw noises on constant bearing, Captain."

"I asked for decoys, people! Our lives are at stake! *Get them launched!*"

"It will be a few seconds, Captain."

"Stop all engines."

"All engines stop."

"Left full rudder. Come left another sixty degrees."

"Left full rudder," the helmsman repeated, just as *Admiral Kolchak*'s torpedo struck the stern of the submarine and exploded.

CHAPTER TWENTY-THREE

● JACK INNES SLIPPED up behind the president as he sipped his after-dinner coffee and whispered the news from Sagami Bay in his ear. President Hood made his excuses to the people around the table and stood up. He followed Innes out of the room.

"A destroyer and a submarine—he torpedoed them both. Only a few dozen men from the destroyer survived. The sub was lost with all hands."

"What is he trying to do?"

Hood asked the question in such a way that Innes knew the president didn't want an answer. Finally Hood said, "Better get the Joint Chiefs over here. And the Secretary of State."

The two men walked to the Oval Office.

After Innes called the duty officer, Hood said, "Is this the same skipper who blew up Yokosuka?"

"Apparently so. CIA says the Russians have only one boat left, a *Kilo*-class named *Admiral Kolchak.*"

"What was the skipper's name?"

"Pavel Saratov."

"One obsolete old boat . . ."

"He's a fox, he's in shallow water, and he's been damned lucky."

"What is he trying to do?"

"I don't know, sir."

An hour later, Hood asked the Joint Chiefs of Staff that question. "What is he trying to do?"

Everyone had a guess. Hood waved the guesses away. "Why haven't the Japanese found this guy? It's an obsolete diesel/electric boat."

The CNO answered. "It may be old and have limited capabilities, sir, but battery boats are very quiet. In shallow water they are extremely difficult to detect quickly. The computers have a devil of a time with the bottom echoes."

"Quickly?"

"They have to snorkel every day or two, Mr. President. Given a couple days, trained hunters will find them every time."

"Gentlemen, to get back to it, the question we must answer is this: What trouble can Pavel Saratov cause with his little submarine?"

"Obviously, he can sink a lot of ships," someone said.

"He could have done that without going into the lion's den."

With the help of computer graphics, they reviewed the military situation. "Whatever Captain Saratov hopes to accomplish, sir," the CNO said, summing up, "he had better hurry. He sank that destroyer three hours ago right there." He used a laser pointer. "Even if he dashed away at fifteen knots—and that is a real juice-draining dash—he's within forty-five miles of that position. The Japanese have four destroyers closing that area and they are flying in sonar-dipping helicopters from other naval bases. Regardless of what Pavel Saratov intends, he and his crew are rapidly running out of time."

"Gentlemen," the president of the United States said, "I think Captain Saratov intends to deliver a nuclear weapon. How he will do it, I don't know. My concern is that Japan may be tempted to retaliate if they have nuclear weapons."

They sat in absolute silence as the president looked from face to face. "We have given Japan all the information we possess on Captain Saratov's submarine. I wish we could do more."

"Perhaps, Mr. President," General Tuck said, "we should threaten both Russia and Japan with nuclear retaliation by the United States if they use nukes on each other."

Dead silence greeted that suggestion. President Hood rubbed his temple. "I don't have what it takes to push the button," he said finally. "I couldn't do it. Kalugin and Abe might have the stuff, but I don't. They would know we were bluffing. My daddy always told me, Never point a gun at a man unless you're willing to shoot."

Saratov was bent over the chart of Sagami Bay, measuring distances to Esenin's fault, when the sonarman said, "Helicopter, Captain. He's hovering, I think."

A hovering helo could only mean one thing: a sonar-dipping ASW chopper.

"Pass the word—back to silent routine. Tell the torpedo room to stop reloading the tubes. Absolutely no unnecessary noise."

Saratov glanced at the depth indicator, which registered twenty-five meters. Here in the shallow water of the bay, that was as deep as he could go.

At least the water was noisy. There were fishing boats, ships, pleasure craft, high-speed ferries, all roaring back and forth here in Japan's inland waters. Pavel Saratov donned the headphones and closed his eyes so he could concentrate better. A cacophony of screw noises smote his ears, some of them quite loud.

On the other hand, he had those four damned bomb containers welded to the deck topside. Even at two knots, those things had to gurgle. Not to mention the missing anechoic tiles.

The chopper was there all right, barely audible. The sonarman had good ears.

"Start a plot," he told the *michman,* slapping him on the back.

"I already have, Captain."

"It will take us about an hour to get over the fault. Once we are on the bottom, we will be tougher to find."

The *michman* didn't answer. He knew a great deal about this business and wasn't buying happy propaganda.

"Helo has moved to another location. A little closer."

"Say the bearing."

"Two six five relative."

"Two six five relative," Saratov repeated to the navigator, who drew a line on the chart.

"One rotor or two?" Saratov asked the sonar *michman.*

"One, I think."

That meant the helo was relatively small. Perhaps it didn't carry any weapons.

Five minutes went by. No one in the control room said anything. They stared at a gauge, a control wheel, a lever, something, but not at one another. Saratov thought it strange, but in tense moments, they seemed to avoid eye contact with one another. And they listened. What they wanted to hear, of course, was nothing at all.

"He's breaking hover, fading. Sound is being masked by a speedboat. There is also a freighter going into the bay. He's about a mile from us."

"Turn the sensitivity down," Saratov suggested.

"It is down, sir. It's just damned noisy out there."

"Okay, okay."

Esenin was looking at his watch, now looking at nothing, obviously thinking big thoughts.

The air in the boat was foul. Saratov could smell himself, and he smelled bad.

"Uh-oh. He's right on top of us. He put his sonar pod in the water right over us."

"One knot," Saratov told the chief of the boat. He said it so quietly that he had to hold up one finger to ensure the chief understood.

Several of the sailors were holding their breath.

The beating of the rotors, a mechanical rhythm, pounded against Saratov's ears. The helicopter was very near.

Now he broke hover and moved a bit, not very far.

"He's got us, I think," the sonarman said, biting his lip.

"Listen for a destroyer. He'll be coming at flank speed."

After a few minutes, the helo moved again, to the other side of the boat.

"He's got us," the sonarman said disgustedly, his face contorting. "He really does, Captain."

"Listen for the destroyer."

The sonarman nodded morosely.

"XO, how old were those missiles you loaded in the sail launchers?"

"Twenty years, Captain."

"Much deterioration?"

"Some corrosion on the bodies of the missiles, but all the electrical contacts were good."

Another five minutes passed. The helo moved again. The tension was excruciating.

"Where is he now?"

"Starboard rear. He's dunked his thing in all four quadrants."

"Take us up, Chief. Periscope depth. Sonar, get the radar ready. We'll stick the sail up, shoot at this guy and put him in the water, then dash over to the general's fault."

"How quiet do you want to go up?" the chief asked.

"I agree with Sonar—the jig is up. Let's do it fast, before this guy gets out of range."

As the boat hit periscope depth, Saratov brought up the periscope for a quick sweep. He wasn't interested in the chopper—he knew where it was—but other ships in the vicinity. He walked the periscope in a complete circle, pausing only once for a second or two, then ordered the scope down.

"Okay, gang. He's up there. And we have a destroyer or frigate on the way. He's bow-on to us. We stick the sail out and kill the chopper, then go back to periscope depth and shoot at the destroyer."

"Why are you engaging this ship?" Esenin demanded.

"I'm trying to buy you some time, you goddamned fool. Now shut up!"

To the chief, he said, "Surface. Let's go up fast, hold her with the planes, shoot, and pull the plug."

"You heard the captain. Surface."

As the sail cleared the water, the sonar *michman* fired off the tiny radar on its own mast. He knew the quadrant where the chopper was, and that is where he looked first.

"He's running dead away from us."

"Radar lock!" the sonarman called.

"Fire a missile!"

The antiaircraft missile went out with a roar, straight up, then made the turn to chase the chopper. Being a man of little faith, Saratov fired two more missiles before the sub slid back under the waves.

"I think we got a hit, Captain," the sonarman said, pressing his headphones against his ears.

"Level at periscope depth, Chief. Flood tubes five and six and open outer doors. New course zero four five. Lift the attack scope and stand by for a bearing."

"Helo just went in the water. I can hear the destroyer."

"We'll wait until the destroyer is closer."

"Down the throat?" Askold asked, his brow furrowed deeply.

"We have two fish loaded. We hit with one of them or we die."

"Destroyer is echo-ranging, Captain."

Everything happens slowly in antisubmarine warfare. In this life-or-death duel, the charging destroyer seemed to take forever to close the distance. The men in the control room wiped their faces on their sleeves, checked their dials and gauges, eyed the captain, wiped the palms of their hands on their filthy trousers . . . and prayed.

"Up scope."

Saratov snapped off a bearing, focused the scope, and then dropped it into the well. The scope had been out just five seconds. As it was going down, the XO read the range off the scope's focus ring.

"Five thousand one hundred meters."

"He's going to start shooting, Captain," said one of the junior officers.

"Quiet. Control yourself. Sonar, does he have us?"

"It's hard to tell. He's hasn't focused his pings yet. I think the shallow water is bothering him. Or all the civilian traffic. And he is going too fast."

"Let's pray he doesn't slow down. He won't hear the fish until they are right on him."

"He should be about three thousand meters, Captain."

"Up scope."

"Bearing and range, mark. Down scope." Five seconds.

"He's coming off the power, Captain."

"Two thousand meters."

"Fire tube five!"

"Tube five fired."

One mile. The torpedo was doing forty-five knots, the destroyer slowing . . . maybe twenty. Fifty-five knots of closure. The torpedo would be there in a few seconds more than a minute.

Twenty seconds, thirty . . .

"Up scope."

Saratov grabbed the handles as the scope came out of the well. "He's turning to our left. Bearing fifteen left on tube six."

"Fifteen left, aye."

"Tube six, fire. Down scope."

Aboard ASW frigate *Mount Fuji,* the combat control center crew was well aware that the submarine in front of them was armed and dangerous. They had received a data link from the helicopter before it was shot down and knew the location, even though they hadn't yet located the sub on sonar.

The decision not to focus the echo-ranging signals was a conscious attempt to make the submarine skipper think he was still undetected. *Mt. Fuji*'s captain ordered the ship slowed to enable the sonar to hear better. As Saratov surmised, the sonar operators were having great difficulty picking the submarine out of the background noise.

When the sonar chief petty officer called, "Torpedo in the water," the tactical action officer ordered the antisubmarine rockets fired.

They rippled off the launcher as the frigate turned right, to Saratov's left, to avoid the oncoming torpedo. The ship turned quicker than the torpedo, which missed.

When he was firing his last fish, Saratov saw the rockets' muzzle blast and knew the moment was at hand.

As the scope went into the well, he ordered, "All ahead flank; come right ninety degrees."

He looked at the faces staring at him. "Antisubmarine rockets," he said as the sonarman called the splashes.

The second torpedo went off under the frigate's keel, tearing the bow off. The noises of the sea rushing in and bulkheads collapsing were audible in the sub even without a headset. The men just started to cheer when the submarine shook under a hammer blow.

"Starboard side, Captain. It hit the outer hull. Yes, and holed it."

The chief started giving rapid-fire orders. The holed tank was quickly identified and air pumped into its mates in an attempt to preserve buoyancy and keep the sub from impacting the bottom of the bay.

While all this was going on, Saratov consulted the chart. He used a ruler to plot the course he wanted to the fault, then ordered the rudder over.

The odor of feces was quite noticeable. Someone had lost control of his bowels. Maybe several people had.

Hanging on to the bulkhead, General Esenin never took his eyes off Pavel Saratov.

"It could have been worse," Askold said philosophically.

Amid the confusion, the sonarman said to no one in particular, "We're going to die."

A squalid, shoddy monument to bureaucratic stupidity and inefficiency, the city of Irkutsk in central Asia nevertheless stunned first-time visitors by the spectacle of its setting. The extraordinary waters of Lake Baikal, on whose shores the town sat, were a dark blue, almost black under the shadows of drifting clouds. The lake was so deep that it was once thought to be bottomless. In truth it was a huge inland sea 375 miles long, containing one-fifth of the planet's fresh water. The surface stretched away until it merged with the horizon.

Towering along the western shore of the lake was a range of high mountains, still snowcapped from the previous winter. More rugged, craggy blue mountains lay to the south and east.

Since arriving in Irkutsk, Yan Chernov had not taken the time to admire the view. He spent every minute in meetings with generals and colonels who had flown in from Moscow.

"You will escort a strike on Tokyo," he was told. Amid the transports with Aeroflot markings at the base sat a half-dozen MiG-25s, elderly Mach-3 single-seat interceptors. These planes, Chernov was told, would actually carry the bombs. Of all the planes the Soviets had built through the years, which the Russians had inherited, only MiG-25s had a chance against Zeros. MiG-25s could use their blazing speed to outrun the Japanese interceptors—dash in, drop their weapons, and dash away before the Zeros could shoot them all down.

A Moscow general with an amazing display of chest cabbage held up one finger. "Only one," he said. "Only one has to get through."

Another strike launched at the same time would target the Japanese missile-launch facilities on the Tateyama Peninsula. Chernov knew the colonel leading that strike, although not well.

The problem with the MiG-25s, which was the reason for these meetings and conferences, was their limited range. The bombers would have to be fueled from airborne tankers several times to make this flight, one far longer that anything the Mikoyan designers had ever in their wildest fantasies envisioned for their superfast fighter. Like all Soviet fighters, the MiG-25 had been designed to defend the homeland.

Getting the tankers into position to refuel the MiGs prior to and after their dash was Chernov's job. He was to escort them and defend them from Zeros.

Just listening to the Moscow generals and their staffs explain the mission, annotate charts, assign frequencies and call signs, and talk about the whole thing as if it were possible—indeed, as if it were a routine military operation—Chernov didn't know whether to laugh or cry. The whole thing was ludicrous. At the very start of this exercise in military stupidity, Chernov tried to explain to the staff weenies that the Sukhois didn't have much of a chance against semi-stealthy Zeros: "Zeros are a technological generation beyond our plane. Two generations ahead of the MiG-25," he said.

None of the brass was interested. He would do as he was told—it had all been decided in Moscow.

Now Chernov sat and listened and made notes. He looked out the window and watched the second hand of the clock on the wall sweep around and around, counting off the minutes. Dawn was still several hours away.

An hour before man-up time, the briefers were finished. The pilots were told to relax, make a head stop.

Chernov wandered over toward the barracks and found an empty bunk.

Stretched out, trying to relax, trying to put it all in perspective, he felt the insanity sweep over him. He felt as if he were drowning. Nuclear weapons. Nuke Tokyo. Mushroom clouds. Millions dead.

If any of the MiGs got through, that is.

And afterward, meeting the tankers, trying to get enough fuel to make it back to a Russian-occupied base ...

"What if the Japanese retaliate?" someone had asked the Moscow brass, only to be told, "The Japanese don't have nuclear weapons."

"We hope," Yan Chernov said loudly.

"President Kalugin is absolutely certain."

"Bet he said that in a telephone call from his dacha on the Black Sea," one of the junior pilots said, and his comrades laughed. The Moscow brass frowned, then pretended that they had heard nothing.

The men weren't happy, but they had never heard anyone in uniform suggest Japan might be a nuclear power, so the possibility of thermonuclear retaliation seemed remote. Getting to Japan was the worrisome part.

Well, if the Zeros didn't get them, the usual Russian leadership and efficiency problems would ensure this complex plan ground to a halt well before the planes landed safely back at Irkutsk.

Chernov lay in the darkness, trying to relax. Sleep was impossible. Man-up time in less than an hour.

His thoughts began to drift. Scenes from his youth growing up on a collective farm flashed through his mind. He had wanted something more, and so had applied himself faithfully and diligently to gain top honors in school. The work paid off. He had been noticed.

So what had he gained?

His life had been a great adventure. Truly. The flying, the new and different places, the exhilaration of combat, the thrill of victory—a man would never have gotten any of that back on the collective farm, with that eternal wind always blowing, howling across the plain, scouring away seed, soil, hopes, dreams, everything.

If his father and mother could only see how far he had traveled along this road.

He was seized with the most powerful longing. Oh, if only he could spend another day with his parents, sitting in their tiny cottage, looking out the door at the plowed fields as his father talked about the earth.

All that was over. Gone.

In a few hours, he would be dead and none of it would matter.

The submarine bumped once, scraped along the seafloor for a few feet, then settled into the muddy bottom of Sagami Bay and began tilting ever so slowly to port.

"Captain," Esenin said sharply as the list passed five degrees. Even he was holding on.

Six degrees . . .

"At twelve degrees, we lift her and try another spot."

Eight . . .

"We are so close," Esenin muttered.

Ten degrees . . . barely moving . . . Then all movement stopped.

A sigh of relief swept the control room.

"Fifty-two meters," someone said, reading the depth gauge.

Suddenly Saratov realized how tired he was. He had to hang on to the chart table to remain erect.

"Here we are, General. Wounded, running out of air, with exhausted batteries, and the entire Japanese navy searching for us. I don't know how much time we have."

The tense hours had taken their toll on Esenin. He had to summon the energy to speak. "You have gotten us here, Saratov. That is the critical factor. At this place, we can save Russia."

"Right." The sourness in Saratov's tone narrowed Esenin's eyes.

"We leave this spot when and only when I say." Esenin looked into every man's face. "I am taking two divers with me. We will exit through the air lock. We will open a container and put one of the weapons onto the sea floor. Then we will come back inside and you will move the boat one mile west along the fault, where we will do it again. When the last weapon is on the bottom, you will take us out of here."

Esenin glanced at his watch.

"When will the weapons detonate?" Saratov asked.

"In twelve hours. Planting each weapon will take an hour, plus an hour to move the boat—seven hours total. That will give us five hours to exit the area."

"We don't have seven hours," Saratov told him. "You might have one or two. Three at most."

"You think they'll be on us by then?"

"I guarantee it."

Esenin's lips compressed into a thin line.

"The warheads are armed now, aren't they?" Pavel Saratov asked.

"Do you know that, or are you guessing?"

"The box." He nodded at the box on Esenin's chest. "It could only be a trigger."

"We decided that detonation of the weapons at sea would be preferable to letting them fall into enemy hands. Fortunately for us, that necessity did not arise. Still, it might. If it does, I have faith that Major Polyakov will do what has to be done. He will have custody of the box while I am outside the boat."

Esenin took off the box and placed it on the chart table. He opened it.

"As you can see, there is a keyboard for typing in a code." He punched in a four-digit number with a forefinger. "There," he said. "The code is entered. Now the circuitry is armed."

Saratov stepped forward for a look. "You armed that goddamned thing?"

"It was too dangerous to sail around with the bombs armed. They are armed now."

Esenin's hand came up. He had a pistol in it. He jabbed the barrel against Saratov's chest. "No closer, Captain. You have had your fun at my expense. From here on, this is my show."

Polyakov and the naval infantry *michmen* also had their pistols out and pointing.

The major grinned at Saratov. "I will guard the box, Captain."

"You have brought us far, Pavel Saratov," Esenin said, flashing his Trojan Island grin, "yet we still have far to go. You will let us down if you let anything happen to you."

"You don't really give a damn if you live or die, do you, Esenin?"

"Sometimes it is easier that way."

Saratov got back onto the stool where he had spent the last twelve hours. "You people better get at it. It is just a matter of time before the Japs arrive."

The dinner hour had passed when Janos Ilin made an evening call on Marshal Stolypin at military headquarters in Moscow. He found the old man in a sour mood. When the door closed and they were alone, the soldier said, "Fool! Incompetent! Bungler!"

"What can I say?"

"This morning he gave the order to launch nuclear strikes against Japan. He sent three planes to bomb Tokyo and three to bomb the Japanese missile facility at Tateyama. And, of course, there is the submarine with four weapons aboard trying to put bombs on the ocean floor outside Tokyo Bay. I argued against it, told him no, no, a thousand times no, and he almost sacked me. Ran me out."

"Oh, too bad. *Too bad!* Have we heard anything from *Admiral Kolchak?*"

"Not a word. From all the intercepts of Japanese traffic, it appears Captain Saratov has gotten into Sagami Bay. Against all odds. It's an amazing feat."

"What does Kalugin say?"

"He doesn't believe the Japanese have warheads on missiles that they can use as ICBMs. Refuses to admit the possibility."

"I was hoping you had an appointment with him in the near future."

"Umph."

The old man sat looking out the window. He looked ten years older than he had a month ago.

"You have done what you could, Marshal."

"I should be home in my garden." Stolypin sighed. "My legacy to Russia—I argued futilely against a suicidal course already decided upon by a dictator. Fifty years of soldiering I did, and he wouldn't listen."

"Perhaps it *is* time for the garden."

"I just sent an aide over with a letter of resignation effective at midnight tonight. I should go home now and be done with all of this." Stolypin looked at his watch. "I have my last staff meeting in a few minutes. Perhaps I should sit in on it, say farewell."

"How goes it? Truly."

"The situation is not as bleak as Kalugin believes. We are building an army; we are equipping it, finding food and fuel and transportation. ... We could whip the Japanese this winter. We will have half a million men to put against them. With air superiority, we will crush them."

"Kalugin refuses to wait?"

"He says the UN will give the oil fields away before spring. Maybe he is right. The world has changed so."

"I must see Kalugin tonight."

"I tried to explain.... Time is on our side. Every day that passes, we get stronger. Six months from now, they will be losing troops wholesale; we'll be bleeding them mercilessly; the Diet will be arguing about how much money the army costs.... *Then we could have them!*"

The telephone rang. Stolypin sat looking at it, listening to the rings, before he finally extended a hand and picked up the instrument. "Yes."

He listened a bit, then said, "Janos Ilin of the FIS is also here. He would like an audience, too. May I bring him along?"

He listened a bit more, grunted, then hung up.

"One of Kalugin's flunkies. The president wants to see me about the letter."

"Of resignation?"

"Yes." Stolypin ran his fingers over the desk, put the telephone exactly where it was supposed to be, and flipped off an invisible mote of dust.

"They said you could come, if you wished."

"Thank you."

"Don't thank me. He'll probably have me shot for treason and you for being in the same room."

As they walked into the courtyard, Ilin put a hand lightly on the marshal's arm and brought him to a stop. "Have you any indication that Kalugin suspects you or me of trying to kill him?"

"None. So far."

"Kalugin will purge the bureaucracy, the military, and the Chamber of Deputies as soon as the military situation is looking up."

"I am an old man. I am resigned to my fate. Rest assured, I will say nothing."

"I wasn't thinking of you or me. I was thinking of one hundred and fifty million Russians who deserve better than Aleksandr Kalugin."

With that, Ilin walked on toward the car.

The soldier holding the car door saluted the marshal, and he returned it. Stolypin and Ilin seated themselves in the limo and the soldier closed the door behind them.

There was a glass between the passengers and the driver of the car. "Can he hear us?" Ilin asked.

"No."

"I want to tell Kalugin personally of some critical intelligence reports that I have just received."

"With me there?"

"You might as well hear it now. Both Japan and the United States know of Kalugin's determination to use nuclear weapons. The missions he has ordered may well fail."

"How do they know? A spy? A traitor?"

"The Japanese call him Agent Ju."

"You know this person's identity?"

"It is someone in Kalugin's circle, I think. Someone very close to him." This was a lie, of course, but Stolypin didn't know that.

Stolypin goggled. "Why, for Christ's sake?"

"Money, I think," Janos Ilin told him. "Originally. Now, I do not know. Power? Insanity? I intend to tell Kalugin about this agent, tell him what I know. And tell him, again, that Japan has nuclear weapons."

"A traitor! In times like these!"

"Especially in times like these," Janos Ilin replied.

The foul, stale air inside the boat was dead, unmoving. All the circulation fans were off to save the batteries and minimize noise. Each man was trapped in a cloud of his own stink.

The boat had been lying on the bottom for an hour. Esenin and his two divers had gone out through the air lock twenty minutes ago.

During the past hour, several ships had passed near enough to be heard without sonar. Only Saratov and the sonar operator knew more than that, because only those two wore headsets. Saratov had just concluded that there were six ships within audible range when the sonar operator whispered that there were seven. They were going back and forth near the location where the frigate had gone under, probably pulling sailors from the water.

Right now *Admiral Kolchak* lay on the bottom six miles from that position.

The number of planes was a more difficult problem because the beat of their props came and went. There had to be several, perhaps as many as four.

The ships and airplanes would find the submarine before too long. Although the sub was sitting on the bottom, a MAD would go off the scale if a hunter came close enough.

Pavel Saratov sat looking at Major Polyakov, who was seated on the navigator's stool, facing the captain's right.

Without Esenin around, Polyakov had become lethargic. Saratov thought he had little imagination. He was not stupid, just unimaginative, without ambition or ideas. There are a lot of people in the world like that, Saratov reminded himself, and they seem to do all right. It is certainly not a crime to leave the thinking to others.

Given all of that, the question remained: Why would Polyakov push the button, killing himself and every man on the boat?

"You would kill yourself, would you, Polyakov?"

"I will do what has to be done for my country, Captain. I believe in Russia."

"And you are the only one who does?"

Polyakov eyed Saratov suspiciously. Apparently he thought this some kind of loyalty test. "Of course not," he said. "Aleksandr Kalugin loves Russia too."

"I see."

"I don't want to talk about these things."

"These subjects are uncomfortable."

"I am a soldier. I obey my superior officers. All of them."

"Is Esenin a soldier? A real soldier?"

"What else would he be?" Polyakov's brows knitted.

"You've met him before in your career, have you?"

"No. The naval infantry is a big outfit. Of course there are officers I do not know."

"And *michmen*?"

"Plenty of *michmen* I don't know."

"Where are you from, Polyakov?"

"St. Petersburg, Captain. My father was a shipyard worker."

It went on like this for several minutes. The major answered the captain's questions because he was the captain, but his answers revealed no inner doubts. The faces of the sailors standing and sitting in the small room reflected the ordeal they had been through, and the horror of the abyss at which they found themselves. They looked at Polyakov as if he were a monster, which seemed to bother the major not at all. Esenin had chosen well.

Just then, the screw noises of a ship became audible. Saratov glanced up at the overhead, as did most of the people in the compartment, including Polyakov. The noise became louder and louder.

As the ship thundered directly over the sub, Pavel Saratov removed the Tokarev from his pocket and shot Major Polyakov in the head.

The major toppled sideways off the stool and fell onto the deck. The box remained on the chart table. Saratov reached for it with his left hand as he pointed his pistol at the naval infantry *michman* standing openmouthed facing him, his rifle in his hand. The chief of the boat reached for the *michman*'s rifle and pistol, took them from him.

"This is where the road forks, Chief. Are you with me or not?"

"We're with you, Captain. All the men."

"Go disarm the infantrymen forward. Collect all the weapons and bring them in here. And send *Michman* Martos to me. Hurry. We don't have much time."

The navigator swabbed the sweat from his face with his sleeve. He was near tears. "Oh, thank you, Captain. I'd rather die than start World War Three."

"If we don't have some luck, son, we may do both. Now take the major's pistol and disarm the infantrymen in the engine room and battery compartment."

"And if they won't give me their guns?"

"Shoot them, and be damned quick about it. Now go."

Saratov hefted the box. It was very light. He used a pocketknife to pry off the back, which was held on with just three screws.

The box contained only a battery. No transmitter. It was a dummy.

"Captain," said the sonar *michman*. "A helo just went into a hover off our port side. He is very close. He must have dipped a sonar pod."

CHAPTER TWENTY-FOUR

●THE TOKYO BOMBERS took off first, three MiG-25s, one after another. The four Sukhoi escorts, with Yan Chernov in the lead, took the runway as the last MiG lifted off. Chernov and his wingman made a section takeoff, Chernov on the left. Safely airborne, Chernov turned slightly left so that he could look back over his shoulder. Yes, the other two Sukhois were lifting off.

In less than a minute, the four fighters were together and climbing to catch the three MiGs, which were climbing on course as a flight of three aircraft, spread over a quarter of a mile of sky.

The Tateyama strike was scheduled to follow ten minutes behind. Alas, this whole evolution hinged on successfully rendezvousing with tankers at three places along this route. The tankers had been launched from bases farther to the east hours ago.

Or so a Moscow general said, after much shouting into a telephone.

A coordinated strike, precision rendezvous, over a dozen aircraft moving in planned ways over thousands of miles of sky—the Russians hadn't even attempted exercises this complicated in years. If the tankers weren't at the rendezvous points, if the equipment in the tankers didn't work, if the tankers or strike planes had mechanical problems, if a tanker pilot screwed up, if the Japanese attacked with Zeros—any of these likely eventualities would prevent the bombers from reaching Japan.

The Moscow general with the chest cabbage didn't want to talk of these things.

The morning was cool, but the day was going to be hot. Already clouds were forming over mountain peaks and ridges and drifting over the valleys, portending rain. Here and there a cumulonimbus was growing in the thermals, threatening to develop into an afternoon thunderstorm. All these clouds were below the fighters, which were cruising at forty thousand feet.

The oxygen tasted rubbery this morning. Yan Chernov sucked on it, glanced at his cockpit altitude gauge, and tried to rearrange his bottom on the ejection seat to get more comfortable.

As briefed, Chernov split his flight of four planes into two sections. He stationed himself and his wingman three miles ahead and to the right of the strike formation, and the other section in a similar position on the left side.

He looked at his watch. An hour and a half to the first tanker rendezvous.

The major sat listening to the electronic countermeasures equipment and watching the clouds in the lower atmosphere. There were dust storms down there, opaque areas that hid the land. Amazing how good the view was from this altitude. God must see the earth like this, he thought.

After a careful scrutiny of their credentials, the car bearing Stolypin and Ilin was allowed to cross the small bridge at the main entrance of the Kremlin and discharge its passengers. The two men then entered a nearby room to be strip-searched.

First, each man emptied the contents of his pockets into a plastic bin: watch, money, keys, credentials, everything. Other security officers began examining the attaché cases they carried.

They disrobed in separate cubicles in full view of two of Kalugin's loyal ones, who then scrutinized their naked bodies. They stood naked in the cubicles while their clothes were examined under a fluoroscope, a device much like the machines used in airports to examine hand baggage.

The security men fluoroscoped every item of clothing, including shoes, belts, and ties.

When they brought his clothes back, Ilin put them on. Then he left the cubicle and went to a table where an officer was playing with his keys and glasses. The officer, who was about forty and fat, examined the comb, looked at the pictures in the wallet, then turned the wallet inside out and ran it through the fluoroscope again.

The examination was as thorough as Ilin had ever witnessed.

Another officer handed back his money, keys, and watch, then sat looking at the FIS identity card and pass. He ran the ID cards through a black light, ensured they were genuine, then scrutinized both cards under a magnifying glass before passing them back.

Ilin had brought two pens with him that evening, one a ballpoint and the other an American fountain pen. The fat officer sat there pushing on the button of the ballpoint, running the point in and out, *click, click, click*, as he passed each of Ilin's cigarettes through the fluoroscope. When he finished with the cigarettes, he put them back in a tin cigarette case bearing the KGB insignia and laid it on the table. He made a few marks on a scratch pad with the ballpoint, then laid it down and picked up the fountain pen. He uncapped it and scrawled a bit, looked at it under a magnifying glass, then put the cap back on and placed it beside the ballpoint.

Ilin had been wearing two rings, one with the old KGB insignia engraved on an opal, the other a plain gold wedding ring that had belonged to his grandfather. He normally wore the wedding ring on his right hand since he wasn't married.

The KGB ring fascinated the security guard. Of course he studied it under the fluoroscope. Then he began picking at the stone with a penknife, trying to get it out of the setting.

"You are going to destroy my ring?" Ilin asked, his temper showing a little.

He motioned to the supervisor. "This officer is trying to destroy my ring."

"He is just doing his job."

"You pay him to pry stones out of settings?"

"Let me see the ring." The supervisor pulled out a magnifying glass and studied the stone under it.

"If you want, I can leave it with you and pick it up when I leave," Ilin suggested.

The supervisor passed the ring to him and put the glass away.

Meanwhile, the security officer at the table tackled Ilin's cigarette lighter, a crude souvenir bearing a Nazi swastika. He ran a fingertip over the swastika and looked at Ilin with an eyebrow raised.

"My father's," Ilin said. "He killed the German officer who owned it."

The guard flipped the lighter several times: A flame appeared. He then took it completely apart. He removed the cotton packing, examined the wick and the wheel, then put the thing back together.

Finally he shoved the pile across the table for Ilin to pick up. He didn't say anything, just sat there staring at Ilin as he pocketed his items and adjusted his tie.

The marshal took a bit more time getting dressed. When he came out of his cubicle, the officer in there followed along and watched him pocket his personal items and put his watch back on his wrist.

None of the security officers said a word.

When the marshal was dressed, he picked up his attaché case and looked at Ilin.

"This way," one of the guards said.

They had a long hike—across several courtyards and up two flights of stairs, then down several long, long hallways filled with paintings of long-forgotten eighteenth- and nineteenth-century noblemen.

Finally, they entered Kalugin's reception area. Two plainclothesmen frisked them again while a male secretary watched.

Only then were they shown into Kalugin's office. One of the security men closed the door behind them and stood inside, his back against the door.

Aleksandr Kalugin raised his gaze from the paperwork lying on his desk. "Ah, Marshal Stolypin. Janos Ilin. I have been waiting for you."

The first Russian tanker rendezvous went off like clockwork, which shocked Chernov a little. One by one, the MiGs queued up on the tanker and got a full load of fuel, then made room for the Sukhois. Even though the MiG pilots hadn't flown two flights in the previous six months, they hung in proper position as if they practiced every day.

There were three tankers: one for the Tokyo strike, one for the Tateyama strike ten minutes behind, and one spare.

The Tateyama strike team showed up as the Tokyo strike team departed the rendezvous racetrack on course.

The strike teams were passing a hundred miles north of the American base at Chita. From here to the next rendezvous, they were within range of the Zeros at Khabarovsk. Chernov turned up the sensitivity of his ECM.

When they had walked out to their planes two hours before, one of the pilots asked another, "How is it going to feel to bomb Tokyo?"

Chernov overheard the question, but he didn't hear the reply.

The real question, Chernov mused now, was how each of them was going to live with the knowledge that he had helped slaughter millions of people. Ten million? Twenty? Thirty?

Thirty million human beings was certainly within the realm of possibility, he decided. Perhaps more.

What in hell were those fools in Moscow thinking?

Was Siberia worth that much blood?

He shook his head wearily. He was a soldier. It was shameful to think these thoughts, treasonous thoughts.

He adjusted his oxygen mask and checked his engine instruments and the fuel remaining and the position of his wingman, Malokov, or something like that. Chernov had never flown with him before. He was a new man, from a squadron near Moscow. The whisper was that the idiot had volunteered for this mission.

Maybe he wanted a medal, a promotion, recognition, his picture in the newspapers as a hero of the Russian Republic. Or was he filled with hatred for the treacherous archenemy, Japan? One of the civilians from Moscow had addressed the pilots, and that is the way he'd referred to the Japanese.

Chernov craned his head and searched the high sky until he had located all three of the MiG-25s, lying out there like fish in an invisible sea. Sharks.

His mother—what would she have said about all this?

Maybe Malokov felt like Chernov. Maybe he was just tired of living and wanted to die.

"Come in, gentlemen, come in." Aleksandr Kalugin gestured toward the seats in front of the desk. He picked up a sheet of paper. "What is this, Marshal? A resignation?"

"Mr. President, I think it is time for someone else to serve as chief of staff."

Kalugin sat back in his chair, hitched up his trousers. "Stolypin, you have served your country well. You are building us an army, one we need. There is a war on. You cannot be spared."

He said all of this as the guard watched from his post at the door. The man stood with his arms folded across his chest.

"I disagree completely with your decision to escalate this conflict. The Japanese may have nuclear weapons and they might use them on Russia. That is a risk we cannot take."

"Your objections have been noted. Yet *I* decide what risks we shall run. *I* am the man responsible."

"This is no small matter, Mr. President. I feel that I must resign. You need soldiers who, even if they disagree, can support your government's policies. I can't."

"Marshal Stolypin, the Japanese do not have nuclear weapons. I do not know who whispered this false information to you"—he held up his hand—"and it is no matter. Nuclear weapons are my concern."

"Sir, I disagree most vehemently."

"Your resignation letter says you have been in the army since you were seventeen years old. Fifty-four years."

Stolypin nodded.

"Everyone in uniform obeys the orders of their superiors, including the chief of staff. You know that. I don't care about your support. You have expressed your opinion, I have decided the issue, and now you will obey and soldier on. You will serve on until I release you from your obligation."

Kalugin seized a pen and wrote across the letter, "Denied. Kalugin." Then he passed it across to the marshal.

"National policy is mine," Kalugin said, his face devoid of expression. "We cannot wait six months to fight the Japanese on even terms. Nor can we give up a piece of our country. The Japanese must be violently expelled. They must shed their blood. *Now!*

"The Russian people are united as they haven't been since World War Two. This is our opportunity to weld these desperate, hopeless people into a nation. If we fail to seize this opportunity, we may never get another. One powerful, united nation, with the dissenters silenced at last—we owe this duty to Mother Russia."

Kalugin sneered. "On the telephone minutes ago, the American president threatened an economic and political boycott, 'total political isolation,' he said, if Russia uses nuclear weapons on the Japanese aggressors." Kalugin shook his head balefully. "The man doesn't understand that the very life of Russia is at stake. *This is our moment.*"

Stolypin took a deep breath, then exhaled. He glanced at Ilin, who had been paying strict attention to Kalugin.

Ilin half-turned to see what the door guard thought of all this. The man was still standing with his arms crossed. His eyes met Ilin's.

Stolypin muttered something inaudible. He drew a handkerchief from his pocket and wiped at his hands and face.

"What did you say?" Kalugin asked.

"I think you are wrong, Mr. President," Stolypin said flatly. "However, I took an oath many years ago. I will obey."

Kalugin decided to be satisfied with that. His gaze shifted to Ilin. "Why are you here?"

"Mr. President, I came with Marshal Stolypin," Janos Ilin said, "to share some critical intelligence with you. As you know, the Americans are aware of your plans to use nuclear weapons. The Japanese also. A spy told them."

Kalugin blinked several times, like an owl. Or a lizard.

Ilin drew his chair closer and leaned forward. "I believe this traitor is on your staff."

"Who is it?"

"The Japanese call him Agent Ju, or Agent Ten. He has been giving the Japanese information for years. Now he is passing secrets to the Americans."

Kalugin almost snarled. "Can you find this man?"

"We are looking, Mr. President. I came today to warn you."

"I suspected it," Kalugin shot back. "But we will root him out. You are to cooperate with my loyal ones. Give them everything they ask for."

"Yes, sir."

"We must reinstitute political background checks. Find out what people believe, what they are saying privately. We must know who is reliable and who isn't. I see no other way. Your agency will be tasked with much of this new mission, just as it was in the old days. The modern reforms didn't work." Kalugin crossed his hands on the desk. "A lot of people did not believe in the new ways. This will be a popular move."

"Yes, sir."

"Have your director arrange an appointment with me for tomorrow. We will not waste time on this."

Kalugin leaned back in his chair and levered himself erect. "Gentlemen, I wish to thank you for your devotion to your nation, and to me." He came around the table and stood before them. "I embody our country now. *I* am Russia, its spirit and its soul. I shall guard her well. That is my sacred trust."

Ilin was on the president's right side, and as Kalugin stepped for the door, he kept pace. The moment came as the guard turned and reached for the knob. For just a few seconds, his back was turned.

Janos Ilin had the fountain pen in his hand. He thrust it a few inches from Kalugin's mouth and pushed in hard on the refill lever. A cool, clear spray shot from a pinhole just under the nib of the pen.

Startled, Kalugin inhaled audibly. "What—" he demanded loudly.

Then his heart stopped. As he fell forward, Ilin caught him, lowered him to the floor.

Ilin dropped to his knees beside the president. He felt his carotid artery. "My God, his heart has stopped! He's had a heart attack!"

To the guard, he said, "Quick, call the medics! The president has had a heart attack!"

As the guard rushed from the room, Ilin squirted another charge from the pen into Kalugin's mouth just to be sure. The pen then went into his pocket. He pulled off Kalugin's tie, ripped open his coat and shirt, and began cardiopulmonary resuscitation.

He was pumping hard on the dead man's heart when the medical team rushed in thirty seconds later. Ilin had already cracked some ribs; he felt them go.

The white-coated professionals quickly checked the president's vital signs as five loyal ones gathered around. A medic jabbed a needle straight through Kalugin's chest into his heart and pushed the plunger in. Then they zapped him with the paddles.

The body twitched.

Again with the paddles.

Nothing.

Janos Ilin blotted the perspiration from his brow with the sleeve of his suit jacket. Marshal Stolypin stood watching the medics with a thoughtful expression.

Three of Kalugin's lieutenants were hovering. One asked the guard, "What did you see?"

"He had a heart attack. That man caught him as he collapsed. It *was* a heart attack. I never took my eyes off him."

At length, the medics decided the case was hopeless. They packed their gear and left the room. Kalugin was still lying on the floor, his shirt and coat wadded up on the floor beside him. The guard was nowhere in sight. The loyal ones followed the medics. The last one glanced at Ilin and Stolypin, shrugged, then hurried after the others.

Stolypin picked up the telephone and placed a call. It took several minutes to get through to the person he wanted. Meanwhile, Ilin closed Kalugin's eyes and draped the dead man's suit jacket over him.

"This is Marshal Stolypin. I am calling to rescind the order given by President Kalugin to attack Japan with nuclear weapons. . . . He is dead. . . . Yes, the president is dead. A heart attack just a few minutes ago. . . . There is no mistake; I swear it . . . Don't give me that! I've known you for twenty years, Vasily. I order you not to launch those planes."

Stolypin listened a moment, then covered the mouthpiece with his hand. "He can't stop them. They took off two hours ago. Five loyal ones are still in his headquarters, armed to the teeth. The pilots were specifically ordered not to turn back for any reason."

Stolypin listened for several more seconds, then grunted a good-bye.

Ilin wandered out of the room into the reception area. Marshal Stolypin followed him.

The reception area was empty.

The men walked along the corridor the way they had come in. They met no one. At the head of the grand staircase there was a window. Through it they could see the lighted grounds of the Kremlin and the main gate. The loyal ones were walking quickly toward the gate. Even as Ilin and Stolypin watched, the grounds emptied. Not a single person remained in view.

"The pilots were ordered to bomb Japan, then return to Irkutsk."

"Will they do it?"

"If they have wives and children, I imagine it will not occur to them that they have a choice."

"Perhaps, Marshal," Ilin said, "we should use the hot line to call Washington. The American president may be able to help."

Side by side, they walked the empty corridor back to the president's office.

"He was mad, you know," Stolypin said.

"Yes."

Pavel Saratov stood under the air lock in the forward torpedo room, watching *Michman* Martos check his scuba tanks and strap them on.

"Three against one," Saratov said. "I wish we had someone to send with you."

"It will be all right." Martos was trying to concentrate on checking out his gear, getting it on correctly. The captain obviously had other things on his mind, which was okay. That was why he was the captain.

"Try to figure out how the timers work and turn them off."

"It may take a few minutes."

"Nuclear war, the end of the world . . . I won't be a part of it."

"I understand, Captain." Martos glanced at Saratov, who looked years older than he had a month ago. These last few weeks had aged them all, Martos reflected.

"You're all traitors," one of the naval infantrymen put in. He had been disarmed and was sitting on a nearby bunk, watching Martos get ready. "General Esenin will—"

Saratov glanced at the senior torpedo *michman,* who backhanded the infantryman across the mouth.

"Any more noise, tape his mouth shut."

"Aye aye, sir."

The *michman* wearing a sound-powered telephone headset spoke up: "Captain, Sonar reports two destroyers at ten thousand meters, closing quickly."

Saratov smacked Martos on the arm. "Hurry."

"Aye, Captain."

Martos pulled his mask over his face and scurried up the ladder into the lock. As the torpedomen sealed the hatch closed, Saratov headed for the control room. White faces watched him every step of the way. He tried to keep his gait under control, but the sailors must have thought he was galloping.

"Two destroyers," the sonarman reported. "About ninety-five hundred meters. And two more helicopters."

"Are they echo-ranging?"

"Yes, sir."

Askold had been wearing the extra sonar headset, and now he passed it to the captain without a word. He looked very tired.

As he waited inside the dark lock while the cold water rushed in, Martos felt the dogged-down hatch above his head. Esenin had closed the hatch once he was outside the ship. Had he left the hatch open, no one else could have used the air lock. Was closing the hatch a tactical error, or was Esenin waiting for someone to come out through the lock?

Locked in this steel cylinder as the water rose past his shoulders, Martos recalled that Esenin and one of his men had gone out first, then the third man. That third man must have closed the hatch behind him.

The cold water shot into the lock under pressure. This small, totally dark steel chamber with cold seawater flooding in was no place for a person suffering from claustrophobia. Martos had conquered his fear of the lock long ago.

The water was over his head now. Breathing compressed air from the tank on his shoulders, Martos waited until the sound of water coming in had stopped completely. He could just hear the pinging of the Japanese sonars probing the dark waters.

Saratov was right: they were running out of time.

Martos reached above his head and grasped the wheel on the outer hatch. He applied pressure. The wheel resisted. Martos braced himself and grunted into his mask as he twisted with all his strength.

The wheel turned ninety degrees, and he pushed on the hatch. It opened outward.

Martos flippered up and out.

The light was dim, visibility in the murky, dark water was very restricted. He could see, at the most, ten feet.

He had his knife out now, in his right hand, ready. He cast a quick glance in all directions, including upward.

Keeping his chest just inches off the steel deck plating, Martos swam aft.

The first two containers loomed into view. They appeared to be closed, with the metal bands that encircled them still attached.

As he got closer, he could see someone between the containers, someone in a semierect position, facing aft. The other two men must be beyond this guy.

Martos's adrenaline level went off the chart. He was ready.

He flippered up and over the left container, which was about four feet high, so that he came at the man he could see from behind his left shoulder. As he closed he saw the other two, their heads bent. They had the container behind this one open and were bent over, working on whatever it contained. A light source near what they were working on silhouetted them in the murky water.

Martos took in the scene at a glance as he closed swiftly on the nearest man, still motionless. The head of the man across from him jerked up just as he stabbed with the knife, burying it to the hilt in the side of the nearest man's neck.

With a ripping, twisting motion, he jerked the knife free as dark blood spouted like ink. Martos used his left hand to slam the victim away. His momentum carried him toward the man who had jerked his head up.

He slashed with the knife, but the man kicked backward, so the knife missed its target.

As he went by the third man, Martos slammed an elbow into his mouthpiece, causing it to spill out.

Scissoring hard with his legs, the Spetsnaz fighter shot toward the second man and slashed again with the blade. This time, the knife clanked into a wrench the man had in his hand.

The man dropped the wrench. The human shark that had attacked him bored in relentlessly. Another slash with the blade at his oxygen line bit deep into his shoulder.

The panicked man got a hand on Martos's goggles and snatched them away.

This time, Martos drove the blade deep into the man's abdomen and ripped it free with one continuous motion, then pushed the dying man away and spun to face his last opponent.

"Eight thousand meters, Captain. They were making at least thirty knots. Now one of them is slowing. The other is charging toward us."

Ping! That damned noise.

"The helos? Where are they?"

"One is overhead, sir. I think he has dipped a sonar pod."

Saratov could hear the steady *whop-whopping* beat of a helicopter in his earphones. It *did* sound as if the chopper was in a hover.

Ping!

"How long has Martos been out?"

"About a minute, sir."

Everyone in the control room was looking at him, waiting for him to hatch a miracle, pull a rabbit from the hat. Pavel Saratov made a show of reaching into Askold's shirt pocket for a cigarette, lighting it, and taking a deep, slow drag.

Esenin was no amateur. He fought like a trained professional, without wasted effort, making every move count. He kept his eyes on Martos's abdomen, not his face. He had his knife in his right hand. And the bastard was grinning! Martos saw the flash of white teeth just before Esenin placed the scuba mouthpiece back in his mouth.

For the first time, Martos felt fear.

Was the general grinning because he was going to kill Martos with a knife, or was he grinning because this damned bomb he had been working on was now set to explode?

Esenin slashed with the knife and Martos countered, but in slow motion, because all their movements were slowed by the water. At first

336 • STEPHEN COONTS

blush, avoiding a slow-motion attack seemed easy, until you realized that your movements were inhibited to the same degree. Then underwater hand-to-hand combat became a horrible, twisted nightmare.

Martos got his left hand on Esenin's right wrist and gripped it fiercely. Before Martos could deliver a killing thrust with his right, Esenin seized his wrist.

Locked together, they struggled.

Martos was the stronger of the two. He could feel Esenin yielding, and at that moment, Esenin got his feet up and kicked. The two men flew apart.

Martos had to look at the bomb. There was a panel with glowing numbers.

Esenin launched himself off the front of the submarine's sail. Martos flippered hard to avoid him and slashed with his knife as Esenin went under him. He felt the blade bite flesh.

Esenin whirled to face him. The shoulder of his wet suit was leaking dark black blood, or perhaps Martos only imagined it. In the dim murk it was hard to tell.

This time as Esenin came forward, he held the knife low, ready to slash upward.

Martos used his hands to move himself backward, waiting for his moment.

Something rammed itself into his left shoulder. Stunned by pain and shock, Martos looked down at his shoulder. Protruding from the wet suit was the tip of a knife blade, gleaming in the watery twilight.

CHAPTER TWENTY-FIVE

●THEY WERE WAITING when Atsuko Abe entered the war room in the basement of the defense ministry. The foreign minister, Cho, was there with four other ministers and half a dozen senior politicians from the Diet. The chief of staff of the Japanese Self-Defense Force, General Yamashita, stood in their midst.

"What are you doing here?" Abe demanded of the group as they bowed. Without waiting for an answer, he walked around them. He went to the prime minister's raised chair and climbed into it.

"A Russian submarine is in Sagami Bay, just outside the mouth of To-kyo Bay," Abe said. "I suppose you've heard. Come, let us see about it."

They turned to face him. The raised chair resembled a throne, Cho thought, annoyed that such a thought should intrude at a time like this.

"The submarine can wait, Mr. Prime Minister," Cho replied. "We have come about a more serious matter."

Abe looked from face to face, scrutinizing each.

"My conscience forced me to violate the security laws," Cho contin-ued. "I told these gentlemen of your plans to use nuclear weapons to destroy the American air base at Chita. My colleagues decided that verification must be obtained before any decision was possible on a matter this serious. General Yamashita agreed to meet with us. He confirmed that you ordered this attack."

Abe's eyes flashed angrily. "Without air superiority, gentlemen, our position in Siberia is untenable. We cannot resupply our forces through the winter. Does anyone dispute that?"

No one spoke.

Abe bored in. "General Yamashita? Do you concur with my assess-ment?"

Yamashita gave a tiny affirmative bow.

"We must eliminate the American F-22s or lose the war. If we lose the war, this government will fall. If this government falls, Japan will lose its last, best hope for greatness. Surely you see our dilemma. Desperate situations call for extreme remedies—I have the courage to do what must be done."

"Mr. Prime Minister," Cho said, "sometimes defeat is impossible to avoid. The wise man submits to the inevitable with grace."

"Defeat is never inevitable. Our resolve must be as great as the crisis."

"To struggle against the inevitable is to dishonor oneself."

Abe flared at that shot. "How dare you speak to me of honor!" he roared.

Cho gave not an inch, which surprised Abe. He didn't think the old man had it in him. "I speak of our honor, ours collectively, yours and mine, the honor of the people in this room, and the honor of Japan. We must choose a course worthy of ourselves and our nation."

"And that is?" Abe whispered.

"We must withdraw from Siberia. Nuclear weapons are abhorrent to the Japanese people. To have them as a deterrent is one thing, but to use them on a foe when the life of the nation is not at stake is quite another."

"The life of Japan *is* at stake." Abe looked again at every face, trying to read what was written there. "We are a small, poor island in a vast ocean bordered by great nations. We are caught between China and the United States. With Siberia, Japan can also be great. Without it . . ." His voice trailed off.

"Your failing, Mr. Prime Minister," Cho said slowly, "is that you have never been able to admit the possibility of visions other than your own. But the time for discussion is past. The decision has been made. The Japanese government will not betray the ideals of the Japanese people."

Abe seemed to shrink in his large chair.

General Yamashita stepped forward and presented a piece of paper. "Please sign this, Mr. Prime Minister, canceling preparations for the nuclear strike."

Abe made the smallest of gestures, motioning the paper away. "I cannot," he said in a hoarse whisper. "The strike was launched a half hour ago."

"Call it back," one of the senior politicians said harshly.

Atsuko Abe smiled grimly. "The possibility always existed that weak men might lose their resolve. The pilots were ordered to ignore any recall orders."

The politicians stood in stunned silence, trying to comprehend the enormity of the step taken by Abe.

Cho was one of the first to find his tongue. "Come with me," he said to General Yamashita. "We will call the American president."

David Herbert Hood was still on the telephone with Marshal Sto-lypin when the call from the Japanese defense ministry came in. Hood listened in silence to the translation of the words of Foreign Minister Cho. When he realized that Cho was saying the nuclear strike against Chita had been airborne from Vladivostok for forty-two minutes, Hood pushed the button on the telephone that allowed everyone in the room to hear the translator, and in the background, the voice of Cho talking rapidly in Japanese.

Hood was horrified. The news that a nuclear strike couldn't be recalled struck him as complete insanity. The Russians had done the very same thing.

"Mr. Cho," Hood replied, trying to keep control of his voice. "I just got off the telephone with the Russian chief of staff. Are you aware that Russia launched a nuclear strike via aerial bombers against Tokyo and the missile-launch facilities on the Tateyama Peninsula two hours ago?"

The translator fired ten seconds of Japanese at Cho, who asked in horror, "Tokyo?"

"Tokyo," thundered David Hood. "And the crazy sons of bitches sent planes without any way to recall them."

Cho said something to try to get the message straight.

In a moment, Hood continued: "Yes, sir. The Russians did do that. They are doing it now. Six MiG-25 bombers, three for each target, with Sukhoi-27s for escort."

He handed the telephone to Jack Innes. "Tell them where the Russian strike is. They may be able to intercept it."

While Innes talked, Hood scanned the giant display that covered most of the wall in front of him. It was a presentation of raw data from the satellites, massaged by the best computer programs yet devised. What Hood focused upon were the symbols marking unknown airborne targets in eastern Siberia. There were several. One of the formations the Americans were watching was undoubtedly the nuclear strike, probably that one a hundred miles north of Khabarovsk.

The chairman of the Joint Chiefs, General Stanford Tuck, was standing beside him. "Nukes," Hood told him. "The bastards are trying to nuke each other."

"What are the targets?"

"The Russians are sending two strikes, one against Tokyo, one against the missile-launch facilities on the Tateyama Peninsula. Meanwhile, the Japanese are trying to nuke the F-22 base at Chita."

Tuck was horrified. "Tokyo..."

"The F-22 squadron," Hood said, pursing his lips. "There are hotheads in Congress who will want Japanese blood if they use a nuke to kill Americans."

"How did we get to the edge of the abyss?" Stanford Tuck asked.

"How do we keep from falling in?" Hood countered. He pointed to the computer presentation on the wall. "The Russians are too far east to be intercepted by the F-22s. It would be a futile tail chase. The Japanese are going to have to take care of themselves. Our only option is to scramble the F-22s to intercept the Japanese strike headed their way."

"The planes near Khabarovsk must be the Japanese," Tuck said. He grabbed a satellite telephone.

Stunned by the agony of the knife that had been rammed through his left shoulder from behind, *michman* Martos almost lost his scuba mouthpiece. His instinct and years of training saved him. Without conscious thought, he turned and grabbed his assailant's throat with his left hand and buried his knife in the man's stomach again. Continuing the same movement, he then spun the man toward Esenin and flippered as hard as he could.

The agony in his shoulder was extraordinary, so bad that he could barely stay focused.

Esenin tried to push the dying naval infantryman out of the way so that he could get at Martos, but while he was using his hands for this, Martos pulled his knife from the human shield and stabbed Esenin under his left armpit.

Esenin twisted away before Martos could withdraw his weapon. He floated away, looking down at his left side, reaching with his right hand.

Martos turned back toward the bomb.

Lights...numbers...Where was the on-off switch?

As he looked for it, the sheer volume of the pinging noises got his attention. And a noise like a train. Martos looked up, toward the surface a hundred feet above.

He saw the destroyer speeding over, and splashes. Out to either side of the racing ship's hull, splashes.

Depth charges! The Japanese destroyer was dropping depth charges!

"Depth charges in the water, Captain."

"All hands into life jackets. Let's pray these charges are set too shallow. If we survive them, we'll blow the tanks, surface the boat, and abandon it. Pass the word."

Every man in the boat was talking to someone, reaching for something, bracing himself.

"Close all watertight fittings."

Saratov heard the hatches clanging shut. He reached for a life jacket and pulled it on, fumbling with the straps.

He was still at it when the first depth charge exploded.

The detonation rocked the sub, causing circuit breakers to pop and emergency lighting to come on.

Another blast, like Thor pounding on the boat with his mighty hammer.

Then the worst of all, three stupendous concussions in close succession.

Silence. "Damage reports?" Saratov shouted the question into the blackness. Even the emergency lights were out.

The reports came back over the sound-powered telephone. The boat was still intact.

"Emergency surface. Blow the tanks. All hands stand by to abandon ship."

Martos had only a few seconds, so he looked again at the panel on the bomb still sitting in its cradle on the transport container. Esenin and his helpers had merely opened the container by releasing the two steel bands that held it together. Surely these damned fools weren't arming the thing before they got it off the submarine?

But it *was* armed.

Martos tried to remember—as he knifed the first man, Esenin had been on his left, and doing something to this panel. What?

Which is the power switch?

Running out of time ... Which one is it?

He heard a powerful click, and instinctively he slammed his knees into the fetal position and hugged them.

The concussion smashed into his left side like a speeding truck. For a second or two, he lost consciousness.

Another blast, and another. These blasts were above him and to his right, farther away than the first, which had almost opened him up like a ripe tomato.

Martos concentrated on staying conscious and keeping his mouthpiece in place as the shock waves from the explosions hammered at him.

The knife buried in his shoulder helped. The pain was a fire that burned and burned, and his mind couldn't shut it out.

Then the explosions were over.

Amazingly, he was still alive. And deaf. He could hear nothing. His eardrums must have burst.

He tried to find the warheads, the containers, but couldn't. The water was opaque.

The rising submarine hit him, carried him upward on an expanding tower of bubbles, a universe of rising bubbles.

Instinctively, Martos used both hands to grasp the slippery tiles of the deck, which was pushing him up, up, toward the light.

He was going upward too fast. He was going to get the bends. He could feel his abdomen swelling. Oh, sweet Christ!

More and more light, coming closer and closer . . .

When the submarine surfaced, Pavel Saratov used the public address system. The emergency power was back on, so the loudspeakers worked.

"Abandon ship. All hands into the water."

Already the control room crew had the hatch open to the sail cockpit.

"Let's go. Everybody out," Saratov roared. Amazingly, the sonar *michman* held back. "I'm sorry, Captain. What I said—"

"Forget it, son. Out. Up the ladder."

He waited until the last man was out of the control room and conning tower area, then Pavel Saratov climbed the ladder to the cockpit. The daylight shocked him. The men that preceded him were in the water, wearing their life vests, paddling away from the sub. Men were still coming out of the torpedo room forward and the engine room aft. The swells—they weren't so large, but they were lapping at the open engine room hatch.

The destroyers were circling. One was coming back with a bone in its teeth. The choppers were out there circling. . . .

Saratov's attention turned to the bomb containers welded to the deck forward of the sail. Three of them were still sealed. One, however, was open. The top of the container was missing, but the steel straps were there, loose. Entangled in one was a body in a wet suit, wearing a scuba tank. Saratov climbed down the handholds on the port side of the sail to the deck and carefully walked forward on the wet tiles.

The man entangled in the strap moved. Esenin.

The hilt of a knife protruded from under his left arm.

Saratov lifted Esenin's head. "Where is Martos?"

"Captain, over here."

The cry was from beside the sail, on the starboard side.

Saratov went aft. Martos was trying to get erect. He had found a handhold on the sail to hold on to as the sub came up from the depths; otherwise, the water would have washed him away.

The point of a knife was sticking out of Martos's shoulder. "Don't pull it out," Martos said. "I'll bleed to death."

"Can you get in the water and swim? The Japanese may start shooting."

"I can barely hear you. I think my eardrums are ruptured."

Saratov raised his voice, "I said—"

"We must check the bomb. I think Esenin armed one, started a timer. Help me."

The two men went over to look, Saratov half-carrying the Spetsnaz fighter.

"See the numbers, ticking down."

"We need something to break into this, to cut the circuits."

"The knife in Esenin," Martos said. "Get it."

Saratov moved the three steps and pulled the knife from the tangled man. He handed it to Martos, who raised it in the air with his right hand and jabbed it into the electronic box with all his strength. The knife went in about three inches. Martos pried with the blade.

"Captain!"

The call came from the water. Saratov looked in that direction. Askold was calling. Now he pointed. "Water . . . the engine-room hatch. The boat is flooding."

Now he could feel the deck shifting. The bow was rising.

"Quickly," he said to Martos.

"I—" Martos passed him the knife and ripped at the top of the control box that he had pried loose. It gave. He bent it, trying to enlarge the opening. The deck was shifting, rising from the sea and tilting.

"Help me," Martos gasped.

Saratov grabbed the Spetsnaz fighter with his left hand and used his right to slash the exposed wires.

"Keep me from falling and give me the knife," Martos gasped. Saratov handed over the knife and grabbed Martos with both hands.

Martos sawed with the blade against the wires. Several parted. He sawed some more.

The bow was completely out of the water. Nearby, sailors in life-jackets were shouting.

Saratov looked up. A Japanese destroyer was coasting to a stop less than fifty meters away. Faces lined the rail. Someone on the bridge was using a bullhorn, shouting and waving an arm. Beside him were men with rifles.

"The boat is going to go under, Captain," Martos said.

"Cut the last of the wires."

"The suction will take us down."

"Perhaps. Cut the damned wires."

"I am trying."

The bow rose higher and higher into the air. Saratov heard a bulkhead inside the submarine tear loose with a bang.

When the angle of the deck got to about sixty degrees, Saratov lost his grip on Martos, who was still holding the clock part of the mechanism. He dropped the knife and grabbed the clock with both hands.

Then the wires holding the clock mechanism tore away and Martos slid down the deck into the sea.

Holding on precariously, Saratov checked the mechanism. The clock was gone, all the lights off.

Then he could hold on no longer. He started to slide down the deck, then kicked away with his feet and fell into the water.

As the boat loomed above him, he stroked for Martos.

Towing the diver by his oxygen hose, Saratov turned his back on the boat and paddled away as hard as he could.

He hadn't gone far when he heard shouting. He looked. *Admiral Kolchak* was going under.

As the boat went into the depths for the last time, Esenin was conscious, trying to free himself from the steel cable that held him trapped.

With a huge sigh as the last of the air rushed from the boat's interior, the bow of *Admiral Kolchak* disappeared into the sea.

The swirling undertow dragged Saratov under. He held on to Martos's oxygen hose with a death grip.

When he thought his lungs would burst, he opened his eyes.

He was still underwater, rising toward the surface.

Gagging, he sucked the air, then pulled Martos up and got his head above water. "Breathe, damn it! Breathe."

Martos coughed, gagged, spit water, then sucked in air.

"Don't die on me, Martos."

"Yes, Captain," Martos said, and passed out, still in Saratov's grasp.

The Sukhois and MiGs were thirty minutes away from the second tanker rendezvous when Major Yan Chernov flipped his radar switch to the transmit position. He and the other Sukhoi pilots had been listening passively for radar transmissions by Japanese Zeros and not radiating themselves. So far, they had heard nothing.

Now he adjusted the sensitivity and gain on the scope, ran the range out to maximum, and watched the sweep go back and forth, back and forth.

The scope was empty, of course, just like the dusty sky. The dust in the atmosphere diffused the sunlight and limited visibility. Maybe six miles visibility here, he decided, but worse to the south.

Perhaps the damned tankers would not show up. Screwups of this order were an everyday occurrence in Russian life. That the first set of tankers had showed up in the proper place, on time, was a minor military miracle, worthy of comment wherever uniformed professionals gathered. A similar miracle two hours later was too much to expect.

So Chernov's thoughts went. He turned his head and looked for all his charges, the bombers and the escorts. When he squinted against the glare, he could just see the second section of Sukhois, about four miles away to the south, at this altitude.

And of course his eyes dropped to his fuel gauges. He had enough to get to the tanker rendezvous and fly for another fifteen minutes. That was it.

No doubt the other fighters and bombers were in a similar condition.

Without fuel from the tankers, the three MiG-25 bombers and their Sukhoi escorts would flat run out of gas. The Tateyama strike would suffer a similar fate.

Chernov looked at the chart of this area that he had folded on his lap.

The rendezvous position was plainly marked. Unfortunately, there were no runways within range if Chernov and his charges didn't get fuel.

Watching the radar sweep was mesmerizing. With the plane on autopilot, Chernov had time to study the scope, twiddle the knobs, search the vast sky visually, look at his chart.

Finally he saw it, a dot on the scope, well left of course, 140 miles away. It was moving slowly across the scope toward the extended centerline of Chernov's airplane.

This blip was the tanker formation, of course. Right on time. Right where they should be. And not a Zero in sight.

At a hundred miles, the tankers turned toward the oncoming fighters. They were now in their racetrack pattern. They would spend five minutes on their present heading, then do a 180-degree turn to their right to the reciprocal heading, where they would do another five-minute leg. The fighters would rendezvous on them.

The distance to the tankers was only twenty miles when they began their 180-degree right turn. What had been one blip on Chernov's radar was now three separate, distinct targets.

Jiro Kimura had been awake for thirty hours. The night before, he had lain down but sleep was impossible. He thought of his wife, Shizuko, of Bob Cassidy, of duty, honor, and country and tried to decide what all of it meant, if anything.

He was trapped, like a fly in amber. He had too many loyalties to too many things. There was no way to resolve the conflicts.

The sun fell softly from the dust-filled lemon sky. Windstorms in Manchuria had lifted dust high into the atmosphere, limiting visibility. Here between Vlad and Khabarovsk, the dust was particularly thick. The forecasters said that the dust would thin when the flight rounded the corner of Chinese airspace at Khabarovsk and headed west for Chita.

Three miles ahead and a mile to the right, cruising several thousand feet below, was the converted Boeing 747 tanker that would pass fuel to the four Chita-bound fighters after Khabarovsk was passed. Jiro could just make it out in the yellowish haze. He and his wingman were stationed in the tanker's left-rear quadrant to guard against American or Russian fighters lining up for a gun or Sidewinder shot. The flight leader, Colonel Nishimura, had also stationed himself and his wingman behind the tanker, on the right side, in the quadrant that he felt it most likely the F-22s would attack from. That the F-22s would attack the four bomb-carrying Zeros before they began their bombing run on Chita, the colonel regarded as a fact barely worth discussion. Of course the Americans would attack!

Jiro also thought an attack highly probable. At the brief the colonel had made the classic Japanese warrior's mistake—he underestimated his Western opponent. He seemed to think that Bob Cassidy and company were going to be easy kills, even made a half-joking, disparaging reference to them.

Jiro hoped that somewhere his old friends killed by F-22s were having a good laugh at Nishimura's naïveté. Or stupidity. Whichever.

When Cassidy came slashing in, Nishimura was going to get a quick education. He would probably die before he realized his folly.

Jiro had recommended that the Zeros use their radars until they were fifty miles from Chita. "Only at Chita have we encountered anti-radiation missiles, which must be ground-based. We must use our radars to find the F-22s before they find us."

Nishimura refused. "Athena will prevent them from seeing us. If we leave our radars off there is no way they can detect us."

"Sir, I respectfully disagree. We must rely on Athena for our protection, and use our radar to detect and kill the F-22s before they get within Sidewinder range."

Nishimura refused to listen. He knew better.

Jiro looked down and left, at the tip of the bomb just visible under his left wing. The weapon was a white, supersonic shape.

At seven miles, Yan Chernov located the Russian tankers visually. They were in a trail formation, each plane a mile behind the others and stepped up a thousand feet. The lead tanker was the designated donor for the Tokyo strike.

Instead of swinging in behind the lead tanker, Chernov climbed several thousand feet and lined up a mile or so astern of the third tanker in line, Tail-end Charlie, the spare.

His wingman, Malakov, was on his right wing, of course, but much closer than he should be. Now less than a hundred feet separated them. When Chernov looked over, Malakov was signaling madly with his hands. No doubt in the next few seconds Malakov would break radio silence.

Chernov patted his head, then pointed at Malakov, the hand signal for passing the lead. Malakov patted his own head, confirming the lead change.

Now Malakov added throttle and his plane moved out in front of

Chernov, who flipped his armament selector switch to "Gun." He didn't waste time. With Malakov moving away, Chernov eased the stick ever so gently to the right to turn in behind him. As the crosshair in the heads-up display approached the cockpit area of Malakov's fighter, Chernov squeezed the trigger on the stick. A river of fire vomited from the cannon at the rate of fifty 30-mm shells a second. Chernov didn't waste shells—at this point-blank range, a quarter-second burst was quite enough.

He released the trigger and pulled up abruptly.

Malakov's Sukhoi nosed over in a gentle parabola toward the earth 42,000 feet below.

A wave of fear and horror and self-loathing swept over Yan Chernov.

By an exercise of iron will, he forced himself back to the business at hand.

Armament selector switch to "Missile," green lights on all four missiles, radar lock on Tail-end Charlie, squeeze the trigger on the stick and wait one second.

Whoosh—the missile on the outboard station was away. It shot across the mile of sky separating the tanker from Chernov's fighter, then exploded in the area of the tail. The left wing of the tanker dropped precipitously; then the nose went down.

Chernov didn't have time to watch it fall. He had already locked up the middle tanker with the radar, and now he launched a missile at it. Four seconds later, the third missile left the rail, aimed at the lead tanker.

That missile, the third one, struck the first of the MiG-25s joining on the lead tanker to get fuel. The fighter exploded.

"Zeros," Chernov shouted into the radio. "Six Zeros."

The Russian fighters scattered like flushed quail.

Chernov took his time. He doubled-checked the radar lock-on, ensured the last missile was slaved to it, then carefully squeezed the thing off.

It left with a flash, trailing a wisp of smoke, then turned toward Mother Earth seven miles below and disappeared into the haze at Mach 3.

Chernov switched back to "Gun." He was out of missiles.

Throttles forward, burners lit to close the distance quickly ... at a half mile, he had the HUD crosshairs on the tail of the large, defenseless four-engine tanker.

At a quarter of a mile he pulled the trigger. Like a laser beam, the streak of flame from the gun reached out and touched the tanker's fuselage. Chernov held the trigger down for a long burst.

Fire! A lick of fire from the fuselage, still absorbing fifty cannon shells a second.

The tanker's right wing dropped. Chernov was out of burner now, still closing, only a hundred meters aft. He pulled the crosshairs out to a wing, touched the trigger, then watched as the cannon shells cut it in half.

He released the trigger and slammed the stick left, trying to roll out of the doomed tanker's slipstream.

As he did a stream of tracers went over his head, just a few feet above the cockpit.

Yan Chernov didn't want to kill any more Russians. He rolled onto his back and pulled the nose straight down.

Several miles below, he saw a tanker—this must be the second one— descending in a circle and trailing a stream of fuel that stretched for a mile or so behind. He yanked his nose over and pulled the power back, deployed the speed brakes. He had to be sure. If one of the tankers survived to give fuel to a MiG-25, all this pain and blood would be for naught.

Even as he pulled the nose toward the tanker, the stream of fuel pouring from the injured tanker caught fire. Two seconds later the big four-engined airplane exploded with a dazzling flash.

Yan Chernov plummeted earthward. Somewhere above him, one of members of the second section might be coming down behind, angling for a shot.

Chernov didn't look back.

When the call came from the White House on the satellite telephone, the duty officer took it. He handed it to Paul Scheer, who listened carefully, jotted some info on the duty officer's desk tablet, then said, "Yes, sir" three times before he put the instrument back in its cradle.

"Four Zeros are on the way, all of them carrying nuclear weapons. They plan to nuke this base."

"Where?" Cassidy asked.

"Right now they're just south of Khabarovsk. The White House wants us to intercept them and shoot them down."

"The White House?" Cassidy asked when the shock of hearing the word *nuke* wore off a bit.

"You won't believe this, Skipper, but the voice sounded like President Hood's to me."

That had been an hour ago. Now, Cassidy, Scheer, Dixie Elitch, and one other pilot, a man named Smith, were on their way eastward.

Before Cassidy manned up, he vomited on the concrete. Jiro was out there—Cassidy knew it. He *knew* it for a certainty.

He was living a nightmare.

"Are you okay, sir?" the crew chief asked.

"Must be something I ate," Cassidy mumbled.

When Yan Chernov leveled off a few hundred feet above the ground, doing Mach 2, he looked over his shoulder. He was only human.

Nothing to the right, nothing to the left, nothing behind. The sky appeared empty. Where the other Russian fighters might be, he didn't know.

He scanned the terrain ahead, then the sky behind.

Nothing. ECM silent.

Fuel? The warning light on the instrument panel was lit. A thousand pounds remaining, perhaps.

He was in a valley headed north, with mountains to the east and west. The land below was covered with pines. There were no roads in sight, just an endless sea of green trees with the mountains in the distance.

He pulled the power to idle and pulled the nose up, zoom-climbing.

At five thousand feet, he saw the wandering scar of a dirt road through the forest.

He advanced the throttle to a cruise setting and picked the nose up to a level-flight attitude. He was doing less than five hundred knots now.

He should just jump out and be done with it. Wander in the forest until he starved or broke a leg.

He had his left hand on the ejection handle on the left side of the seat pan, but he didn't pull it.

Four hundred pounds of gas.

The road was beneath him now, running northwest toward the distant mountains. He turned to follow it.

A road would lead somewhere—to a place where there were people.

He didn't think consciously about any of this, but it was in the back of his mind.

The gauge for the main fuel cell still read a few hundred pounds above empty when the engines died.

Chernov let the plane slow to its best glide speed.

He straightened himself in the seat, put his head back in the rest, and pulled the ejection handle.

CHAPTER TWENTY-SIX

● THE FLIGHT OF four F-22s leveled off at 38,000 feet, conning in the dust-laden sky. Bob Cassidy wasn't worried about the white ice crystals streaming behind the engines—visibility was so bad the Japanese wouldn't see the contrails.

He played with the satellite data down-link and adjusted his tac display. The screen was blank. That worried him. With the dust and the thermals, maybe the satellites weren't picking up the Zeros.

He looked longingly at the on-off switch for the radar. He badly wanted to turn it on, sweep the sky.

If the Americans missed the Zeros in this crud, everyone at Chita was going to be cremated alive. Assuming the brass in the White House war room knew what they were talking about.

This whole thing was insane. Nuclear weapons? In this day and age?

He was fretting, examining miserable options, when he realized he wasn't strapped to his ejection seat. Oh, he had armed the seat all right, just before takeoff. Unfortunately, he had forgotten to strap himself to it, so if he ejected he was going to be flying without wings or parachute. Even an angel needs wings, he thought.

He engaged the autopilot and began snapping Koch fittings, pulling straps tight. There.

Amazing how a man could forget that. Or maybe not. He had too much on his mind.

"Hey, Taco! Any word from Washington?"

Taco Rodriguez was the duty officer, sitting by the satellite telephone in Chita. The encrypted radio buzzed, then Cassidy heard Taco's voice.

"They rounded the corner at Khabarovsk, Hoppy, and left the tanker. Four of them, they say. About five hundred miles ahead of you. Call you back in a bit."

"Thanks, Taco."

The F-22s were making Mach 1.4, better than a thousand knots over the ground. Presumably, the Zeros were also supercruising. Five hundred miles—the flights would meet in about fifteen minutes.

A quarter of an hour. Not much. Just a whole lifetime.

He had just four F-22s to intercept the Zeros. Cassidy would have brought more along if he had had them. His only other planes, exactly two, were being swarmed over by mechanics. Several more planes were inbound from Germany, but this morning he had just four flyable fighters.

The ground crewmen had been pretty blasé about the whole gig when the pilots manned up, Cassidy thought. The word went around the base like wildfire: *The Japs are on their way to nuke us!* Still, the men did their jobs, slapped the pilots on the backs, grinned at them, and sent them on their way.

Just before the canopy closed, the crew chief had said to Cassidy, "Go get 'em, sir." Like it was a ball game or something. Like his ass wasn't also on the line.

Good-looking kid, the crew chief. Not Asian, of course, but he did look a bit like Jiro. About the same age and height, with jet black hair cut short.

Jiro wouldn't be out here in this dirty sky with a nuclear weapon strapped to his plane. Naw. He was probably back in Japan someplace, maybe even home with Shizuko. Sure.

Bob Cassidy wiped his eyes with a gloved hand and tried to concentrate.

The tac display was still blank.

How good was that info the brass in Washington passed to Taco Rodriguez? Could Cassidy rely on it? There were two hundred Americans and several thousand Russian lives on the pass line at Chita. Just how many souls should you bet on that Washington techno-shit, Colonel Cassidy, sir?

Bob Cassidy lifted his left wrist and peeled back the Nomex flap to get a squint at his watch.

Fourteen minutes. He had fourteen minutes left in this life.

Dixie Elitch lifted the visor on her helmet and swabbed her face with her glove.

The dirty sky irritated her. Dirt at these altitudes was obscene, a crime against nature.

The Japs infuriated her. Nukes.

She checked her master armament switch, frowned at the blank tac display, and flicked her eyes around the empty yellow sky.

Maybe I should have stayed in California, found a decent man, she thought. God, there must be at least one in California.

"If I live through this experience, I am going back to California, going to find that man." She told herself this aloud, talking into her oxygen mask over the drone of the engines reaching her through the airframe.

Well, Dixie, baby, that's a goddamn big if.

Paul Scheer was the calmest of the F-22 pilots. When he'd been diagnosed with a fatal disease three years ago, he had worked his way through the gamut of emotions one by one: denial, rage, lethargy, acceptance.

The comment that had struck him with the most impact during those days of shock and pain was a quote he had seen in a magazine in a waiting room: "We are all voyagers between two eternities."

Out of one eternity and into another. That's right. That's the truth of it.

Scheer sat relaxed, his eyes roaming the instrument panel.

Layton Robert Smith III, riding Scheer's wing, was an unhappy man. He shouldn't be here. He had been in the *United States* Air Force for nine years, nine peaceful, delightful years, cruising without sweat or strain toward the magic twenty. Eleven years from now he planned to retire from the blue suits and get a job flying corporate moguls in biz jets. Weekends in Aspen, nights in New York and San Fran, occasional hops to the Bahamas, he could handle it. Fly the plane when the paycheck man wanted to go, then kick back.

His mistake had been volunteering to fly an F-22 from Germany to these idiots at Chita. Praise God, if he lived through this he was going to get NEVER VOLUNTEER tattooed on his ass. In Chita, that damned Cassidy had shanghaied him, called Germany, said he needed Smith III "on his team."

And Colonel Blimp in Germany had said yes!

Layton Robert Smith III was scared, angry, and very much a fish out of water. He stared at his master armament switch, which was on.

Holy shit!

The Japanese were going to try to kill Smith III. The prospect made his blood feel like ice water pulsing through his temples.

He should have told Cassidy to stick it up his ass sideways. *Now* he knew that. What would Cassidy have done? Court-martial him for refusing to join the *Russian* air force? Hell, there was nothing Cassidy could do, Smith told himself now as he lawyered the case, then wondered why he hadn't thought of that two hours ago.

Maybe he should just turn around, boogie on back to Chita.

Look at this dust, would you! You don't see shit like this floating over the good ol' US of A. Or even in Germany. What the hell kind of country is this where you fly through dirt?

Smith III told himself he should quit worrying about the injustice of it all and concentrate on staying alive.

Jiro Kimura adjusted his infrared goggles. They were attached to his helmet above his oxygen mask, and they were too heavy. He would have to hold the helmet in place with his left hand while he pulled G's, or helmet, goggles and all, would pull his head down to his chest.

Maybe he wouldn't have to pull any G's. Perhaps the colonel was right about the radar. At least he had a plan.

Jiro looked at his watch. Shizuko was teaching at the kindergarten this morning. She was there now, telling stories to the children, singing songs, comforting the ones who needed a hug.

He had been so very lucky in his marriage. Shizuko was the perfect woman, without fault. She was the female half of him.

He loved her and missed her terribly.

With the goggles on, Jiro Kimura scanned the dusty sky. He suspected he would have only seconds to see the Americans and react—and not many seconds at that.

The forecasters had been wrong about this dust. There seemed to be no end to it.

He checked his watch again. Yes, it was time. Jiro gave a hand signal to his wingman, then pulled the power back and began a descent.

"Call the Japanese and Russian ambassadors," President David Herbert Hood told the national security adviser, Jack Innes. "Ask them to come to the White House again as soon as possible." It was one o'clock in the morning in Washington.

Innes didn't ask questions. He got up from the table and went to a telephone in the back of the White House war room.

Hood turned to General Tuck, the chairman of the Joint Chiefs. "It's time for us to get in the middle. Congress has been loath to get involved. Things have changed. We've got to step between these people before they trigger something no one can stop."

"Yes, sir."

"I want to get on television later this morning, when the sun comes up, talk to the nation and to the Japanese and Russian leadership."

The secretary of state asked, "Sir, shouldn't we get the congressional leadership over here first, get their input?"

"They can stand behind me when I talk to the nation. Putting out fires is my job, not theirs. And let's raise U.S. forces to Defense Condition One."

"Whom are we going to fight?" General Tuck asked.

"Anybody who doesn't like the gospel I'm going to read to them."

Bob Cassidy was breathing faster now, although he didn't notice it. As the minutes ticked by, he was sorely tempted to use the radar. What if the satellites couldn't pick the Zeros out of this goo? Maybe the Zeros' Athena gear wouldn't work.

"Taco, talk to me."

"Hoppy, Washington says they are at your twelve-thirty, three hundred miles. Space Command is having some difficulty, they say . . . but they won't say precisely what."

Cassidy growled into his mask, shook his head to keep the sweat from his eyes.

He checked his watch again. If the Zeros were transmitting with their radars, he should pick up the emissions. Maybe the Sentinel batteries had educated them. Perhaps the Zeros were running silent, as were the F-22s. In that case, the advantage would go to the side with outside help. The satellites were Cassidy's outside help, and just now they didn't seem all that reliable.

He played with the tac display, trying to coax a blip to appear on its screen. Nothing.

"Two-fifty miles, Hoppy."

"Can the satellites see us?"

"Wait one."

If the satellites could see the F-22s, Cassidy could safely divide his flight into sections, secure in the knowledge that the other three F-22s would remain on his tac display even though the dust blocked out the laser data link between planes. Of course, the question remained: If the satellites could see the Zeros, why weren't they appearing on the tactical displays?

And if the satellites were blind, the F-22s had to stay together to ensure they didn't shoot down one another.

Was it or wasn't it?

A minute passed, then another.

The tension was excruciating. Unable to stand it any longer, Cassidy was about to fire a verbal rocket at Taco when he got a bogey symbol on his scope, way out there, 260 miles away. He put the icon on the symbol and clicked with the mouse.

Zero. Quantity one plus. One thousand seventy-nine knots over the ground. Heading 244 degrees magnetic. Altitude four hundred, which meant forty thousand feet. Distance 257 miles . . . 256 . . . 255 . . . The numbers flipped over every 1.8 seconds.

"Stick with me, gang," he said into the radio, and turned left thirty degrees. He would go out to the north, then turn and come in from the side, shooting at optimum range as the F-22s flew into the Zeros' right-stern quarter.

When he was ten miles or so to the north of the Zeros' track, Cassidy turned back to his original course. The two formations rocketed toward each other.

Please, God. We need to kill these guys. It's a hell of a thing to ask you for other men's deaths, but these guys are carrying nukes. If even one gets through, they could kill everyone at Chita.

His formation was where it should be, spread out but not too much so—everyone in sight in the little six-mile visibility bowl.

Cassidy wondered what his wingmen were thinking. Perhaps it was better that he didn't know.

Still only one plus on the quantity of Zeros. *Damn the wizards and techno-fools!*

Fifty miles . . . forty . . . thirty . . . At twenty, Cassidy spoke into the radio: "Okay, gang, get ready for a right turn-in behind these guys. Try for a Sidewinder lock. On my word, we will each fire one missile. Then we will continue to close and kill survivors."

"Two, roger," replied Dixie.

"Three's got it," said Scheer.

"Four," Smith answered.

Cassidy would not have brought Smith if Taco hadn't been trying to get over a case of diarrhea; the idiot drank some water from the shower spigot. Joe Malan was fighting a sinus infection, the others were exhausted: Cassidy had kept planes in the air over the base every minute he could these past few weeks.

Smith had no combat experience, none whatever. Still, he was the only person Cassidy had to put in a cockpit, so he had to fly. Life isn't fair.

"Turn . . . now!"

Cassidy laid his fighter into the turn. The Zeros continued on their 244-degree heading. After ninety degrees of turn, the Zeros were dead on his nose, ninety degrees off, five miles ahead, and two thousand feet above him, according to the tac display. Cassidy looked through the heads-up display and got a glimpse of one, then lost it.

Damn this dust!

He got a rattle from his Sidewinder. It had locked on a heat source. Cassidy kept the turn in. His flight was sweeping in behind the Zeros.

Through his HUD, he saw specks. Zeros. Two.

Two?

Were there other Zeros? Where were they?

"Let 'em have it, gang." Cassidy touched off a 'winder. "There's only two Japs in front of us. They've mousetrapped us."

"Red Three, the Americans are behind us. I have them in sight." Colonel Nishimura made this broadcast over his encrypted radio, and fifteen miles behind him, twenty thousand feet below, Jiro Kimura heard his words.

Jiro and his wingman turned their radars to transmit.

Yes. The four F-22s appeared as if by magic.

"Five miles at your four-thirty position, Red One," Jiro said into the radio as he locked up the closest F-22 and pushed the red button on his stick. The first missile roared away.

As he was locking up his second target, his wingman fired a missile.

They alternated, putting six missiles in the air.

Meanwhile, Colonel Nishimura turned hard right and his wingman turned hard left, pulling six G's each, trying to evade the missiles the Americans had just put into the air.

Bob Cassidy knew for certain he had been ambushed when his ECM indicators lit up. The strobe pointed back over his left shoulder; the aural warning began deedling; the warning light on the HUD labeled

"Missile" lit up, then seconds later began flashing. The Japanese planes behind him had just launched missiles.

Cassidy already had fired his first missile. As the targets in front of him separated, he squeezed off a second at the target turning right, Colonel Nishimura, although he didn't know who was in the plane.

Cassidy's chaff dispensers kicked out chaff bundles and the ECM tried electronically to fool the radars in the missiles aimed at him. All this was done automatically, without Cassidy's input.

Bob Cassidy was busily trying to turn a square corner to force any missiles chasing him to overshoot. He lit his afterburners and pulled smoothly back to eleven G's, two more than his airplane was designed to take. His vision narrowed, he screamed to stay conscious, and the two missiles behind him overshot.

Nishimura's wingman signed his own death warrant when he turned left, a flight path that carried him out in front of the Americans. Two Sidewinders were aimed at him, and they had no trouble zeroing in. The first went up his tailpipe and exploded; the second went off twelve inches above the main fuel tank, puncturing the tank with hundreds of bits of shrapnel and shredding it. The plane caught fire in a fraction of a second.

Without thinking, the pilot pulled the ejection handle. He died instantly when the ejection seat fired him from the protection of the cockpit. A sonic shock wave built up on his body and disemboweled him before he and his ejection seat could slow to subsonic speed.

Nishimura was lucky. Two of the missiles fired at him went for decoy flares that he had punched off. The other failed to hack his turn. Unfortunately, his flight path was taking him into the area directly downrange of the Americans.

Jiro Kimura's first missile smashed into Paul Scheer's airplane several feet forward of the tail. Scheer knew something was wrong when he lost control of the plane—it simply stopped responding to control inputs. Instinctively, he glanced at the annunciator panel, which told him of problems with the plane's health; he saw that every light there was lit.

What the lights and engine gauges could not tell him was that the plane had broken into two pieces. The tail was no longer attached to the main fuselage.

He glanced at the airspeed indicator. Still supersonic.

The nose was falling and the stick position had no effect. It was then that Scheer glanced in the rearview mirror and realized the tail was gone.

The attitude indicators showed the plane in a steepening dive. He retarded the throttle to idle and popped the speed brakes open. They came completely out and would probably have slowed the plane below Mach 1 had it not been going straight down.

Then the plane began to spin like a Frisbee.

Paul Scheer fought to stay conscious. He wanted to experience every second of life left to him.

Layton Robert Smith III never realized Japanese planes were behind the Americans, so the explosion that blew off half his left wing was a complete surprise.

He had managed to get one Sidewinder in the air and was preparing to launch another at Colonel Nishimura when the explosion occurred under his wing. He had his ECM gear on and the audio warnings properly adjusted, but in the adrenaline-drenched excitement of shooting missiles to kill people, he never heard the warnings or saw the flashing lights.

Shooting to kill *was* exciting. He had never felt so alive. He had never even *suspected* that the joy of killing another human being could be this sublime.

Then the Japanese warhead went off under his wing and his plane rolled uncontrollably, faster and faster and faster. He blacked out from the G, despite the best efforts of his full-body G suit. When the G meter indicated sixteen times the force of gravity, Layton Robert Smith III's heart stopped. He was dead.

The coffin of steel, titanium, and exotic metals containing his corpse smashed into the earth forty-two seconds later.

One of the missiles missed Bob Cassidy by such a wide distance that its proximity fuse failed to detonate the warhead. There was another radar target beyond Cassidy, one slowing to subsonic speed in a very hard turn. The missile might have missed it—the angle-off and speeds involved were beyond the missile's guidance capability—had not the target turned toward the oncoming missile—turned just enough.

The proximity fuse in the missile detonated this time. The shrapnel penetrated the cockpit canopy and decapitated Colonel Nishimura. The hit was a one-in-a-million fluke, a tragic accident.

Dixie Elitch somehow avoided the shower of missiles that killed Scheer and Smith. She had also turned a square corner, and now she found that she had a head-on shot developing with one of the Japanese planes far below, one of the two that had fired the missiles. Both these planes were now on her tac display. She locked up a Sidewinder and fired it, then another.

One of the missiles guided; the other went stupid.

Dixie didn't have time to watch. Her ECM was wailing, so she pulled straight back on the stick and lit her burners. She wanted to get well above this fur ball and pick her moment to come down.

Jiro Kimura knew that if he remained in this dogfight, the odds of being the last man left alive were slim. The Zeros had come to bomb Chita, not to shoot down American fighters. Kimura rolled over on his back and pulled his nose straight down. Going downhill, he came out of burner in case one of the Americans was squirting off Sidewinders.

He rotated his plane onto the course he wanted, 260 degrees, and began his pullout. He would get down on the deck and race for Chita while the Americans milled about with Nishimura and the others.

The last Japanese pilot in the fight was Hideo Nakagawa, who had the reputation as the best fledgling pilot in the Japanese Self-Defense Force. He came by it honestly. He was very, very good.

And he was lucky. The first Sidewinder Dixie Elitch triggered in his direction went stupid off the rail; the second lost its lock on his tailpipe and zagged away randomly after six seconds of flight.

The instant Nakagawa realized the second missile was not tracking, he pulled his plane around to target Bob Cassidy, who had come to the conclusion that both the Zeros in front of him were fatally damaged and so was completing his turn toward the threat in his rear quadrant.

Both pilots were in burner—Nakagawa in a slight climb, Cassidy in a gentle descent. And both were almost at Mach 2.

Nakagawa managed to get a lock on Cassidy, whom he saw only as a radar target. He squeezed off the radar-guided missile, then pulled his infrared goggles down over his eyes to see if he could locate the American visually. There he was! At about five miles. Nakagawa switched to "Gun."

Cassidy saw the flash of the missile's engine igniting under Nakagawa's wing or he would never have been able to avoid it. He pulled the stick aft into another square corner while he punched off decoy chaff and flares.

The missile maintained its radar lock on Cassidy's plane, but it couldn't hack the ten-G turn. It went under Cassidy and exploded harmlessly.

Nakagawa pulled with all his might to get a lead on Cassidy's rising plane. As the two fighters rocketed toward each other, he squeezed off a burst of cannon fire, then overshot into a vertical scissors.

Canopy-to-canopy, Bob Cassidy and Hideo Nakagawa went straight up, corkscrewing, each trying to fly slower than the other plane and fall in behind. The winner of this contest would get a shot; the loser would die.

Nakagawa dropped his landing gear.

When he saw Nakagawa's nosewheel come out of the well, Cassidy thought he had the stroke. Nakagawa drifted aft with authority.

Cassidy shot out in front. He jammed both throttles to the stops, lit the burners, and pulled until he felt the stall buffet, bringing the plane over on its back, all the while waiting for cannon shells to hit him between the shoulder blades.

Nakagawa had a problem. The designers of the Zero had placed a safety circuit in the gun system to prevent it from being accidentally fired with the airplane sitting on the ground. Only by manually shifting a switch in the nosewheel well could the cannon be fired with the gear extended. Another peculiarity of the Zero was the fact that the pilot must wait for the gear to extend completely before he reversed the cycle and raised them again. Nakagawa sat in his Zero, indicating 240 knots, waiting for the gear to come up while watching Bob Cassidy dive cleanly away. Furious, he screamed into his mask.

He stopped screaming when a Sidewinder missile went blazing by his aircraft, headed for Mother Earth. He looked up, keeping his left hand under the infrared goggles, just in time to see an F-22 turning in behind him.

Fortunately the gear-in-transit light was out, so he turned hard into his attacker.

The slow speed of Nakagawa's Zero caused Dixie Elitch to misjudge the lead necessary. Her first cannon burst smote air and nothing else.

She was going too fast. She overshot the accelerating, turning Zero. With engines at idle and speed brakes out, she pulled G to slow and stay with her corkscrewing opponent.

This guy was damned good! Amazingly, his nose was rising and he was somehow gaining an angular advantage.

The G's were awesome, smashing viciously at her. She fought to stay conscious, to keep the enemy fighter in sight.

He was canopy-to-canopy with her, descending through twenty thousand feet. He was close . . . too close. Somehow she had to get some maneuvering room.

She slammed the stick sideways, fed in forward stick. The other plane kept his position on her as she rolled. She stopped the roll and brought the stick back a little. Instantly, the enemy plane was closing, canopy-to-canopy . . . fifty feet between the planes. She looked straight into his cockpit, looked at his helmet tilted back, at him looking at her as they rolled around each other with engines at idle and speed brakes out. She saw the infrared goggles and in a flash realized what they were. So that is how he kept track of the invisible F-22!

What she failed to realize was that Nakagawa was trying to hold his helmet and goggles in position with his left hand while he flew with his right. What he needed was a third hand to operate the throttle.

Then he was above her, on his back . . . and too slow, out of control. He released the stick with his right hand and reached across his body to slam the throttle forward.

Dixie realized Nagagawa had stalled as his plane fell toward her. Before she could react, the two planes collided, canopy-to-canopy.

Bob Cassidy had pulled out far below and relit his burners to climb back into the fight. He was rocketing up toward the two corkscrewing fighters—two on his HUD, but he could only see the Zero. They were too close together to risk a shot.

Just as he caught a glimpse of the F-22 alongside the Zero, the two fighters embraced.

The planes bounced apart, then exploded.

Jesus!

Cassidy rolled and went under the fireball.

Jiro Kimura was on the deck, streaking toward Chita with both burners lit. His radar was off. His GPS gave him the bearing and distance: 266 degrees at 208 miles.

Using nuclear weapons was insanity, but Japan's lawful government made the decision and gave the order. Jiro Kimura had sworn to obey. He was going to do just that, even if it cost him his life.

Right now imminent death seemed a certainty: He was hurtling toward it at 1.6 times the speed of sound. The odds were excellent that more F-22s would intercept him very soon. They were probably maneuvering to intercept at this very second.

Even if he dropped the weapon successfully, he would not have the gas to get back to the tanker waiting over Khabarovsk. He was using that gas now to maximize his chances of getting to his drop point. He was going to be shot down or eject. If he ejected, the Siberian wilderness would kill him slowly. If by some miracle he lived, the nuclear burden would probably ruin him.

All this was in the back of his mind, but he wasn't really thinking about it; he was thinking how to get to the weapon-release point. He had F-22s behind and F-22s ahead, he believed. And at Chita, the Americans had those missiles that rode up his radar beam.

Jiro Kimura didn't think he was going to get much older.

Where, he wondered, was Bob Cassidy? Was he in one of the F-22s that had been shot down, or was he in one of the planes waiting ahead?

A warning light caught his eye. Athena! The super-cooled computer was overheating. He turned it off.

At that moment, Cassidy was fifty miles behind.

The last Zero was not on his tac display. The dust in the air must have screwed up the satellite's ability to see planes in the atmosphere, he reflected.

According to the White House, there had been four Zeros, each carrying a bomb. Three had gone down; the last had escaped. If the pilot abandoned his mission and returned to base, there was no problem. Knowing the professionalism and dedication of the Japanese pilots, Cassidy discounted that possibility.

If the pilot had gone on alone to bomb Chita, there was no one there to stop him. So Cassidy zoomed to forty thousand feet and lit his afterburners. Just now he was making Mach 2.2, maximum speed, toward Chita.

The blank tac display was a silent witness to the fact that the three F-22s he had taken off with were no longer in the air.

The radio was silent.

He had to find that enemy plane. Dixie Elitch was certainly dead, killed in the explosion of those two planes just a moment ago. Smith III and Paul Scheer . . . who knew? Maybe they managed to eject. Then again, maybe not.

He had to catch that Zero. He checked his fuel. If that plane reached Chita . . .

Cassidy reached for the radar switch, turned it on. It might not help, but it couldn't hurt.

He wondered which plane Jiro had been in.

Jiro was one of the best they had, so he was undoubtedly one of them. Even as Cassidy thought about it, the question answered itself. The best pilots always find a way to survive. One Zero was still in the air. With a growing sense of horror, the possibility that Jiro Kimura was in the cockpit of that plane congealed into a certainty.

Yes. *It must be Jiro!*

The ECM indicated that an F-22 was behind him. Jiro watched the strobe of the direction indicator. Yep!

The American probably hadn't seen him yet, which gave him a few options. He could turn right or left, try to sneak out to the side. Or he could turn and engage. If he kept on this heading, the American would get within detection range before Jiro got to the drop point; then he would launch a missile.

Jiro turned hard left ninety degrees, as quickly as he could to minimize the time that the planform of his airplane was pointed toward the enemy reflecting radar energy.

Cassidy saw the blip appear. Forty-three miles. It was there for a few seconds; then it wasn't.

The enemy pilot turned.

Right or left? At least he had a 50 percent chance of getting this right.

Right. He turned twenty degrees right and stared at the radar. In a minute or so, he would know. Luckily, he was faster than the Zero, but only because he was high. The thinner air allowed him to go faster.

The seconds ticked by. He couldn't afford to wait too long for this guy to appear, or he would never catch him if he went the other way. But he had to wait long enough to be sure.

Cassidy swabbed the sweat from his eyes.

The enemy pilot must be Jiro.

If he turned left too soon, before he was certain that Jiro wasn't ahead of him, he was giving Jiro a free pass to kill everyone at Chita—all of them.

Dixie was already dead. Scheer. Foy Sauce. Hudek.

When the sixty seconds expired, Cassidy turned forty degrees left. He had made up his mind—one minute. Not a second less or a second more.

Steady on the new course, he wondered if he should have stayed on the other course longer.

Dear God, where is this Zero?

By the time Jiro realized the American had turned back toward him, it was too late. The American fighter was too close. If he turned now, the American pilot would pick him up for sure. Yet if he stayed on this heading—once again he was pointed straight for Chita—the American would see him before many miles passed.

Perhaps...

He applied left rudder and moved the stick right, cross-controlling. Perhaps he could make a flat turn.

Cassidy was beside himself. He couldn't think, couldn't decide on the best course of action. The Japanese fighter had escaped him.

Every decision he had made had turned out badly. His comrades were dead, a Zero had escaped... and a boy he loved like his own son was either dead or was flying that plane and going to kill everyone at Chita—with one bomb.

He swung the nose of the plane from side to side, S-turning, watching the tactical display intently. If the radar picked up anything, it would appear there.

Nothing. Bob Cassidy came out of burner to save some gas and laid the F-22 over into a turn. He would do a 360-degree turn, see if he could see anything. If not, he would go to Chita and sit overhead, waiting for the Zero to show up. Of course, the Zero pilot would probably announce his presence by popping a large mushroom cloud.

There it is! *There!* A coded symbol appeared on the radar screen and on the tac display.

Cassidy slammed the throttles into maximum afterburner. The fighter seemed to leap forward.

Although Jiro Kimura didn't know it, the F-22 Raptor was so high, looking down, that its radar had picked up a return from the junction between his left vertical stabilizer and the fuselage.

He realized the enemy pilot had him when he saw the ECM strobe getting longer and broader. The F-22 was closing the distance between them, and that could only mean that he was tracking the Zero.

Jiro had no choice. He dropped a wing and turned to engage.

Since he had the nuclear weapon taking up a weapons station on his left wing, Jiro had had only two radar-guided missiles, and he had shot them both. He had also fired a Sidewinder, leaving him one.

As the two fighters raced for each other, he got a heat lock-on tone and squeezed it off.

Cassidy was already out of burner and popping flares. He didn't have the Zero visually, but this guy wouldn't wait. He would shoot as soon as possible, and Cassidy was betting that since he wasn't using his radar, he would shoot a Sidewinder.

When the missile came popping out of the yellow haze from almost dead ahead, Cassidy rolled hard right, then pulled the stick into the pit of his stomach.

Pull, pull, fight the unconsciousness trying to tug you under while the chaff dispenser pops out decoy flares.... And the missile went off behind the F-22.

The Zero was turning back toward Chita. Cassidy had him again on the tac display.

How far is Chita?

Holy ... it's only thirty miles.

This guy is almost there!

With his nose stuffed down, Cassidy came down on the fleeing Zero like a hawk after a sparrow.

At six miles, he visually acquired the Zero, which appeared as a small dot against the pale, yellowish sky.

The speed he gained in the descent was the only edge Cassidy had or he would never have caught Jiro Kimura.

Perhaps he should have launched his last missiles at him, or closed to gun range and torn his plane apart with the cannon. He did neither.

Cassidy came down, down, down, closing the range relentlessly.

He knew Jiro was flying the Zero. He had to be.

He wanted it to be Jiro.

Looking over his shoulder, holding his helmet and infrared goggles, Kimura saw the F-22 at about three miles. The pilot kept the closure rate high.

There is time, Jiro thought. *If I yank this thing around, I can take a head-on shot with the cannon.*

But he didn't turn.

He was flying at four hundred feet above the ground. He put his plane in a gentle left turn, about a ten-degree angle of bank. He glanced over his shoulder repeatedly, waiting for the approaching pilot to pull lead for a gun shot.

And he waited.

It's Cassidy! He's going to kill me because I couldn't kill him.

The distance was now about three hundred meters.

Two hundred ...

One hundred meters, and the F-22 was making no attempt to pull lead. It was still closing, maybe thirty or forty knots.

Jiro realized with a jolt what was going to happen.

He grabbed a handful of stick, jerked it hard aft.

The damned helmet ... He couldn't hold it up, so he lost sight of the incoming F-22.

Bob Cassidy's left wingtip sliced into the right vertical stabilizer of the Zero.

The planes were climbing at about fifty degrees nose-up when they came together.

Jiro felt the jolt and instinctively rolled left, away from the shadowy presence above and behind him. This roll cost him the right horizontal stabilator, which was snapped off like a dead twig by the left wing of the F-22.

Two feet of the left wingtip broke off the F-22, which was in an uncontrolled roll to the right.

Bob Cassidy's eyes went straight to the airspeed indicator. He'd had enough time in fighters to have learned the lesson well—never eject supersonic.

Fortunately, the climb, the lack of burner, and the retarded throttles—he had pulled them to idle just as his wing sliced into the Zero—combined to slow the F-22. In seconds, it was slowing through five hundred knots.

Amazingly, Cassidy regained control. He automatically slammed the stick left to stop the roll, and the plane obeyed. He dipped the wing farther, looking for the Zero.

There! The enemy fighter was slowing and streaming fuel.

Get out, Jiro! Get out before it explodes!

Jiro Kimura fought against the aerodynamic forces tearing at the crippled fighter. He had no idea how much damage his plane had sustained in the collision, but at least it wasn't rolling or tumbling violently.

He glanced in the rearview mirror, then looked again. The right vertical stab was gone!

And the right horizontal stab!

Even as the damage registered on his mind, the plane began rolling. He saw the plume of fuel in his rearview mirror.

Jiro tried to stop the roll with the stick.

The roll continued, wrapping up.

Sky and earth changed places rapidly.

The airspeed read three hundred knots, so Jiro pulled the ejection handle.

When he saw the Japanese pilot riding his ejection seat from his rolling fighter, Bob Cassidy devoted his whole attention to flying his own plane.

With full left rudder and right stick, the thing was still going through the air.

Chita was fifteen miles northwest.

Bob Cassidy gently banked in that direction. He looked below, in time to see Jiro Kimura's parachute open.

He pulled the power back, let the badly wounded fighter slow toward 250 knots. As the speed dropped he fed in more and more rudder and stick.

He sensed that the airplane would not fly slowly enough for him to land it. Forget the gear and flaps—he would run out of control throw before he slowed to gear speed. He was going to have to eject. And he didn't care. A deep lethargy held Bob Cassidy in its grip.

Ten miles to Chita.

After all, in the grand scheme of things, the fate of individuals means very little. Nothing breaks the natural stride of the universe.

But he was still a man with responsibilities. "Taco, this is Hoppy."

"Yo, Hoppy."

"All four of the enemy strike planes are down. I am the last one of ours still airborne."

"Copy that."

"Relay it, please, on to Washington."

"Roger that."

"And tell the crash guys to look for me. I'm about to eject over the base."

"Copy. Good luck, Hoppy."

"Yeah."

He kept the speed up around three hundred. The plane flew slightly sideways and warning lights flashed all over the instrument panel as the base runways came closer and closer.

When he was past the hangar area, with the plane pointed toward Moscow, Bob Cassidy pulled the ejection handle.

CHAPTER TWENTY-SEVEN

●Two mechanics driving a Ford pickup found Jiro Kimura in an area of scrub trees on the side of a hill ten miles from the air base. Jiro had broken his right leg during the ejection. When found, he was still attached to his parachute, which was draped over a small tree.

After the mechanics got the Japanese pilot to the makeshift dispensary, Bob Cassidy went to see him. He just stood looking at him, trying to think of something to say.

"I figured it was you flying that plane, Jiro."

"And I knew it was you behind me."

Cassidy didn't know what to add.

"The doc is going to set your leg. They'll give you a sedative. We'll talk tomorrow."

"You should have killed me, Bob."

"Shizuko would have never forgiven me."

Jiro didn't say anything.

"I would have never forgiven myself," Bob Cassidy said to Jiro Kimura. Then he walked away.

Cassidy sat down on a rock outside the building and ran his fingers through his hair. He could hear a television that someone had turned up loud. The satellite dish was in the lawn in front of Cassidy.

President Hood was speaking. Cassidy could hear his voice.

The sun was warm on his skin.

He was sitting like that, half-listening to the television, imagining the faces of his dead pilots, when he realized Dick Guelich was squatting beside him.

"Hoppy, I was thinking perhaps we should send the Cessna to look for survivors. The others who went with you this morning? Did anyone . . ."

"They're dead." His mouth was so dry, the words were almost impossible to understand. He cleared his throat and repeated them. "They're dead."

"Dixie?"

"Midair with a Zero," Cassidy whispered. "In a dogfight. Didn't see a chute."

"Scheer and Smith?"

"Hit by missiles, I think. At those speeds..." He gestured to the east. "Send the Cessna. Let 'em look."

"I'm sorry, Colonel."

"Get those other two airplanes up. Have the pilots go out at least a hundred miles. Make sure they are no more than twenty miles apart, so one can help the other if he's jumped."

"I've briefed them, sir."

"When those planes from Germany land, fuel them and get them armed. Send the pilots to me for a brief. I don't think the Japs will try it again but they might."

"Yes, sir," Guelich said, and he was gone.

It felt good to sit. He had neither the energy nor desire to move.

Poor Dixie. Now, there was a woman.

The sun seemed to melt him, make him so tired that he couldn't sit up. He slid down to the grass, put his back against the rock.

"I did my best, Sabrina.... Honestly..."

When the tears came, there was no way to stop them. Bob Cassidy didn't try.

The bayonet was in excellent condition even though it was old. The army issued it to Atsuko Abe's father when he was inducted in 1944 at the age of sixteen. Of course, the elder Abe never saw combat. If he had, presumably the bayonet would now decorate the home of some American veteran's son. The boy soldier spent his military career guarding antiaircraft ammunition dumps in northern Japan. The army disintegrated after the war. Abandoning his Arisaka rifle, young Abe hitchhiked back to his home village. For reasons that he never explained, he kept the bayonet and the scabbard that housed it.

Almost a small sword, the bayonet was about eighteen inches long, with a straight, narrow blade. It had a wooden handle, which suited it admirably for military tasks like slashing brush and opening cans. Originally the blade was not very sharp, but as a youngster Atsuko had ground a keen edge on the steel, including the tip. In a nation with strict laws on the ownership of handguns, the old bayonet made a formidable weapon.

Abe always displayed it on a small wooden stand designed to hold a samurai sword, across the room from his shrine.

This evening Atsuko Abe sent the servants away. He ensured the doors to the prime minister's residence were locked, then retreated to his chamber, where he bathed and donned a silk kimono that his wife had given him years ago, before she died.

He spent some time sitting on a mat in front of his shrine writing letters. He wrote one to his sister, his only living relative, and one to the emperor, Hirohito, son of the late Emperor Naruhito. He apologized to them both.

He asked his sister's forgiveness for shaming the family. He begged forgiveness of the young emperor for failing Japan. The Japan of which Abe spoke was not the workaday nation of crowded cities, apartments, factories, and tiny farms where he had lived most of his life; it was an idealized Japan that probably only existed in his dreams.

The brush strokes on the white rice paper had a haunting beauty. Oh, what might have been! Abe finished the letter to the emperor and signed his name. He put each letter in an envelope, sealed it, wrote the name of the recipient, and placed the envelopes on the shrine.

The final letter was to his father, who had been dead for twenty years. He explained his dreams for Japan, his belief in her greatness, and bitterly told of the shipwreck of those dreams. He had misjudged the Japanese people, he said. They had betrayed him. And themselves. It was shameful, yet it was the truth, and future generations would have to face it.

That letter also went into an envelope, but after putting it on the shrine and praying, he dropped it into the incense burner, where it was consumed. Abe lit a stick of incense and watched the smoke rise toward heaven. He wafted some of the smoke toward him so he could get a sniff.

Finally Atsuko Abe realized he just wanted to get it over with. He was ready for the pain, ready for whatever comes after life.

He bared his belly, then drew the bayonet from its scabbard. The ancient and honorable way to commit the act of *seppuku,* or *hara-kiri,* is to stab deep into the belly, pull the blade across the stomach, severing the aorta, then turn the blade in the wound and pull it upward. The cuts lead to massive internal hemorrhaging, and death soon follows. The disadvantage is that few men have what it takes to inflict this kind of injury upon themselves. To preserve their honor, condemned samurai in olden days equipped themselves with an assistant, the *kaishaku-*

nin, usually a close friend, who would decapitate the warrior after he had made the ritual cut, or before, if the assistant glimpsed the slightest indication of pain or irresolution.

Of course, Abe had no *kaishaku,* for his honor demanded that he suffer.

Atsuko Abe reached forward and grasped the handle of the bayonet with both hands. He took several deep breaths, readying himself. To fail here would dishonor him still further.

Sweat popped out on his brow. He said one last prayer and, using both hands, rammed the bayonet deep into his gut.

The pain about felled him.

With steadfast courage, he pulled the sharp blade across his belly. He got it about halfway when his strength failed him. The pain robbed him of his resolve. He summoned all his will and courage and twisted the blade.

The agony was astounding.

The final cut and it would be all over.

Moaning, gnashing his teeth, and trying to stifle a scream he felt welling up, he pulled the handle upward.

His hands slipped.

There was only a little blood seeping out of the wound. If he didn't get the blade out, he would suffer here for a week.

With one last mighty heave, he pulled the bayonet free of his flesh. The little sword got away from him, flew halfway across the room and landed with a clatter.

The blood came better now, although the pain was only a little less than with the blade in.

Try as he might, he could not remain sitting upright. He toppled slowly onto his side.

He bit his lip, then his tongue. Blood flowed from his mouth, mixed with the perspiration that covered his face.

He should have drunk more wine. That would have dulled the pain.

At least honor was satisfied. He had failed Japan, but not his honorable ancestors, whom he soon would join.

Time passed. How much, he didn't know. His mind wandered as he slipped in and out of consciousness.

Then he heard a man's voice. Doors opening. A questioning voice. His senses sharpened; the pain in his stomach threatened to overwhelm him.

The door to his room slid open. He tried to turn to see.

Abe caught a glimpse of the face. It was the chief of the domestic staff. A civil servant in his fifties, the man had risen through the ranks of the domestic staff since joining it as a young man. Now the staff chief stood wordlessly, taking it all in, then left, closing the door behind him.

Atsuko Abe moved, trying to ease the agony. Nothing seemed to work.

When he realized he was groaning, he began actively chewing on his lips and tongue. Anything to keep from shaming himself further.

Episodes of the past few months played over and over in his mind: the meetings with his ministers; General Yamashita; Emperor Naruhito; speaking before the Diet. The jumbled, mixed scenes ran through his mind over and over again.

Oh, if only he had it to do one more time.

A door opened below. The sound was unmistakable. What was the time? The small hours of the morning. The staff chief had been here— what? Two hours ago, at least.

Who could this be?

The door opened.

A woman was standing there. Abe tried to focus.

She came across the room, stood in front of him.

Masako. Empress Masako.

Shame flushed Atsuko Abe, then turned to outrage. That a woman should see him like this! The staff chief had dishonored him, the prime minister.

"Your Majesty," he managed. Summoning every ounce of strength he possessed, he managed to lever himself into a sitting position. "Please leave me. You shame me with your presence."

She stood before him, looking around, taking in the blood-soaked white mat, the bayonet, the shrine, saying nothing. She was wearing a simple Western two-piece wool suit, white gloves, sensible shoes, and a stylish matching hat. In her left hand she held a small white purse embroidered with pearls.

She looked down at the purse and opened it. Using her right hand, she extracted a pistol.

"Your Majesty, no. I beg—"

"This," she said evenly, "is for my husband. And my son."

With that, she leveled the pistol and shot Atsuko Abe in the center of his forehead. His corpse toppled forward.

Empress Masako put the pistol back in the purse, snapped the catch, and walked out of the room without a backward glance.

The two weeks after the untimely death of Aleksandr Kalugin were busy ones for Janos Ilin. He helped with the security at Marshal Stolypin's inauguration, and he assisted police in rounding up and disarming Kalugin's loyal ones. He whispered long and loudly to prosecutors about which loyal ones should be brought to trial. He argued that Kalugin's key lieutenants had to answer for their crimes. Private armies, he thought, were bad for democracy and bad for business. President Stolypin helped carry the day. He didn't think much of private armies, either.

One evening Janos Ilin sat in his office, trying to assess the pluses and minuses of the late Russo-Japanese War. Tomorrow Captain First Rank Pavel Saratov and the surviving crewmen of the submarine *Admiral Kolchak* were flying in from Tokyo. President Stolypin would meet them at the airport and decorate every man. Saratov would be declared a hero of the Russian Republic and be promoted to rear admiral. From the reports Ilin had seen, Saratov richly deserved the honor.

Today the American president had announced a new foreign-aid bill for Russia, the largest in American history, one that for the first time gave substantial tax credits to American firms that invested in Russia. And soon American firms would have money to invest. The last two weeks had been the biggest in the history of the American stock market. Everyone, it seemed, had suddenly decided that peace was wonderful.

Atsuko Abe's death led to a new government in Japan, one that Ilin thought might be more attuned to the future than the past. The inescapable fact was that Russia was rich in natural resources and Japan had capital and technical know-how. Put together in the right kind of partnerships, there should be something there for everyone.

Something for everyone was the way the world worked best, Janos Ilin thought. Soon it would be time for Agent Ju to send another message to Toshihiko Ayukawa. This time Ju would point out the best people in Russia to approach for Siberian joint ventures, people who could make things happen.

For a while there, Ilin thought Ju's message reporting the destruction of all of Russia's nuclear weapons had backfired. For months the outcome of that gambit had looked grim indeed. Still, looking back, he thought as he had thought when he drafted the message—that enormous risks were justified. Russia had little to lose and everything to gain if a foreign enemy forced her to fight.

The nuclear raids on Japan had been a close squeak. He had never suspected Kalugin would go over the edge, order the use of nuclear weapons. Fortunately, nothing had come of it, but Kalugin certainly had tried.

Yuri Esenin and the bombs on board a *Kilo*-class sub—that was an effort doomed from the beginning. Only the skill and courage of Pavel Saratov had allowed the sub to get as far as it did.

The air raids on Japan were another matter. When they were launched, the spymaster thought his worst nightmare had come true. Then the planes just disappeared.

Ilin, of course, set out to discover what had happened.

After reading the reports of the interrogations of the survivors of the Tokyo/Tateyama Peninsula raids, Ilin thought it likely that Yan Chernov had shot down the Russian tankers, dooming all the planes to crash landings. It was his voice, two survivors believed, that warned of airborne Zeros, yet not a single enemy fighter had been seen.

One of Ilin's agents in an American seismic exploration unit working in Siberia said that a man answering Chernov's description had shown up two days after the raid attempt with only a flight suit on his back, nothing else. The Americans fed him and gave him a job. He was still there, the informant said.

Either Chernov or the Japanese had shot down the Russian tankers, dooming the strike planes. Whichever, Ilin thought the nuclear strike on Japan was a matter best forgotten.

Poor Russia, a land without hope. Now it had some. With Kalugin gone, with the government rejuvenated and foreign nations willing to make investments, hope was peeping through the rubble.

Perhaps hope would continue to grow. With all this hope and billions in foreign capital, Russia might even grow into a country worthy of its patriots, men like Yan Chernov and Pavel Saratov.

Time would tell.